On Brassard's Farm

On Brassard's Farm

A Novel

DANIEL HECHT

BLACK STONE
PUBLISHING

Copyright © 2018 by Daniel Hecht
Published in 2018 by Blackstone Publishing
Cover and book design by Kathryn Galloway English

Printed in the United States of America

First edition: 2018
ISBN 978-1-5047-9771-9
Fiction/Literary

1 3 5 7 9 10 8 6 4 2

CIP data for this book is available
from the Library of Congress

Blackstone Publishing
31 Mistletoe Rd.
Ashland, OR 97520

www.BlackstonePublishing.com

The minute I heard my first love story,
    I started looking for you, not knowing
    how blind that was.
Lovers don't finally meet somewhere,
    they're in each other all along.

                    —Rumi

"You are an *animal*! You know how to do this!"

                    —Kit Gates

"Farming looks mighty easy when your plow is a pencil
and you're a thousand miles from the cornfield."

            —President Dwight D. Eisenhower

Chapter 1

IF I HAD to give a name to what kind of tale mine is, I would certainly have to call it a love story. But it's not the kind of story we usually think of when hearing those words. The difference is not only what's meant by "love," but also who or what is loved, and how one goes about it.

The only sensible beginning place is the land itself. It is the foundation of everything that has happened to me: the physical solidity of the granite and earth I placed my feet on. That inarguable material presence allowed me to brace myself. It was there I felt the Earth's gravity for the first time as an embrace in which I was not held down but simply *held*.

I first saw the land in early spring. From the interstate exit, I had driven about twenty miles on the paved road, then another six on dirt. This was hardly wilderness, but it was pretty wild for a woman who had lived in the city all her life. I passed through several towns and hamlets, but mainly it was trees and more trees, in a mist of palest pink or pale yellow-green from near-bursting buds. A darting deer, farms with mud-smeared, disinterested cows, shambling houses settling to earth deep among flaking apple trees. Snow-broken, sway-backed abandoned barns. Some badly cut-over woods. Derelict mobile homes. Muddy ruts. My hosts at the bed-and-breakfast had told me that in Vermont this is called "mud season," and correctly warned me that the back roads would be soupy. In spots, my car skated and bogged and I wasn't sure I'd make it through.

At the top of a forested ridge, I turned and started downhill on a yet narrower road that was little more than a slot between overhanging branches.

Soon, the woods opened up and gave me a better view of the valley in which Brassard's farm lay. To the left, pasture sloped gently down to a small stream, then steeply up again, the fields yielding to forest that rose to a wooded ridge. Mottled black and white cows—I didn't yet know a Holstein from a rhinoceros—ranged on the near slope. To the right ran a narrow strip of ragged untended field, last year's milkweeds parched and tufted above dead brown high grass. Above this field rose a steep, flat-topped forested hill, an unlikely arm projecting from the main ridge. It thrust up from the sloping valley in the shape of an ironing board or a submarine just emerging from the depths.

Coming down the hill, I got a good overview of Brassard's place: a cluster of sheds big and small, silos, an old barn with a ramp to its gable-end door, and a house. Scattered among them were trucks, tractors, and two cars that had seen some use.

A pleasant scene, I thought. Remote enough. I had looked at two disappointing parcels of land, but here my pulse picked up. Maybe this was it, maybe I was now looking at my future. It was not postcard pretty, but ruggedly comely in its curves and proportions. Close enough for jazz, as my ex-husband might have said, and I liked jazz. When I could fool myself enough, I liked to think of this whole thing as an upbeat jazzy urbanite taking an improvisatory turn into new territory.

A mailbox with "Brassard" painted on it reassured me that I'd found the right place. I pulled up between house and barn and turned off the car. My windows were open to the spring air, so that a wet smell of manure and mud came to me. The house had white clapboard siding with dark green trim around the doors and on the shutters, and a covered porch faced the road. The nearer barn was a looming ark of faded red paint with a row of small white-trimmed windows along its lowest level. Between house and barn, the driveway faded into a functional dirt yard, where a blue-and-white tractor sat, surrounded by various farm implements. A man in mud-stained jeans and T-shirt was doing something to the tractor's motor, but he extricated his arms and put down his tools as I pulled up.

I got out, suddenly feeling citified and naive about country life and farms and machines and men like the one who was now looking questioningly at me. He wasn't tall, probably my height, but was wide and thick in all his parts, his bare arms muscular. With his deep copper skin and blunt facial features, he was hardly the gaunt, long-faced Yankee I'd unconsciously expected: Brassard would be Uncle Sam in coveralls, the dour pitchfork-wielding farmer in *American Gothic*. This guy was Mexican, I thought, or maybe Native American.

"Are you Mr. Brassard?" I asked.

He turned toward the barn door and bellowed, "Jim! That Boston gal's here." To me: "He's in there somewhere."

He went back to the tractor, wedging his arms into a narrow part at the front of the motor. I stood there, feeling the give of mud beneath my suddenly wildly inappropriate white running shoes, not knowing what was expected of me. I didn't really want to walk toward the barn and muddy the shoes further. The wide man's wrench clanked, and a cow bawled down in the pasture. Otherwise, silence.

After a long minute, an older man emerged from the barn, wiping his hands on a rag. He did wear denim coveralls over a checked shirt, but he was no dried-up Puritan. He was a tall man in his sixties: big in the chest and belly, clean-shaven fleshy pink face, thinning hair cut short and gone mostly gray.

"You're Miss Tanner?"

"Turner, yes. Thanks for taking the time to see me, Mr. Brassard."

"Well, I ain't gonna sell the piece if somebody don't come look at it.

I'd shake your hand, but you don't want to get what I got on your hands. Come all the way from Boston this mornin, did you?"

"No. Just from Montpelier. I'm staying at a bed-and-breakfast. It's …" I felt a need to flatter the landscape, but Jim Brassard probably didn't need my approval for the place he'd lived all his life. But now I had to finish: "… lovely here."

His face remained expressionless. "You want some coffee or something, use the facilities? Or you want to just go on up and take a look?"

"I'm fine with just looking at the land. If this is an okay time for you."

"Good's any other."

A yellow Lab-mix dog came up to nose my jeans. I roughed him around the ears and he licked my hand.

"Yep, Bob, he's a friendly one," Brassard said. "Now you've got him as your best buddy for life, won't leave you alone. Throw a stick and he'll be at you to do it again all day. Won't you, bud?"

Bob went over to Brassard, who worked his pelt down his spine until the dog's back leg twitched up. Brassard's hands were huge, each finger thicker than my thumb.

The man at the tractor took his arms out and wiped his hands on his pants and looked on as Bob nosed me again and Brassard fished in his pockets to jangle keys. The wide man smiled. Native American, I decided.

Spring smell: You think you know it, but you can't until you're out on a small farm in the woods of New England. Break a stalk of celery and put your nose up to it; that's a bit of the smell. Add a touch of lime, when you take the wedge and squeeze it into your Corona. A little rosewater and the dry smell of ice. A wet earth smell like the one that rises from the pots when you water your houseplants, here supplemented with the murky sweet of manure. Those things I instinctively recognized, though my experience of them was largely limited to a much weaker version along the river in Cambridge. It was a distillation of newness and optimism and another start after the snows.

BRASSARD POINTED OUT the land I'd come to see: that ironing board or emerging submarine above us to the west. It was his opinion that taking a tractor up would be our best bet. Perhaps he was considering the burden of his own heavy body—he walked with a hitch that suggested sore joints. Or maybe he saw my obvious unreadiness for a steep uphill trek in spongy earth and mud. He went around the barn to get another tractor, leaving me alone with Bob the dog and the unnamed man wrestling with the blue tractor's engine.

"So," I hazarded, "you work for Mr. Brassard?"

He grinned back at me. "Looks that way."

"I'm Ann Turner. What's your name?"

"Earnest Kelley. I make myself useful when Jim needs a hand. Think you'll buy that land?"

I heard an engine fire up, popping and clattering on the other side of the barn. "Thinking of it, yes."

"What for?" Earnest didn't look my way. Whatever he was working on under the engine compartment of the tractor was giving him trouble.

I was sure I wore my desperation on my face, obvious as a billboard, but I hesitated for only a heartbeat. "Just a place to get away to once in a while. I thought I'd build a cabin, spend some time there in the summers. I'm a middle-school teacher. Just moved to Vermont."

I could have said more—this explanation, tossed off to others and to myself, was somewhere between a convenience and a lie—but this wasn't the moment, and this guy wasn't the person. In any case, Jim Brassard was coming around the barn driving a green and yellow tractor, and it was time for me to go figure things out in more pragmatic and present-tense ways. We were going to ride this contraption up the ridge to the forty-acre parcel he was selling.

"Best you ride the hitch rack," he called down to me. "Put your feet on the two bars there and hold on up here. It gets steep. You want to hold on good."

A sort of shelf of steel bars stuck out behind the tractor's cab, offering a pair of flat blades between the big cleated wheels. I put one foot on each, found it reasonably secure, and got a good grip on the bars that supported the canopy over the seat. He checked my position, asked Earnest to hold

Bob until we were over in the other field, and moved a lever on the steering wheel. The tractor's motor clattered faster and the wheels began kicking up slats of mud.

We crossed the road and chugged between two posts holding sagging barbed wire, then up a dirt track through the strip of scrub. Brassard had to holler back at me over the engine noise: "This here would be your access road."

In the muddy places, the tractor sashayed from side to side and it felt dangerous—those enormous wheels churning close on each side, my Adidas joggers keeping a tenuous grip. I wedged my feet into the welded joint to keep them from slipping.

"Forty acres, never could farm em—can't get a truck or a cow up there. Lots of ledge, no good for pasture. Some good timber, though. Figured I wasn't usin it anyways, maybe somebody'd put up a hunting camp. What'd you want with it anyway?"

"Yes, just a little cabin," I yelled at him. "For summer."

I didn't think conversation was possible, given the noise. And now I was becoming distracted by the delight of riding the tail end of a tractor grinding through spring mud and by the valley view that opened as we got higher. It was like starting out on a carnival ride. An adventure! The newness of it cut through the layers of caution and doubt and angst and ennui to a quickening down at the center of me. I was already touching something real.

The bristle-cut back of Brassard's head half turned. "You okay back there?"

"I'm fine," I screamed.

He moved the throttle and our speed picked up. "Yep, it's not for livin on, not for farmin," he bellowed. "Can't get a car up there. Cuts its sale value. Maybe you could swing a right-of-way from the folks at the top of the ridge, but knowin them it's a slim-to-none chance. Need a hell of a long access road, power and phone, forget it unless you're a millionaire. Cell phone, maybe—don't know, but we don't get reception down at the house. You want to get away, this'd be the spot."

I didn't try to respond. The engine noise coming through the bobbing cap on the exhaust stack was too loud. We ground up to the first steep rise, where the trees began, then turned left and followed a pair of ruts that ran parallel to the ridge. A rugged, near-vertical face of granite reared on our right. The ground was drier here, better traction, and now the tractor swayed not from the yield of mud but from hard uneven ground knuckled with bumps of granite. I held on until my fingers ached as we took a hairpin and angled up the other way. Soon we were above the cliff, and through the trees I could see the farm below. When the breeze shifted, the diesel exhaust blew straight back into my face. Between it and the rolling motion, I began to feel a little sick.

After another hairpin and a longer curve, the track began to level out and we emerged on top of a sort of plateau, forested but clearly once inhabited: on a patch of brambly open land, a few ancient apple trees surrounded a stacked-stone cellar hole, mostly filled in and grown up in blackberry cane. Once we got onto the flat, Brassard ratcheted down a brake pedal and cut the engine. I stepped down, but he stayed in his seat above me, a florid-faced knight on his mechanical steed.

"Well, this's it. Property line on the far side, west boundary, is about where the hill comes down. Down to the bottom there you'll see the old stone wall, that's the start of Hubbard's land, next farm over. Up to the top, you go until you hit the big jumbled boulders on the slope there, that's about the end. Goslants own everything above the rocks."

He took off his billed Agri-Mark cap and scratched his head. "You want me to walk it over with you?"

It was clear that he didn't want to. I wouldn't have minded a better sense of where the land began and ended—I understood that borders were important in property transactions—but more than anything, I wanted to be alone here. I'd hoped I would know my refuge when I found it, that there'd be a certain pull from the soil or the trees, some song of recognition, to assure me that this was my place to go to ground. I needed to listen for it without distraction.

"I'm fine walking around by myself. I can explore and I'll come down on my own. You don't need to come up for me, or anything."

He was frowning off uphill. "Some water up here," he said doubtfully. "Had to've been for someone to live here back when. Seems I saw a spring once. Couldn't tell you where, you might want to scout it out. Good to have water."

Then he set his cap firmly on his head, pushed the button on the tractor dash. The exhaust cap bounced and the motor rattled to life. "Yep, fine with me. Got enough to do, that's for sure. Just you walk around. You can't find me when you get down, look for Earnest. Be a nice piece up if you don't mind walkin in. Four-wheeler could do it. Winter, you could get up with a Ski-Doo."

He turned the tractor in a half circle, one wheel motionless as the other pivoted around. He waved once as he headed away. He was gone from sight as soon as he made the first bend. The tractor noise dwindled until it became inaudible.

I was alone on an almost-level forested hilltop where I'd never been before in my life. Through the trees, I could see other hills rolling away to a distant backdrop of mountains.

I turned in a slow circle to get a quick view in every direction and felt a tick of fear. I knew there were bears and bobcats out here, and I'd watched *Deliverance* back whenever.

But I loved it. Not yet so much the land itself, which I'd barely seen and which seemed only ambiguously acceptable; I loved this moment. Just being here, having this adventure. Or just *being*—awareness of *being* itself kindled in me.

Chapter 2

I KNOW, PERSONAL stories are supposed to begin with some kind of life history, but I don't want to tell you a great deal about the person I was before I found the land. Much of it's boring. Some of it's awful. I was the *Hindenburg* going down in flames when I first arrived. And now it strikes me as a distraction from what matters.

But, of course, any present or future has its roots in a past. I could pretend that my seeking a patch of wild forest was a typical back-to-the-land impulse, a sort of ordinary thing to do. But there was more to the tropism. I'd had two wretched, horrid years and was in abject retreat from my prior life and aspects of the world and myself that I despaired of ever coping with.

I was also moved by some better impulses, unrevealed to me despite my self-probings. I now know that our lives are moved equally by the lash of circumstance and the pull of unrecognized longings, and both can steer us true. Both were required to lead me to Brassard's farm.

At the time, I had an ordinary neo-Freudian way of looking at myself: I was a product of my parents' personalities, our domestic life, my early social experiences, and so on. Now all that seems surficial. I don't mean irrelevant, just shallow—the outer skin of a more robust and profound onion.

But here's how the narrative would have gone. My name: Ann Turner. My age: some years before the onset of menopause and the end of the choice of having children. The proverbial clock was ticking, but I wasn't counting the beats, because the idea of having kids had never loomed large in my life's agenda.

I was my parents' second child; they had lost their first in a late miscarriage. I didn't come along until seven years later, because it took them that long to muster their courage and try again. My survival gave them more confidence, so two years later I was joined by my brother, Erik.

We lived just outside Boston, where my father worked as director of facilities at a prep school. My mother taught photography at a community college, but only part time, so she was at home enough to maintain a reasonably ordered domestic life. Our house was full of conversation, benign commotion, humor. With their combined income, they paid off our house, I took dance lessons, and we went on vacations to Maine or Vermont. But they worried about our cars' repair costs, rising property taxes, and my college tuition. We lived a reasonably secure life, not affluent but by no means poor.

I mention all this because, with loving, attentive parents and a stable, happy home, I had no obvious failures of nurture or genetic inheritance to blame for my becoming a quirky, desperate woman prone to bad decisions.

My brother was what, as a child, I called a little rat, and he later morphed into what I called a stoner, Mom called a rebel without a cause, and Pop lovingly called a ne'er-do-well. But I adored Erik, and we played a typical sibling duet: sometimes harmonious, sometimes dissonant, sometimes competing for parental attention, sometimes in league against them. He was "brilliant but an underachiever," his teachers said—a fast learner who picked up any skill quickly but usually lost interest just as fast. He finished high school a year early and headed off to the West Coast and a life we didn't hear much about.

I went to college, graduating with a degree in education that didn't prove especially useful for the waitressing jobs I took afterward. For a couple of years, I shared an apartment with my dearest friend, Cat, then moved in with my boyfriend.

Four years after I graduated, my mother died of breast cancer. That was a dark time. Her absence wounded us all. Erik came back and cried hard with Pop and me at her funeral. Grief pulled the three of us close for a week before Erik left again.

Eventually, we got as over her death as anyone gets. My father soldiered on and remarried when he was in his midsixties. I got along well with my new stepmother, Elizabeth, but I had a life of my own and no great interest in developing a deeper relationship with her. That was reciprocal, given that she had two adult children from her first marriage, who, reasonably enough, took emotional precedence over her husband's daughter and invisible son.

My father and I grew closer as he aged. After he retired, he acquired by degrees a certain gravitas and a stillness that made him a good listener for his daughter's rants and confessions. When he died at seventy-three, I missed him terribly. Erik came for the funeral, but he returned to California far too soon, and anyway he had been remote for a long time. I felt very alone in the world, untethered. My stepmother inherited my father's house and much of the money he had put aside, leaving me with no geographical axis for my life and not enough means to establish another. Besides Erik, my only relatives were an aged aunt in Schenectady and some distant cousins whom I'd barely met.

Pop's death made me realize how spare a landscape of familial security I lived in, how meager my connections. Suddenly aware of the importance of blood relationships, I began calling Erik a lot. Crass-sounding girlfriends or male buddies answered the phone, clashing rock and roll played in the background, and Erik often sounded distracted, in the style of a druggie. He spoke evasively of his personal life, and I got the sense his work involved something illegal. Still, he was always sympathetic in his way: *Yeah, I hear what you're saying, Annie. I gotta get out east sometime, but work here, business ... you know how that is.*

At some point, I called Erik to find that his phone had been disconnected. I contacted old friends of his and did online people searches, but couldn't find him. I didn't think he was dead—surely somebody would have let me know, some sixth sense would have whispered the awful truth to me. I figured maybe he was on the lam from the law or women or bill collectors, or had gone back to the land and off the grid. I even searched the online inmate database for the California Corrections Department, but there was no record of his arrest or incarceration. Eventually, I gave up trying to find him. Either I would hear from him when he wanted to be heard from, or I wouldn't.

Yes, I felt orphaned, but it wasn't really so bleak. While my parents' deaths and Erik's vanishing act made a hollow in me, they occurred within the context of a satisfying social milieu and a consuming professional life. By then I had a job teaching middle school kids at a public school in Brookline. I was part of a group of newer teachers in a demographically diverse and economically challenged district—idealists who took pride in our battle against ignorance and social inequity. We gave up a lot of free time to meet with troubled kids after class. With the school budget too tight to afford extracurricular activity, we spent our own money to pay for field trips and books and musical instrument rentals. My comrades-in-arms helped make up for the absence of family in my life.

And then I fell in love with Matt, who did a great job of either filling, or further distracting me from, that void. He was a graphic designer for a firm that manufactured a chic line of purses, hats, sandals, and scarves that hit the marketing sweet spot among the twentysomething "hipnoscenti," as he labeled their customer base. He was hip and smart, with a square chin, red-brown hair, and an intriguing scar on his cheek that he told people he'd gotten in a gang rumble in New Jersey. In fact, he got it when he was nine years old, by hitting his head on a wrought-iron fence while trying to do wheelies on his bike.

We had a big laugh together when he confessed, and I loved that scar as a symbol of our intimacy. Also, it gave him a slightly rakish look that I liked. His style was a little like my brother's, which may account for the strong sense of connection I felt.

I really fell for him, and I loved every minute of the plummet. We got married six months after we met.

Looking back, I see that the deaths of my parents and my brother's disappearance nudged me into that inward-spiraling orbit toward some solid thing in a life increasingly defined by loss and uncertainty. Those losses also made me cleave—I can't bear to say "cling"—to Matt more than I should have. And made the crash of that relationship all the more disillusioning and injurious.

Death, absence, and disillusionment: Between them, I felt unmoored, desperately wanting not only something certain, solid, but also a departure from my life as it had been.

BUT NONE OF this entered my thoughts as I explored Brassard's land that day. I felt only a breathless exhilaration, devoid of thought. There was so much to see.

The air warmed as the sun rose higher above the neighboring hills. I was perfectly comfortable in my fleece jacket. Tendrils of steam rose wherever the light shone directly on bare earth or granite. As I walked I occasionally entered pockets of surprising cool, frigid ghosts of the winter just past. In the occasional open patches, where grasses and scrub held the ground, green spears of new growth pierced the snow-flattened thatch. Low-growing bushes were tipped with swelling beads of green and purple.

I wasn't even thinking about whether this was the right land, whether I felt the intuitive tug, whether I'd make Brassard an offer. I was too absorbed in the small facts of the place, an awareness of detail I'd never experienced. It was as if my eyes had become magnifying glasses, as if local space were occupied by a medium more transparent than air, so that everything visible registered with startling clarity.

The knobs of rough gray granite that humped through the weave of dead grass or wet leaf detritus wore scaling pelts of lichens and brilliant green moss that looked exactly like a rain forest seen from an airplane. Small birds flicked in the trees and among the bushes, picking at dried berries left on the branches despite winter's winds. A couple of spent shotgun shells lay on a granite shelf, their plastic red and glistening brass startling and incongruous. The sunlight, slanting through almost-bare branches, cast a shifting lacework of pale shadows over the ground. A solitary bottle-green beetle trundled along, sluggish with cold, on a rotten log. My running shoes got mucked, and I was pleased to punish them for their prior naïveté and hubris. The air was so fresh, I wanted only to inhale and never have to exhale.

I started by walking along the plateau toward the uphill end. Here the trees thickened, the slope steepened. My way was often barricaded by whipping saplings, fallen trunks topped by tangles of branches, rearing earthen walls made by the upended root masses of blowdowns. Thickets of brambles encircled the little open patches, and after my first attempt I learned not to mess with them. My jacket picked up knots of burrs; my hair gathered twigs. I stepped unexpectedly into ice-water puddles that soaked my shoes. I slipped and stumbled and tangled my way along.

I was a little surprised by all this. I'd probably absorbed too many images of idealized pastoral life from old paintings in museums. I had certainly watched too many romantic movies about nineteenth-century England, where forests were so spacious that one could gallop sidesaddle on a runaway horse until the scion of some other wealthy family dashed up on his steed and grabbed the reins. Unconsciously, that was what I had been expecting, not this raw, muddy, hard-bitten place. Farther along, facing a particularly dense thicket made by two fallen trees, I began to feel discouraged and irritable.

I was sitting on a rock, retying my wretched shoes, when a sudden racket of footfalls and crackling erupted close behind me. I was so startled, I swear I felt an artery throb in my brain. In unfamiliar deep woods, primal paranoia reasserts itself instantly.

I whipped around but couldn't see anything through the snarled brush. A bear, a wolf—were there wolves in Vermont? Maybe one of the mountain lions said to hide out around here! A moose? I'd heard the bulls are aggressive and terribly dangerous when they're in rut. *Did* moose rut in spring, or was it fall?

The noise moved farther away, and though I waited expectantly, nothing devoured or even mauled me.

Now I know the difference between the drum of a deer's hooves, a bear's heavier, twig-breaking tread, the measured thump of a moose, the footless rustle of a porcupine or skunk. Also the bipedal beat of a man moving in the woods. I didn't then. I stood for another minute in heart-pounding, hand-tingling paralysis before I could resume my uphill trek.

The scariest part—the saddest—was that in that startle and long moment of trembling, part of me welcomed catastrophe. Invited it. I felt a savage, cruel yearning for injury or death, punishment or atonement. Some kind of finality.

Chapter 3

By the time I married Matt, I had lived with two men and was by no means unfamiliar with the ups and downs of cohabitation. People are all a little crazy; my boyfriends were and I was, too. You joked, confided, argued, figured out the other gender's laundry, learned each other's sexual preferences, talked about your respective pasts. You drifted distant and then worked back closer, or didn't. You accommodated—or didn't—the inevitable eccentricities and neuroses. Sex was sometimes great, sometimes less than. Men coped with PMS and women dealt with fragile male egos beneath hard but brittle exteriors. And you wondered whether your bond was strong enough, your affinities adequately synced, for the long haul.

But marriage turned out to be different from mere cohabitation. Maybe the biggest difference is, what with that legally stipulated long-term commitment, you dissolve into a collective identity. You become a sugar cube melting gratefully in a cup of warm tea. It's not about *me* anymore; it's about *us*. Home decor that began as an eclectic mix of two collections pulls together in a consensually determined style. Your finances merge;

your circle of friends is winnowed to those both of you can enjoy or at least endure. You confide your life histories until they become a shared possession, until you're telling each other's stories at parties. Your friends say "you" not in the singular anymore, but as in "you guys," "you two."

I let myself dissolve more than Matt did. With no family beyond my invisible brother and my Schenectady aunt, I was more susceptible to this blending. Maybe I needed sure connection or a defense against loneliness more than Matt did. Or maybe those are tendencies shared by all women.

In any case, by the time our marriage ended I had dissolved too much and I seemed unable to become solid again. I fled to Brassard's valley in large part to pull myself back together. To congeal, to cohere again. Given my proven, pitiful tendency for melting, I knew it had to be a solitary process.

But this was not the only factor propelling me toward the land. From my father, I had inherited a romantic's belief that living close to the earth was righteous and good, and the vacations we took when I was a kid affirmed that notion. We would pack the car and drive to Maine or Vermont to set up a miniature household in a canvas army tent at some state park. Campfire, hissing Coleman lanterns, showers in a concrete-floored bathroom shared by strangers, fishing with my father from a rented aluminum canoe. All four of us sleeping in the same cozy space. At night, Erik and I ran with other flashlight-wielding kids among the trees and glowing tents. In our sleeping bags, hearing the murmurs of other campers conducting their bedtime rituals, we felt an embracing sense of common humanity.

These were the best of times. My parents lost their workweek edge and became expansive, accommodating. I loved our hikes, the white, muscular calves of my father pumping along in front of me, my brother behind me, Mom bringing up the rear to motivate stragglers. We were like a little railroad train, exploring nature's splendors.

Pop, in particular, blossomed when nourished by woods and sky. By the time he died, he had achieved many of the things he wanted, but finances had denied him one important fulfillment: owning a little forest home away from home. It became one of those mythological regrets built into the family identity, like *Yeah, I had a chance to buy into Apple back in the day, but ...*

Yeah, we've always wanted some land, but ... became one of ours. Certainly, that yearning, and memories of those camping trips, helped bring me to Brassard's place.

But there's another reason, too, harder to explain. My attempts to talk about it always come across as a political polemic when, in fact, it's a personal confession. I haven't a name for it, but *environmental angst* comes close. I mean our political, social, cultural, economic, and, yes, environmental milieu—the larger situational brine we marinate in every day. To me, it felt increasingly like a toxic immersion.

My parents raised me to have a passion for social justice, and a suspicion of materialism and unbridled striving after wealth. They believed in respect for others, sticking by your values, practical and emotional self-sufficiency. But I saw the country, the world, mutating, moving in a direction diametrically opposed to these values. Matt reminded me that it had been doing so for decades, that there's not much any individual can do about deterministic trends, that it's best to develop a thick skin and get on despite them. I knew he was right, but it didn't help much.

At times, I worried about getting crushed beneath the rubble of a decadent society crumbling under its own weight. I had read *Collapse* and could not doubt that, like the Easter Islanders, Americans would cut down the last living tree just to make some one-percenter the wall paneling he simply had to have. America was fighting two ugly wars, and even our veteran friends admitted that they were unwise, unwinnable, unnecessary. Bush the younger had seemed to feel contempt for the Constitution and any dissenting citizen—easily half of America. Obama was trying hard, but his election had aroused the awful snake of racism and xenophobia that coiled around America's heart. We ate food grown on factory farms and brought to our tables by machines burning fossil fuels. We had no idea how to feed ourselves, no connection to the soil, no relevant skills, and too little respect for the people who did have those things.

I was by no means a rabid survivalist, buying guns and hoarding cases of Spam. As for food, I enjoyed nothing more than a fresh ripe mango, Asian cooking seasoned with curry and saffron, tender mesclun lettuce from California fields. And beef fed on a mix of genetically modified corn, Saudi Arabian oil, and what little was left of the Ogallala Aquifer. But what could I do about it? We all knew things were going to hell in a shopping cart, and like everyone else, I soothed the pangs of this awareness with the balm of cynicism, resignation, and a high tolerance for my own hypocrisy.

I didn't often wail or rage about this. But it was certainly one piece of the puzzle, one of the reasons I found myself scrambling and tangling around Brassard's back forty that day: *There's got to be a more honest, less divided way to live.*

Chapter 4

I COVERED A lot of rugged ground that first day. I made it to somewhere near the upper property line—just as Brassard had said, a wall of boulders tumbled against a steep hill. They ranged in size from a microwave to a minivan, and white birches thrust up through the ramparts here and there. I was unwilling to get too close to the dark gaps and shallow caves between rocks, worried that creatures might take offense at my intrusion. It looked like the kind of place that animals hibernated or denned or whatever it was called, and gave birth. I had no desire to startle a she-bear guarding her cubs. Also, I remembered that there were copperheads in Vermont, and these rocks seemed just the sort of place they would hang out. I paused for one uneasy moment at the boulder wall before deciding I had located the upper border precisely enough.

I headed back toward the submarine's prow, then cut down the west-facing slope to look for the border with Hubbard's land. At the bottom, I found an old knee-high stone wall and followed it along. Stretches of rusted barbed wire, deeply embedded in the trees that held them, assured me I had found the property line.

By early afternoon, I was getting tired, so I angled back uphill to the flat top where I'd started. That exquisite awareness of small wonders had long since faded. The morning's fresh sun had stealthily faded into a thin, bright but sullen overcast. My feet were numb and my shoes thick with mud; my fleece was torn and bristled with burr fuzz. The constant tangling and slipping and fighting with vegetation had made me irritable.

More, it made me despondent: I didn't really like the outdoors that much. Buying some land wasn't going to fix what was wrong with me, but I had no other idea what might. Here was yet another example of my inanity. The remorseless engine of self-flagellating introspection started up in me.

Enough. I slogged down the tractor trail back to Brassard's farm, unsure whether I should go through with my grand stupid plan, and distinctly ambivalent about this particular place.

I crossed the road and walked past my car to the tractor Earnest had been working on. There was no sign of either man or Bob the dog.

I walked to the barn's broad doorway and leaned in. "Mr. Brassard? Earnest?"

No answer. I went to the end of the yard to where the pasture fence met the corner of the barn, scouted the field and saw no one except tranquil cows.

"Mr. Brassard?" I yelled.

Behind me I heard the stretch of a storm-door spring and turned to see a woman coming out of the house. She was gray-haired and barrel-shaped, wearing a floral housedress, down vest, and tall rubber boots. She shut the inner door behind her and let the outer door slap shut.

Bob had followed her out and immediately came to me to review my scent in a friendly way.

"Bob, get your nose the *hell* out of that woman's privates!" she roared. When the dog backed away, she visored her eyes with one hand to look at me. "You want the men, they've gone to get a tractor part and some other indispensables. Said you'd be down after a while."

"Are you Mrs. Brassard?"

"Sure hope so. After thirty-five years, I'd be dismayed to discover I'd been living in sin all the while. My name is Maureen—one hell of an awful name, so people call me Diz, and don't ask how that happened. How'd you like the property?"

I crossed the yard and driveway to shake hands with her. "It's really nice. I had a good time walking around."

Behind her glasses, shrewd eyes scanned me up and down, taking in my dishevelment. "Looks like you did. Think you'll buy it?"

"Well, I've got to think about it. Consider the money side a little more. But it's the nicest I've seen so far."

Mrs. Brassard, Diz, gathered up a pair of empty galvanized buckets and started toward the barn, tipping her head for me to follow.

"I get up there a couple times a year. Chase the bears out of the brambles and take about five gallons of blackberries, come August. Lose about the same in blood from the thorns. Pretty piece of property, but no good for a year-round house. What d'you want with it, anyway?"

I sloshed behind her for another few steps. "Build a little cabin and have a place to get away to once in a while." Then I surprised us both by confessing, "That's what I've been thinking, anyway. Actually, I'm not sure exactly why."

She'd gotten to the door of the barn but now turned around, buckets clanking. My last comment had kicked it up a notch, suggesting that my purpose was more than recreational.

She looked at me with heightened interest, and lips compressed in a hard smile. Behind the glasses, her blue eyes narrowed. "I wondered the same thing when I hooked up with Brassard and came out here. And often enough I still do. *What the heck, Diz?* And I say, *Couldn't tell ya, get back to work.*"

I laughed. Diz was obviously a "character," a woman who enjoyed the role of conversational provocateur. I liked her, and feared her slightly. "Can I ask a question?"

"You can certainly give it a try."

"Why do you want to sell that land? I don't mean to pry, I'm just—"

"Need the money. Things're thin right now, milk's down and fuel's up, Brassard's not gettin any younger. We could log it off and get some money from the timber. But Brassard doesn't want to see it go that way. Likes his picturesque view, I guess, doesn't want to look at the mess that's left over after the trees're down and the skidders've dug ruts all over. Got a sentimental streak, or else he's got too much pride to make our place look like the trash that lives up the hill."

She winced up her glasses on her nose and turned back to the barn. Disappearing into the dark, she called back, "Brassard'll be home by four or five. You give a call if you want to talk about it."

Chapter 5

I'D BEEN PRONOUNCING the name "Bruh-*SARD*," accent on the second syllable, because in college I'd known a Jill Brassard and that's how she said it. But Diz pronounced it to rhyme with "bastard"—hard A, emphasis on the *brass*. I wasn't sure whether that was the accepted way of saying it hereabouts or another eccentricity of hers—maybe some habitual jab at her husband. On the drive back, I decided she was a former alcoholic, one of those early-sixties, witty, sarcastic, seen-it-all, don't-give-a-damn-what-anybody-thinks women with practical haircuts and mannish clothes that declared they were beyond all that business about wanting or needing males. They'd cleaned up their act but, like Diz, still had the husky voice of the ex-alkie, ex-smoker. I'd met them on both sides of the desk in the legal aid office where I worked, and I'd volunteered alongside them at park clean-ups or tree plantings. Whether still married or widowed, if they spoke of their husbands at all it was without a shred of sentimentality.

Back at my B and B, I managed to get into my room without the owners seeing what a mess I was. I would have collapsed on the bed, but I

carried too much organic material on my clothes and didn't want to ruin
the bedspread. I took off my clothes intending to take a shower, decided
I'd lie down to recharge a bit first, and woke up almost three hours later.
Without once even thinking about it, I called Brassard and said I wanted
to buy the land.

"Okay."

"Would you take sixty for it?" He had advertised it for seventy
thousand.

He paused. "I guess I would."

I was pretty sure he meant it in the Vermont vernacular, that is, "yes."

We arranged for him to come up to Montpelier on Friday so we could
meet with his lawyer to complete the transaction.

And there it was. My irrational determination had culminated in an
equally irrational decision. Why? Perhaps it was that clarity of detail, the
seeing I'd done for that first half hour, a rare spirit or feng shui that had
spoken to what was still bright and unsoured in me.

But, sadly, I have to admit, it was mainly my three-hour harried hike
along the borders, the scratches on my hands and cheeks and the soreness
of my calves, the mucked shoes and ruined jacket, that decided the issue.
That was the real deal. The land promised a harrowing that I needed
and deserved, some hard, skin-thickening, making-do woods living, a
taste of the ascetic's life. Look, I even have the stigmata!

To the extent that I had any real hopes for personal growth, I also
knew that here was what needed confronting: my own bramble patch, my
own deep woods. Brassard's land was its perfect external manifestation.

WITH LESS THAN five thousand dollars to my name, I was hardly rich
enough to afford such a purchase. What made this whole idea marginally
possible was that my aunt Theresa had died and had left me sixty-five
thousand dollars. I'd received most of it, with about ten thousand due
to me in another few weeks, when the last of her bonds were liquidated.
Brassard had kindly agreed to owner-finance that bit. When he met me at
the lawyer's office, I handed over a cashier's check for fifty thousand, and

Brassard, after carefully reviewing Aunt Theresa's portfolio statements, had me sign a short-term promissory note for the remaining ten grand. The lawyer tried to force a celebratory joviality on the process that neither of us really felt. Brassard didn't want to part with his woods; he just needed the damned money.

When I had shaken his big hand and left the office and got back into my car, I immediately felt that I'd done something really, profoundly stupid, like getting pregnant from a one-night stand. Another act of self-destructive impulsiveness.

My plan, if one could call it that, had been to buy some land and live off the remaining ten grand while I looked for a job nearby. I'd build a little cabin on the cheap. I'd live in the woods for the summer and move into an apartment in town when winter came. Even then, I'd still make pilgrimages out there, in the snow. I needed physical hardship. I would build the cabin with my own hands. It would show, or require the acquisition of, independence and grit. My cell phone would keep me connected. If I really felt the hunger for human company, I would make new friends in town or invite my few remaining Boston friends up for a taste of roughing it. Any man who might enter the picture would by necessity have to share my longing for primitive living, a hankering for physical hardship. It would provide a good filter for unsuitable suitors.

I knew this was a radical departure for a person with my background, and I relished the thought of the courage and discomfort it would demand of me. Maybe over time I would ease into an earthier, more rooted rural life, growing some vegetables, cutting some firewood, and learning at least a few self-sufficiency skills. I would manage the world on my own terms. I pumped myself up and swore that nothing would dissuade me.

Chapter 6

May 21

*It's been a while since I kept up with my journal, mainly because there's no
way my scribblings can adequately describe what I've been doing or feeling.
Why am I bothering with this? Who am I writing to? I ask as I sit here and
flail at the blackflies that torture me.*

*To myself, of course. Basic principle: Leave tracks so you can find your
way back. What idiocies led you here? Remember and avoid them next time.
Assuming you bother to read your own diary, which I don't—lousy handwrit-
ing, too much whining. Thus am I condemned to repeat history.*

*I am camping on my land, alternating three or four days out here with
a partial day and a night at a cheap motel near the interstate where I can
shower and watch TV, enjoy indoor plumbing and the absence of dirt, and
make phone calls—there's no reception on my hill. Also to escape the pressure
of insects who want to suck me dry as a mummy. Little pestilent shits! I
kill every one I can slap, determined to reduce their available DNA in*

proportion to the nutrition they extract from me, which would otherwise go to breeding new ones.

It's been very hard. Goodie! I felt at first, with each new difficulty or discomfort. But I failed to anticipate the effect of prolonged subfatal, insufficiently dramatic discomfort. It erodes even masochistic impulses. And I hadn't taken fear into consideration—not the urbanite's comfortable, self-imposed existential fear, but a primal, irresistible terror springing from the deep caverns of instinct. Fear has been hard.

Writing about the last few weeks is an exercise in answering the question "What's the hardest part?" Answer: All of it. Mostly it's been a bastard. It's been murder.

There have been some wonderful moments, but nothing has ever been easy. I realize now that the camping trips we so enjoyed were nothing more than luxurious fantasies of rugged living. We set up our tent on a flat piece of mowed grass with our car fifteen feet away. We were surrounded by other families, never all alone in the deep woods. Running water, toilets, sinks and showers, firewood for sale at the ranger's office, a coin-op laundry room. Clothes and food kept safe in the back of the station wagon. Not a wild animal within a mile. Hardly any bugs. We thought we were roughing it, but we were just playing house. But I fell for the fantasy, and now I'm stuck with my own foolishness.

My tent has turned out better than I expected. I had no idea tent technology had advanced so far. It's tall enough to stand up in, big enough to tuck my sleeping stuff out of the way and to keep my old sea chest here, full of clothes and other necessities. I keep food in a strongly built wooden cabinet covered with galvanized sheet steel to keep mice and porcupines from chewing their way in—Earnest taught me that trick—nailed to a tree near my campfire circle. But the tent had its "hardest part" moments.

The night of my first heavy rain, two weeks ago, began as one of the greatest delights I've ever experienced—lying in the dark, listening to the varying patter and thrum of the rain on the tent's fly, hearing it hiss and roar in the trees in every direction, hundreds of layers of distance and intensity. Rain comes and goes in irregular waves, and you can hear a heavier fall moving through the *trees toward you. I was ecstatic and less afraid than usual—surely no bears or mountain lions or deranged hillbillies would be out in this. The sound was symphonic in complexity, sometimes a murmured susurrus, then swelling to a bass waterfall sound, grand and sometimes martial, even threatening. And the air was exquisite, as if the rain carried down cool, pure, rarified atmosphere from high altitudes, tinged with ozone.*

Drifted off in a heavenly state. Woke up well before dawn to find that my sleeping bag and pillow were sopped and cold, the floor was slimy. The seams had leaked and humidity had condensed on the ceiling and fallen on everything inside, a baby rainfall birthed by its big mother.

I spent a miserable day wearing a plastic trash bag over my last dry clothes as the rain came and went. I couldn't retreat: I was ashamed to go down the hill and risk having anyone at the farm see me in my bedraggled condition. So I spent a second horrible night shivering in my ever-wetter sleeping bag, getting up now and then to mop the hanging droplets off the ceiling with paper towels.

When I finally came down, Earnest was there—he's often not, off working as a tree surgeon up in Chittenden County. He's started to call me "Pilgrim"—either an allusion to the old John Wayne movie or a subtler comment on my purpose for being here. "You look like shit, Pilgrim! Don't know enough to come out of the rain?" He explained that if you're tent camping for any extended period, you've got to make sure you've sealed your seams. And you have to build a wooden floor, even just a few inches off the ground, and set your tent on top of that. That way, the air circulates beneath, the ground moisture never touches your tent, everything ventilates better, no condensation. He took me to the lumberyard that morning and we brought the boards back in his pickup. We strapped it all to a flat trailer that the faithful tractor dragged up to my eyrie. He lent me a hammer, carpenter's square, tape measure, and handsaw, then left me to figure out how to build it.

I think of myself as fit, but putting together the platform taught me how weak my wrists and forearms are. Jogging and biking don't use them much. It was almost impossible to cut the wood by hand and to drive the big sixteen-penny nails through two-by-fours. But when it was done, I was satisfied with it. Not a cabin, but at least a first step toward an education in carpentry.

I set up the tent on the platform and it was great. Flat floor, dry, more civilized. I felt clever and capable for two days. Then a big wind came up—no rain, just one of those robust, ebullient spring winds that come in to make sure winter is thoroughly swept away. It bent the trees frighteningly and flapped my tent fly with a sound like machine-gun fire that stopped suddenly when the thing ripped loose and flew away in the darkness. Without a waterproof covering, the tent was fully exposed to any rain that might come, and I spent a night of high anxiety wondering if a thunderstorm would drown me out completely. At times, the arched aluminum poles swayed and the nylon wall ballooned so much, I was sure the whole thing would lift up like a box kite, with me still inside, a woman blown away into the night sky.

Didn't blow me away, didn't rain. In the morning—beautifully fresh and clear, ringing blue sky, winter absolutely combed out of the woods—I found the fly, snarled high in a tree about a hundred feet from camp, inaccessible and badly torn. I had to buy another for almost as much as a whole new tent would have cost. When I mentioned it to Earnest, he told me you really had to use every one of the loops for a guy wire that would hold the fly tight. He also had a little secret, a way to use a marble-size pebble to make extra tie-down grommets on the nylon, with short ropes that could tie to the platform and pull the fly closer to the inner shell. Less room for the wind to get under.

The tent has been much nicer and since then has handled rains and winds in fine shape.

Earnest: I've enjoyed our times together. Turns out he's an Oneida, born on the tribe's lands near Green Bay, Wisconsin. They were originally a New York tribe, he says, but they were kicked out by the governor in eighteen-something and marched to their new "nature preserve" (his term)—but not before Gov. Schuyler fathered twenty-seven kids by Indian women. When I asked him how he ended up in Vermont, he told me that he and Brassard served together in Vietnam in the early seventies and when they got back to the States Earnest had no big plans or prospects, so Brassard hired him to work on the farm.

"I didn't like working for Jim," he explained. He seemed a bit uncom-fortable telling me this. "Anyway, after a few years I got to a head place where I needed some distance from the farm and went up and started my own

business." He went on to tell me he set up as a tree surgeon up near Burlington, but realized he had gotten attached to the farm, and started coming down to help out: *"Now when I come down, I'm not getting paid, so he and Diz can't tell me what to do."* He smiled at that.

Earnest is the equipment fixer and major project manager. It's a marginal farm, no extra money, the nineteen-year-old kid Brassard hires is a pretty dim bulb, and a lot of the machines are getting old and cranky, so his skills are badly needed. He's also strong as an ox and doesn't have any physical problems. I'd guess Earnest is in his midfifties. Brassard is probably ten years older and has arthritic joints, so he can use the help. I get the sense there's some bond between the men, some exceptional basis for their loyalty to each other. From what I can gather, Brassard spent five years in Vietnam while Earnest only served there for the last humiliating, stumbling year of the war. Maybe some act of heroism, one saving the other's life or something.

Another bastard hardest thing: For the first two weeks, I brought my water up the hill in plastic gallon jugs. It was agonizing, but I can only prevail upon the Brassards' help so many times. Two jugs, one in each hand, leaving my arms and shoulders and hands aching by the time I got to the top. Relished the discomfort the first few times, proof I was living hard, then got fucking sick of it. Finally I set out and did a methodical search for the water source Brassard said might be up here.

And I found it. It's about two hundred yards uphill from camp, a little channel about six inches deep and two feet wide, clear water running off toward Brassard's valley. The bottom is made up of clean rocks. I tracked it back up the hill almost to the boulder wall, to a point where it bubbles up out of the earth. It's crystal clear and tooth-achingly cold, the best water I've ever tasted. It's never been in a pipe, never languished in a plastic bottle absorbing carcinogens. Brassard says the fact that it's a real spring and not a runoff stream is a very good thing. Comes from deep underground, no germs or cow poop in it. I look forward to washing in it every morning, even though the cold burns my skin. I'm sure it's good for your complexion.

Hardest bastard parts: On the physical side, bugs rank at or near the top. Blackflies are the worst. Each is about half the size of a grain of rice. They bite *every exposed part, particularly blood-rich areas like behind my ears, where the bites itch intolerably. They create a dive-bombing cloud around your face that drives you to madness. You get virtually hysterical, and the state is not optional; it's your body, not your brain. Slathering my face and arms with insect repellent reduces their biting but doesn't diminish their frenzied activity all around me. And some still get through. Eventually, they drive me screaming to the shelter of the tent. Another way to diminish their bloodthirsty ardor is to light a fire. I have come to smell like wood smoke from cooking, warming myself in the chilly evenings, and hovering in the smoke of the dying fire to escape them. They're bad in the morning, absent during the middle of the day, and intolerable in the late afternoon and evening. Earnest says they'll be mostly gone by mid-July.*

There are mosquitoes, too—not as many, but another maddening irritation at night. Several always get into the tent, whining around invisible in the dim light and biting me when my guard is down. I splat them when they land, and thwack their little flat corpses off my skin with one finger. Hundreds more hover and press frantically at the tent's window screens with a high urgent screamy whine. The sound creates an uneasiness at a primal level, awakens an instinctive aversion to biting insects that's built into the human genome. Impossible to ignore. Makes me feel under siege, eases off when I blow out the candles.

There are bugs I'd never heard of and didn't believe existed until they bit me: no-see-ums. No-see-ums are semitransparent flies about as big as a comma, and they bite painfully. You're going about your business and are startled by a sharp pain, like a splinter. When you look for the source of the pain, you can't find it at first. Then you spot the tiny bastard and smear him into nothing. How can such a minute thing cause such pain in a creature as big as, relatively, a mountain? Fortunately, the bite doesn't itch afterward. And they can't get at me inside the tent. I was lucky I bought superfine-mesh tent screens, or they'd drive me out of here.

Then there's fear. Sometimes, when the weather is just right and the bugs are momentarily absent and the woods do look like serene glades in the sun and the birds are singing all around, there's no nag of fear at all; it's sweet and good. But at times, even during the day, I get spooked when I head up to the spring and into the deeper woods. I always feel I'm being covertly watched, and I probably am—animals live here. I realize I am a stranger here. It's like walking in an unfamiliar neighborhood and some local gives you more attention than you'd like. The woods are a community, and I don't know its residents.

At night, I'm always afraid. The dark is mysterious; I am blind; my little outpost of candlelight seems very isolated. Earnest swears that Vermont's black bears are harmless, but I am deathly afraid of them at night—I nearly threw up after watching Grizzly Man *last year. I strain my ears to hear the night noises beyond the mosquitoes' shrilling. And there are always things moving out there. A crackle in this direction, a leafy scraping there. The stealthy progress of some creature moving over last year's leaf litter. Shiftings. A stick breaking. Once, a series of hellish shrieks in the distance that literally brought up the hair on my arms.*

A couple of times, I swear I've been stalked by a human. Regular, two-legged-sounding quiet footfalls from uphill coming closer, a zipping sound like fabric scraping past a twig. Then silence charged with horrible imminence, expectancy. Maybe one of the Goslant "trash" up the hill, who heard about this woman camping out where no one could hear her scream. I haven't seen one of the Goslants yet, but picture them as a tribe of leering, gap-toothed, twitchy-eyed sinewy men with evil intentions about everything.

I may have a death wish, but if I'm going to shuffle off this mortal coil I'm going to do it my way, not subject myself to some other creature's or human's perverse preferences. So I go to sleep with a set of defensive weapons carefully arranged where my hand can find them in the dark: flashlight, sheath knife out of its sheath, hammer, shovel. Anything and anyone could come through the thin nylon with ease. Wake up in the night but am too afraid to go out to the outhouse hole I dug, about a hundred feet away among the trees, so I wait until my bladder's about to explode, and then I scuttle out and pee right next to the tent.

Like so much else I feel up here, this fear transcends conscious or rational control. My body must remember being a timid little hominid in a big predatory world. It knows the harsh laws that govern nighttime in the deep woods. Sometimes I lie with suspended breath so I can hear noises better.

And, I hate to write this down—an admission I'll feel stupid about later, when I've escaped this situation: I fear supernatural dangers. It's as if I sense movements in mental space, unnamed creatures of the air or earth, sentient but inhuman beings that all outdoor-living peoples acknowledge and fear. If I could say where they came from, it would be the boulder tumble uphill, out of the crevasses. I don't even know that they're malevolent, only that being around them could destroy me, or that our kinds have always been enemies.

Each dawn I chide myself for these imaginings. I rationalize them as stemming from the same species proclivities that led people to invent gods, demons, ghosts. I almost laugh at myself. And as night falls I become aware of the gargantuan stupidity, the hubris, of such skepticism. Of such profound ignorance of the world's real ways. The source of the fear is vast, ancient, deeper by far than reason and the easy lies of daylight.

And yes, I am lonely. This loneliness is not a godlike presence, like the fear, just a cringing small thing dwelling close to my heart. Each night, I think of Mom and Pop, and Erik wherever he went, and Cat and even friends from grade school, and I miss them unbearably. I cry a little and feel sorry for myself. I feel unprotected and disconnected. At these moments, I curl up on my cot, more like a grub than a fetus, cringing away from my distance from everyone. "Where are you?" I ask everyone I ever loved. Then, as I drift off to sleep in my curl I think of the comfort of spooning back-to-belly with your loved one, and of course it's Matt, and then I wake and fling his memory from even my loneliness. I will be lonely for the whole human race, but not him.

It hurts to be this lonely curled grub.

This process is the woods prying me open, can-opening me, to expose fears and senses and awarenesses and feelings and instincts that have always been in there. That's good, isn't it? Isn't that what I wanted in coming here?

No. I was supposed to come to a hard-won understanding of myself, a tough-love relationship with my life. Atone for past sins. True, in the background I harbored carefully suppressed, more optimistic aspirations. To the extent I hoped for any deeper self-awareness, I was supposed to serenely discover insightful but conventional perspectives on my past, my family, my relation-ships—all the usual. It was also about remaking myself as bolder, sturdier, independent, more capable. Maybe, my most idealistic inner voices piped, I'd even get healed by unexpectedly touching a nurturing Gaia, learning earthy wisdom, accepting nature's gentle embrace. Hasn't worked that way. I am over all that.

And I'm striking out on the job front. Applied for a couple teaching positions, didn't get called for interviews. I can only wonder what my recom-mendation letters say.

I am considering leaving, calling the experiment a bust. Maybe Brassard will let me off the hook and give me some of my money back. Maybe I'll move back to Boston, try for a job at some other school. Get real again, pretend to be like real people.

Chapter 7

I DID NOT buy my land with the intent to totally isolate myself. While I badly wanted some distance from my prior life, I never intended to become a hermit.

I'd closed my Facebook page the year before, at the peak of my catastrophes, so I didn't have to read my friends' happy inane postings. But I still drove to the public library in Montpelier to check in on friends' pages, make telephone calls, and send emails inviting people to visit me "in my new digs." I even wrote an actual paper letter to my friend Cat—Catherine—which I actually put into Brassard's mailbox. I put up the little red metal flag, and the US Postal Service actually picked it up and delivered it. (The Postal Service cars here are privately owned, typically back-road-weary SUVs with nothing to differentiate them from any other car but their jerry-rigged right-hand drive and some yellow flashers on their roof racks.)

Cat thought getting a paper letter was a hoot. Never reciprocated, but said she'd love to visit.

We met in eighth grade, made it through high school by protecting each other's back from the daggers of other girls, went to different colleges but shared an apartment for a year or so after graduation—the first place either of us had lived "on our own." She has brittle blond hair that makes her look caffeinated and frenetic even when she's not. She's skinny, runs half marathons, eats a lot of meat, drives an old BMW that costs more in repairs than she'd pay on a new car loan. Her cynical outlook helps make her a superb middle school teacher: that withering ironic wit gives voice to the students' contempt for government and convention and adults and racists and routine, and they love her for it.

She'd been through more boyfriends than I had in our years as friends—a diverse lot. One was a tubby, shy, big-bearded hospice nurse who tended to mumble and grope for words yet was a marvelous poet; another was a buff Harley rider who managed a car-detailing shop. She spent a year with a Pakistani man, Sandeep: smart, great sense of humor, handsome, a financial advisor at some big firm. And others. She was almost always the one to break it off with them.

Ordinarily, one is well advised to avoid commentary on another's choices in love. Cat and I were always candid about men, jobs, families, and our bodies, but over the years we'd developed an unspoken compact that if one of us didn't offer to talk about something, the other didn't press the issue.

With Sandeep, though, I felt compelled to say something. They just seemed to fit. He was clearly devoted to her, and from what she told me, they really hit it off in bed. They seemed enthusiastic about each other until the day she cut him off.

I approached it with trepidation: "Cat, I love you, right? I like to think I know you pretty well. So forgive me for sticking my nose in, but, I mean, of course I don't know all the nuances of your relationship with Sandeep, but—"

"Spit it out," she said. "Let's get this over with."

"I think you're making a mistake. I really think you're doing the wrong thing this time. I think you're being ... like, crazy." I kept eye contact with her to make sure she knew I meant it. Then I went ahead with the hard part: "Sometimes I think you're ... running away from something."

Deadpan, she gave it a couple of beats and then said briskly, "Good. Forgiven. Thanks for being honest with me, sweetie." As she left the room, she couldn't help but call back one little jab: "Let me know if you want his phone number."

Life went on, and eventually that water went under the bridge to merge with the ocean of other forgiven and forgotten things. I treasured the resilience of our friendship.

In my emails, I described my land and state of mind without minimizing the discomforts, fears, and doubts. At least I thought I did. When Cat said she'd like to visit, I assumed she understood about the bugs, the hole in the ground that served as outhouse, the ice water carried back to camp by hand, the squatting in the dirt around the fire, the gut-clench of fear that came with hearing something moving in the midnight dark. I figured she'd have enough ironic distance to enjoy Diz; she'd rather admire Jim Brassard as the man-of-few-words professional that he was, and she'd probably get a crush on Earnest. Maybe she'd even pick up on some of the deeper charms of the situation, understand the difficult, transformative magic it was working on me.

I admit that I was a bit proud of my new hardihood and my radical divergence from the mainstream—what else was there to be proud of?— and I was looking forward to showing it off.

I gave her directions to the right interstate exit and to a general store about six miles from the farm; after that point, navigation on unmarked dirt roads was too complex to explain. We arranged to meet at the store at one o'clock on a Tuesday afternoon so I could lead her to my new home.

She got there before me. I came trundling down the road, and there she was: a skinny, frizzle-headed blond leaning against the hood of a funky BMW, wearing a vivid pink tank top, tight black jeans, and flip-flops. She was eating something plastic-wrapped and complicated that required licking her fingers at intervals.

"Hey, baby," I called as I pulled alongside her. "Want to come up to my place?"

She had her mouth full, and her hands were gummed with pastry and cream. When she had swallowed, she said, "What's with this place? You're the third person to ask in the last five minutes!"

I got out and we hugged and she finished her food, which she declared "the best whoopie pie I ever ate! No label or anything, homemade!"

I got gas at the pump while she headed back into the store. When the nozzle chunked, I went in to find her at the counter with a twelve-pack of Heineken. She was chatting with the cashier, an obese fiftyish woman who didn't look as if she laughed often.

"I can't believe you keep worms in there with the groceries!" Cat said.

"Crawlers have to be kept cool," the cashier said. "Or they die."

Cat turned to me: "They're in Chinese take-out boxes! Right in with the beer and cream cheese and everything!"

"People fish. Need bait." She handed over Cat's change and took my gas money.

We caravanned back to Brassard's farm, with Cat's car sometimes lost in the dust my tires churned up. At the top of the hill, where you get the first glimpse of the farm and its valley and my own little ridge, I stopped and went back to explain the layout.

She got out and looked. "Very bucolic."

"It's pretty, don't you think?"

"Totally pastoral," she said with marginally more enthusiasm.

Brassard's nearer cows swung their heads toward us as we passed the upper pasture, and then I led Cat into the turnout where I always parked. From there, a pair of tractor-wheel ruts cut through the scrub field to the bottom of my hill, the access route Brassard had provided as part of our deal.

I figured I'd start by introducing her to the Brassards so they would know what the unfamiliar car was doing there. But from the powerful manure smell, I knew that Brassard himself was out with the spreader, and Earnest's truck wasn't there. So that left Diz. As we crossed the road and headed into the farmyard, I felt a twinge of anxiety about the impending chemistry between the two women.

There was no sign of Diz outside, so we stood on the porch and knocked. Bob wandered amiably over to say hello. After a bit, Diz came to stand behind the screen. I made introductions, and Diz said, "A visitor!"

"Yep!" Cat piped. "Hi!"

"Well, no woman is an island, I guess—not even our Ann, apparently. Welcome to Brassard's Farm, Cat, and God help you."

"Thank you."

Diz came out so she could look Cat over more closely. The door whacked shut behind her, and she scanned Cat up and down, taking in her naked arms and shoulders and back, the thin elastic fabric of her tank top, her bare ankles and feet.

To me, dryly: "How're you fixed for bug dope up there? Got some here if you need more."

"We're good," I said. "Thanks, though!"

Diz nodded, checked her watch. This was not a gesture of impatience but a real concern for the relentless cycle of a dairy farm's chores.

"Friends for a long time?" Diz asked Cat rhetorically. "You don't strike me as the deeply introspective, overly sensitive type. Unlike—"

Cat laughed. "Got that right! We met in, what, seventh grade? She was the brainy girl."

"So you're, what, the antidote?"

"Diz is very insightful," I warned Cat. I was afraid that some comment of Diz's would constitute one barb too many, and that Cat might reciprocate. And then it would get unpleasant.

But Cat was loving it. To me she said solemnly, "Good to know. I'll be careful around her." To Diz she said, "Yes. And she's mine. My antidote."

Diz chuckled, then said, "Well, enjoy your stay. And now, as the radio guy says, I gotta get back to work."

As Diz turned away, Cat added, "But we're not gay!"

That cracked Diz up. She slapped her thigh and gave us a *get outta here* wave and stumped off toward the lower pasture.

I was pleased they had hit it off. Cat has a kind of momentum to her personality, and like it or not like it, it tends to sweep people along. She's not judgmental of individuals, and she doesn't care much about other people's judgments of her. Perhaps that's the definition of "irrepressible." I envied her clear sense of self and the freedom it gave her, and I wondered whether Diz might have been a bit like her in her younger years.

We'd spent all of five minutes on the farm, and my three days with Cat had gotten off to a great start.

We crossed the road and Cat went to her car and got in the driver's seat. When I asked her what she was doing, she looked puzzled and asked, "Aren't we going to drive up now?"

"Drive? I thought I mentioned that. We have to walk from here on." I pointed out the paired wheel ruts, the ground humped high between.

We unloaded her little backpack and a large duffel and her purse and a huge rolled Coleman sleeping bag and a fat copy of the *Boston Globe* and the twelve-pack of Heineken. Cat's flip-flops proved unworkable when we hit the first steep part, so we stopped for her to dig some running shoes out of her luggage. The manure odor swelled up from the fields here—a dark, deeply fermented smell that I'd learned to tolerate but Cat almost gagged on. A couple of deerflies found us, swinging in tight elliptical orbits and landing surreptitiously to bite, and I realized that my insect repellent was up at the camp.

Cat stayed game, though. When we started walking again and the flies didn't leave us, she growled at one of them: "Keep it up, asshole. I am going to squish your guts out of your crispy little exoskeleton. Believe it." But we couldn't swat them with our arms so full. The best we could do was to toss our hair. One got in a good long suck just behind Cat's ear before I spotted it and elbowed it away.

Cat was fit, but slogging on uneven ground, steeply uphill, carrying armfuls of irregularly shaped things, was not easy for her. The twelve-pack was particularly hard to clutch. We had to sit and rest our arms. The bright side was that with our hands free we were able to take several deerflies out of the gene pool.

And it gave me a chance to show off the valley. From the first hairpin turn of the track, you get a lovely overview of the farm. Looking to the right, you have a longer view over the fields and copses and hillside forests.

You can follow the meander of the stream on the far side of Brassard's land, and then, as the valley broadens in the distance, a few silos and, beyond them, several strata of higher hills, hazed successively paler blue even on clear days.

Cat nodded approvingly. "It's not *The Sound of Music*, but I can see how this could grow on you."

Up at the camp, we dropped her stuff and had beers. We sat on my fireside logs as she caught me up on her life and our immediate circle of friends. But the blackflies began to find us, more and more until it seemed we were in the center of an aerial dogfight between scores of tiny fighter planes. We sprayed each other with repellent, got some on the lips of our beer cans, spat when we drank again. Cat went to pee and came back with dirt on her elbows that told me she had found the woods squat difficult. I had, too, at first: brace your legs on either side of the hole, drop your pants into a wad around your ankles, hunker down, try not to lose your balance, hold the clothing out of the way so you don't piss on it or your heels. It takes practice.

We went for a walk; I introduced her to my spring, and we brought back water for cooking and washing. As we talked, I began to assemble the campfire. I had planned our first dinner with the idea of impressing Cat that you could live in Stone Age conditions yet still enjoy decent cuisine. So I'd bought some locally made fresh linguine and a can of clams, a box of already washed spring salad with lots of baby arugula, and some white wine. In retrospect, I realize I was romancing my friend, trying to seduce her into accepting my ... what, choices? Lifestyle? Life?

As night seeps into dense woods, a fire is a lovely thing. It puts the palette all into contrasts and complements: orange against deepening green, bright against dark, motion against stillness. The air slides down from the higher places, chill, but the fire's warmth holds it at bay. Its vital pulse and flicker promises warmth, food, light, companionship. There is no appliance, no computer or TV or microwave or lamp, with comparable powers and assurances.

Dear Cat got it. She really did. She fell into the spell, and as I tended the fire and the pasta we talked as we hadn't in years. Neither of us was by any means a mate-seeking single—we scorned that trope—but we both thought that eventually we'd like to be with one person and explore the depths of intimacy rather than the range of options.

When the mosquitoes drove us into the tent, I lit candles and a gas lantern and we had a truly delicious dinner. We killed the bottle of wine, and Cat produced a little bottle of brandy. After a couple of toasts, she looked drowsy—she'd had a long day, what with the drive—so we laid out her bedding. Then we both needed to use the "outhouse." It proved complex in the pitch dark. We both were unsteady, so we stumbled and thrashed through the undergrowth. And it's impossible to hold a flashlight when you're using both hands to stabilize yourself and manage your clothing, so I went with her to assist with lighting. Then she did the same for me. Not much privacy. Lots of mosquitoes. The whole exercise took probably twenty minutes. We were in absolute stitches throughout.

When we got back, Cat had to remove her contacts, and we discovered how hard that was without bright lights, a sink, smooth surfaces, a good mirror. She had brought silky pajamas to sleep in, but I told her she'd freeze to death, so she wore her sweatpants, socks, and hoodie pullover to bed.

We blew out the candles, and when I turned off the hissing Coleman lantern the night sounds came around us for the first time. I could hear Cat shifting uncomfortably, scratching at bug bites.

"It's like this every night?" she whispered.

"Sometimes it's windy or there's rain. Then it's very different."

"Do you ever get … nervous?"

"Like, afraid of the dark? Always."

A long silence, a distant owl quoting the Beatles: *goo-goo-ga-joob.*

"Are there animals?" she asked.

"I've seen deer. Raccoons. Mice. Cute little snakes. Mostly I see porcupines. The buggers come into the camp and chew on things, so sometimes I have to get up and chase them away."

"So that's why you sleep with the shovel by your bed?"

"Yes," I lied. It was there for wolves and mountain lions and serial killers and, when the night fears were upon me, chupacabras and aliens and demons of the earth. "There aren't any animals that'll hurt humans here in Vermont."

Another long silence. "Don't you get lonely?"

I was going to say, "Of course!" because I was very much, increasingly, missing the company of other people, Cat, a man, my Boston friends, my long-lost brother. At night, I cried for the absence of everyone I ever loved, and I felt small and anguished by my solitude.

But I had also realized that in the woods there's another set of feelings that we mistake for more familiar emotions. Sometimes the loneliness here was a feeling for which I had no name. It had to do with being supremely aware of existing as a separate, unique self, not a cell in a larger social organism. I suspect that many people spend their entire lives without once experiencing that. In a way, "loneliness" demeans it, stressing the absence of others, but this feeling is a keen, strong sense of self-presence, of standing sharp and clear and fully defined. Imagine you're a small, bright fountain of light, urgent and utterly distinct against the night sky. That feeling. It is acutely solitary, disconcerting, but for me that particular species of loneliness is more like what we call "reverence."

So I said something like, "Yeah. It can get really bad. But sometimes it's in a kind of good way."

She said, "Mm," thoughtfully or wearily. After a while, I heard her snoring. I cherished the human sound as it folded into the night symphony.

WE AWOKE TO the clang of a cooking pot outside the tent. It was pitch dark, dead black.

"What?" Cat whispered.

We heard a thump and a ripping and dragging sound, and then a deep whuffle of breath and some more ripping.

"Porcupine?" Cat asked hopefully.

I groped for a flashlight, flicked it on and saw Cat sitting up wide-eyed, then shined it out toward the fire pit. Four orange eyes reflected it back, and it took me a moment to see that they belonged to two bears.

From fifteen feet away, they looked gigantic. They had something on the ground and they'd been ripping at it with their claws.

They looked away from the light, as if unsure what to do.

"Oh, shit," Cat quavered. Then: "I've got some pepper spray! It's in my pack!"

Then we realized it was her pack that the bears were opening out into a scattered mishmash.

"Hey! That's Cat's!" I called irrationally. "Cut it out!"

The bears shied like horses at the sound of my voice. Then I found the shovel and beat the handle of my Buck knife against it, making a metallic racket, and they turned in place and moved quickly away into the woods. I kept my flashlight on until the crackling of twigs faded out of hearing.

"I forgot to mention the bears," I said, pretending to be used to this. But my heartbeat was banging in my throat and wrists.

"Jesus, Ann! Fuck me, I thought we were gonna get killed! Get *eaten*."

"They never hurt people. They've never come to camp before."

I heard her breathing hard in the dark. "*Fuck*," she said.

"It's my fault. I should have told you about not leaving your pack outside. I was too pickled. I always bring everything inside with me so the critters don't get at it."

"That would have been worse—they'd have come in here for it!" After a pause, she said, "There goes my surprise. I brought a bunch of those good sausages you like. Thought we'd have them for breakfast."

I was touched, and thanked her. We both took a long time to find sleep again, but probably for different reasons. I'm pretty sure Cat remained frightened they would return, but though I still trembled with adrenaline, I felt elated: I'd seen *bears*! Close up! They hadn't killed me! There were bears on my hill! I had bears for neighbors.

We awoke in the morning to a steady drizzle. Cat's pack was a mess, the sausages gone along with a box of granola bars. Her swimsuit and other essentials were ripped and soaked. The rain turned my tidy campsite into a sloppy mess. I made coffee and fried eggs on the Coleman stove in the tent. The eggs were great, but the bread I'd bought to go with had grown mold overnight, so we ate them with saltines and used our tongues to mop up the yolks.

There's not much to do in heavy forest when it's raining. Walking is muddy and slippery, and every low-growing tree or bush soaks you as you pass. The boughs sag and a haze rises, so views are short: more trees, more bushes, without the relief of windows onto sky, distant hills, fields. We stayed in the tent, chilled, until we got too claustrophobic, then gave up and hiked down wearing black plastic garbage bags for raincoats. We changed to dry clothes in the car, then drove to Montpelier, where we had lunch in a restaurant. Cat's fly bites were swollen and must have itched like crazy.

I suggested that we spend the night at a motel, but Cat was determined to get a full taste of my lifestyle. We trudged back up the hill, ate some cold Chinese take-out, finished off half the remaining beers, and got sloshed enough not to care much about physical discomforts.

Chapter 8

THE RAIN STOPPED that evening, and by noon on Thursday the sky cleared up, so we decided to take a walk. I figured we'd walk the borders of my land, then explore some of the country to the west.

"Let's go on a *real* hike!" Cat suggested.

"Like …?"

"Like when you pack pemmican and water and spend all day. And have a compass and binoculars."

"Pemmican?"

"That's what we called it at Camp Watitoh. The Indians used it when they went on long hunting trips. A mush of nuts and raisins and M&Ms."

"Indians had M&Ms?"

"They put in jerky instead."

I had no pemmican ingredients and no compass or binocs, but we packed saltines, bananas, a chocolate bar, and two beers. We filled two water bottles. I put all remaining food in my metal-lined cabinet, and we went off uphill.

We found my uphill property boundary, the wall of tumbled boulders, then turned left and followed it as the slope descended toward Hubbard's land. After the rain, the forest was sparkling, fulsome, glorious: brilliant green leaves sunlit through and translucent like stained glass, the shifting mottle of the forest floor, jack-in-the-pulpits, trilliums, ovoid pellets of deer scat, red squirrels skittering out of view and then, unable to contain their curiosity, peeping around a tree at us. Close to us, the birds went silent, but in the near distance, their songs rioted. Lots of blackflies, but we had doused ourselves thoroughly.

Cat got snagged and scratched more than I did, but she stayed game. Our conversation took on rhythms that varied with the terrain, the typical back-and-forth interrupted by silence when we had to navigate down tricky sections of slope or clamber uphill on all fours.

Matt had another new girlfriend, a total slut. Our friend Tom, a talented weekend sax player, had decided to make a career of it, going for a master's degree in music from Indiana University; I should come down for his goodbye party in July. The new teacher filling my slot at Larson Middle School was okay but would never be able to fill my shoes.

We talked about Megan's announcement that she was pregnant—twins, according to the ultrasound—and about Tomás' alcohol problem, which had gotten to the stage of a yanked driver's license and loss of custody of his daughter. Valerie's car got impounded for unpaid parking tickets, which we all had warned her would happen.

Cat looked at me sideways as we descended to the edge of a rolling cornfield and began skirting it. "Don't you miss it? Miss everybody?"

"Some of it."

"I mean, I still don't get why ... Was it just getting away from that shit at Larson? Or, what, like, pique? At Matt?"

I ignored her question about events at school and answered the part I felt more confident with. "Matt? Fuck, no! Jesus!" A bit later, I grumbled, "'Pique' is hardly the right word." This was understatement to an extreme degree. For me, our ending had been like shoving a beef joint through a meat grinder.

"I know," she said apologetically. She understood the many levels of heartbreak and disillusionment it had meant for me.

"Actually, I'm still not sure I can stick this out. If I don't find a job, I can't live in the woods in winter, I'll have to bail. I'll still have to pay off Brassard, but I can scoot by with my savings until I sell the land."

"You still owe him money!"

"Just ten grand. There's some more money due from my aunt's estate." She frowned.

"Everything was totally fucked, Cat! *Everything!* I needed to do something *different.* Something not in the city, not safely … ensconced among friends. Or trapped among *former* friends! Something out of my own ruts. I know, doing this doesn't make sense, but it …"

"… seemed like a good idea at the time," she finished.

Neither of us laughed.

We circumnavigated the field, putting in half a mile on the forest verge, coming out on a dirt road near a barn and house that I assumed were Hubbard's. We headed south on the road. At noon, we stopped to eat some of our rations, resting on a tumbledown stone wall among the flurry of blackflies, nodding to the occasional passing cars.

After a few minutes of silence, Cat surprised me. "And what about men?"

"What's a 'man'?"

She laughed. "Personally, I'd think after Matt you'd want a torrid affair. Rinse the little shitbag out of your system."

"I don't have much 'torrid' in me at this point. Once I get a job, rent a place in town, I'll be in contact with the human race. I'll check out my torridity then. Vermont is very hip."

She nodded equivocally. "So I've heard."

EVENTUALLY, THE SUN'S heat wore us down and we turned back. We'd seen some lovely views, climbed a bit of cliffside overlooking the river, skinny-dipped in the cold clear water. When we headed back, we were tired enough to follow the roads rather than go overland. We walked past

Hubbard's farm again, then uphill to where our road intersected the ridge road.

I hadn't explored the larger area much, because I'd been too busy setting up my domestic functions and inspecting my navel. In fact, I had never gone past the turnoff to Brassard's valley. So I'd never actually seen "the trash that lives up the hill," as Diz called the Goslants.

I think our encounter with them upset Cat even more than me.

Along the ridge road, the forest was heavy for a quarter mile, but just around a bend, the landscape changed shockingly. Suddenly, we found ourselves in a cut-over wasteland of stumps and brush through which blackberry canes and scrub trees had snarled themselves. You see this kind of place here and there in Vermont, looking like a World War I battlefield after the dead have been hauled away. Earnest had explained that the owners of this kind of land had clear-cut the trees and sold them off as logs or firewood—an indication of financial distress, trading the forest's long-term productivity for quick cash. Just what Jim Brassard had refused to do. It's no longer an ecosystem, but an aftermath of a place, ugly and desolate.

We heard the Goslants before we saw them: raised voices, emphatic and angry sounding. Then we saw their house: two conjoined mobile homes that sagged in the middle. Someone had tacked on a front porch made of two-by-fours and plastic sheeting, and odd tar-paper-covered sheds stuck out at random angles. Next to the house stood a caravan-type mobile home and a newer-looking garage with two bays, one with the rolling door jammed at an angle and the other open to reveal heaped plastic bags, cardboard boxes, car parts, TVs, broken aluminum lawn chairs, piled as if they'd been flung blindly through the door.

The yard was covered in random scatter: disemboweled snowmobiles, a toppled refrigerator, a sun-faded plastic kids' minislide and wading pool. Piles of concrete blocks, stacks of firewood, a dilapidated rain-soaked couch, a rusted-out barbecue grill. The ground beneath was a mix of scrub grass and smaller trash. Torn plastic fluttered over the windows of the trailer. A big, shiny pickup truck and a couple of cars were parked up in the driveway.

Two young men leaned against the side of the pickup, one of them looking bored and talking into his cell phone, the other arguing with a very obese middle-aged woman who stood on the front porch, shouting.

"Give me the goddamned keys! I'm not going to say it again!"

One of the young men, dressed in jeans and a T-shirt, held out some keys. "Why don't you come down and get them? Because you can't move your lard-ass butt that far!"

Off to the side, a pretty adolescent girl, maybe fifteen years old, yelled out in an acid voice, "Bobbie, I said GET your ASS over here!" This was to a toddler wearing only a paper diaper, who was teetering out toward Cat and me. "I said NOW!"

We walked faster, wishing we were invisible. The yard exhaled the smell of mildew. We were embarrassed to witness a family argument, and frightened by the malevolence of the combatants.

The obese woman started down the stairs toward the man with the car keys. "You don't want to do this, Johnnie. You really don't want to fucking go here, you little shit."

Johnnie laughed and tossed the keys in the air, caught them, and moved quickly around the truck as the woman came off the steps.

Cat and I were abreast of the driveway by then, slinking by, looking forward but unavoidably glancing over at them. The young man on the cell phone put it away from his face long enough to stare defiantly back at us. "What the fuck are you looking at?" he snarled.

"What did I SAY!" the girl snarled at the toddler. She had come forward and now grabbed its arm and jerked it so that the kid spun around. She dragged the child screaming back toward the house. "SHUT UP! Or I'll give you a real good reason to cry!"

Johnnie had gotten into the truck and fired it up, and the huge woman beat on the hood. "Don't come home tonight, you little bastard. The door'll be locked and all your shit will be out in the yard."

"Don't fuck with my stuff, Ma. Don't even think about it."

We were past the place by now, power walking, and couldn't see them anymore. But a moment later, the truck roared up behind us, too close, and the cell-phone guy made moronic bug-eyes at us as they zoomed past.

We didn't say anything for a long time. I was nauseated and ashamed: My little paradise had revealed an ugly underside. The Goslants' lives were deeply destitute in uncountable ways, lived without any apparent control of circumstance. A broken chair was too complex to cope with except to toss into the yard and forget about. A damaged relationship was too complex except to vent rage and frustration at it.

We turned onto my road, the road to Brassard's farm. When we came to the top of the hill and the view opened, I almost wept with relief. But our comfortable fatigue had become a poisoned exhaustion.

We talked that night, over the campfire, mainly about social issues, demographics, poverty, education. We were less comfortable together. Cat asked me if I wanted to talk about what had happened at Larson at the end—some catharsis—and I told her no. We hit the sack early. In the morning, we packed her up and walked down the hill together. She praised the beauty of the day and how tranquil it was, but the comment seemed rather rueful.

Whatever fun we'd had, the Goslants had polluted the memory of it. I desperately wished that Cat could meet Earnest, wanting to show her a decent, solid, intelligent person, but still his truck was not there.

We stowed her stuff in the car, hugged, kissed. Head against my shoulder, she said, "Honey, you know I love you. And I have no right to tell you how to live. But I think you're making a mistake with this. I really think you're doing the wrong thing this time. I'm sorry. It just seems … like, crazy to me."

She had quoted my words about Sandeep almost verbatim. But she wasn't being ironic or cruel. She was trembling with apology, offering it with all the sincerity in the world.

I hugged her harder. "I know. I know. Thank you."

"Just tell me you're going to take care of yourself," she said. "You don't have to do this, you really don't … Promise me you'll think about that? Promise me."

I promised. And at that moment, I completely agreed with her. When she drove away, I felt her absence instantly, a hole in me. Loneliness, the little cringing kind, came rushing back into my days and nights. Between the emptiness after Cat, and the horrible poverty of the Goslants, I spent the next couple of days thinking through the logistics of my retreat.

Chapter 9

I CAN'T PUT it off any longer: I haven't been revealing the full scope of the desperation that hurtled me off the tracks in Boston. I came to my land and to Brassard's farm in more abject retreat and internal imbalance than I've been willing to admit.

Back in Boston, I got into serious trouble for unprofessional conduct at Larson Middle School. I fucked up. I'm sure this was why I had a hard time finding a teaching job in Vermont.

I made inappropriate physical contact with one of my students.

This is the first time I have actually written those words, and they scream off the page in accusation.

There's context to what I did—and ultimately, the context is more important than the act. Context: I didn't feel "pique" against Matt. I was damaged by our ending, and I was heartbroken, not just about losing him and losing the marriage I thought I'd been constructing pretty well, but about life and, in fact, about losing the idea of marriage itself. I won't pollute this recounting with the sordid details of what Matt did or said, but life was more about loss and betrayal than I had ever imagined. It wasn't just that Matt didn't love me; it was more that nobody loved anybody. Grim.

As I've said, back at Larson I was part of a group of teachers who had some progressive approaches to education. We encouraged the kids to be more expressive, more honest about their anger and frustration, about their family life.

We knew that the biggest impediment to their future success wasn't school, but the society they lived in, the families they lived in. Too many came from single-mom households. Too many had witnessed violence, divorce, drug use by parents or siblings, crimes committed on them by others. Some had committed crimes themselves and lived with whatever psychic residue that leaves. Some came to school hungry, and not just for food. They came starved for a reasonable degree of love and trust—the emotional security we generally assume should be built into kids' homes.

I'm not saying there weren't kids who were happy, lived in complete families, and led wholesome, sufficient lives—there were. This was not a deeply troubled, crime-ridden, impoverished inner-city school district of the kind that's so popular in all those redemptive, feel-good teacher movies. But as one eighth-grader told me, there were so many kids with "issues" that it was almost a social stigma not to have a few.

We kept our antennae up for problems that might warrant intervention, and we maintained frequent contact with the guidance office and social services agencies. And when it seemed the best course, we also put our own shoulders to the wheel.

We knew that better teacher-student ratios equals better grades and fewer behavioral problems, and we knew that our school couldn't afford more teachers. So we changed the numerators: More teacher *hours* per kid equals better everything. We spent a lot of time with our students, individually, often after class. We believed we could make a difference. And I'm sure we did.

Larson was a big brick pile built around 1940, a central building three stories tall with two-story wings projecting into an asphalt playground.

It occupied its own block in a residential neighborhood of three-story apartment buildings, some fairly well kept up and some getting rough around the edges.

I loved that place. It had an agreeably worn quality, pleasingly rounded and sculpted by the river of young lives gently eroding its halls and classrooms over the decades. What it lacked in modern amenities, it made up for with an old-fashioned charm. In front, concrete entry columns flanked three sets of big double doors, capped by an arch with *William J. Larson Middle School* proudly carved into it. The wooden staircases creaked, and they were still framed with the kind of banisters that kids could slide down despite the age-old prohibitions against doing so. The building's aura was that of an elderly, kindly aunt.

Every classroom had high ceilings and tall windows along one side. Teacher's desk up front beneath a big clock that ticked loudly, blackboard behind. The students' desks were two-person Masonite-topped tables with separate chairs, circa 1990. Video setup on a rolling trolley. The computer lab in the library had some recent, decent equipment, but otherwise the old ambience was alive and well. It smelled of chalk dust, hair gel, adolescent body odor and deodorant, the stink of photocopy toner mingling with the whiff of sloppy joes from the cafeteria.

As my colleagues did, I often stayed on after the school day to tutor, console, confront, or interrogate one kid or another.

So there I was in that last year, and I'd been divorcing Matt for most of it, and here comes yet another kid: Omar, about fifteen, in eighth grade and with a life that was a disaster. I first asked him to stay after class to discuss a quiz on which he'd answered "Bite me" for every question.

We met so I could explore the reason for the answers he'd given. I told him, "This says to me that either you don't know—which I don't get, because you and I both know you're smart. Or it says you don't care, when I know you're actually interested in some of this material. Or it says you have contempt for school, or for me, but you seem to have an okay time here and I thought you and I got along pretty well. So what's up?"

After some digging, I learned that his father had recently gone "crazy" on drugs and gotten arrested and that his mother couldn't stop crying. His older brother, seventeen, just took off and they didn't know where he was, and his little sister had started sucking her thumb again, at the age of eleven.

We were sitting in my big, bright room, door open to the hall, a few stragglers passing, voices bidding each other goodbye in the echoing hallway, and Omar broke into tears. I was facing him across his desk, right in front of him, and when he cracked I reflexively leaned over and hugged him awkwardly. His sobs pounded against my chest. It was so complex and so big that the only way to name or say it was to cry. A howl from the heart. My cheek was wet with his tears. This is no small matter: For a teenage boy, to cry is to surrender a lot of machismo, to admit that his swagger has been pretense.

Then he said, "So now I'm fucking up school just like everything else is fucked up," and that broke the rest of my heart. I told him that he wasn't fucking up, he just needed to acknowledge the problems and come up with practical strategies to overcome them. Eventually, he calmed. When he left, I handed him the card of the head of guidance and pleaded with him to contact her and see if there was anything the school or social services could do to help. I also told him he could always talk to me if he needed to; I was in my room for at least half an hour after school on most days.

Omar was tall for an eighth grader—he'd been held back. He had a faint mustache and a chubby, childish face with full, expressive lips over uneven teeth. During my months observing him, he struck me as a bit clumsy physically, in an endearing kind of way. But he was pretty good at maintaining the jivey persona required by his fellow students, and so he seemed to me, from my distance, to be reasonably popular. On the other hand, middle school is largely an education in the theater arts, immersive training in doing an impersonation of a peer-determined idea of "normal," so his persona didn't necessarily reflect his inner state.

My home life was such a mess that I took refuge in my work, spending more and more time after school. I felt cruelly betrayed by

Matt's infidelities and his hurtfulness and his emotional indifference to figuring out how they affected our relationship. I had been cut by all the raw edges, both paper cuts and deep slashes, that go with the rancorous ambivalences of divorce, especially if it has dragged on too long and the wounds are reopened daily. Ironically, one of the most painful aspects of it all was realizing that he didn't *need* me. I needed to be needed! Being needed allows you the opportunity to provide succor, to demonstrate love, to be the balance and the ballast. To prove you can be the strong one. It is a good thing to feel.

You can see where this is going. Omar stayed after class again, cried, talked. We hugged. Et cetera. He was so grateful. I felt good about myself: the Samaritan teacher. After a few such meetings, he had stopped crying and our encounters became more reciprocal, less charged conversations. He showed himself to be more intelligent than I had first assumed, and I felt we were developing a special relationship, communicating on a level beneficial to both of us. I began to look forward to seeing him. I was confident that our talks had helped him, and in my divorce-battered condition I welcomed the pride that gave me. I was no doubt blind to other signals. We hugged, but only briefly, when he took his leave.

But then one afternoon, I was leaning, half sitting against my desk, and he rather spontaneously came up to me and hugged me. God help me, this is how starved I was: I relished the feeling of a body pressed to mine, somebody goddamned well needing contact with me. He was a big kid, about as tall as Matt; all the parts and places fit the same. Neither of us made any suggestive movement, but yes, okay, yes, there was probably a bit more frontal contact than is appropriate for such hugs. And I let it go on for too long before I shrugged away.

Was it erotic? For him, maybe. As for me, I don't know what I thought or felt. I wasn't sleeping at night and I was taking caffeine pills to get through my workday. In any case, I have never been good at distinguishing the precise dividing lines between companionship, the pleasant pressure of friendly touch, and erotic contact.

I didn't see Omar after class for a few days, and I had no reason to ask him to stay on—no bad test results or papers so wretched they required personal follow-up.

But one day, he lingered after the others left. He seemed to be relapsing into another tough phase. He didn't cry, but he spoke darkly and hopelessly. I made sympathetic noises. He came to the desk and we hugged and it went on too long and his hand drifted too low in back and cupped my buttock and I was slow to react, and that's when I heard muffled snickering from the doorway and looked up to see a little crowd of boys and girls, leaning in to watch. Obviously, Omar had been talking up his adventures with the horny Ms. Turner, bragging about his cougar conquest, and had invited them to the show.

It went through the whole student body overnight, manifested in suppressed smirks in class and, in the hall, a different kind of glance, followed by averted gazes.

The administration heard about it. The principal, vice principle, and faculty council chair interviewed me. I told my version, skipping the part about my inner confusion. They believed that I had been moved only by compassion and that my oversight was due to an excessive expression of it. But it was a serious lapse. They had no recourse but to remove Omar from my class and put me on a kind of probationary status. When the school year ended, budget cuts eliminated a couple of positions, and I was one of those whose contracts weren't renewed.

I couldn't blame them. I had let my personal life interfere; my control had slipped. I looked like hell, with bags under my eyes, split ends, lost weight. I walked around in an exhausted haze from the emotional wear and tear, and by then I was preoccupied with the hellish logistics of the divorce endgame: doing the awful paperwork, sorting possessions, finding a new place to live. During that last term, my colleagues' responses segued from sympathy to concern to professional disapproval, to a subtle ostracism as, one by one, they distanced themselves from the contaminated one. I lost some good friends because, when they tried to offer condolences or advice, I told them they could shove it up their condescending asses.

As bad as my external circumstances were, the internal ramifications of the Omar event were worse. I had started to trust him, assumed that it was reciprocal. I had started to enjoy our afternoon chats and believed he did, too. And his betrayal, his *exploitation* of these simple faiths, echoed everything Matt had done. It reiterated the duplicity, cruelty, disrespect—the whole Dumpster of disappointments and disillusionments. It branded me with an unhappy outlook on life in general and my life in particular.

That pathetic episode—not so much what I had done as what I'd felt—constituted a rude awakening. Was I really so desperate that I needed, and could take, affirmation from a fifteen-year-old boy? Was I really so lonely or hungry that I couldn't resist the need for physical contact? When I felt his hand slip to my rump, my response should have been instantaneous, but what I really felt was a sort of helpless puzzlement about the sensation that seemed to deserve a couple of seconds to process.

It sickened me that I had let myself become such a miserable wreck, had let a creep like Matt, or Omar, jerk me around, let myself become that vulnerable, that weak. When I left for the Vermont woods, I wanted to get the hell out of there. I wanted to punish myself, and I wanted some goddamned hardship that would toughen me up enough that I would never *ever* get so lost and so weak.

Chapter 10

WHICH AT LEAST partly explains why, despite the increasingly clear hopelessness of my little experiment, I didn't leave right away. I had burned every bridge behind me, and my past seemed too spoiled to return to. I had acquired a Pavlovian aversion to Boston and the person I had become there.

Also, it seemed that every time I made up my mind, something would offer an argument for staying.

A few days after Cat left, I awoke to another brilliantly clear day. Up here they have a saying: "Don't like the weather in Vermont? Wait ten minutes." There had been a little shower during the night, which now brought up the wonderful smell of soil from the forest floor. The leaves glistened, and the morning's negligent breezes brought down an irregular patter of heavy drops from the tree canopy. The forest seemed pleased with itself, like a cat after it has groomed its coat satisfactorily.

I was sitting on my fireside log, listening to the day as I blew across the top of a cup of instant coffee. I was missing Cat and wondering gloomily at my meandering life, when I heard a voice call from below: "Are you decent?" It was Earnest.

I checked. I had put on running shorts and a dirty T-shirt, and I had been scratching at the blackfly bites on my ankles, leaving red welts. "As much as I'll ever be," I called back.

A moment later he came into the clearing, wearing a khaki T-shirt and army pants and a Castro-esque hat tipped back on his head. He tossed himself down, at his ease on the ground across the fire pit from me.

"Too late to meet your friend, I guess. Too bad. Diz says she's a real firecracker."

"That she is. You'd like her. You want coffee?"

"No, just drank a quart of it down below. So ... what's on your clock for today, Pilgrim?"

I had been asking myself the same thing. "Sounds like you have a suggestion."

"I've got a problem that I'm hoping you'll help me with. It's a paying proposition."

His regular assistant for his tree surgery business had called in sick—most likely hungover, Earnest thought. He'd called others, with no luck, so he was desperate for someone to help him bring down a big tree in Essex Junction. When he described the job—a huge old elm in someone's backyard—I warned him that I had brought down only a few trees in my life, all of them in the past month, none of them thicker than my arm. I doubted I should help with a tree near a house.

He dismissed my concerns with a wave. "All it takes is brains and brawn and good luck," he told me.

Working for Earnest: Caravanned behind him up to Essex, left my car at the park-and-ride near the interstate, rode in his big truck—not his regular pickup but an old warhorse of a stake-sided dump truck—out to a suburban residential district. Big trees along the streets, including some elms that had miraculously survived the midcentury blight. They were going one by one, Earnest explained, and today we were going to take down a behemoth that had started dropping branches on a house.

Earnest was in an ebullient mood, his big face shiny. He drove with a huge thermos of coffee in one hand, handing it to me to share occasional swigs, and explained that if this went as he hoped, he'd make out like a bandit and I would get a generous cut.

When we pulled up at the client's house, I saw that the old elm was truly a monument. Its massive branches rose and curved up and out in the shape of an inverted umbrella or the bell of a trumpet, overhanging the house and the power lines. Earnest backed the rig up the driveway, shut it down, and got out to appraise the scene.

"You getting pretty good with that chainsaw up at your camp?" he asked.

"Not so bad, I guess." Despite my minimal experience, I was proud of my growing mastery of the whining, ripping thing. I hated the stink, but even that had its uses: the blue smoke kept bugs away. "But I—"

"Well, let's get to it. First we gotta unload the gear."

There was a lot of gear. The most important tools of the trade are the ropes: huge coils of inch-thick oiled sisal that chafed my forearms as I dragged them off the truck's dented steel bed. I could hardly carry them. Earnest had brought along a bundle of leather straps with steel fittings, thick as draft-horse tack. Back to the truck for the chainsaws. I grabbed the first one, about the size of mine, then saw the other two: engines the size of a lawn mower's, bars longer than my arm.

"I'll saddle up if you bring the rest of the stuff," Earnest told me.

I lugged the saws to a part of the lawn well away from the tree and laid them out in a neat array as Earnest instructed. These were the surgeon's tools, and they needed to be ordered and ready to his hand. Back to the truck for cans of gas mix and chain oil, a hard hat and headphones for me, a metal toolbox, smaller ropes.

"Saddling up" meant putting on gear that would delight a leather fetishist. He started with a heavy belt around his waist, two thick straps connecting front and back through the crotch, leather suspenders that crossed his chest and back, carabiners here and there rattling from grommets. Then he buckled leather greaves onto his shins, each mounted with a steel spike that extended well below the inner arch of his boot. A heavy canvas strap about ten feet long, with clips attached at intervals and at each end: He hooked one clip into a steel loop on his belt and slapped the doubled-up remainder of the strap over his shoulder. As he girded himself, he meticulously inspected each strap, buckle, fitting.

"I'm a relic," he explained. "This is how they did it in the Stone Age. Nowadays, a team of guys come in with a cherry picker, go up and knock off a branch here and there. Ground guys chip the little stuff as fast as it comes down, blow it right into the truck. Load the big stuff on with a grabber. I can't afford the equipment, only way I get clients is by under-cutting their prices. And having the skills to do the ship-in-a-bottle jobs."

Under the tree, he explained that I was going to be his rope man, who has two primary duties. One is to send things up to the tree man as he needs them: chainsaws, other ropes, whatever. You tie them to a slender rope and he pulls them up. I figured I could manage that part.

The other is handling the big ropes to direct the fall of the branches he cuts off.

"How do I do that?"

"It's easy. I climb up to the branch above the one I'm cutting, put the rope through a crotch so it works like a pulley. You hold one end of the rope, I tie the other end to the one we're going to drop. When the branch starts to go, it'll swing, and your job is to hold it up until it swings to where it'll fall clear, won't hit the house. Or power lines."

The idea appalled me. "Earnest. I've never done anything like this in my life. I don't think I should—"

"Yeah, if you get it wrong, it could be a major fuck up. I've had helpers drop em right through the roof. One guy brought down the phone lines for half a block." He cackled, putting on a redneck twang: "He don't work for me no more."

"I'm not strong enough!"

"Outdoor living has built up your constitution. You'll be fine."

I protested again, but he wasn't listening. Burdened by his leathers, he waddled over to the tree, carrying one end of a light rope that I'd coiled on the ground. He swung his canvas strap around the trunk at shoulder height—the tree was easily four feet thick—clipped it to his waist belt on the other side of his body, leaned back hard against it, and began to climb. He stepped up, stabbed his ankle spikes firmly into the wood, shifted his weight to his feet, leaned in, flipped the strap up, leaned hard against it, stepped up again, *jab, jab*. His arms and shoulders rolled and swelled each time he hoisted himself. With the leather and metal fittings and muscles, he looked like a Roman gladiator girded for arboreal combat. In less than a minute, trailing his thin white rope like spider silk, he was at the first big juncture of branches, level with the peak of the house roof.

"Okay. Big rope." He flicked a ripple down the little line. I lugged over the carefully coiled rope, and Earnest gave me instructions on how to tie the right knot. "No. Yeah. No, no! The other way—under. There. No, the other loop."

"You should have shown me before you went up!"

"Oh, come on. You like the challenge, admit it." He was in irrepressible high spirits, coffee in his blood and a mountain of a tree to take down.

Once I had it right, the big rope rose up and up until it was in Earnest's hands. Seeing him up there, I began to understand the true size of the tree. Each of its main branches was thicker than the trunk of the biggest tree on my land, and looking up into it felt like standing in a centuries-old church, vaulted and ornate. It was dying but still had enough green on it to make this inner landscape a lovely, dappled, airy place. We earthbound people tend to think of trees in terms of their trunks; when we're kids we draw them as upright cylinders with a solid ball of green on top—lime lollipops. In fact, a tree is a thing of air, a thing with an interior. Birds probably think of trees as lattice-filled balloons anchored only mysteriously to earth.

Earnest climbed higher and higher until he found a spot he liked. He tossed the heavy rope through a crotch above him, grabbed the end as it swung back. Then he startled me by leaping delicately into the air. He arced away through the air-forest to another branch. At the right instant, he let rope slip through his hands so that it deposited him just where he wanted. Then he pulled the end of the rope back to him and did it all again.

I watched from below, astonished. This man was built like a fifty-five-gallon oil drum. On the ground, he walked with a bearish stride, a weight that was easy to mistake for clumsiness. When he worked with the cows, he often seemed to rely on strength more than finesse. But in the tree, he became weightless and graceful. He moved around easily, swinging and alighting, climbing quickly, balancing effortlessly as he gathered in rope. For five minutes, he glided and swooped through the lacy canopy in complete freedom, until he had reconnoitered every branch, every angle, every anchor place.

"Okay. Send up the Stihl," he called.

That was the smaller of the two big saws. I tied it using the loops as he directed, and he pulled it up.

To move around on the branches, he'd been running the big rope through a loop in his harness and holding it with both hands to let out line. Now he tossed the rope through a high crotch, tied one end to a branch about the thickness of my thigh, and dropped the other end to me. He told me to keep at least twenty feet of it behind me so I'd have slack if I needed it.

"Okay. Get ready to boogie." He positioned himself at a fork on one of the big branches that stretched out well over the house.

"Earnest, I can't! It'll go through the roof!"

"It'll swing toward you because of the angle I cut and where I set the rope. You hang on hard until it swings clear of the roof, then move toward the tree and play out rope as fast as you can, before it swings back. But don't just let go of the rope, then you don't have any control. Just step quickly forward and let it slip through your hands fast when it's the right time."

I was terrified. But I couldn't protest again, because he lifted the chainsaw in one fist and started it with a mighty yank of the other hand.

The chain bit into the underside base of the branch, spewing a waterfall of chips. A wedge of wood dropped down. Abruptly, the branch bobbed and shivered, as if it had felt pain or a sudden presentiment of its fate. Then another minute of sawing, from the top side, and the branch convulsed and began to fall, pivoting toward me. It groaned and swung like the arm of a construction crane, gathering speed as Earnest cut through the last fibers.

Then it was free and its weight came onto the rope, dragging me toward the tree. I held it back as well as I could, and when it seemed right, I let it slip. The branch bowed to me and swept down and crashed to the ground. The cut-off end had stayed well up in the tree, but I was able to ease it down without killing myself.

Earnest shut off his chainsaw and looked down with satisfaction. "Not bad for a rookie!"

"I gotta go pee," I yelled back at him.

"Use the back door. Nobody's home, but they said they'd leave it open."

"I was kidding, damn it!"

I began sawing, starting from the twig end. And that was the rhythm. We would drop a branch, and I'd cut it into sections that would fit into the truck, while Earnest flew to a different part of the tree and made his next set. Each time, I would drag the debris out of the way before the next branch came down, so that we didn't end up with an impossible tangle and the danger of snagged ropes.

We had started at around ten, and by three o'clock we'd taken three truckloads of smaller branches to the town stump dump. The great trunk of the tree and its main branches, tragically shorn, remained upright, but it was time for lunch. I had packed a peanut butter sandwich and a banana. Earnest had bought an enormous sub from a stop-and-shop cooler, and a bag of chips big enough for both of us. He also had two canvas-wrapped army canteens, having kindly filled one for me.

It was nice sitting there on the broad flat seat, windows open. Earnest possessed a massive serenity, didn't need to talk all the time: "It's an Indian thing," he had told me. Silence was easier with him than most people. My back ached, and my lunch looked inadequate. We both stank of sweat and oily exhaust.

"How'd I do?"

His cheeks were full, so he just nodded, *pretty good.*

Between bites, he told me more about the art of tree pruning and felling. I asked him where he learned to do it, and he joked about the Indigenous Peoples' deep knowledge of nature, ancient lore handed down from father to son. He loved making these digs at Whitey's romanticization of Native Americans. Rain dances, tepees—I'd started telling him to cut it out, and he enjoyed that just as much.

Actually, he had learned by working for a tree surgeon out in Wisconsin, during high school.

We'd been eating for a couple of minutes before he thought of taking a drink. He opened one of the canteens, tilted it to his lips, and immediately spat it out.

"What?"

"It's hot! Sitting in the sun all this time."

I didn't care, but Earnest wouldn't drink it. He fired up the truck and we headed off to find some ice.

We pulled up at a crossroads general-store gas station on the edge of town. A half-dozen customers' cars were parked in the lot, and along the side a dozen beaters were lined up with their prices and virtues posted on signs behind the windshields: *Loaded! 150K. $2,995.* Earnest went inside, then came out and took a big bag of ice from the quilted silver cooler.

When he got back to the truck, I asked him why he hadn't just bought a cold drink.

He shrugged as if it had never occurred to him. He ripped the plastic with a thick finger and took out a cube. He intended to put it into his canteen, but it wouldn't fit—just sat there obdurate on the round aluminum opening. He looked irritated for a moment and then did one of the most amazing things I'd ever seen anyone do.

The ice cube was balanced on the mouth of the canteen. Earnest held the canteen with his left hand and then, with his right index finger, drove the cube into the hole with one sudden, precise stab. The cube disappeared and ice chips showered the cab. He did it six or eight times, then sloshed the water around. My lap was covered in a light snow.

He took a trial sip and nodded. "Better," he said.

He didn't seem to think he'd done anything out of the ordinary, but I was speechless. I had just witnessed an astonishing act of strength and skill, each blow so savagely hard yet so well aimed that his finger went knuckle-deep into the hole after the cube. One rigid finger, held at right angles to his fist, stiff as a railroad spike.

We went on eating. After a while, I asked, "So what did you do in the army?"

"MP. That's Military Police, basically where you have to break up bar fights among the enlisted men."

"I take it you got some martial arts training."

He had a huge mouthful. When he'd swallowed, he said, "Some."

I didn't probe further. When we finished, we balled up our wrappers and threw them into the trash can. Then we were on our way back to work.

We had barely swung out of the parking lot when Earnest stiffened, swore, and shifted gears quickly. He was staring at his side mirror.

I looked in the mirror on my side but didn't see anything alarming.

"Fuck!" he snarled. He pounded the steering wheel. "Fuck!"

"What?" I craned around to look again. This time, I saw a police cruiser making a three-point turn in the parking lot. We were about half a block away now, and Earnest was flooring it, the old truck roaring and rattling. "What, the cop?"

He didn't answer.

A UPS truck cut off our view of the parking lot, and the moment it did, Earnest yanked the wheel and we took a hard right onto a side road. "There, dickhead," he growled at the police car. He smiled evilly because the truck and the line of cars following it had trapped the cop in the lot. "But he's on the radio right now, you can bet on it."

I got scared then. I had no idea what this was about, and I had no desire to get in trouble with the law through some guilt by association, aiding and abetting, accessory to a crime, or something. I craned around but didn't see any sign of the cruiser.

Earnest swung a hard left at the next intersection, then barreled down a dirt road that dipped into a steep valley where the forest came up around us. We crossed a narrow bridge, came up the other side, rumbled along for a mile, ripped through a four-way stop without slowing, then turned past an abandoned barn and slowed to cruise past farms and auto junkyards. Earnest calmed. A final big puff bulged his cheeks, and then he chuckled.

"Okay," he said as if I'd pressured him for information. "No big thing. Deputy sheriff. Name's Dick Wilson—Puddin Head. Dick Head. Classic honky small-town sheriff. Got a bug up his butt about me."

"Why?"

"Five, six years ago, we had a disagreement. He's this great big guy, foot taller than me, ex-marine. I guess he thought he was tough. This was at a bar."

I could see where this was going. The thought of anyone fighting with Earnest—one finger under the rib cage would surely kill a man.

"What'd he do?"

"He made disparaging remarks and I reciprocated. He's well known for his attitude around here. Plays he's big stuff, gives everybody a hard time. He wanted to get physical with me."

"So …?"

Earnest grinned.

"Didn't go his way, I take it," I said.

"Well. Everybody at the bar had a good laugh. Hurt his reputation. So whenever I'm up this way he magically appears, to pull me over and ticket me for whatever—speeding, inspection out of date, taillight not working. It's like he's got a sixth sense, knows when I'm within ten miles of him. Third time, I made a mildly unflattering comment and he told me he was going to kick my ass. That a bunch of other cops around here would help him. He wasn't kidding. About six months ago, he pulls up behind me in the mall parking lot over on Suzy Wilson Drive. I can't back out. Two other sheriff's cruisers pull up, five guys in all. Dick introduces me to them and they give me the evil eye, just letting me know how it is. So now I try to stay out of their sight. They'll get me legally—you can always find something wrong on an old truck like this. I can't afford any more fines. Or they'll gangbang me. That's what Dick really wants, hands-on gratification. That's a no-win for me because if I let them kick my ass, it hurts, and if I fight back, I go to the big house for assaulting an officer, breaking half a dozen necks."

"Wow," was all I could say. Then: "Why didn't he have you arrested after that first time?"

"Drinking on duty—he didn't dare call in. Plus, too many people heard him being provocative. Came over and pushed me off my stool. Plus, he needs a more personal kind of vengeance after his public humiliation."

We drove for a while before I thought to ask, "Provocative how?"

He waved his hand dismissively. It was clear that he had enjoyed our adventure just now, Brer Rabbit outwitting his pursuers once again. He was humming, a totally non-sequitur tune like "Some Enchanted Evening."

"What'd he say to you?" I persisted. I figured it had to do with race.

"Said I was fat." Earnest barked a laugh. "Also that my girlfriend was ugly, that she was actually a guy." He laughed some more, slapping his thigh. "She *was* ugly! Pancake makeup, bad dye job, three packs a day. But she wasn't a guy. Anyway, you don't talk like that. It's rude."

IT TOOK US until sundown to drop the main trunk. Earnest had to walk all the way around it with his chainsaw to cut through the bole. The last segment of the blunt-shorn pillar dropped with a *whump!* that literally shook the earth. Earnest sawed it into slabs.

"Just toss them on the truck while I finish," he yelled. He was joking: on edge, the bigger bark-rimmed wheels stood as high as my chest and probably weighed three hundred pounds each. Instead, I raked and bagged the mounds of sawdust while he droned and roared on. When he was done cutting, he backed up the truck and, amazing me again, flipped the slices effortlessly onto the bed, one after another.

HE TREATED ME to dinner at a steak house in a commercial district on the outskirts of Burlington, out of Deputy Dickhead's jurisdiction. After so many weeks in the woods, it felt strange to be surrounded by built structures, shiny cars, signs, floodlights, modern architecture, flat masonry surfaces, asphalt-covered ground. The place bustled, *festered* with humans and their vehicles. It struck me as at once futuristic and atavistic.

We sat at a booth in our honorable filth and dishevelment. He ordered the biggest piece of meat on the menu, I ordered a smaller version of the same, and we crammed food into our faces as he told me more about himself and the Brassards.

He was born in Wisconsin to an Oneida Indian father and a half-Menominee, half-white mother. His father had fought in the army during World War II, then returned and used the training he'd received to work as an electrician. They lived near the tribal lands but not on them, so Earnest grew up going to public school. Their small house was about twenty miles west of Green Bay, where the smoke from the Fort Howard paper mills blanketed the flat farmlands for days at a time. It stank like rotten cabbage, and because his mother hung the laundry outside to dry, he often smelled it on his pillowcases and sheets even when the air had cleared. He rather liked it.

I was a bit loopy with exhaustion, and Earnest was an easy guy to goof with. "You mean you're ... you're part *white*?" I asked, appalled.

"Yeah. You wanna see which part?"

We laughed and he went on: Most of the kids at his school were "of German and Scandinavian extraction" and there were a few fights, but he didn't think it was any worse than what white kids faced when they went to the mainly Indian schools. It helped that he was both "hardy," which I took to mean tough, and "one of the eggheads," the smart kids, in advanced placement classes. He had a younger brother, who died while driving drunk when he was around twenty, and a younger sister, who lived in Milwaukee and had a couple of kids.

"Married a white guy!" Earnest said, keeping the joke going.

I shook my head, saddened at the state of things.

Earnest pulled a bad number in the draft lottery when he turned nineteen, "joined" the services, showed talent, got a year of special training, and went to Vietnam in 1973.

When his tale got that far, he moved along briskly, mostly skipping two years and revealing nothing about what he did in the war. Met Brassard there. Came back to the States in 1975 as the USA ingloriously folded up its Vietnam tent, and spent some time on base as an MP, left the army. He went back to the Midwest to deal with his brother's death, then moved east to get the hell away from there. Meanwhile, Brassard had returned from service and taken over his family's farm and he needed help and Earnest was available. Earnest moved to Vermont, worked for him for a few years, then quit and made his money doing tree surgery.

"How come you keep working for Brassard?"

He chewed and swallowed before answering, taking his time as if the answer required some consideration. At last, he said, "Jim needs work done. Couldn't afford to keep the farm if he had to pay somebody. Plus, I owe him. And I do 90 percent of my tree work in town and I get sick of it. I feel more at home out in the boonies. I've got my own bedroom at the house. Diz is a good cook."

Earnest had made an even thousand dollars bringing the big tree down, and he'd given me two hundred for the day. His appearance at my campsite that morning had rescued me from a day of difficult second-guessing myself. I hadn't had time to think about anything other than the work all day, and his good mood was still buoying me along.

"What do you owe him for?"

He looked at me soberly. "Nothing all that interesting."

"So why are you reluctant to talk about it?"

"It's nothing heroic, if that's what you're thinking. No battlefield dramas, Ann. In fact, it's not flattering to either of us." "Now I'm *dying* to hear it." I put my chin on my hand and leaned forward across the table.

He shifted uncomfortably, irritated. "Is this why you're still single?"

I was enjoying myself too much to feel hurt. "Come on. Fess up."

I could tell he was genuinely peeved with my persistence, but he indulged me. I promised Earnest then that I'd never tell, so I won't reveal all the details—and I'm sure he didn't tell me all the details—but it had to do with a brothel where Earnest did something that got him into trouble with the management. Brassard, also a patron that night, saved his bacon and got his ear sliced almost off for his efforts.

I choked down my laughter and tried to remember whether I'd seen anything strange about Brassard's ears.

"I was eighteen years old, okay? And a virgin when I first got to Vietnam."

"Did I say anything? Any comment at all?"

"At that age, a guy—"

"I'm not judging!"

"You're the one who brought it up."

I chuckled into a forkful of mashed potatoes, and Earnest went back to eating in a huff.

After a couple of minutes of silence, he added, "And don't tell Diz about it. And don't mention it to Jim. Or anybody."

I swore I wouldn't, and I never have until now.

He drove me back to the park-and-ride, dropped me off, and I drove back to Brassard's. My muscles were sore and stiffening, but I felt better. Maybe I'd stay with this project, this choice, a little longer. There were good people here, there was a lot to learn, and it all felt new and refreshing.

Chapter 11

BUT THAT WAS just another zig or zag, dip or bounce, of the cosmic roller coaster. By the next day, I had relapsed into indecision once again, and by sunset had more or less resolved to bail out, despite the forest's being so very lovely.

In any case, unbeknownst to me, it had become a moot question. The dimensions of the choice changed radically only a week after Cat's visit.

Brassard and the lawyer and I had all felt safe with my delaying payment of ten thousand dollars until Aunt Theresa's broker sold some remaining stocks. We had reviewed the papers; we all knew it was just a matter of a few technicalities required to liquidate and release the funds. Brassard had kindly given me ten weeks to hand him the last of what I owed him.

But there was a little glitch in the plan: the great recession, that deep malfunction in the machinery of the American economy. Of course, I knew about the financial markets' collapse and the bank bailouts and the suddenly obvious divide between Main Street and Wall Street. But it had never occurred to me that it would affect me personally. I'd never had any money to lose, no mortgage to get into over my head.

But those vibrations in the machine, those grinding bearings and blown head gaskets (Earnest's way of expressing it) affected my inheritance. My aunt's canny local broker had invested some of her money in funds that paid extraordinary dividends. Turned out they were packages of subprime mortgages or some financial instrument associated with them. That's why he'd had a hard time liquidating the last of her stock assets.

All this had been metastasizing while I was blissfully and miserably toughing out life on the hill. The end result was that not long after Cat's visit, six days before my final payment to Brassard was due, the cosmic magician whipped aside his handkerchief to show that—*ta-dah!*—the ten thousand dollars had all but disappeared. Less than two thousand remained.

By then my own savings had dwindled to about three thousand. I knew I needed some pittance to live on, at least some transition money to move back to Boston.

It appeared that the string of disasters of the past few years had followed me even here. What had I been thinking? That putting some geography between me and the site of my mistakes would put them behind me? I would suddenly get less stupid? My penitential hardships in the woods would atone for past sins? Of course this stuff doesn't shake off that easily. I was a fuckup, and here was the proof. Again.

All that was hard. But the toughest part was still ahead: telling Brassard. I had gotten the definitive word from my lawyer while sitting unbelieving in my car at the top of the ridge, where my phone could get a signal. No, no, no, I argued, for sure? Yes, sorry, yes, my lawyer said, final word, sorry.

So there it was. Six days. Brassard would need to know as soon as possible, because he'd built his own plans around my payment. It would be unconscionable to delay telling him. The shame I felt is indescribable. Here was another terror: the thought of facing the Brassards. I postponed the moment. Parked my car, walked back up to camp, numb and empty.

Beautiful day. Birds raucous in the trees like a crazy orchestra tuning up. A benevolent wind gently tossing the leaves so that sunlight and leaf shadows swam like fish, light and dark, schooling on the forest floor. My campsite looked lovely and dear. There it was: the sum total of my feeble and misguided attempt at making a home. A little era of my life, for whatever it was worth, past and gone. I cried at the imminent awfulness of telling Brassard. I figured I could give him two thousand and then let him decide whether to take the land back and sell it to someone else, or maybe agree to a new payment schedule despite the fact that I had no income. Or he'd sue me. Or whatever happened in cases like this.

I washed my red face in my bucket and marched down the hill. Cruelly, that magical clarity had returned, and the forest was unbearably beautiful, a rich embroidery in perfect focus. It was surreally divorced from my state of mind.

Down the hill. A new stab of terror as the house came into view. Across the ragged strip of scrub field, across the road. Late morning. Didn't see anybody, and Brassard's truck wasn't there. So I'd have to start by telling Diz.

Pigeons cooed and warbled as they courted in the barn. A sweet breeze tugged at my hair, and a cow lowed contentedly far out across the pasture. I was crossing the yard to the back door when Earnest pulled up in his truck. The parking brake ratcheted and he stepped out grinning.

"What a day!" he called to me. "This is what you live for up here. Makes it all worthwhile." He went around to the tailgate to rummage in the bed.

When he pulled in, I had stopped, paralyzed, unable even to say hello. Still smiling, Earnest turned and started toward me carrying a pair of red toolboxes. "So how're you doing up there, Pilgrim?"

At the sight of his broad smiling face and solid, square body, I burst into tears. In my pursuit of self-punishment, I had never let his simple kindness and camaraderie fully penetrate, I'd kept them out because they were at odds with my goal of feeling rejected by the world, suffering universal disapproval. Another shameful thing. I exploded now. Tears sprayed from my eyes, I coughed on sobs. And crying was yet another shameful thing. I was a cliché, the classic fragile woman with no recourse besides emotional breakdown.

Earnest looked alarmed. "Is everything all right? Is Diz okay? Where's Jim? Jesus, Ann, what—"

"I have to leave. I've totally screwed up. Shit, shit, *fuck*! I've screwed everybody up!" Choked out between wrenching sobs.

"Whoa! How?" He set down his toolboxes but didn't come any closer, as if I had something that might be catching.

"By doing everything! By being who I am! By being stupid my whole life."

Earnest looked toward the house, then came forward and took me by the arm and led me back to the other side of his truck. He propelled me toward the rear fender, where I leaned, moaning and burbling.

Eventually, I got to the money stuff.

"Oh, man." He peered over the hood at the back door again, and I realized he was worried that Diz would see all this. "Jesus."

He hovered uneasily while I cried and snarled at myself and leaked. After a bit, he opened the cab door and found a rag and gave it to me. I blew my nose in it and smeared my eyes with the oil on it. I was nearing empty, moving beyond caring what happened next.

"I don't know if anybody can *totally* fuck up," he said. "Not totally. Even me, and I've done a better job than most."

"Well, you've met someone now." I looked up at him and felt suddenly impatient with him. "I've just screwed your best friend! You should be mad at me! What's the matter with you?"

"I guess I must be fucking up again." His face became impassive for a moment, but then his eyes widened suddenly. "Here's Diz," he said. And there she was, coming out of the barn. Not in the house after all. We were in full view. My heart began to pound, my terror instantly renewed.

"Earnest! What are you doing to that poor woman?" she called. She chuckled and came toward us. When she got closer and could really see what a mess I was, she gave a resigned sigh and lifted her eyes heavenward. Still being sardonically funny.

"What *now*?" she asked.

THAT WAS A hard day.

When I told Diz, she was speechless, aghast, before the fury hit. Rage filled her face. She spun away, then turned back: "How could you? How *dare* you! When we went out on a limb to give you your little exercise in self-pity? Your little masochistic haven? I *told* Jim we shouldn't do it! I *told* him you were a narcissistic twit without the character, the *sand*, to follow through on anything in your whole spoiled yuppie life! But I never, *never* dreamed it would be our money—*our money!*—you'd flake out on."

"Diz—" Earnest began.

"No! She needs to hear it! Who does she think she is? We're running a *farm* here, not a rehab spa for troubled orphan girls! We need the damn money! That's why we sold the goddamned property. It wasn't *optional!*"

She stopped there, literally sputtering, unable to find words adequate to the task.

I didn't say anything. First, I deserved it. Second, I was stunned at how well Diz had scoped me.

Earnest took Diz's arm, and though she tried to jerk it out of his grip, he forcibly turned her around and led her back toward the barn. He didn't let go as he bent his head toward hers and made her listen. Eventually, she answered back. They conferred, Diz vehement, Earnest steadfastly calm, determined.

After a minute or two, Diz went over to the pasture fence, kicked it, then leaned on the topmost rail and looked out over the fields.

Earnest came back to me. "It's bad timing for them. I told her we should wait till Jim gets home, try to talk it over and figure out what to do so it's not a disaster for everybody."

I nodded.

We waited. Diz went into the house. Beautiful day, getting hot. I held myself and shivered, waiting for Brassard to get home.

Chapter 12

So, PARADOXICALLY, MY financial nosedive was what kept me there.

One day, I was on the verge of quitting—giving Brassard the last ten grand from my inheritance, then putting the land up for sale and heading back to Boston. The next, I was broke and a debtor who owed money to good people who needed the cash I'd promised and who had no wherewithal to take up the slack. I couldn't just walk off and leave the Brassards ten grand in the hole. Even putting the land up for sale wouldn't help: Earnest had said it had been on the market for two years before I came along—too hard to get to—and with the economy the way it was, nobody had the liquid capital to invest in marginally useless land. Not in time to get money to Brassard anytime soon.

I considered calling Cat and other friends to see if they had some cash I could borrow, but I didn't. I knew that none of them had that much to squander on me, and I was too ashamed to let them know the whole situation. Anyway, I wasn't even sure who my friends were anymore: I had burned too many bridges back there. I had said things, warranted and otherwise, that I couldn't unsay.

The solution, brokered by Earnest, was for me to enter a kind of indentured servitude as a farmhand. Franklin, their main regular hand, was going to quit in August to start at the technical college in Randolph. The Brassards would be looking for help anyway.

And that's how I got initiated into farm life, farmwork. Sort of a birth trauma. The deal was that I'd give Brassard two grand and then work off the remaining eight. Diz said I'd never manage it, I wasn't physically strong enough, I was a quitter, I'd bail and leave them high and dry just when they needed farm help the most.

"Franklin isn't exactly Rhodes scholar material," Earnest reminded her. Diz couldn't deny that Franklin wasn't the best hand. He wasn't bright, he wasn't motivated, and it seemed as if he was always breaking equipment or forgetting to do assigned chores.

"You managed it," Brassard added quietly. Diz gave a disgusted snort, but that quieted her.

So I BEGAN dairy farming. I would come down the hill just before dawn, go to the house for a cup of coffee, then head out to the cowshed, a long metal-roofed recent structure that was the biggest building on the farm. At first, I shadowed Franklin and Diz, learning how to move cows around and deal with the manure they left in the milking parlor and holding paddock. Only when I'd mastered that did I graduate to the milking routine and equipment cleaning. Earnest taught me to drive the Ford tractor and the little Bobcat skid-steer, to attach various implements to them, to use the tractor's PTO—short for *power takeoff*, a shaft that can drive other machines—and to use their buckets or forks to move around hay bales, watering tanks, and heaps of feed grain.

Just as I'd had imbecilic notions of the forest, I had childlike misconceptions about farms, farming, and farmers. I had an imaginary "farm" in my mind.

I *knew* that most of our food is grown on factory farms run by giant corporations. I *knew* that growing lots of a single crop or raising lots of a single kind of animal was the rule. I *knew* that the self-sufficient family farm was a dying institution. I'd read about these things in the *Boston Globe* and *New York Times*.

But as a kid, I had learned my letters by poring over picture books that depicted cozy farms with red and white barns, some friendly horses and sheep at the paddock fence, the fuddy-duddy farmer and his plump wife, the rows of vegetables, the henhouses, all surrounded by fields thick with grain. I loved *Charlotte's Web*. At school, we sang "Old McDonald Had a Farm." Every TV ad for cereal still reinforces the myth: A hale middle-aged farmer sits to his breakfast—whatever cereal is being marketed—in his sunny kitchen. Behind him are flowery curtains and a counter displaying other totems of rural life: a colander piled with just-collected pure-white eggs, a bowl of blueberries, a bunch of fresh carrots, and some greens ready for the missus to chop for dinner. Cut to him heading out, full of vigor, to his spotless small-farm compound, then fade to a close-up of the nodding heads of golden grain in his wheat field.

The myth lives on in our beguiled minds; it resonates inside us, a template of all that is good and honest. I have a theory that we grow much like trees, that every period of our lifetimes remains fully intact inside us, just covered over with the next layer and the next. Later layers may not accord with the early ones—we know there's no Santa Claus, but the five-year-old is still in there, waking on Christmas morning delirious with expectation.

So I came to Brassard's farm with that blurry-edged cameo image still underlying my expectations.

I had begun acquiring a truer sense of things even before my *Hindenburg* imitation. I literally got an overview, because I'd sometimes sit in a comfortable glade just above the steep cliffs facing the farm, where, through gaps in the trees, I could see everybody's comings and goings. I'd go there to write in my journal and then get distracted and just watch, pages unmarked.

If it were a film played fast, you'd see humans zipping here and there, trucks and tractors whipping about. In summer, you'd see a mottled tide of cows funneling into the milking parlor, then spraying out again across the pasture. In winter, as I learned later, the cows moved indoors and then you'd see manure being moved, piled, and spread on the fields, stall bedding and silage being carted here and there. And snow being pushed and heaped.

Inside the barn, there's no three-legged stool and bucket: Milking is done by machines. You usher the cows into the milking parlor—they don't need much coercion, because their udders ache and they know there's relief in there—where you attach suction devices to the four teats. Once all the cows have been drained, you have to purge the whole apparatus with near-boiling water, scrape up the fresh manure, and then hose the whole area.

The milk in the holding tank gets picked up every other day by a big stainless-steel tank truck that holds thousands of gallons. That's the Agri-Mark truck, from the farmers' cooperative that processes and markets the milk. It idles for a while as it pumps the stuff out, and the driver hands Brassard a computer-generated receipt. The milk goes to the processing plant; Brassard gets a check.

Brassard didn't spend his time stroking the velvety noses of his horses and giving them sugar lumps, because he didn't have any horses, and his pockets had keys and tools and rags in them, not sugar lumps. In fact, he spent hours each day in his office, once a first-floor bedroom, at his computer, working his spreadsheets, juggling cash and debt, writing checks for equipment loans, reviewing the price of milk and feed on the exchanges. Farming is a business, and he was a capable businessman.

Manure was a big part of his day. In colder months, when the cows lived inside, the manure flowed to a sort of pond; Brassard periodically pumped the pond's contents into a special tank trailer that he towed behind the tractor across the fields, spraying the stuff onto the soil. The shed for the younger cows, those not yet lactating, was set up so the manure fell into straw on the floor, creating a more solid form that he moved around with the bucket on the front of his tractor. He piled it in a big U-shaped concrete berm he called the "stack," and in spring he loaded it into another specialized trailer that flung the stuff out in lumps as he drove. Both activities trailed a plume of odor that filled the valley.

He bought hundreds of tons of feed grain, but he also raised a lot of his own cow food. Think of it as a recipe for a cake or loaf of bread: To a hundred and ten acres of soil, sift in manure and chemical fertilizers. Whisk with spades and harrows, mix in corn seed. Let stand until it rises. Baste as needed with insecticides or herbicides. Bake in sun.

This wasn't sweet corn, so it was never harvested for human consumption. The cobs dried on the stalk, and in autumn the golden-brown fields were felled by a combine that chopped both cob and stalk and hurtled the mixed chaff into a high-sided trailer. The fields were left with uniform rows of stubble, and the stuff was blown into the silo to feed the cows during the winter.

Brassard also grew ninety acres of hay, which he cut several times a summer, left in windrows, and then raked to fluff and flip it so it dried uniformly. He baled some but rolled most of it into huge wheels that he wrapped in heavy white plastic, leaving the fields scattered with six-foot marshmallows.

Diz did grow vegetables, in a fenced plot right behind the house, but mostly they bought their green stuff at the Grand Union and kept it in the refrigerator or a freezer in the basement.

Diz was a stickler for "respectability," keeping the house and immediate grounds well tended and pretty. She maintained a fringe of lilies and poppies and chrysanthemums, three mountainous lilacs, and some apple trees. Morning glories climbed a trellis near the door. She mowed the lawn and weed-whacked the taller grass along the road.

But the farmyard, just to the side of this island of order, wasn't pretty. It was shapeless and often muddy and marked by the braided ruts made by tractor wheels. Tractors and tractor attachments sat haphazardly when not in use, along with various cars and Brassard's truck—a massive red double-cab Dodge Ram that he washed often and took great pride in. Earnest's regular pickup was often there, and sometimes his big old warhorse stake-side, the one he used for his tree business, decorated the place as well.

Beyond the farmyard and the near paddocks, though, lovely pasture opened up, green and inviting. Brassard's cows grazed freely there during the warm months, contentedly lounging or strolling along meandering trails they'd worn in the grass to favorite grazing spots.

So cows, manure, machines, and corn are the most obvious elements of the small dairy farm. Diz didn't even raise chickens—she used to but said she got sick of having to go out to the henhouse with the .22 to "pop" raiding weasels, raccoons, and fisher cats. She bought her eggs from a "hippie" couple who ran an organic vegetable farm about two miles down the road.

I wasn't exactly disillusioned by the realities of Brassard's operation, but for a while it did leave a hollow in me where the ideal farm used to glow. The six-year-old in me, you could say, mourned the dream's passing.

AND YET. AND yet—another example of why we should be more patient with life—despite modern farming's hard pragmatism and reliance on technology, I found that there is strength to be gained from having feet on the ground and hands (or at least tools) in the earth. Your psychic clock is set by the sun's year and by its day, and I do believe our lives are better when we acknowledge and live by the power of those cycles. Otherwise, we get out of step with the world and with ourselves, our rhythms wrong, then wonder why we're stumbling and off balance.

And I believe that we know ourselves to be real when we experience ourselves as creatures—as animals. Every woman I know who has had a baby, who has suffered through the burden of carrying and then the pain of birthing, says that this holding and cleaving wakened her to her life. I was there when my friend Terri gave birth, and I remember her screams and mounting fear when it seemed the baby's head simply would not crown. I remember what the midwife said so fiercely to her, what pulled her out of her dive into despair: "You are a *female animal*! You *know* how to do this!"

And Terri was. And she did.

Similarly, waking to the red-tinted sky and getting your work-stiffened limbs moving, and going outside to the first tentative bird calls, and inhaling unapologetic animal and earth smells, and getting cold if it's cold and wet if it's raining, and looking a large fellow mammal in her long-lashed eye—these things are basic, natural, foundational. They make you strong, and at times they can still the jittery yammering of the urban monkey-mind. No meditation practice has ever granted me such long stretches of productive emptiness, such single-pointedness of mind.

Mucking out the parlor and holding area, giving a no-nonsense shove to a recalcitrant cow, wiping dew off the tractor seat so my butt wouldn't be wet all day: I simply *was* the task, the manure, the cow, the tractor.

I liken my initial dislike of farming to the way, back in Cambridge, I hated trying to get fit after an urban winter. Padded out with insulating fat, I found the initial jogs laborious, uncomfortable, even painful. And embarrassing: to be seen clunking along in clothes that don't fit your flabbier frame.

But then after a couple of weeks, you forget to bitch at yourself as you jog, or you catch your reflection in a storefront window and don't recoil.

Farming did that with my soul, or my "character," as my father called that inner thing we all supposedly have. After a while, it wasn't so difficult, and I didn't flinch so much when I glanced into the mirror inside me.

You are a working animal, I told myself, *and you know how to do this.*

I SPENT THE last two weeks of July numb with fatigue. I was wary of introspection because I didn't want to awaken the shame and sense of rudderlessness. I told myself I had made stupid choices, had done bad by some good people, but I had sorted it out and was working off my debt. I was on a reasoned trajectory to … somewhere.

My life divided into two completely different tracks: daytime, working on the farm, and nighttime, living my solitary life up in the woods.

During the day, I did what I was told: mainly moving cows around, then milking them, then cleaning the milking apparatus and dealing with manure. Between milkings, an unending stream of odd jobs: hand-feeding the calves, unclogging culverts, putting out feed grain, towing feed wagons loaded with hay out to the pasture, helping Franklin repair fences.

My favorite times were the hours I spent with Earnest. Sometimes, he would corral me to help with the tasks he'd taken on, usually involving fixing trucks, tractors, harrows, combines, pumps, conveyors, balers, blower fans, and motors. I'd serve as his surgical nurse, handing him tools as he lay beneath a vehicle or entwined in some machine's innards. He would explain his diagnoses, outlining the mechanical or hydraulic or electrical systems, and, through either his adroit teaching or my heretofore unnoticed engineering instincts, I actually did get a good sense of how things worked.

When we weren't talking about the job at hand, he told me a little about the Brassards. And because he never seemed judgmental, it was easy for me to talk about myself. I was careful not to abuse this privilege, not to overindulge in confession.

But he seldom offered much when I asked him about himself. When I pointed that out to him, he answered, deadpan: "The American Indian is taciturn by nature."

Chapter 13

AFTER SELLING ME my forty acres, Brassard had three hundred acres, about thirty forested and the rest divided between pasture, hay, and corn. By Midwestern standards, not much, but in Vermont it's a pretty good spread. You can spend a day walking on it, and you can get lost in the surrounding woods because many of the borders aren't marked. And parts of it are rugged, making it seem bigger. They say that if you pressed Vermont flat it would be big as Texas.

I'm sure I would have learned more about Brassard and Diz earlier if I hadn't betrayed them. It took many weeks, which I spent desperately showing how hard I could work, before Diz could say more than a few words to me.

What I did learn came from Earnest. He always seemed to get a little evasive, which I took as a measure of his respect for their privacy and his contempt for gossip. So what I gleaned was pretty bare-bones, and the exact chronology was never clear to me. Brassard married young and had a daughter, Jane, who now lived out west. I deduced that she would be around forty. His first wife died, and at some unspecified point Diz appeared on the scene. Diz and Brassard married and had a son, Will, who was about my age and lived in Rutland.

When I asked Earnest if the kids ever came to visit, he said that Will managed to swing by the farm fairly often, and I'd likely see him before long. Jane, the daughter, "doesn't get along with Diz." His tone told me this was an understatement best left unprobed. I could easily believe that Diz was an unforgiving enemy and that she would cultivate a similar outlook in others.

My rhythms were even more closely linked with those of the sky and the forest than the Brassards'. Each morning, I awoke in a tent in a small clearing in the woods, already aware of the temperature of the air and the movement of the wind. I got so I could tell the time of day, whatever the weather, by the relative glow of the tent nylon under the morning sky. I lived among the blackflies and by their life cycle. I knew when the birds' chicks hatched and fledged, because I heard them piping in their nests and found the shells of their eggs at the base of the trees and eventually saw their first plummeting attempts at flight, and their parents' hopping, shrieking exhortations to get the hell back up in the air.

Important revelations, I learned, often come at you with a left-handed, offhanded, slow spiral. Insight frequently requires preparation in the form of a gradual melting of habitual stupidity. And when real revelation comes, it may not be something you can name; it may not make sense except in the deep places where our souls forge coherence from the world's various pieces.

My epiphany about water is a good example.

While I loved drinking and cooking with and washing in the water from my spring, it was a little thing that dwindled as the warm season ripened and the snowmelt left the water table. I filled my jug by sitting at the stream's edge and scooping water with a small saucepan. Scoop, pour, scoop, pour, spilling half of it over numbing fingers and back into the stream: It took ten minutes to get my day's supply into containers I would then lug back to my campsite. I washed the same way, ladling the crystal ice liquid onto myself. Or, if I felt really felt begrimed, I humped the jugs back to the tent and heated the water on my fire before washing.

Getting water took a long time. So during one of my free afternoons, I decided I would dam the stream to make a basin deep enough to dip the water jugs in, filling them much faster. I brought a trowel and found a spot twenty feet or so below the spring head, where the water passed between two good-size rocks (each the size of a big couch pillow or, as I tended to think by then, the size of a porcupine) that could anchor a dam. Watching the play of light on the braiding surface of the stream, so energetic and silvery, I felt reluctant to obstruct such a vital thing. But practicality won out.

First I scooped out gravel, fine silt streaming away in delicate tendrils, to make a basin. When it was about the size of a bushel basket, I cast around to find rocks that would fill the gap between the two porcupine rocks. I figured that a range of sizes and shapes would give me a choice when I got down to the stonemasonry puzzle. They would have to fit tightly. After ten minutes I had assembled twenty stones ranging from the size of my hand to the size of a shoe box. I anchored the larger ones in shallow holes I dug in the streambed, and then filled the gaps between, fitting progressively smaller stones into progressively smaller chinks. My hands froze wax white, but after an hour I had made a curved dam about fourteen inches high and two feet across. It looked well constructed, and I was proud of my work.

The stream didn't notice it, though. The water slithered and shimmied through, undismayed. It didn't rise in the basin at all.

But, I warned the stream affectionately, we hominids are very smart. We have clever minds and clever fingers! I collected still smaller rocks and wedged them into still smaller holes until I was working with pebbles the size of lima beans. I didn't hope to make a miniature waterfall over the top, just to delay the flow enough to fill the basin to maybe eight inches deep—enough to dip the jugs or my big pot into and not have to ladle them full. But still the water refused to tarry.

Taking a cruder approach, I heaped gravel and sand on both sides of the dam. The water tarried for a few moments and then simply, cheerfully removed the gravel and kept going. So I gathered leaves, reasoning that the leaf membranes would span gaps and be pressed against them by water pressure and thereby seal the dam. They did—a little, for a while. Before long, the water had discovered all the gaps and lifted things away here and there, and the net gain in the basin was no more than an inch.

I kept at it for another hour before I understood that water's fingers were far cleverer than mine. The water seemed newborn, so clear and quick, but it knew its job well. I was a rube, a dude, and this lithe, innocent silver snake had billions of years' experience moving with gravity and meticulously probing everything it encountered and passing through every obstacle. The insight resonated deeply in me. The elements are subtle and profound and ancient and powerful. At this epiphany, the pieces of the world slid into a kind of order and provided a perspective of my own being and nature in relation to the world. It was both humbling and strengthening.

The next day, it rained and the stream swelled so that on the day after, when I visited the dam there was no indication that anyone had tried to build anything on the spot. I recognized a couple of my largest stones a few yards downstream. Even a little stream has unexpected muscle not to be underestimated.

Only later did I encounter the real force of Vermont's hill waters, when an unusually heavy thunderstorm washed a four-foot diameter, twenty-two-foot-long corrugated culvert out of one of Brassard's logging trails on the property's east side. That stream, bigger than my spring but usually lazier, had become a car-size fist. It punched the culvert out of its position and tumbled it fifty feet downstream, leaving it cocked at a steep angle against a boulder. Earnest and Will and I dragged it back using the tractor's winch. It took us all day to reseat the thing, and another few days to dump twenty yards of crushed rock and gravel on it to keep it there for another while.

So: humility. Brassard had suffered enough of it in his lifetime to be immune to notions about how spiritually cute it is when nature shows you

you're small and it's big. Hail destroys your corn, cold ruptures the pipes from the well in the middle of winter when the ground's too damn hard to dig them up, windstorms pull up sections of barn roof, ice brings down trees on the powerlines so there's no electricity or phone for three or four days. It all costs money that isn't there, requires time and energy you don't have, and tests patience long since exhausted.

But I was still new enough and urban enough that I found it existentially reassuring. Earnest found my outlook amusing and made sure I knew it.

Chapter 14

I WAS NERVOUS about meeting Will Brassard, because I was still terrified of Diz and because I didn't know what judgments he might have of me as a result of my Great Betrayal.

I also knew myself as an inexplicable person living a chaotic life. I didn't mind Earnest's seeing me that way—I knew he enjoyed my company and forgave my failings—and was used to Brassard and Diz knowing the sad truth. But I hadn't spent much time in the proximity of other human beings during my months on Brassard's farm. I had only gotten stranger, more contradictory and not less, and didn't relish the idea of others catching wise.

When Will swung into the driveway, I was wresting with a coil of four-inch drainage pipe that we planned to install below the barn to help dry out the near paddock, where the cows had churned the soil into hock-deep muck. He unfolded from his Jetta and nodded at me over the roof of the car: a pleasant-faced guy with a reddish mustache, wearing khakis and a checked shirt rolled up his forearms. He was as tall as his father but carried much less weight in the shoulders and gut, and he walked with a light stride toward the house. Diz had come out on the porch and, for the first time since I'd known her, wore a big smile that was not crimped with a sardonic tilt. Will swayed her left and right as they hugged, and then they went inside. After a time, Brassard pulled up in his truck, nodded to me, and also went inside.

Hundred-foot rolls of perforated drainage pipe aren't that heavy, but they're four feet in diameter and about the same tall—awkward to grip or lift, prone to tumbling out of the tractor's bucket. I opted to roll them, one by one, through the gate and across the paddock to the ditch Earnest had dug last time he was here. The big, uneven wheels teetered and toppled unexpectedly, or suddenly veered off course; moving them was like shepherding large, strangely built toddlers. I went back and forth feeling something sour in me that took a moment to acknowledge: I felt left out.

This was the first time since I'd been here, even living as the object of Diz's disdain, that I felt the circle of a family close around the house and exclude me. Whatever sense of inclusion I'd had was thanks to Earnest: He wasn't a blood relative, but he stayed and worked like one, and it was easy for me to tag along in his wake. But with Will and his parents in the house, I felt envious and suddenly alone. They were in there, relishing that intimacy that only families know. I was out here in my mud boots, working to pay off the debt I owed, more of an indentured laborer than a hired hand, a woman alone and without a family to embrace her. Or any kind of plan for her life.

Hard work is the best antidote for self-pity, I told myself. As Diz had said when I first met her: "What the heck? Couldn't tell ya, get back to work." Being a Hardheaded Woman is not so bad. Sometimes I think our extreme sensitivity to our own emotions is an indulgence that only the urban and solvent—people with too much time on their hands—can enjoy.

So I stayed at my task. I positioned three rolls of pipe at hundred-foot intervals along the newly dug ditch. Earnest had closely analyzed the slope here and had planned the pipe's route carefully. The trench ran across the bottom of the paddock and then took a curve downhill, getting shallower and shallower until it emerged from the ground a hundred yards below the barnyard. Earnest had explained how to stake the pipe as I unrolled it, so it wouldn't just curl back up. I toppled a roll into the ditch and cut the strapping with my pocketknife. Suddenly, the whole thing shrugged and slithered and expanded, startling me and becoming a still more awkward, uneven mass.

I worked in a series of forceful jerks and resentful shoves, a purse-lipped frown in my brain because seeing the Brassards together had reminded me how much I missed having a family. I cursed my brother Erik for abandoning his only sister. Where was the little bastard? I cursed Matt for being a shit and liar and skirt chaser and for thinking so highly of himself that *he* could jilt *me*! I tried, staunchly but in vain, to keep that ever-present loneliness at bay. I cursed myself for having missed the boat of life as it left port with all the more sensible people aboard.

After I'd tugged loose ten feet or so, the whole pipe unwound and became a huge, unwieldy series of big loops that made a plastic racket as their ridges shifted over each other. I wrestled it back into the ditch, working my way along its length, anchoring it with stakes whenever it arched or curled, then opened the next roll, coupled the ends, and repeated the process. When I'd gotten three hundred feet of it in place, I went to get the tractor to lay some gravel. My internal soliloquy went something like, *I'll show them! I'll show how hardworking and capable I am, how good I am at solitude. I don't need you, and I especially don't need your attitude, Diz. Don't worry, you're getting your money's worth out of me.*

I wasn't allowed to drive the newer Deere or the hulking Harvester, but that was fine because I liked the old Ford tractor better anyway. It was clanky and worn and Earnest had repaired every part of it at one time or another, but it was more my size, and sturdy. I liked that the seat was metal, not padded, and there was no canopy or fancy dashboard— that the whole thing was so simple. By now I was feeling good about my tractor-driving skills and had come to love the double brakes that allowed such tight turns. Once, when I thought I was out of view of the farm, I spun the Ford a few times just for the fun of it, to feel the centrifugal force. But Earnest had seen me, and when I got back to the barn he grinned and made some comment that made us both laugh.

I'd gotten pretty good at handling the bucket, too. Earnest had said that when I was "ready"—this in the mysterious tone of some wise philosopher–kung fu master—he would teach me how to attach other implements and then how to use the digger attachment—"the backhoe arts."

I revved it up, lowered the bucket, and charged at walking speed toward the pile of crushed rock. When the bucket engaged the mound, the engine labored, but I continued to rock the beast forward against the slope, raising the bucket by degrees until it had a reasonable load. Then I backed away, more carefully now because the back end of the tractor seemed awfully light with all that weight up front. Through the gate. Over the softer soil of the paddock area. Up to the brink of the ditch so that the bucket hung over the pipe, then a delicate touch with the hydraulic levers to tip the bucket. The egg-size stones rained down onto the pipe more or less centered in the ditch—we would level it all by hand later—and covered the pipe with a pile about ten inches deep and four feet wide. When the bucket was empty I backed away and turned to survey my work.

Not too bad for a spoiled city twit with an identity crisis, huh, Diz?

I returned to the gravel heap. My first bucket had not made much of an impression on it, and for the first time I understood just how much there was to carry and dump. I rammed the tractor forward again, working the hydraulics, striving for a fuller bucket. The exhaust darkened with blue smoke as the engine strained, the hydraulics whined as they labored, and I knew I had a good load.

Back to the ditch. Carefully maneuver the tractor up to the edge at a right angle to the ditch, just where the first load ended, then inch forward until the bucket overhung the pipe, then slowly tilt and lower to sift the stuff off. The gravel seemed to cling inside the bucket, and the back end of the tractor rose disturbingly, but I jiggled the lever and got it bouncing, and at last the load avalanched off and made a tidy mound just where it should be.

Doin' good! I told myself. I savored my own prowess and inhaled the diesel fumes deep into my lungs as if they were full of vitamins.

The gravel had been heaped at the end of the driveway, at the pasture end of the old barn—a small mountain that represented twenty dump-truck loads. We all had gathered to watch the first truck empty itself. When I asked why they didn't just dump it down by the ditch, Diz had explained with excessive patience that the truck would sink to the door handles in the mud and stay there forever and "we'd use the damn thing as a planter, put our begonias in there maybe."

Of course. A loaded ten-yard dump truck would weigh many, many tons and would indeed have a hard time in the wet soil of the paddock.

"Or end up in China," Earnest said. "Then we'd have a problem with Immigration."

Diz had scowled at him for interjecting genuine humor into the situation.

Screw Diz, I told myself grimly. When I came up to the pile the third time, I was thinking about how little my last bucket had taken. At this rate, it would take all day and Diz would say something about what a sensitive tractoring style I had. So I really worked the bucket in, getting the angles just right so that when I lifted it free the rocks were mounded above the bucket's rim. I congratulated myself.

Chug-chug back to the ditch, the tractor crushed low in front and daintily high off the ground in back. I was fuming inside but I took it slow, mindful of the weight differential. I positioned myself, edged out over the ditch, and tipped the bucket. Only a few stones fell. The gravel had lodged itself in there pretty well. So I joggled it up and down, the tractor clanking and rocking front to back, and inched a little closer, and then the edge of the ditch gave way and the tractor tipped forward and the front wheels went down so that the full bucket lay flat on the far bank. The Ford's back wheels floated just off the ground. The whole thing was locked in place, canted at a hard forward tilt and pinned by the bucket full of half a ton of gravel. The bucket couldn't lift and the tractor couldn't reverse itself out of the trap.

I shut off the engine. For a moment, I sat there, leaning forward, holding myself off the steering wheel with my arms. It was a fine day. Birds making a lovely cacophony in the woods. Cows unperturbed on the green slope. A tranquil bucolic scene. My mind racing like a panicked rat in some gruesome lab experiment.

Truly, literally, I thought of just sprinting to my car, getting in and driving away and never coming back. Leave all my stuff up on the hill. Send the papers back to Brassard and they'd never hear from me again.

But I didn't. This was my cross and I was destined to be crucified on it and was apparently to drive the spikes myself. So I walked along my wheel ruts back to the yard and up the porch steps. I went through the mudroom and tapped on the inner door, mortified at having to bring this awful news into a happy family get-together.

Brassard called from the living room: "In here, Ann."

I left my boots on the porch and went through the kitchen and into the living room, where I was surprised to see no family gathering but just Will in Brassard's recliner, reading a magazine while Brassard, wearing his reading glasses, did some paperwork. Diz wasn't in sight.

"Did you meet Will?" Brassard asked. "Will, this is Ann, our neighbor and our hand for the time bein."

Will leaned the recliner upright and stood up, and we shook hands. He smiled; I smiled. I covertly examined his face for signs of the contempt he would feel if he'd heard much about me, but couldn't see anything definite.

"Diz is up taking a nap," Brassard said. "I've got to get these bills paid, but you can sit if you'd like. There's coffee." He turned in his chair and looked at me over his glasses, and his eyes widened. "What?"

"There's a problem," I said.

It wasn't as big a problem as all that. Brassard looked out over the pasture fence at the distant up-canted back end of the Ford and said to Will, "You want to do the honors?" Will said he would. Brassard went to fire up the Deere, then brought it around to where we stood. He clambered down, Will swung up, I climbed onto the hitch rack, and we rolled at a leisurely pace out to the ditch. Over his shoulder, Will told me not to worry, he'd done the same thing more than once.

Will positioned the Deere, and I hauled out the winch cable and attached the hook to a steel loop on the Ford's frame. I started up the little tractor and put it into reverse, and when Will said, "Go," I let up the clutch. The Deere effortlessly pulled the thing out and there it was, done. The indestructible Ford was none the worse for wear. I dismounted and checked and found to my relief that its front wheels had not crushed the plastic pipe; then I got back in the saddle and dumped the damned bucket. Will and I chugged back on the two tractors like a tiny parade. At Brassard's invitation, I joined them for a cup of coffee at the kitchen table.

When Will asked me about myself, I gave him a heavily redacted history: from Boston most recently, middle school teacher but out of work so far, glad to be learning about farmwork.

Brassard mentioned that I was the gal who'd bought the land uphill, and Will just smiled and asked how I liked it.

"It's beautiful," I told him. What was most beautiful at that moment was realizing that Will had not heard about my transgression. I could sit here without the stage fright that comes with being a bad actor and not knowing your lines. Better yet, I'd gotten away with my tractoring faux pas without Diz knowing about it! The coffee was bracingly hot and excellent.

Will said he and his friends used to camp out up on my hill when he was a kid. He told me he had seen moose a couple of times, and bears in the blackberries. I told him about the bears Cat and I saw, but said I'd mainly seen just porcupines and blackflies. He said he'd seen them often enough, too.

Then Diz was clumping down the stairs. She came into the room wiping her glasses on her shirttail, touched her son's shoulder as she passed, poured herself a cup of coffee.

She sat heavily and without inflection said, "I see you've met Ann." Then she looked at me. "Supposed to fill it with gravel, not tractors."

Chapter 15

July 16

I am so tired I can hardly sit up to write. Today was the first time I've operated a tractor for so many hours straight. Every muscle hurts. I stink of diesel and am too tired to heat water to wash up. I conked my knee a dozen times dismounting, exactly the same place again and again, and now there's a bruise the size of my hand, so tender something must be seriously damaged in there. I could hardly walk back up the hill. No wonder Brassard's got such a gimp, after fifty-some years of that kind of wear and tear.

I astonish myself with my immaturity. Remind me, when's that hard-bitten self-sufficiency supposed to kick in? I have been a devoted follower of the discipline. I have left sacrifices of my own flesh on the altar. Yet today I spent the entire day seething with juvenile resentment, feeling rejected, angry at Diz, pissed at myself, fuming and confused and out of control.

Trying to prove my worth as a human being up on the tractor, rather than just getting the job done—that was my first mistake. In the unlikely chance I ever read these scribblings, here's a memo to my future self: Do. The. Job. Skip the extraneous emotions. The work is real. It's simple. It's Zen. It is necessary and it is good and it is enough.

Yeah, therein lies respite, absolution, clarity, yadda yadda, but you can take this philosophy too far.

And here I sit, still knotted and seared and all acid, despite being in heaven on Earth. The evening is gentle and sweet. Twilight comes early here among the dense midsummer trees, and it's a serene time. The light is going blue and soothing, the air moves with decorum in the woods, scented with some blossom's sweetness, the birds have gone drowsily quiet except for one—I should learn my birds—that makes a particularly liquid reveille: whirly-whirly-whirly-whirly. I have everything I need in my tent and my porky-proof storage boxes; I have a good book to read by lantern light. I can't even complain about the bugs, because my diesel-skunked skin repels them. And I'm squandering all of it. Something else to detest about myself.

Today I was dumping gravel into the ditch and tipped the tractor into it and Will Brassard is visiting and he pulled me out and I thought I'd escaped without shame but Diz saw it from the upstairs window and got in a jab at me and I let it hurt me.

To his everlasting credit, Will smiled and pointed out that he and she and Brassard himself and Franklin and probably every other farming person in the history of mankind had done something similar at one time or another. In fact, he related the time Diz herself had been towing a stake-side trailer full of the big rolled-hay marshmallows and one got loose and rolled downhill, gaining speed until it bounded over the stone wall at the bottom of the field and landed on the hood and windshield of Diz's car, which then needed eight hundred dollars' worth of bodywork and glass.

Brassard chuckled and chimed in with some details here and there and affectionately covered his wife's hand with his baseball mitt of a hand. Diz sipping her coffee with indifference. I liked Will for taking on his mother with good humor and no mercy.

After a bit, the conversation turned to other things, and the family seemed to wrap around itself, so I took my leave and went back out to finish the job.

I covered three hundred feet of drainage pipe, back and forth dozens of times on the trusty Ford. I worked until I was so tired I was afraid I'd mess up again, then shut it down and hobbled back up here. The valley was darkening and the windows of the house came alight behind me. I walked up into my dark woods knowing that it would be one of those nights of missing kin and connection, and I dreaded it.

Slumped on my fireside log, the lantern giving light to write by, the most resonant image in my exhausted mind is Will. It's the way he looked when he and I were hooking up the winch cable. He's slim, rangy, well proportioned, with medium-length brown hair. He was wearing jeans and an old checked shirt with the sleeves rolled up, and for a few seconds he just stood straight and looked around the family's acres, nostalgically appreciative. At that moment he struck me as very handsome and somehow familiar.

Which is the worst, the most middle school, dumb-ass fairyland thing of the whole goddamn day. I was wondering if Will Brassard is married or not, and if maybe destiny has brought me here so I'll meet my soul mate at last. And I wondered how I'd struck him, if he'd found me gross or if maybe my muddied, sweated, dieseled, sunburned, ragged-denim-covered inept self had a certain je-ne-sais-quoi appeal.

I can hardly stand to write this. I'm too disgusted with myself. This situation is not about Finding One's Will Brassard At Last. It's not about a man, it's not about a "relationship." I am appalled to discover this awful Cinderella wannabe still living inside me. How readily she rears her ash-smudged little hopeful prince-seeking head when she gets within arm's length of a man her own age.

I'm going to sleep now.

I DID NOT go to sleep. At some point, I got up and dutifully heated a pot of water, soaped myself down, standing naked in my little clearing to rinse the stink and grime off me. I put my clothes into a plastic trash bag so their smell wouldn't pollute the night air. Then, scoured skin thrilled and goose-bumped with the cold, I sort of danced. I danced gestures of apology to the night woods for ignoring their grace and generosity, and I requested their friendship again and felt as though I received it.

I assure you this was not at all a New Agey sort of thing. I didn't try to commune with some wise, vastly serene and maternal Gaia—I doubt this dear planet has ever been either serene or particularly concerned with any one creature's misery. What this was: a tired, desperate human being trying to regain some sense of connection to herself and to some part of the world, and resorting instinctively to something like prayer—a prayer to no being but to the whole damn thing.

Really, I had nothing else. It's that simple.

But there it was again: necessity. The mother of invention, they say, but also the mother of resiliency. After my ablutions and dance of supplication, I felt renewed.

Chapter 16

AN EXPOSITION ON manure is not a digression. On dairy farms, it is a central and continuous concern. Manure requires pushing, scooping, hoeing, shoveling, pumping, relocating, hosing, piling, and spreading. In winter, with the cows in the barn, it's a major daily undertaking, but even in summer the poop needs to be removed after the cows have sashayed into and out of the milking parlor. It's part of every working day.

Over the years, I had walked in pastures and stepped around cow pies, those neat nests of ground-up fibrous material. So I always assumed that cow poop came out with a texture like horses'.

In reality, it emerges as a thick liquid the color of soy sauce. Deposited in the pasture, its water drains into the soil, leaving only the residues of grass and feed in that nice pie shape, solid enough that you can throw it like a discus. But on concrete, with nowhere for the water to soak away to, it lingers as a wet, soupy slurry. You spend a lot of time removing it with hoe, shovel, or the tractor's bucket or scraper blade.

I mention this now because Will came to chat with me while I was cleaning off the concrete pad where the cows congregated as they waited their turn in the milking parlor. When I thanked him for deflecting his mother's contempt for my tractoring, he just laughed. He acknowledged that Diz was an acquired taste.

I had recovered from the psychological stumbles of the day before. The largesse of the night woods had soothed me and allowed me to accept myself a bit. I'd landed in the new day with some measure of grace and balance.

I had even forgiven Cinderella. I figured that, like any creature in the woods, no matter how noxious, she had some rightful niche in the ecosystem. If I encountered her, I would respectfully replace the rock I found her under and trust that she had some odd but indispensable place in the scheme of things.

Yes, when Will came to lean in the doorway, Cinderella was there, and I let her into the conversation, let her check him out, seek clues about his personal life. She found none. He didn't offer any. He didn't wear a wedding ring, but then, neither had my father or Matt.

Did I bat a conversational eyelash? I don't think I did—I was shoveling and hosing cow shit. My rubber coveralls were splattered with it, and I was hardly in a position to feel, or be, flirtatious.

He told me he was up this way because had some business in Burlington, working on an agricultural video project in partnership with UVM's farm extension service, just for the day, and then had to get back to Rutland. He had a nice face, long in the jaw, showing none of his mother's hardness. He seemed interested in me in a courteous way, not as a woman but as a person who happened to be coexisting with his parents on the farm where he'd grown up. His comfort with himself, the absence of posturing, suggested he wasn't paying much attention to my gender.

We talked for ten minutes, then he said so long. We exchanged jaunty waves. I went about my work.

EARNEST CAME THE next day to help Brassard and me finish the drainage project. He and I worked in the ditch, shoveling the gravel around—those ice-cube-to-egg-size irregular chunks collectively make a stubborn medium, so in reality you're sort of raking it, kicking it, digging at it—as Brassard unrolled a fabric silt screen over the top and used the Deere's backhoe to fill in soil on top. It got hot and my entire T-shirt, starting at the armpits and working outward, turned dark with sweat.

Earnest just took off his shirt. It was the first time I had seen his broad, copper-colored torso without clothing, and I was stunned. His body was gently rounded by a layer of hard fat, but when he raked and jabbed with the shovel, the muscles of his back rolled and stood in ridges, and his biceps and shoulder muscles bulged and balled. His body seemed a locus of great power, radiating it, and I found myself stealing glances at him, at once fascinated and intimidated. It seemed an elemental phenomenon. My scratchings and scuffings accomplished virtually nothing, but when Earnest told things to move, they *moved*. Brassard smiled as he worked— the pleasure of a man glad to see a job getting done. I'd noticed that the mood at the farm always brightened when Earnest was there.

That night, up the hill, exhausted again, my mind turned to the day's activities, conversations, images. And my thoughts returned again and again to Earnest—the power of him, the sun-warmed color of his glistening skin, his pleasure in the effort of the work. The masculinity of his form.

It was the second time in two days that my thoughts had lingered on a man, on a man's physical self, and I realized abruptly and completely that I had just come up hard against another challenge or problem with my choice to seek land and live in the woods and be utterly self-sufficient in every way. Eros is a river, I realized, and just like my little stream, it will not let itself be dammed for long.

Chapter 17

WITH THE DRAINAGE system installed, I returned to my regular work routine. Maybe it was Will's comment about Diz's own farming faux pas, or my imagination, but I thought I detected a slight softening in Diz. We worked together for the afternoon milking, and she didn't scowl the entire time. We became an efficient team, trading off tasks and tools without hesitation. I had studied her various techniques of getting an animal ten times your weight to do what you wanted, and was getting pretty good at them. I think she noticed.

Against the daily, unchanging rhythm of milking, another slow and subtle longer beat had been playing: The corn came up. The hay came up. The off-cycle fields of clover came up. Brassard's brown-earth soil disappeared under robust green.

AND SO MY first summer passed.

I spent every night at my camp, and I worked on the farm for about twelve hours, five days a week, depending on the needs of the herd and the season and the availability of other help. By late August, life on my hill had become downright civilized. I dug a deeper hole and erected a rickety structure with a roof over it, and made a sort of chair of scrap lumber, to which I nailed a store-bought toilet seat—almost a genuine outhouse. I built a kitchen consisting of two-by-fours tied to two trees, with boards across for a counter, then put my Coleman white-gas stove there so I could sometimes cook standing up instead of crouching in the dirt. The biggest luxury was the aluminum sink I installed in my counter. I still hand-carried water from the spring, but now I could plug the drain and use the basin to wash vegetables, and myself, well clear of the soil floor. When I was done, I'd pull the plug and the water would pour out onto the ground and slither away in a little runnel I had dug. It felt very high-tech.

BRASSARD WAS PAYING me eight bucks an hour. By the end of August, I had earned $3,325 and, after my living expenses and car payments and first-ever property tax bill, had paid back about $1,900. At that rate, factoring in the 4 percent interest I was paying him, I would finish off my debt in sixteen more months. That is, I'd work the coming fall and winter, all the next summer and fall, and be paid up by January of the following year.

I loved living in my tiny palace, loved making shift to see to basic needs, and the woods did strengthen and smooth me. I learned to manage my nighttime fears somewhat better, and the knowledge that I could challenge them, or at least weather them, also helped reconstruct me.

But I had no intention of working on the farm for sixteen more months. It was occasionally fun, but mostly it was difficult and boring and uncomfortable. My hard-used hands ached at night. So I kept looking for jobs. I read the help-wanted ads in the newspapers, and when I had some time off I'd go to the Montpelier public library and search the online jobs site run by the Department of Labor.

It was a time of budget cutbacks at Vermont schools, and there were very few teaching jobs. I applied to three and didn't even get an interview. I had to believe that the recommendation letters my principal had promised were less than lukewarm, so after a while I quit looking for a teaching position.

I considered jobs at day-care centers, nursing homes, burger franchises, but either the math or the morale didn't work out. Commuting from my hill was out of the question, so I would need to move to some unfamiliar town and then pay rent, and salaries in Vermont were low. Even if I put my land on the market, I'd need to keep paying Brassard until it sold, which certainly wouldn't happen this year. I simply couldn't afford to live anywhere else unless I had a steady job at a respectable salary.

Anyway, by then my half-made decision to sell my land was faltering.

My land? Yes, I had begun merging with it in ways that I hadn't anticipated. And I was earning it by enduring inconvenience and discomfort and nighttime fear and, on the farm, by the sweat of my brow. And I felt a tinge of pride. For the first time, I began to understand the true dimensions of rural people's fierce attachment to their lands, the determination of small farmers to honor the soil they work and their own labor and that of their parents. One becomes *loyal* to that earth, those trees, the swell and fold of field and hill.

So fall was coming, and it appeared that I would stay on at the farm.

EARNEST SAID THAT fall would be glorious, absolutely the best time to be in the woods, but that by sometime in October the cold would drive me from the hill and into a former chicken coop the Brassards had set up as a guesthouse or bunkhouse for temporary workers. It was divided into two tiny apartments side by side and had all the amenities. Diz, determined to keep up appearances, had even put flower boxes on the windowsills.

Earnest was right: It got cold and sorrowful up on the hill. While the leaves were turning it was splendid, the air filled with a dry pumpkin scent, a rust-orange scent, invigorating. The biting insects vanished and it was lovely to sit or walk without their harassment. But soon an unease came to the woods. The breezes seemed to shiver the remaining leaves, tremble them rather than toss them. Fewer and fewer birds sang among the trees, until one day they were gone and the woods were silent.

Loneliness haunted my silent woods. It was as if the absence of living things around me heightened my need for the company of human beings. With the forest now stark, loneliness encompassed me, threatened to swallow me; at times I felt I would vanish into it. And the hunger for contact became more physical. I yearned for the assurance of a companion's arms around me.

For a time the crickets kept on, a silvery shimmer of sound, but they, too, dwindled in number until at last there was only one, a solitary dry creak at the base of a boulder near my camp. And then it, too, ceased.

That day truly signaled the end of my summer. I started getting cold at night despite covering myself with every piece of fabric I owned, and when I awoke, the water in my bedside glass would be skinned with ice. The light got bleak, and by the time I'd return to camp after the evening milking it was full dark.

One mournful day after the last leaves had fallen, I borrowed the Ford and a little utility trailer, labored up the switchbacks to my clearing, and carted down my possessions. Seeing it piled there—two big steamer trunks, a few watertight plastic tubs from Walmart, two wooden chairs I'd bought at a yard sale—brought home to me the sheer lack of stuff I owned. I had a weak grip on materiality, no ballast. I felt fragile again.

With my tent gone, my little platform looked forlorn and incongruous in the naked autumn light. Before I chugged out of the clearing, I blew it a kiss and made a fervent promise to return.

AFTER BEING OBLIGED to move down from my eyrie, the next most difficult thing that fall was saying goodbye to Earnest. He had an annual seasonal cycle, too: When it got too cold to do tree work in Vermont, he followed the warmer weather south, taking tree jobs as far down as North Carolina, wherever he had friends, cousins, old military buddies, or former clients to help find him jobs. He planned to be gone about six weeks, so before he left he worked hard to batten down the place for winter: getting the cowshed ready, putting up storm windows on the house, preparing the tractors for their winter chores. He and I cut six cords of firewood up on the far side of Brassard's valley—most of it from dead trees and already dry—and then brought it to the house, split it, and stacked it in a roofed crib near the back door.

The day he trundled his old stake-side flatbed out of the farmyard, saluting me goodbye, a void seemed to open at the farm. I missed his warm presence instantly and almost feared the next six weeks with only Diz and Brassard for company.

Chapter 18

MOVING INTO THE repurposed chicken coop increased my daily contact with Diz, and I knew a showdown of some kind was inevitable.

Even when we weren't working together, I could see her comings and goings from my windows. She was a thickset woman, strong, given to out-of-date floral pants mismatched with her denim jackets or checked wool hunting shirts that got increasingly layered as the weather cooled. Knee-high muck boots, always. She worked continuously and vehemently, and I came to realize it was her unrelenting labor that kept the farm functioning. She did the work of at least two people, saving the cost of another hand. She personally knew every cow and every machine, and she also saw to the domestic chores of cooking and laundry, gardening, shopping, and housecleaning.

The windows of my apartment looked directly out onto her vegetable garden, so I couldn't help but see her working. I watched her dig up the potatoes and clip off the stalks of the brussels sprouts and load wheelbarrows full of pumpkins and winter squash. She attacked the compost heaps, stabbing and turning the stuff in huge forkfuls, carrying buckets of the ready loam and raking it into the garden rows. She tore down bean and pea vines and hacked them to bits and mixed them into the compost along with the fallen tomatoes. Earlier, she had picked apples from the trees in the yard and blackberries from the cane at the edge of the property, and now she put up applesauce and preserves. When she was canning, the kitchen windows turned white from the steam.

She managed all this in bits of time between major farming chores.

Most of the time, her face wore a focused frown, sometimes interrupted by a wince of pain, as if some joint suddenly complained. There were moments, though, when I suspected she'd gone off into a meditative, contented state during a task, kneeling or gathering or raking, because her face smoothed and her movements lost their perpetually hurried gracelessness.

No such tranquil state was evident when we worked together. Clearly, she intended to punish me. For example, when the blackberries were ripe, I had picked a couple of big bucketfuls off my land and brought them down and left them in the kitchen for her. It was a not-so-oblique request for some token of reconciliation, but she had never thanked me or even mentioned it. I didn't know if she'd even used them.

I got sick of being afraid of her, and given that I'd made every other mistake in life, I figured I had little to lose by making some more with Diz.

My first success occurred during a lunch break. I was munching on a sandwich and unavoidably observing as she pushed her wheelbarrow and carried other burdens back and forth through the garden gate. The gate had a flip-down peg designed to hold it open, but a stiffer-than-usual wind was blowing, today at just the right angle so that the peg dragged and the gate swung shut behind her every time she went through it. Often, the lift latch snapped shut again. This meant she had to put down her burden to open it again, then lift everything once more and push on through. Or she would back through while elbowing the latch down and banging her rump against the boards. This inefficiency surprised me—she should have given up on the peg and propped something heavy against the gate—but she was apparently so preoccupied, she didn't notice the recurring bother.

After a while, I couldn't bear watching. I put down my sandwich, went out, and opened the gate for her as she approached pushing a garden cart mounded with coiled watering hose.

She glared at me before coming through. "Go finish your lunch."

She went on past, down around the house. When she came back, she was surprised to find me still there. "I don't need your help, thank you. Find something useful to do."

"I'm going to open the gate or help you carry stuff," I told her.

"No, you're not. What did I just say?"

I stayed in front of her, blocking her. "I can't eat my lunch while watching another person work this hard. So I'm helping whether you like it or not."

"Get out of my way."

I crossed my arms and didn't move. "Or what? You gonna fire me?"

Her face stuttered: started to take on an expression, failed to achieve it, tried another, lost that one, too. I knew I couldn't be fired, because if they didn't have a hand right now they'd never get the fall work done. And given that I had no other income to pay off my debt with, they'd never get back the money I owed. Diz was stuck with me.

I felt cranky and was determined to slug it out with her if need be. But her face stabilized into a small, unwilling smile. She nodded and said, as if in revelation, "Ah! You're embracing your Inner Diz."

I almost laughed. It was such a clever satire of my supposed New Age psychology, such good comedic timing. Her grin tightened. I opened the gate, and she pushed through. We did some garden chores together.

I was elated.

My Inner Diz? What had empowered me to confront her was my unwillingness to endure any more of my own fear, my determination to prove myself of value and to not take shit off anyone. If she recognized herself in that attitude, it explained the core of her, the hard way she'd had to take to live her life.

It suggested that Diz had come a long way from some difficult place, and the journey had forged her into the warrior I saw every day. What was that place? I wondered. It was six months before I learned more about her surprising, hard, broken path to becoming Diz Brassard.

I became bolder. A week later, I asked after the blackberries.

"So," I hazarded, "I take it you got the berries? Some weeks ago?"

"Of course I got them," she snapped. "They were sitting on my damn kitchen counter."

Her attitude rankled and I said, "You're welcome, Diz."

She started to bristle but then decided to take the high, if utterly sarcastic, ground: "You're right. I should give you some of the preserves. How thoughtless of me."

Those weren't by any means the only exchanges that took the starch out of Diz's resentment. But we had neither a big blowout nor a heart-warming reconciliation; her hackles went down hair by hair. Throughout the fall, we had many small collisions that were overcome by many little grudging concessions and acknowledgments. Most of these slipped past because we were simply too busy to deal with them except by forgetting. We segued into a functional relationship.

Fall struck me as a season of rituals. Within just a few weeks, certain tasks simply had to be completed, in a certain order. Get up the last of the hay, bale some, roll the rest and cover it in white plastic, stack the rolls along the side of the cowshed and the fence of the near paddock. Move the cows inside and latch the outer pasture fences. Check the NO HUNTING posters tacked to the trees around the borders. Complain about the out-of-state leaf peepers, gawking at the rusticity of it all, whose slow-rolling cars choked the roads closer to town.

Then there was harvesting the feed corn. The combine was a creature unto itself, and Brassard had a tractor, an older International Harvester, just for dragging this and the other large tilling and planting equipment. It was much bigger than the Deere, not a "utility" tractor but one designed just for towing things. I thought of it as a kind of elephant, tall and gray and massive, with a dusty dignity.

When Brassard explained the logistics of harvesting to me, he also provided an exposition on tractors. Their brand names have a legendary ring to them: Massey Ferguson, International Harvester, New Holland, Allis-Chalmers, McCormick, John Deere—the tractor equivalents of famous guns such as Colt, Smith & Wesson, and Winchester. He had no faith in the Japanese and Korean tractors—the Kubotas, Hinomotos, and Kiotis—that had flooded the market in recent years. I pictured them as futuristic, streamlined things—ninja tractors. His father had been partial to Fords and Harvesters and had purchased my beloved little Ford back in 1979.

He didn't let me drive the Harvester, because managing turns and repositionings with the combine behind took considerable finesse. Instead, I drove the Ford alongside, pulling a high-sided trailer that received the stream of chopped stalk and grain. At intervals, Diz trundled out on the Deere to bring an empty trailer and pull away the full one. Back at the barnyard, she worked the machine that blew the mealy chaff up a long chute and into the top of one of the silos.

Finally, the fields were stripped. The corn stubble stood in rows, looking like a military graveyard seen from the air. The naked hayfields struck me as sad and vulnerable looking. The white rolls of hay along the fence suddenly looked like deep snowdrifts. After sleeping in my woods all summer, I felt claustrophobic in my tiny apartment and missed those sweet, green days and nights. I no longer felt the Great Fear at night, but the loneliness still wormed its way into my heart, my bed, despite my physical proximity to others.

I THINK EVEN Diz noticed that I was a better hand than Franklin, the young man who had gone on to Vermont Tech. He was strong but always seemed a little at sea. Diz once said, "Kid's so dumb he couldn't find his own ass if it bit him on the ass." Unlike him, I could generally see the larger objective behind minor chores. My ability to stick to a sequence of tasks allowed me to sync efficiently with Diz and get a lot done.

This was especially important during milking. Cows *like* getting milked, so in summer they spontaneously drifted toward the barn and convened in the concrete-floored paddock near the milking parlor at the appointed time. In winter, when they lived in the cowshed, they needed very little goading to get them to milking.

The Brassards' setup was an eight-station "herringbone" parlor into which groups of cows were ushered and arranged in two rows of four. Between the two rows, down the center of the room, ran a waist-deep alley—Diz called it "the pit"—that allowed us milkers to stand, rather than crouch, as we attended to eight cow behinds.

Overhead pipes ran the length of room, and above each station hung a flexible hose ending in the apparatus that actually drew the milk. Once the cows were in position, I went the rounds with a cup of iodine solution, dipping each teat. Then I went around again, wringing out a squirt of milk from each, then went around one more time to wipe off excess disinfectant with a clean rag. When I was done, I'd get out of the pit to move cows in or out, and let Diz hook them up—she didn't yet trust me to get the milking cups settled right. She turned on the vacuum and attached the milking cups, *shup-shup-shup-shup*. Diz called the milker a "claw"—to me, they looked more like robotic spiders—a set of tubes that ended in four cups, each about the size and shape of a flashlight. They applied a pulsing vacuum that brought milk surging into a glass bulb at the bottom. From there it was sucked up into ceiling tubes, its flow measured by an electronic monitor about the size of a shoe box.

The machines took about six minutes to drain each cow, then pulled off automatically when the flow tapered. By the time the last of the left-side four was hitched up, the right-side four would be finished. I would release them, shoo them out the far end of the parlor, and bring in four more from the holding area.

Each group took about sixteen minutes, so milking the whole herd took about two hours. Eighty cows with four teats each. Twice a day. After the first hour, it became mind-numbingly repetitive. Even then, the job wasn't done—we still had to clean the whole pipe system and remove manure from the parlor and antechamber. Diz had very high standards for cleanliness and made sure I lived up to every one of them.

Diz avoided personal conversation, but she often expounded on the economics of dairy farming. Brassard's farm operated on a razor's edge where the costs of operations intersected income from milk sales. Brassard had bought the current equipment in the 1990s to increase production and meet federally mandated dairy hygiene standards. Diz didn't like the parlor design, because there was no splash guard and runnel, so if the cows urinated or shat it went onto the floor or into the pit. But this setup was the best their finances could manage.

I was appalled when Diz told me they were still paying off the loans Brassard had taken out back then. As he was for the Deere and the truck and the bulk milk storage tank and an extension of the shed in 1998, which had allowed them to take on another twenty cows.

Like every other small farmer, they were perpetually trying to find the elusive sweet spot of milk production, where sales offset debt enough to leave some net income. When milk prices are up, this works. When prices fall, farmers can lose money on every gallon they produce. They have no choice but to keep producing, because the cows need to be milked and supply contracts have to be honored. Brassard had lost almost ninety thousand dollars the year before I came, because milk prices were so low.

No wonder Will had taken up a different line of work and swore he'd never work on the farm.

Last year's loss explained why they had sold me my land, and when Diz told me this, I realized just how seriously my default had put them at risk. I was appalled, horrified, to understand what I had done.

To her credit, though, Diz explained all this without directing her rancor toward me. She was angry at "the system." As she saw it, they were personally, anonymously—and thanklessly—putting that milk on America's tables at direct expense to themselves.

She told me this at five in the afternoon, when we were about half an hour into the milking routine. She started the vacuum, affixed the next four cups, then leaned back and said, "All I can say is, thank God for Earnest."

"How so?"

She slumped, despairing of me. "Take a wild guess, sweetheart."

I stared stupidly at her.

She tipped her head toward the holding area door to remind me to get the next group of cows moving. "Paid your bail." She watched me process that. "Put up ten K to keep us afloat while you paid us off with labor. We were up against the wall. Had to make a balloon payment on a revolving credit line, and it was either take Earnest's money or default and screw ourselves up the be-hind."

We worked for another half hour before I could find any words: "You know I'm sorry, Diz, right? I really want you to know how sorry I am."

"Not sorry enough yet, but I'll make sure you get there."

"Why would Earnest ... I mean ..."

"Saint Earnest," she said to the next claw. "Another ten of him, the world wouldn't be in such a mess."

Chapter 19

Nov. 6

Observations of late fall: The fields are dark brown for a time, but then comes a morning when they're hazed over gray with a surface frost—the night's dew, frozen. As the sun rises, later and later, the shadows of the hills stretch farther across the fields, and the soil stays white-gray in the shade while the sunlit areas turn brown again, a distinct melt line.

The forested hills turn gray-brown except where, suddenly, clumps of pine and fir appear, dark green, almost black, as if they'd sneaked in from somewhere else or just now stood up from the earth.

The mud in the paddock and driveway crusts over with ice, so that when you walk on it your boot crunches through to the taffy-like partially frozen soil beneath. Dressing for your day takes longer as you layer things on under your coveralls; Brassard warns you not to put on your long johns until January, or you'll get used to them and have no further recourse when the serious cold hits. Your exhaled breath turns dazzlingly bright when you're working in the sun.

On windless days, the Brassards' chimney releases a perfectly vertical stream of white smoke, and the delicious smell of burning hardwood fills the barnyard. One morning your Toyota won't start and you put a new battery on the list of other purchases to be made on the next town run.

A fox, bright rust red against the gray forest, trots purposefully along the edge of the pasture.

More chainsaws in the far distance: getting up the last of the firewood. Deer-hunting season starts, gunshots echo in the hills. You wear a fluorescent-orange stocking cap even when working in the barn or close to the house. Diz replaces Bob's collar with a neckerchief of the same color.

A late and straggly V of geese angles across the sky, changes direction for a time, then reorients with more confidence. Later a solitary goose flaps uncertainly, first this way, then that, honking lost and mournful, and you feel a sudden pang in your chest: that's me.

Chapter 20

LIFE IMPROVED AS the tension ratcheted down between Diz and me. I had to ask myself how I would have treated someone who had put me in such jeopardy, had forced my husband to prevail upon the charity of his old friend. And I had to admit, I probably wouldn't have done any better than Diz. I doubted that my capacity to forgive, or to handle sudden extreme pressure with grace, was any greater than hers.

And looking back at what I've written, I realize I've painted an incomplete portrait of Diz and Brassard. Diz is only snarly, Brassard bland and rather absent. To be fair to them and honest about my own feelings, I should round out the picture.

Unlike my time with Earnest, my interactions with them were generally brief, always functional, never intimate, so I got only glimpses and can capture only vignettes. But those moments can be telling.

From midsummer: Brassard's place, like every farm, has barn cats, which provide an essential service by controlling rodents. They're feral, but if you approach them with the right noises and body language, some will warily let you pet them. The number varies depending on how many kittens get born and how many get eaten by owls or fisher cats, the giant murderous weasels that prowl Vermont's hills like forest sharks. When I first came that spring, there were two (feline) cats, but one gave birth on an empty burlap bag in a corner of the hayloft: five kittens in a wild array of stripes and calico patches.

The strict policy, Diz had told me, was that they never fed the cats. Otherwise, the farm would be swarming with them, and they'd want to get into the house, and they'd get run over by tractors, and so on. Anyway, there was plenty of wild game—best keep them hungry for it.

But by July, when the kittens were big enough to roam around the whole barn, I spotted Brassard putting out a pie tin of dog kibble soaked in milk. The kittens came and set to it like lions on a fresh-killed zebra. He stayed bent and rubbed the back of their necks as they ravaged their prey.

He glanced over when I came into the room, and looked caught out. I said something like: "Mr. Brassard! I'm shocked!"

He grinned weakly as if he wasn't sure I was kidding, and creaked back upright—his knees were almost kaput with arthritis, his lower back in continuous pain—and said seriously, "Just don't tell Diz!"

We chuckled and went about our work. Later, I passed by the spot and noticed that the pie tin was gone. Brassard had hidden the evidence.

What made this so amusing is that a few days later, I came into one of the sheds to find Diz doing the same thing. Kibble, milk, Bob's outdoor dog dish. She looked mortified, then angry, that I'd caught her. "For Chrissake, don't mention this to Jim!" she warned me.

That litter got too tame. They had Bob figured for a softy, and they had no reservations about coming to the house door. We had to take out an ad in the weekly advertiser to find homes for them. I personally handed them away to the happy Volvo- and Subaru-driving families who found their way to the farm in response. As soon as they were gone, I missed their mischief around the place.

Another vignette: Brassard and Diz, early fall afternoon, the forested hills just barely starting to show splashes of yellow here and there. I spied on them through a window in the barn as I did some cleaning in the equipment room. A moment between chores, they came out of the house and sat on the porch swing, side by side. Brassard in his denim bib coveralls with a T-shirt underneath, Diz in an oversize flowery Walmart shirt and camo pants. Plastic mugs of coffee. Two aging people, catching their breath together. Bob the dog came and stuck his head onto Brassard's lap, got a good working over, then moved on to Diz, who gave him an attentive scratching.

After a while, Brassard gave Bob a gentle shove with his knee and told him something like "Enough now," and Bob obediently lay down. The man and the woman then chatted sparingly as they sipped coffee. Diz's hand idly came up and massaged the base of Brassard's red, bristly neck, and he gratefully leaned his head back, left, right, into the pressure of her fingers. When she stopped, his big hand moved to Diz's knee, and they just sat, gazing out across the road at nothing much, the swing moving back and forth like a slow breath, in and out, in and out.

What's in a moment like that? Is it any different from two draft horses in the same harness, standing wearily until their driver urges them on again? I can't speak for horses, but in this case I saw it as two human people, being on the planet in a particular moment of their allotted time, which they have agreed to share until the end. This is what that only-ever time consisted of: this moment, this farm, each other. And, it seemed to me, at that moment they were aware that was what they were doing, and were cherishing it. Were grateful for it.

A few minutes later, Diz checked her watch, leaned over to Brassard, who by then was drowsing. She briefly put her forehead against his chin, then stood and half hoisted him to his feet. He followed her obediently back into the house, and a few moments later they emerged from the side door and went their separate ways back to the demands of the farm.

Chapter 21

Nov. 12

Haven't seen Earnest in too long. Brassard told me he calls every now and then, mainly to say he's been very busy, got a lot of jobs, isn't sure when he'll return. I've been thinking about how, or whether, to talk to him about his lending Brassard the money I defaulted on. So far, I haven't decided. Would it be better for him to think I didn't know? And what would I say—thank you? I still think there's more to their relationship than Brassard saving Earnest's bacon in a Saigon whorehouse.

Will comes by every few days but seldom stays long; still, I relish these brief contacts with a person other than Jim and Diz, someone my own age and with more connection to the world beyond Brassard's valley.

Something happened today that in retrospect startles me. I know absolutely that I am a hired hand, not family, not a friend (except to Earnest). But I used the plural first-person pronoun. It just slipped out. I'd been doing an inventory in one of the supply rooms and told Diz, "We're going to need more iodine dip pretty soon."

"Write it down," she said, preoccupied.

I jotted it on the clipboard where, as it occurs to us, we write down tasks to remember to do and supplies to buy. Then I went on without noticing, "Oh, and Jim says we're low on diesel. He said I should remind you to call Agway." The tractors are refueled from a pair of 250-gallon tanks on the other side of the old barn, which Agway refills from a tanker truck every now and then.

Diz nodded, putting it on her mental to-do list. Neither of us noticed my grammar at the time. Of course, I had many times used "we" in reference to Diz and myself, as in "Do we need to bring a shovel?" But this time, I'd used it in reference to the farm itself, the collective effort, which in some recess of my mind had apparently come to include me.

Now I am wondering about it and marveling at it. So many questions to ask myself. What does "we" mean? Who is "we"?

Chapter 22

DEER HUNTING IS another of Vermont's important fall rituals, and like so much else that first year, it demanded some adaptation on my part. Having grown up in the city, I was at first taken aback at the sight of people openly carrying guns. There was also more visible blood and guts than one would hope to see on a city street: eviscerated, empty-eyed deer lolling and leaking on truck tailgates or hanging outside the general stores that serve as Fish and Wildlife Department weighing stations. And some of this gore I experienced at much closer range, in more personal circumstances, than I would have preferred.

Once the rifle season opens, you see pickup trucks and station wagons pulled onto the shoulders of every rural road. Men in brilliant neon orange vests and hats, rifles over their shoulders, stalk the roads, looking for sign. Gunshots pierce the quiet. Conversation at the hardware store shifts from baseball to guns, scent lures, skinning tools, venison smoking techniques, and tales of magnificent bucks sighted from afar.

Will gave me an overview of how it works: By the time the season opens, there's usually a little snow on the ground, so it's easy to follow a line of paired-crescent tracks. The trees are bare, so you can see a long way through the woods, and with binoculars you can spot a deer before it spots you. You want a clean shot through the lungs because otherwise you have to follow a blood trail for who knows how long, and carrying the carcass back to your car can be tiring. When you bag a deer, you field-dress it: You slit it lengthwise along the soft belly, then scoop out intestines and organs until the abdomen is empty. This makes for a lighter load on the trek back.

Some hunters track deer, but others put up blinds in trees at places where they know deer will pass. They crouch, "freezing their butts off," and if they've correctly scoped the deer's habits, they get their buck. Most seasons, you can only "take," or "harvest," bucks, not does, and the more "points"—branches of the antlers—the greater your glory. Easily half the importance of the ritual is social: Groups of friends spend weekends at somebody's shack deep in the woods, hunting during daylight and drinking into the night.

Will seemed like a gentle guy, and I was surprised at how casually—callously, to my urban perspective—he related the bloody ritual. I had often seen deer weaving delicately through my woods and bounding across the roads, and could not imagine killing these graceful, timorous creatures. Then again, I was new up here, and I was a hypocrite—I was perfectly happy to eat a pig or cow if somebody else did the gory work for me. Will said Vermonters ate the venison they brought home; he didn't know anyone who hunted just for the trophy.

According to Will, the law says that unless a landowner posts the borders with NO HUNTING signs, hunters can roam freely anywhere. Knowing my sentimental tendencies, Earnest had bought me a fat roll of brilliant yellow plastic-paper signs and lent me his staple gun, and in the weeks before the season opened I had signed each one of them with a laundry marker and posted them around my borders.

I had still been making occasional pilgrimages to my land, because I missed the place and because I wanted to witness it in all its seasons, its varying raiment and mood.

During hunting season, I dressed in orange from head to foot before heading out. That day was unseasonably cold, the snow brilliant but only an inch deep. Heading up, I found the bends and switchbacks of my trail utterly unfamiliar, as if the topography, the geology itself, had been transformed by the leafless trees and blinding white carpet. A starker, simpler place.

My little clearing was especially strange to me. Without leaves, it had no real borders. The sense of its being an enclosure of any kind, a sort of room, was gone. It was just an area without bare tree branches overhead. Plumped by snow, my tent platform looked like a big mattress somebody had left outside.

But the beauty of it grew on me. Spacious, keen, Spartan. Trees dark but certainly not dead. A sense of latency: I could feel the plants hiding and hoarding their vital force, all the creatures burrowed and curled somewhere, wrapped around winter dreams as they began to ride out the harsh caloric economy of the cold season.

The only sign of animal presence was a deer trail that I followed up toward my spring, one set of split-hoof prints joined by another and then another, their tracks braiding together and then apart again. I almost couldn't find the spring—it was just a long, shallow dent in the snow. But when I scuffed at the surface, I found a thin, rippled layer of ice with the water running quick and vivid as ever just below. Bubbles meandered quicksilver on the underside of the ice, and I could hear a quiet chuckle of water moving.

My heart swelled with affection. Then I wondered whether a stream is the water in it, or the bed in which the water travels. The bed is a place and is always there, but it has no life or function without the water. But the water is transient, here now but miles away by tomorrow ... I have no answer except that what I love is the whole, both the thing that stays and the thing that goes, which ultimately cannot be understood except as a unity.

After a time, I continued uphill, and in another hundred yards I came to an inexplicable and ghastly sight: an area of disturbed and trampled snow, with red stains and spatters toward the middle and a horrific pile at the center. I recoiled but couldn't help moving closer to study it. Lumpy, tangled ropes of viscera, branching veins, yellow and purple and red-brown globs. A mound about a foot deep, two or three feet across. Guts and organs. Frost only just forming on the surface fluids.

I fell back away from it, two steps, five. Then I saw the tread marks of boots heading up the hill.

Someone had poached a deer on my land and field-dressed it and made off with the carcass. And I knew it must have been one of the Goslants.

I came down the hill feeling shaky, angry, sick, violated, utterly out of my depth again. I had posted the land! I had relished the idea of creating a little refuge for deer in this season of wholesale murder.

I wondered whether I should tell the Brassards about it, but given Diz's hatred of the Goslants, I was afraid that would set off repercussions that might lead to trouble. Also, I worried about getting into some kind of range war with these people, whom I'd never met but had glimpsed and found frightening on so many levels.

At the same time, I couldn't have people coming onto my property and doing whatever they pleased, taking anything they wanted. Brassard said the Goslants weren't too worried about borders when it came to cutting trees, either. Then I wondered whether they had visited my campsite in my absence, scouted me out, maybe even come stealthily at night. It was deeply unsettling, an unfamiliar sense of violation.

I asked Will about it while milking that night. He paused for a moment, frowning, before he went back to his task. "Poaching? Hm. It could be more complex than that. If a hunter wounds a deer, he really should follow it and finish it off, even if it strays onto posted property. Actually, I don't know if that's what the law says, but it makes moral sense, don't you think?"

I could understand that perspective. But that night, the image of the pile of guts, a living deer turned inside out, was hard to shake. It kept returning to my mind's eye as I tried to sleep. And thinking it over, I couldn't recall seeing any blood trail leading to the scene. Surely I'd have seen droplets or spatters on the way or on the periphery of the butchering site. On the other hand, I hadn't been looking for them. And probably the blood would have melted down out of immediate view. I gnawed at this question until my thoughts faded into vivisectionist dreams.

The next morning, after milking and cleanup, I decided I had to know. Had they legitimately pursued an injured deer and put it out of its misery on my land, or had they brazenly poached? I covered myself in orange and hiked uphill again, following my own footsteps. The air rang with occasional distant gunshots.

I didn't get as far as the bloody pile. I didn't do any crime scene forensics, because before I got there I encountered something in some ways worse. When I came into my clearing, I found more boot tracks, new ones, tracks that were definitely not there the day before. I'd stood on my snow-rounded tent platform, and now so had this unwelcome visitor. This same person had prowled around my kitchen setup and had pissed in the snow nearby. And then had headed back uphill, toward the guts and toward my border with the Goslants' land. I didn't follow the trail.

So I TALKED to Brassard about it. It was midmorning by then and he was trimming hooves. With the cows indoors now, he'd taken extra time to check the health of each one and had found a few needing a trim. I wasn't up for dealing with Diz and was glad to find she'd gone to town on errands.

Brassard was hunkered down with a cow whose ear tag read 78. He had tethered her in a stall and hoisted her back leg up onto a plywood box he'd hammered together. Apparently, the hind hooves are hardest to trim—the cow can deliver a kick that requires a visit to the emergency ward—but Brassard was sort of a "cow whisperer." He had cared for those cows throughout their lives, had trimmed them before, so his propping up one hind leg and carving away didn't bother them that much.

The upturned hoof looked like a black, dirt- and manure-crusted lobster claw. It was as hard as a leather shoe sole, but with quick, forceful strokes of his straight-razor sharp, old-fashioned hoof knife, Brassard easily peeled off strips of the stuff.

"Got six or eight grow too much hoof even over summer," he told me. "Grow too long in the toe and rock the ankle back, that's bad, but the heel's more important. Don't get the heel right, you put her lame in no time, especially comin indoors and on concrete all day." He drew the knife again, expertly, and checked the cut. "Nowadays, most use an angle grinder. But I got pretty good doin it this way as a kid, never saw the need."

I started by asking about the Goslants—vaguely, like what kind of people they were.

Brassard kept slicing, peeling off thin slices and taking his time answering. When he'd trimmed the hoof to an oyster-shell white and held a gauge to the heel, he let it down and looked up at me thoughtfully. The cow set her newly pedicured foot on the rubber mat experimentally, found no pain, forgot about it.

As Brassard cleaned off his tools, he gave me the lowdown. The Goslants had been there since before he was born. There used to be a farm-house, behind where the trailers are now, but it had always been in bad repair and burned down twenty years ago. Then they moved the trailers in.

His description didn't match my expectations. He said that the elders of the clan, Homer and his wife, Fran, were about his age, had lived there all his life and had raised their family there. But there was a lot of coming and going, residents changing as a son or daughter or cousin or uncle or grandchild ran into tough times and came to stay on the family estate. He said there was "some intermarrying" between Goslants and maybe that accounted for some of their "problems." There might be as many as eight or ten people crowded in there sometimes, sometimes maybe just three or four; he couldn't keep track.

He moved over his hoof stand and picked up the next cow's right rear hoof—she resisted for a moment till he spoke soothingly to her—then used a thin tool, like an ice pick, to pry out impacted debris. As he probed with his fingers, assessing the health and length of the hoof, he asked me why I wanted to know.

"Do you think I have to worry about them? Like … when I'm up at my camp?"

At that, he stopped working on the hoof. Even the cow, number 32, turned her big head to look back as if wondering what caused this interruption of the trimming rite. She shifted and daintily kicked the box so that it spun out from under her leg and bounced away.

Brassard grunted as he straightened, then faced me, checking my face and then gazing distantly down the row of stalls. "No question but some of em get up to trouble. Don't know the details. Not bein farmers, they don't travel in the same social circles as us. Diz won't have anything to do with em."

But, he said, there's order to the clan. Homer and his wife Fran had had four kids; the kids had had kids, and probably another generation had started up by now—they married young, Brassard said. He described Homer and Fran as good people, honest and steady. "No education, but don't drink and they make room for everyone who needs someplace." Homer had worked for the state highway crew for as long as Brassard could remember, and he figured Homer's income provided the financial ballast for the extended family, whose fortunes fluctuated wildly. Fran was very obese and had diabetes, almost crippled. Two of their kids were "pretty normal," one was truly "slow." "Doesn't stop em from havin kids, though. Startin about fifteen, sixteen." He didn't know how many grandkids—maybe eight. He thought a couple of the grandkids had been born with some problems, and he knew one of them got brain damage in infancy. "Run into Homer at the general store, this's ten, fifteen years ago now, and he was upset. Said his son-in-law was throwin the baby in the air and it hit the ceiling and fell on the floor. Concussion and spine damage, developmental problems after that. You'll see him out front sometimes, can't walk straight?"

I retrieved the hoof-holding box, but Brassard stayed standing, considering the matter further and stroking the cow's hindquarters to calm her. "Another grandkid has that Down syndrome, you might see him sometimes. When I think of what that man has been through—Homer. What he deals with. What're you going to do if you're Homer and Fran? You stand by your family, same as I'd do, anyone would do."

He said that though the kids and grandkids sometimes got into trouble, they respected Homer and Fran and mostly didn't bring it into the house. He spoke of Homer and Fran with respect—he called Homer "gentle" and "steady," Fran "bighearted."

Number 32 began to get impatient, stamping and shifting. A 1,300-pound, head-high animal in close quarters is hard to ignore. Brassard grabbed her right ankle and drew it firmly up onto his little platform.

"She'll settle," he reassured me. "Just needs to know we're gettin the job done and she'll be free to go."

As for whether I was in danger up at my place, he said he didn't think so, but couldn't be sure. He said some of the grandkids had friends who were definitely not upright citizens or obedient to the household rules of Homer and Fran. "If you ever see the sheriff's car up on the ridge road, this far out, you can pretty well guess where they're goin."

Then I glimpsed the authoritative side of Jim Brassard, some of the force that had earned him officer rank in Vietnam. He met my gaze straight on and said, "Better just tell me what's happened to get you worried, so I can figure out what to do about it."

I told him about the guts and my conversation with Will and the footprints in the snow. His eyes went distant. "The deer, it's more likely just habit—I never posted that hill, they've spent their whole lives huntin up there if they wanted. Somebody walkin around, same thing. People generally don't worry too much about walkin in somebody's woods as long as they don't do any harm. When I was a boy, we'd hike around and even sleep in somebody's camp. Nobody locked em back then. People who live out this far, some just live more in the old way."

He went back to work on the hoof. Then, as an afterthought: "In any case, don't bring it up to Diz. She's none too fond of them already, no tellin how she'd react. Whatever else, we don't need Diz on the warpath."

Bob, wearing his neon-orange neckerchief, met me outside and gave me an affectionate nuzzle before he went on to see what the boss was up to. His trust and goodwill made me feel a little better, but back at my little chicken-coop apartment I kept replaying Brassard's narrative in my head, ambivalent. He was probably right about the deer, the visitor. Cat and

I had walked through any woods or fields we came to without thinking twice about whose property it was. In any case, it would be six months before I started sleeping out there again.

But I still felt a deep unease. What had I been thinking? That Vermont was a postcard utopia without crime, poverty, violence, dysfunctional families, genetic disorders, and all the rest of humanity's woes? All the trailers and houses I'd passed on the back roads, with debris-covered lawns and torn plastic over the windows: The lives lived there were probably a lot like the Goslants'. This was just a different kind of desolation from what I'd been accustomed to in the city. In the context of lush forest and verdant fields, it had taken me longer to fully recognize what I was seeing.

Chapter 23

WHEN THE COWS moved indoors, the nature of the job changed radically.

The cowshed is a long, airy thing built mainly of steel beams, with a corrugated sheet steel roof and wooden end walls. The sidewalls are mostly just open to the outdoors—the cows' collective body heat keeps it comfortably warm (for them)—unless the cold gets truly vicious, and then we roll down tarp curtains along the sidewalls. The open structure means it's well lit during the day; it's lit less pleasantly by overhead fluorescents after sunset. The cows spend most of their time standing or reclining in two long rows of stalls, their back ends hanging out a bit into the center alley so their manure falls onto the concrete floor.

This was a "free stall" shed, meaning that cows are not restrained by stanchions but are free to move around. When the urge strikes them, they wander down the central aisle to take a drink from the water tanks or to stick their heads into a separate alley where we put out foodstuffs. Actually, they don't move around much; after milking, they'll grab a bite at the buffet and then are generally content to return to their regular stalls to chew their cud and drowse.

Manure: I thought I knew the basics, but until the cows moved inside I didn't know that a single cow produces about 110 pounds of it a day. That's about as much as the entirety of *me*, defecated by each cow, every day. Brassard had eighty cows milking at any given time, producing six *tons* of manure, daily, that in winter ended up on the shed floor. Six tons that it was my job to remove.

Every day, I'd come along the central alley with the Bobcat skid-steer. This was a small yellow tractorish thing to which Earnest had attached a cut quarter-section of some huge construction vehicle's tire. I lowered the bucket with this scooper-squeegee attachment on it and pushed the soup of manure the whole length of the shed. At the far end, it flowed into a long floor grate and got pumped into the manure "lagoon" outside. After several passes, the aisle was still wet but reasonably clean.

Manure and urine also ended up in the stalls. Brassard kept his cows comfortable—happy cows give more milk and stay healthier—flooring their stalls with rubber mats as well as something soft to cushion their bony bodies when they reclined, mainly sawdust but sometimes ground hay or sand. I had to rake out the wet bedding and replace it every day, in every stall.

Having cows inside also required that we put out feed for them at frequent intervals. One of us would drive a tractor loaded with silage and grain through the feed alley as a second person shoveled the stuff to the floor. A fence kept the cows out of that alley, but they put their heads through rails to get at the goodies, munching happily. And depositing more manure that I had to remove.

All this was in addition to the care of around sixty other cows that lived in their own shed nearby. These were heifers—young cows that hadn't yet been bred—and mature cows that were "drying off," that is, getting their annual two-month vacation from milking. Fortunately, their manure management required far less of me: Their floor was covered with thick straw that stayed there, composting, until warmer weather. I simply had to scoop out the wettest spots and spread a new layer of clean straw on top.

With the added work, I was walking around in a haze of fatigue by early December. I had been putting in longer hours and more days because Diz's lower back was "acting up" more than usual, to the point that her chiropractor told her to stop lifting and stooping, at least for a while. That she would admit to the pain, that she'd take his advice, told me how much it must have hurt.

Twelve to fourteen hours, six or seven days a week: By the time my workday was done, I would fall down on my bed and could barely get up to cook myself dinner. Even so, I couldn't accomplish a fraction of what Diz did. The farm faced a severe shortage of human-power.

Ultimately, Brassard had to hire one of the "hippie" organic farmers from down the road to help fill in for Diz. Lynn and her husband, Theo, grew organic greens that they sold at farmers markets, kept a few chickens, and raised a small herd of goats that they milked to make soap. Their winters were not as busy as those of dairy farmers, so Lynn had time to help with Brassard's cows. Taking on a hand to replace some of Diz's work put a strain on the farm's finances, but it couldn't be avoided.

I liked Lynn immediately: late twenties, slim, pale-skinned, white-blond straight hair pulled back into a short ponytail. She was quiet and struck me as centered and certain of her path—so unlike me. She was optimistic about small farming's future, hadn't had her idealism kicked out of her yet. She'd gone to U. Mass and studied anthropology for three years before dropping out: "And the only anthro I've done since then is field-work, studying my husband and his family." Theo is a native Vermonter, a mild-mannered guy who tagged along with college friends when they went to whoop it up among the big-city Amherst kids. He hadn't done much whooping, apparently, just looked embarrassed by everybody else's lack of decorum, until Lynn talked to him. She had a sly grin that invited confidences and drew me into a conspiratorial sense of camaraderie. I loved the idea of marriage as an anthropological study.

Two can do the milking, but it was better to have three on duty: one person to manage "cow flow," one to work in the pit, and the third exploiting the cows' absence to rake out the stalls and distribute fresh bedding.

Also, the purging of milk pipes and washing of the claws always went faster with more hands. So it helped that Will Brassard's work brought him to the area more often. He'd stay over for a couple of nights, get up to help with the morning milking, drive off to the studio to work on his video project, then return in time for the evening milking.

When I commented on his schedule to Diz, she told me, "Got his work ethic from his old lady." Then she snorted and added a disclaimer: "Huh! Sorta."

He inherited some of her other mannerisms, too. He could be very blunt. Early on, five in the morning, pitch dark outside, he was working his way along the udders as I leaned over the pit railing to chat. Our breath steamed and the coffee was barely starting to perk in our veins and Will said, "I detest this shit. How my parents stand it, I couldn't tell you. This is why I'll never work on a farm." He meant it, but he said it without Diz's scalding bile. "I like clean clothes. I like clean hands. I don't like getting up this early. I don't like freezing my ass off. I don't like animal poop. I don't even fucking *drink* milk!"

Eighty cows, 320 teats twice a day, plus six tons of manure to clean up every day: I could see his point.

I THINK THE first time I realized just how acclimated I'd become to farm living was the moment I came out of the barn and my heart leaped at the sight of Earnest's big stake-side truck in the farmyard. I realized I had an affection for that old funky rig. I liked its lines, the pragmatism of its construction, its dents and scrapes and other evidence of the hard miles it had put in—the same charms of the Ford tractor I drove every day.

I went into the house to find Earnest at the table, telling Brassard and Diz of his misadventures in the comparative tropics. He was sitting with his back to the door, and as I came in I couldn't resist grabbing his ears from behind and tugging them.

"I'm glad to see you, too," he said.

I joined them for coffee. Earnest related how he'd done a few jobs in Maryland, just north of Washington, DC, then worked his way down through Virginia. He had a moment of trepidation when a North Carolina state cop pulled him over for no reason, came to the window, looked at him, and said "*¿Habla inglés?*" And Earnest answered, "Sorry, what? I don't speak any Spanish except *¿Qué pasa?*"

"Jeezum!" Brassard exclaimed. "Could've caught yourself some trouble that way! What'd he do?"

"Asked to see my license and registration. Read my name, laughed at himself. 'Arnest Kelley—Irish, then, are we?' he said. With the accent."

Brassard laughed aloud and slapped his thigh.

"Yeah. His name tag said Officer McGillicuddy. Good sense of humor. We got talking. I ended up giving him one of my cards, he said he'd show it around, see if anyone needed tree work."

Earnest had a small duffel on the floor beside him, and after a few minutes he rummaged in it and presented gifts he'd brought back from foreign climes: "early Christmas presents." For Diz he'd bought a big coffee-table photo book, *Washington, DC: America's Historic Heritage*, which she began paging through immediately. Brassard's was a pouch of pipe tobacco that Earnest had bought near the farm that had grown it—sold illegally and famous for its flavor, sort of like a local moonshine.

Brassard took it, opened it, sniffed it, made a dubious face. "I'll give it a try, anyway," he said.

"Not in the house!" Diz commanded.

Earnest rummaged in his duffel again, then seemed to change his mind and came up empty-handed. "Got something for Will ... something for you, too, Pilgrim. But I'll get it to you later. Right now I think I'd better take a shower and have a nap. Lot of driving the last few days."

He came out to see me a couple of hours later while I was stall bedding. Usually, I'd go through and rake the dirty stuff into the alley and replace it with clean material while the cows were getting milked, but we'd had only two on duty that morning and nobody had seen to it. I was coaxing a cow out of almost every stall to do the job.

Earnest appeared beside me with another rake, and without saying anything, he encouraged number 17 to back out so he could clean out her stall. She acquiesced and stood by to watch the proceedings with mild curiosity.

"You again," I said. My breath steamed in the air.

"How's it going with Diz? She let you in the house—that's a good sign."

"We're totally best buddies. Like sisters now."

He made a few more vigorous strokes with his rake. Within seconds, number 17's stall was empty.

"We get by," I amended. "Her back is killing her, so I've been filling in for her quite a bit. She has to treat me a little better."

His brow furrowed. "Diz? Skipping work? That's a first."

I shrugged and kept pulling out sawdust. Earnest spread number 17's clean bedding from a pile I'd put at the head end of the stall.

"So," he said, "aren't you dying to see the present I brought you?"

"Perishing. Actually, I figured you had forgotten to get me anything and were covering up."

"No. It's something I thought you needed, up there in the wilderness."

"Twenty-minute walk isn't wilderness."

"In the woods, then." He dug in the pockets of his jacket and produced a field guide to New England trees and shrubs, the size of a ham sandwich but twice as thick. He presented it to me with a certain ceremoniousness and a somber expression that struck me as incongruous. I had hoped he'd be as happy to see me as I was him.

"Earnest, that's very sweet of you!"

He dipped his head, moved on to the next stall, which was empty; its occupant was out for a meal or drink elsewhere in the shed. I moved on to my next stall and began raking out clots of manure and wet sawdust.

"I mean," he explained, "you live among the trees, I figured you'd want to know more about them. They're like … the walls of your house."

"True."

"I work with trees every day. Know them intimately. They're really very interesting when you get to know them better. Incredibly complex and diverse organisms."

I didn't know why, but the way he told me this felt sort of stiff, artificial—unlike him. Something had changed in the dynamic between us.

The cow in the next stall along the row was Queenie, the biggest and
orneriest of Brassard's herd. She had an alpha attitude, and facial markings
that looked to me like war paint. I had often seen her humping her sisters
in the pasture. She didn't move when I urged her out, just turned her
head around to show me her sullen expression. I was reluctant—afraid,
actually—to get into a shoving match with her in such close quarters.
Even Diz was wary of her.

"Earnest, what should I do with Queenie?" I asked.

He came over. He squeezed himself up to her head and spoke to her
in a friendly way: "Honey. It's Earnest. You know what happens when you
and I have to get physical. Right? Let's get your place tidied up."

Queenie backed out and went down the aisle to get away from us.

I marveled but didn't say anything. Earnest raked out her stall and
spread the new bedding. But he stayed quiet, thoughtful in what I felt to
be a troubled way. It put me into a similar mood.

"Ann, I have some stuff to attend to," he said. "I might be away for
another while."

"But you just got back!"

"I know."

"Where are you going?"

"Good question," he said gloomily.

I leaned on my rake to frown at him. "Seems like you're avoiding
answering me."

"It's personal, complex, and at the moment it's awkward. Let's leave it.
Want to see what I got Will?"

"Okay …"

He grinned, pulled another book out of his pocket, and flashed me its
cover: *Pretty Good Joke Book*, by Garrison Keillor.

My brain clicked through a selection of responses. I frowned at him:
"What, Will needs a manual for being funny?"

Bronze-colored people do change color when embarrassed.

"Earnest! Are you being unkind?"

"Of course not! But he is sort of … a *reticent* guy, isn't he?" He slipped the book back into his pocket. "You know I love Will. He's practically like a son to me. I just thought he would, it would … be a fun book for him to have."

He worked with me until the job was done, then went back to the house as I pushed the used bedding down the alley with the skid-steer. He headed up to Burlington a few days later and we didn't see him again for almost two months.

In fact, Will did bring that book out to the parlor a couple of times, and he and Lynn and I had a hoot reading jokes to each other at odd moments. It helped break the tedium of those chilly predawn milkings. I put the field guide on my kitchen counter, next to my egg timer and salt and pepper shakers, where it mainly served to remind me of Earnest. It was winter now, and identifying trees would be difficult—no leaves to compare to the lush photos, hard to get to the woods in the snow.

Chapter 24

UNTIL THAT WINTER, I'd only ever done the milking with Diz or Franklin, once in a rare while with Earnest, and I found it much more pleasant with an amiable companion such as Lynn or Will. It's a sort of intimate experience and has its odd charms.

Typical mid-January morning: Alarm goes off at four thirty. I wake up in the dead black, grope my way to the coffeemaker, which I've programmed to start brewing ten minutes earlier. Fill up a huge plastic mug emblazoned with the UVM Catamounts mountain lion logo. The cup holds a quart and has a screw-on top with a sippy slot in it so I can take it around the barn with me. Check the thermometer tacked to the porch pillar: eight below.

Then, tights and shirts and pants and coveralls and a big, dirty, checked wool jacket, stocking cap, gloves, boots. It's usually around forty degrees in the shed this time of year, around fifty in the parlor—tropical compared with outside—but bone chilling after an hour or two.

Stumble out into the dark, which is breathtaking from beauty as well as cold, stars crisp and shivering above. Motion lights blink on over house door and barn. Crunch on brittle snow toward the bare bulb glowing over the milking parlor door. To my left I see a shadowy figure bumbling in the same direction and it's another human being with similar clothes and a cup that's identical to mine except that it's got the Boston Red Sox logo on it. That's Will.

Inside, on with the lights, rows of bovine faces turn toward us. Pause, swig scalding coffee, blow out steam, knowing the other is feeling the same inertia and trying to muster the resolve needed. The cold and dark wrap around you, you're the only two people in the universe, it's muffled quiet except for the shifting of the cows. Then to work: move em toward the parlor, get em in position, commence the ritual.

One morning, Will was particularly fuzzy, and he started talking about his family. I got a picture of him as a freckle-cheeked all-American boy, jeans and a white T-shirt, running wild in the hills and fields when chores didn't require him, shooting BB guns with his friends, swimming in the pools along the creek. But by the time he was fourteen, he decided he had no use for the "agricultural lifestyle." He'd always preferred technology, won science fair prizes, ended up getting into video production.

Picturing their household, Will and his now-estranged half sister, Jane, and Diz and Jim, I asked him when Earnest had come into the picture.

"Earnest?" He looked at me over the back end of a cow. "I figured you'd have heard all this. Thought you two were good friends."

"Well, Earnest is … a man of mystery. Your father is a man of few words, and your mother is … isn't often forthcoming," I said.

He laughed.

Will told me the basics in an offhand monologue with lots of ellipses as memories emerged or milking activities distracted him.

After the two men returned from Vietnam, Earnest moved to Vermont and worked on the farm. Where he met and after a couple of years married Brassard's sister, Charlotte.

"This was before I was born, so all I know is what Dad or Earnest have told me in bits and pieces. From what I've heard, sounds like they were seriously in love, I mean back-on-Broadway big-time. It made Dad happy. Earnest moved in, worked on the farm, Char worked at the bank in town. Dad was glad his sister had landed 'an honorable man.'"

I was stunned. Why hadn't Earnest told me this when I asked him about his history with Brassard, his presence at the farm? Was there any truth in the scandalous tale about the Saigon brothel?

"Yeah, she was quite a live wire, supposedly. Earnest made a 'decent woman' out of her. Which I'm guessing there had been some doubt about previously. There's pictures of her up at the house. The gal leaning against the tractor, with the cheesecake pose?"

I tried to get my mind around this as I moved on—sixteen iodine dips, sixteen squirts, sixteen wipe-downs, get the claws starting their twitchy pumping, then attend to the second row of preposterously swollen mammary bags.

When he came back with the next group, Will told me more: "He and Dad were both totally screwed up when she died. It was a huge thing for them. Driving back from Rutland. Icy road, snowy night. Went off into a ditch, ruptured spleen or something. Didn't find her until morning." Will paused to check my reaction, which was speechlessness. Of course Earnest hadn't said anything about it when I probed him: This wasn't something to talk about with a virtual stranger who casually inquired.

"Hasn't he ... ever remarried? Girlfriends?"

"Earnest? He's had girlfriends. A couple of them really set their caps for him. That's where he's been the last few weeks—up in Burlington. Dad says one of them has persuaded him to give it another try. Earnest is dubious, but he's a soft touch and doesn't want to hurt anyone's feelings. Also, he's not getting any younger, probably worth trying another heave-ho."

I felt a sense of loss, thinking of Earnest taking up residence else-where—everyone seemed happier when he was around, myself included, and winter was getting very long in his absence. Again, I felt irrationally betrayed that he hadn't told me about this part of his life. And again, I realized it wasn't particularly any of my business.

Will released the four cows that were finished, moved in the next four, both of us quiet. We went through another cycle of eight cows before he continued.

"Yeah, that was a bad period," Will said, returning to the time of Charlotte's death. "A couple of bad years. I'm glad I missed out on it. Mom told me the really tough stuff."

I didn't say anything.

"So, you've noticed there's no booze here at the house?" he asked.

I hadn't, but apparently no alcohol came onto the property, because after Charlotte died both men drank hard and the farm went to hell. A couple of cows died from lack of timely vet care. Earnest smacked up his car. One time he drank himself to unconsciousness lying on the woodshed floor and almost froze to death. Brassard and Diz had been seeing each other, and when things went to hell she moved to the farm and took charge. She'd had her own serious problems with booze—my first impression was right about that—and knew the ropes when it came to getting sober. She was the one who pulled them out of it. According to legend, Will said, she literally, physically, fought with Earnest to get the bottle out of his mouth.

"This was no twelve-step program," Will said, chuckling. "It was a one-step program, done Mom's way."

Diz had carved her place on the farm with a hatchet, from day one.

While Will was moving in the next group, one of the cows let go with a rush that almost got him point-blank. He danced away with nothing worse than brown splashes on his legs. "Witch!" he scolded the cow. To me he complained, "Is there any other animal that's so oblivious to its own defecation? You have to wonder if they even know it's happening back there. Christ Almighty."

He hated farm life, but paradoxically most of his video projects were about agricultural subjects, because with his background, those were the jobs he'd gotten early on and now it was his portfolio's greatest strength. So when he wasn't in production meetings or the editing room, he was often on farms anyway, filming. He'd done educational videos about brucellosis for a major interstate dairy organization, another for the Department of

Agriculture about environmental regulations that require farmers to keep field and pasture runoff out of streams. His current project was an ambitious one, funded by the USDA, on "modern dairy practices."

"So," I said, "are you going to do any filming here? I've always wanted to be in the movies!"

He laughed. "This place? If it was in the film, it'd be as an example of out-of-date technology and practices. Nowadays it's all indoors, they never set foot outside. Free-roaming in the shed with on-demand robot milking when the cow wants it, automatic latch-on, computer monitoring of each one's daily output and milk fat content. Hormones to stimulate lactation." He gazed along the row of bovine back ridges, then tipped his head. "But to give my folks credit, the hygiene is pretty good, given the limitations of the equipment. That's mainly my mother's doing. Runs a tight ship. Gotta keep things neat, 'respectable.' Work herself into an early grave."

For a while, we kept on in silence, and it occurred to me that we'd spent many hours doing chores together over the past few weeks, but I couldn't think of one personal topic, aside from his job, that he'd revealed.

So I asked him. "So, are you married?"

He blew out air between his teeth. "Right now I don't exactly have a wife, but I do exactly have a divorce. I also do exactly have a daughter, along with custody issues."

"I'm sorry. That must be tough."

"Actually, the divorce—it's not much fun, about like getting a root canal, but it's long overdue. The hardest part is my daughter."

"How old?"

"Six. Temporary arrangement is, I can see her several times a week. Problem is, with my work, I'm gone so often. Messes up the schedule."

I expected him to reciprocate with comparable questions, but he was, as Earnest had said, "reticent."

Both bored with our roles, we switched positions, Will going into the pit as I managed cow flow. It was quiet again but for the dull thump of hooves, the huff of the great bellows of their lungs. Bright yellow ear tags gave each cow a numerical identity, but, like Queenie, some stood out as individuals and had acquired names. The next group included a skittish cow named Twiggy, who was sometimes reluctant to enter the parlor and whose restlessness could infect the others. I was firmer with her, sweet-talking but also prodding with hips, elbows, or a two-handed shove here or there to keep her moving.

Will observed my management technique and said, "You're getting good at this!" And I felt quite flattered.

That morning, when we'd finished and had cleaned up the parlor, he swatted my many-layered shoulder in a comradely way as we headed back toward our respective quarters, a casual affirmation: *Good on us, huh, one more damn milking out of the way.*

I CAN TELL you about this now only because I have the security of retro-spect and have forgiven myself for my pitiful state at the time. That night, after Will clapped me on the shoulder, I remembered that casual, uncon-scious touch for hours. My response was another demonstration of the drift of my heart and body. Back at Larson Middle School, before my apocalypse, my colleagues and I had routinely shared that kind of touch, men and women alike, an affirmation that we were fellow soldiers fighting on behalf of a good cause. But when Will tagged my shoulder, he brought back full force the longing that had been growing in me.

I knew, or should have known, where I stood on this stuff, and it should not have caused any particular disturbance: I was and am hetero-sexual, and I had pretty well justified Cinderella by acknowledging that I was and am sentimental, full of romantic longings. I also knew that I was instinctively or fundamentally monogamous, always, even when it wasn't fashionable. One at a time is all I can manage.

And when it's with someone I like a lot, someone who intrigues or attracts the whole of me, I love sex. My liberal humanistic parents, coming of age in the sixties, raised me to accept and celebrate my body, my sexu-ality, to forgo the puritanical shame paradigm. They liked my high school boyfriends and allowed us time alone at the house. I may be ashamed of other things, but my body and its yearnings have never been among them.

So, sex: That night, my response showed me that I had a backlog of figuring out to do. I wondered whether it was a factor of my age—when I was younger, I sometimes went a year or two without a boyfriend. Was it so difficult? Actually, that night I couldn't remember. And I knew it didn't matter anyway. That was the moment I was living, and now is always now.

Cat was not as monogamously inclined as I was. She did get into the recreational aspect of sex more than I did, but she agreed with me that it wasn't just about arousal and the mating dance, so much of which is pretense anyway and, eventually, rather too predictable. It wasn't just about fucking. No: There's the whole swirl of physical contact, the mammal need for touch, for rubbing up against a warm, receptive fellow creature. I remember how my father and Erik and I used to wrestle on the living room floor, how Pop would grab my mother's ankle and pull her into the tangle and we'd squirm and tickle and throttle each other and laugh and finally just lie there in a heap, flushed, momentarily exhausted.

My father called it "the mammal pile"—it's just what mammals do, he said, and thank the gods. Erik would chirp, "Mammals are the *best*!"—a proud chauvinist of the class of fur-bearers and milk-givers.

That night after milking, the absence of it ached. It just ached. We hug our parents and friends, we hold and stroke our children, we even comfort hurting strangers with the assurance of body-to-body contact. Feeling another person's heartbeat, just opposite your own heart, says *You aren't alone.* I hadn't felt a moment of such contact since Cat's visit and the hugs we'd exchanged.

But if you're attracted to someone and feel the tug, and you enter the orbit, that swirl spins gently and then inevitably and then urgently around sex, the most intimate and surrendered of physical contacts. When the inward spiral has been graceful, unforced, and without pretense, conjoining in sex is its fulfillment, and it's wonderful.

That night I tried to persuade myself that all I really yearned for was the deep assurance of the mammal pile. But I knew I ached for the whole deal. And there was nothing I could do about it.

Chapter 25

Feb. 27

Earnest returned today as I headed into my apartment to make lunch. I was startled to see him after so long. He waved to me as he went up the steps into the house, I waved back.

I have to confess I've been wondering about his romantic life—perhaps because there's so little to occupy my poor brain. Winter gets wearying out here in the sticks. I guess I'd never thought of it, being a child of the city. We're a long way from any kind of diversion, no movie theaters within thirty miles, no restaurants—and no money to treat oneself to a fancy meal. No malls to stroll, no urban bustle outside the windows, no choice of twenty radio stations—no radio at all, because the reception here between the hills is at best intermittent and full of static. I tend to avoid driving, because the roads are often tricky and my snow tires aren't great. There's farmwork; books from the Montpelier library; still somewhat strained dealings with Diz, who's extra crabby because of her back pain and, I suspect, a secret shame that she's not "pulling her weight." Brassard himself is hardly what one would call a big socializer.

A few pleasant visits with Will, yes, and some fun conversations with Lynn. A week ago I had dinner with her and Theo at their place, a warm and fun evening in their cozy house, a glass of wine. Theo's younger sister Robin was visiting, a sweet, forthright young woman full of tales of college life. That event has lingered in recent memory like a sunny island in a gray sea. Spring is theoretically approaching but is hardly around the proverbial corner. I am desperately looking forward to a release from the clench of cold and the winter routine.

So I was pleased when, after about an hour inside, Earnest came out to see me in my chicken coop abode. He came in, took off his snow-covered boots, gave me a quick bear hug, and agreed readily when I offered to make some tea. When I asked him how he'd been, he tilted his hand side to side, his face saying maybe less than so-so. In fact, I thought he looked a little careworn. As I filled the teakettle, he sat at the counter, fiddling distractedly with the egg timer.

"Rumor has it you've been fanning an old flame up in Burlington," I said.

"'Flame' is a little strong. She and I lived together for a few years, then broke it off. But we kept in touch. A good person. We got talking a bit when I was down south this fall. You know."

I found mugs and my honey bear and a couple of spoons, then presented him with a few boxes of my tea stash. "Peppermint, black, jasmine, hibiscus—name your poison."

"Black."

I decided to be bold: "How's it been going?"

He grinned—a little sadly, I thought. "Kind of like this." He held up the egg timer, the round, retro-styled, hand-winding type.

He gave the knob a halfhearted little twist and set it ticking on the counter. For several seconds I looked at it, at him, puzzled, and then it went "Ding!"

Then I understood: It was done, very short but not unexpectedly so. I wanted to ask more: What didn't work? How did you decide that it had ended? How are you doing with it? Part of me wanted to assure him that she *wasn't good enough for him anyway—absurd since I knew nothing about her, not even her name.*

Instead, I nodded and said nothing. He seemed grateful for my restraint. He commented on the field guide he'd given me and seemed glad to see that I'd kept it close at hand. Then we talked about other things, more easily now, for another fifteen minutes, until I had to get back to chores.

Chapter 26

WHEN SPRING CAME, I moved back up the hill at the earliest opportunity—which meant I took the tractor up with my stuff as soon as the soil dried out. I raked leaves and twigs off my platform and out of the fire pit, reconnoitered, set up the tent. One of my first acts was to double the number of NO TRESPASSING signs all along my uphill border, facing the Goslants, and around the western property line—yellow plastic-paper signs stapled to virtually every tree.

By the time my first anniversary on Brassard's farm came around, I had fallen in love with my land and had in some inexplicable way invested myself in the farm and its well-being. I'd learned a little about the woods, a middling amount about myself, and a lot about hard work. I still counted the days until the end of my servitude, one more year, but not so often anymore.

For the Brassards, it had been a difficult year, and the coming year promised to be harder. Jim's joints just got worse, and the pain really began to slow him down. When I first came, he had occasionally smoked a pipe, outside, but by late spring he no longer did, because his big-knuckled thumbs got so arthritic that the delicate movements of tamping and lighting became more trouble than they were worth. My heart broke when I watched him fumble at the attempt and then, for the first time, give it up. He dropped the book of matches in the slush of the barnyard and didn't bother to pick it up. Bob, who tended to tag after Brassard, looked up at him with a concerned, puzzled expression.

As I write this, I realize I am stalling. I don't want to write the next part.

Over the winter, Diz's back pain had refused to get better. When she finally went in for an MRI, they found that the pain was caused by a tumor at the base of her spine. There was a very confusing month of tests and trying to figure out how to run the farm without Diz and often without Jim, who drove her to and from the various medical appointments. The tumor was too close to the spinal cord to remove surgically. She did chemo, but the cancer went into her organs anyway.

One day she came home from the hospital, gray and grim-faced, and told me, "My Tokuhashi is four."

"What's a Tokuhashi?" I asked.

"It's a Japanese guy. A doctor. It's also a measure of your life expectancy."

"So is four good?"

"'Good' compared to what? It's good compared to two. Bad compared to five. Means I'll be dead in less than four months."

Actually, it was about three months. She was often away from the farm, down at Dartmouth-Hitchcock Medical Center. They sent her home to die, though, with palliative care administered by dear, dear people from the Home Health and Hospice organization. I wasn't in the room when she died, but Jim and Earnest were. Will had made a grocery run into town and so missed the moment of passing.

Her death put the farm seriously at risk. It may strike you as insensitive to talk about the farm's health in the same breath as the death of a person, but it's not. The farm was part of Diz; she was part of it. It was the only thing she owned and one of the few places she'd ever lived—she had devoted her life to it and staked her pride on it. An intelligent woman, she was a fierce advocate of "the small farm life," which she knew to be a dying tradition. A dying part of American identity. One reason she was so tough and worked so hard is that she was by God not going to relinquish her little corner of it without a fight. Coming in her own desperation to Brassard's farm, back when she married Jim, had been her last stand, and we who did not die could not take that lightly.

That all sounds like bullshit, but it's not. One of the last conversations I had with her reveals it unequivocally.

The hospice people had moved a rented hospital bed into the former parlor of the house, downstairs, so it was easier to tend to her needs and get food to her. A big, chrome-tubed thing with motors that raised and lowered it and tilted the head end forward, and so on. It sat in a circle of oxygen tanks and catheters and bags of urine and a wheelchair and a wide range of paraphernalia on little tables brought from other parts of the house.

I was sitting with her as Jim and Earnest were taking a break from tending to her and getting some chores done; Will was upstairs taking a nap, recovering from night duty with her. At Diz's insistence, I was reading local news to her from the *Valley Reporter*. It's basically an advertising weekly, but it's also full of local sports team scores, marriages, births, little news items about farming or business.

She always had me read the obituaries. John somebody, aged eighty-two. Mary somebody, forty-seven, survived by so-and-so. Mrs. Helen something, of natural causes. When I read that last, Diz burst out in a harsh cackle that startled me.

"Ha! That old witch! I prayed to God I'd outlive her and dance on her damn grave. Aah-haha! And I did! Goddamn it, I did it!" Her voice was grindingly hoarse by then but full of vengeful glee.

Mrs. Helen Crutchfield, sixty-three, died of natural causes in her home, surrounded by her loved ones. Diz had outlived her—it wouldn't be for long, true, but the fact gave her enormous pleasure. Diz's obit would be almost verbatim the same.

"Why'd you hate her?"

She puckered her lips, then grinned contemptuously. "Not worth talking about. Nothing that woman did in her life was worth wasting your breath on. But I can tell you I've waited a long time for this moment. A lo-o-o-ong time."

Her satisfaction was absolute. A glint of the old Diz gleamed in her eyes—sardonic, irreverent, implacable, cruelly amused by life. Seeing it for the first time in many months, I realized how I'd missed that furious light.

I paused, not sure I should go on reading or let her indulge the moment longer. Suddenly her hand shot out and grasped my wrist. She jerked me toward her with a startling strength.

"Now, you listen to me. I'm dead. I'm outta here. Sayonara. That means *you are going to have to take care of these men*. You get that? They *saved your pathetic little life*, how many times, how many ways, and *you owe them*. You are going to have to step up and pay your dues *and take care of these men*."

The effort exhausted her and she let go of me and fell back on the bed, but her eyes stayed blazing on mine. She looked like a kamikaze mother wolf or mountain lion in defense of her litter. I had never before experienced such absolute ferocity in a human being. I felt seared, scalded inside. The bruises on my wrist lasted days.

Her eyes stayed, pinning me, beaming a savage fire at me, and bit it off again: "You take care of those good men."

"Oh, Diz," I said. "Of course I will. Of course I will." My voice shook and my eyes brimmed, every indication of the weakness she despised in me, but she just continued looking at me. For once, I saw no judgment or contempt.

A FEW DAYS later, she was dead. I worked the farm chores hard, cooked eggs and bacon for the men, kept the house in order. Brassard was stunned, shell-shocked. He drifted looming through the house, over to his desk to shuffle papers, then realizing he couldn't see without his reading glasses and then discovering he couldn't find his glasses and then remembering that Diz wasn't there to help find them as she always did.

Will and Earnest made all the arrangements. Of which there weren't many. They bought a coffin and a plot in a cemetery near Tunbridge, where other Brassards had been buried. Jim had a stone made but didn't hold a church service, because Diz didn't believe in God or religion and would have disemboweled anyone who suggested doing such a thing. Toward the end, only half-jokingly, she told Jim that she wanted him to put her through the chipper—the farm keeps a big one that's driven by the tractors' PTO—and mix the chunks into the compost. Brassard said he wanted a place to visit her, and insisted on a real plot with a real gravestone.

We had a gathering of remembrance at the house. The group included Lynn and Theo and Theo's younger sister Robin, a couple of the hospice people who had acquired a very moving affection for Diz, Jim's sister Elizabeth, and some other Brassard relatives. Several farming neighbors from down the road came, but no "trash" Goslants from up the hill. I didn't know any of these people and wasn't sure how they were connected, but I noticed that none of them introduced themselves as relatives of Diz. Her long-estranged stepdaughter Jane didn't show. There was one sixty-something guy in a dark green jacket, who skulked uncomfortably on the periphery of the room trailing the reek of stale tobacco smoke. He struck me as the lounge-lizard type, and when I asked Earnest about him, I learned he was "one of Diz's prior husbands."

I grilled chicken outside and prepared trays of other edibles. Mostly people talked about cows, crops, weather, dairy policy, tractors, and other relatives or neighbors who had died. At one point, Will came to help me in the kitchen, where he stood at the counter trying to remember what he was supposed to do, which can to open or cheese to slice, looking so lost that I took his hand. Didn't say anything. Didn't look at each other. He just held my hand with a firm, grateful grip: two lonesome hands there on the Masonite counter.

After a time, I let go because it was time to ferry some bread and cheese slices back to the living room.

Numb, adrift, Brassard gave a short eulogy: "She was my wife. I loved her and I don't know how I'm gonna get along without her. She was my companion and I loved her. I was always very proud of her. Lot of people don't know it, but back fifteen years ago she had the gumption to go out and get a certificate in cosmetology. Worked for two years at it between milkins, can you believe it, at the beauty place over to Randolph, and you never heard that woman complain, not once. I was proud of her. Always proud to call her my wife."

He seemed to have more to say but couldn't put his finger on just what. Will took him by the elbow, led him to a chair, said some words from a grieving son's perspective.

We caravanned to the cemetery, a typical Vermont graveyard on a gentle slope with a few big maples in the lawn, shelves of bedrock rearing out of the ground here and there, gravestones with dates ranging from the 1700s to the present.

The cemetery people had dug the hole. The funeral home delivered the coffin and settled it into the straps, where it hovered for a while at the top of the grave as we said our farewells. Will, wry sorrow on his lips, knocked affectionately on the lid as it began to descend. We threw in flowers and then handfuls of dirt. We left before the backhoe came up to start filling it in, but not before I spotted her gravestone, waiting to get set up. It was a simple rectangle carved out of good Vermont gray granite, polished on the front, rough on the other side.

All this time, I hadn't cried for Diz, had been too preoccupied living up to my promise to her. But I burst into tears when I read the inscription on her stone and abruptly a window opened on this hard-fought life:

In Memory of
Our Beloved Wife and Mother
Maureen Goslant Brassard
"Diz"

Chapter 27

I HAD STEPPED into Diz's functional role even before her death, so the workday didn't change much for me except for the period right after her funeral, when it fell upon me to help deal with her things. Elizabeth, Brassard's widowed sister from Rutland, came to help with this—somehow, as throughout history, certain details of death being left to the women. I doubt Brassard wanted Diz erased so quickly from the house, but Elizabeth, four years his senior and considering herself an old hand at spouse death, said it was the best way to do things, and he assented.

We sorted Diz's wardrobe, a typical bunch of underthings, pants, shirts, and a very small collection of dresses. Mainly, she owned work clothes. Her cosmetics were similarly limited: She had long since abandoned lipstick, rouge, eye shadow. Jewelry: She did have pierced ears, and small earrings appeared to be her only indulgence. There were probably two dozen pairs, inexpensive things, practical and nothing pendulous, because, she'd told me once, they'd catch on things in the course of a day's work "and rip your damn earlobe off." Her wedding ring had stayed on her finger, into the grave.

Diz had kept a shelf of books and periodicals about gardening, including, surprisingly, a few issues of a magazine about orchids. Another shelf held cookbooks and some large volumes of photographs—"coffee table books": *The Wonders of Paris, The Mysteries of Egypt, The Amazon Rain Forest, Historic Savannah*, and Earnest's *Washington, DC: America's Historic Heritage*. I wondered whether he had given her all these, and whether they signified an inner yearning for those faraway places, some hint of a life's unfulfilled longings.

I dwell on these artifacts because in total they were shockingly few. Her collection of personal things was hardly bigger than my own, up on the hill. To me it said that she had been so fully subsumed by the apparatus of life on the farm that there really wasn't time or mental energy left over for a personal life.

This terrified me. Whatever personal transformational trajectory I'd envisioned, it did not include becoming merely a part in a machine, even a machine as worthy as a farm and an inadvertently adopted family. Making Brassard's farm functional had cost her everything. Even my heartfelt vow to take care of the men did not encompass that level of sacrifice. It would not.

THE FARM-RELATED DETAILS of that spring and early summer are vague in my memory because it was all so centered on Diz's dying, and so devoted to work, and the work was so repetitious, that days blurred together. Theo's younger sister Robin graduated from UVM and moved in with them, and we hired her on a regular basis for the afternoon milking rituals. Earnest was there more often, Will came and went but worked hard when he was there. Brassard mainly did tractoring and truck-driving chores and the business side of things, whatever didn't put stress on his joints. Nobody tended to Diz's vegetable garden, so weeds moved in, the lettuce and asparagus bolted early; later, some pest got into the tomatoes so they puckered and paled. The lawn often went unmowed; I forgot to water the flower boxes at the windows and they browned and died. The place wasn't as "respectable" as it used to be, and Earnest said he could hear Diz spinning in her grave.

But cows got milked. Milk pipes and tanks got sterilized. Calves got born, fed, weaned. Corn and hay got put in. Tractors and their attachments got fixed. The Agri-Mark tanker came and went. By unspoken mutual consent, I stopped counting my hours; Brassard knew I was more than repaying him for the land, and I knew I would quit when the payoff time rolled around, late next winter.

But my life had divided into two distinct halves, and if the farmwork got blurry, my life on the hill was distinct and keen. Some nights I was just too tired to hike up, but mostly I made it to the tent in time to enjoy the late sunlight and lush evenings. Also, Brassard knew burnout all too well, and he insisted I take at least one day a week off, two if possible. He quoted some maxim from one of his books on modern management techniques, how having a tired and disgruntled staff cuts productivity.

Eavesdropping from nearby, Earnest nodded sagely. "And is bad for retention," he added. A joke for my benefit: As if I didn't already want to quit! Brassard had no laughter in him.

And as far as disgruntlement went, I was simply too busy to be disgruntled.

LIFE ON MY hill was easier now, in part because I was hardier and in part because, by increments, I was making my camp more civilized. The most important improvement was figuring out how to get running water into my kitchen sink. I couldn't dam my spring, but I did manage to trick it into delivering some of its flow to the campsite. I cut the bottom off a plastic one-gallon milk jug to make an oversize funnel, staked it in the streambed, then attached almost four hundred feet of garden hose that gravity-fed water to my kitchen. The stream didn't seem to mind this borrowing of water as long as I didn't try to stop or slow the main flow.

It was hardly a Roman aqueduct, but I was proud of my ingenuity. And, turning on the faucet for the first time, watching the water spill from the sink drain and soak into the soil beneath, I experienced a lovely epiphany. It's just common sense, but then, the deepest insights usually are: The spring's waters, separated briefly by my hose, would reunite downhill. Eventually they'd merge with all the other waters from these mountains, in Lake Champlain, I suppose, or maybe the ocean. *Things separated connect again.*

Having running water on demand, in my outdoor kitchen, seemed almost embarrassingly high-tech.

IF YOU ARE not already familiar with the woods in summer, I will not be able to convey to you how *alive* they are. Everything moves. The trees sway and billow, shift and shimmer, bees hover and zip as they tend the tiny forest flowers, birds flit and glide and racket in the treetops. Gnats float in clouds above sun-warmed spots, tiny caterpillars swing from invisible threads. A porcupine trundles into the clearing, oblivious, then notices the human presence, hesitates in a befuddled way, and ambles off. Red squirrels scold the human interloper with a machine-gun chattering trill and barking squeaks. The weather seems alive, too, as cloud shadows drift through the woods, and the forest light goes from shy to bold to shy again. When the sun is bright, tossing leaf shadows turn the forest floor into a freckling surface that moves like wavelets on a small pond.

Even on the most windless of days, seemingly dead still, you'll see one single paradoxical leaf waving back and forth, elastic on its stem and caught just so in an imperceptible movement of air.

Most people have hiked in the woods, have cut firewood, gone hunting, taken dogs for walks, but I think too few have spent the purposeless time that allows the forest to reveal its own innumerable purposes. On my days off, I luxuriated in simply being still, observing. My silence and immobility encouraged the woods to resume their normal activity.

Of course, blackflies and deerflies and mosquitoes were among those moving things, and at times they became torture, enough to make me scream. I still fled back to the tent to escape them. Nor was the weather always conducive to pleasant meditations. Storms on my ridge could be frightening in their intensity; there were days of sullen drizzle, and there were hot, hazed days, murky with humidity, so stifling that the most basic camp tasks seemed impossibly difficult.

And still, at night, fear would steal into my little clearing. At times, the image of that pile of guts came back, and I felt as if surely one of the Goslants had to be watching from the dark. One night I was wrenched out of sleep by a horrific screaming, growling, gargling, very close by—some smaller animal being killed by a larger one, probably a fisher cat. The dark forest seemed full of murder.

But more powerful, more imposing by far was the huge, formless terror of darkness and wildness, the abyss staring back at me. It was as big as a god, whether it came from the darkness outside me or inside me, and it was a god heedless of prayer and ignorant of mercy, and my whole body knew that god from ten million years back. Yes, the Fear remained. But it was better counterbalanced now by a slowly growing sense of competence in— and a greater tolerance for the mundane discomforts of—woods living.

Chapter 28

TOWARD THE END of July, on one of my days off, I was sitting on my log clipping my toenails when I heard Earnest call from down near the last trail bend: "Ann! You decent?"

"Come on up and find out!" I yelled back.

He came into the clearing puffing, a barrel of a bear of a man in oil-stained jeans and blue work shirt, sweat sheen on his summer-bronzed face. Like the rest of us, even the mighty Earnest was showing the strain of work. He couldn't neglect his tree business, because it provided green-backs—he was feeding some into the farm's cash flow by now, to help pay for Lynn's assistance with milking—yet he had to be at the farm as often as possible. Now he spent most nights there, coming in his big stake-side GMC so he could go straight to tree jobs.

He had spent the previous afternoon working on the tedder, which had gone awry just when the hay had to be turned. This created an urgent problem. Once the hay's been cut and is drying in its rows, timing is everything: If the weather turns wet when it's on the ground, it can ruin a whole crop. If one of the hay crops can't be used, the farmer has to buy it from someone else, and so if money's tight it gets tighter still. The tedder is a triangular frame mounted with four big spiders that spin rapidly, that you tow behind the tractor to flip and spread the rows of semidry hay. Each of its legs ends in a pronged fork, giving the whole thing a spiny, spiky look. Part of the frame had broken and Earnest had done a lot of urgent clanking and welding to get it functional again.

"Day off," he stated.

"Mm-hm."

He sat heavily on the ground, looking around my site, nodding to himself but ill at ease. "Nice up here." Stalling.

I helped him stall: "How's your hand?" He had burned his wrist on a piece of hot steel while welding the tedder, a mistake he would never have made if he weren't so overworked. I had put aloe on it and taped gauze over it. Maneuvering his arm and wrist to tend to him, I was struck by how thick his hand was through the palm, how startlingly solid, how strange it was to find the instrument of his incredible physical power lying passive in my own much smaller, slighter hands.

He nodded, held up the bandaged wrist, wiggled the fingers to show they still worked.

"Need a favor," he said.

My heart sank, but I knew he wouldn't ask if he had any alternative. And I owed him a great deal.

Earnest planned to spend the night at a motel in Burlington, so I drove behind him up to the park-and-ride lot in Williston, left my car there, and joined him in the truck. Despite our fatigue, we both felt more energized when we got off the main roads, bouncing along together on the GMC's big bench seat, each with an elbow on our windowsill, fresh air blustering in, thermos and bagged sandwiches bouncing between us. It was to be another huge old tree, this time a silver maple that had been hit by lightning and riven and was now dangerous.

"I'm doing this on one condition," I told him.

"Making me an offer I can't refuse?"

"You're in no position to negotiate, no."

He shrugged, resigned.

"I have …" I counted them in my head "… five items on my conversational agenda, and I'll expect you to be forthright about them."

"'Forthright.'"

"Yes."

He groaned, downshifted, cranked the wheel to turn onto the dirt road, rumbled the truck back up to speed.

"Diz," I said. "Maureen *Goslant.*"

"Yeah, Diz. Our Diz. Not closely related to those Goslants up the hill, I don't think. Maybe second or third cousins. With them, though, who knows? A, uh, certain amount of intermarrying among the clans. Lots of Goslants, big tribe—old Vermont backwoods name. Her immediate family came from up near Marshfield."

"She was ashamed of the name. Of being associated with them in any way."

He thought about that, then reframed the issue: "She worked hard to draw a line that distinguished her, yes." He mused for a moment, then chuckled. "Early on, when she first came to the farm, the bunch up the hill claimed some kind of relationship. They wanted to borrow money or a truck or something. Second time they drove up, Diz came out on the porch with Jim's deer rifle."

That was a scary image. "What did Jim think?"

"Of her family tree? Of her cutting loose of it?"

"Either. Both."

He drew a deep breath, exhaled slowly through pursed lips. "At the time Diz moved in, Jim didn't have too many choices. He was … we were having a tough time on the farm right around then. Various problems. Plus, Will was already on the way. Diz whipped us into shipshape, pronto."

It would have been just a short step from there to Earnest's wife and her death and the misfortunes of that era. But I just didn't dare, not yet.

"I have a question for you," I hazarded instead.

"Proceed," he intoned gravely.

"Okay. This is about Goslants, too, but maybe it's about … I don't know, etiquette? Vermont tradition?" I told him about the poached deer, the guts in my woods, and watched closely to see his response.

"When was this?"

"Back in November."

"Why didn't you tell me earlier?"

In fact, I hadn't known what to say about it—he had been gone when it happened, and by the time he returned I had moved onto the farm and the issue seemed less urgent. "Well, I talked to Will, I talked to Jim, they thought I should sort of let it go. Talking about Diz reminded me just now. And fall's not so far off. What if it happens again?"

He winced his eyes shut, a sort of a *please not this* frown. The muscles in his jaw rippled. "'Etiquette' isn't the right word, Ann. Homer and Fran are good people, but some of them are fucking dangerous wood-chucks, PPP. You don't want to mess with them, but you can't let them take an inch or think you don't have borders or limits. It's a real bitch. God damn it!"

"PPP?" I thought he was talking about a drug, something like meth.

"Piss-poor protoplasm." He glanced over to see that my puzzlement lingered, then translated primly: "A term I learned from Diz, meaning lousy genetic inheritance not conducive to high intelligence."

"Earnest, that's really offensive!"

"Diz should know, right? Would you have argued the point with *her*?"

"I don't believe in that! In genetic destiny. It's, like—"

"It's like a good, politically correct, liberal, white, college-educated female schoolteacher believing it's all socioeconomic, cultural deprivation, bias, whatever, and not getting the picture. That's why I worry about you up there, at night, with those PPP fuckers just through the woods from you."

My whole upbringing, and my training as an educator, rebelled against the idea that people fell into "types" determined by race or family history, and I was shocked by Earnest's embrace of this genetic determinism, this eugenicists' rationale. Also, it was the first time Earnest had ever chided me or derided my urbanite's naïveté or labeled me in any way. I felt a gust of anger, then hurt.

"I am all those things—liberal, politically correct, college-educated, and whatever else you said," I told him stiffly. "And I am not likely to change my outlook anytime soon."

He didn't say anything.

When I opened my mouth to speak again, my brain skipped a groove. "And there's no reason to worry about me!" I bit off. "I can take care of myself." Oddly, though, the thought pleased me: It was as if his derision had been a slap, and this a caress.

He just drove, his lips set.

IT TOOK ANOTHER ten minutes to get to the job site, during which we spoke very little. Once we got there, we just let go of the damn discussion, though we both chewed it over in our thoughts. There was work to be done.

The tree was another monument, a tragic one. The silver maple is not like its cousin, the more common sugar maple. They grow huge, wider than tall, with grand random branches—really, multiple trunks—free-form throughout. In a good breeze, the leaves toss and flash their silvery undersides, in the right light a kaleidoscopic effect. This one, a hundred years old, fully leafed, robustly healthy, had been hit by lighting and now showed a white line of ruptured bark from its highest big fork right into the ground. It loomed over a garage on one side and a house on the other. At the top of the split, the weight of the tree had started to pry the wood apart, a widening gap of splintered strands, too far gone to cable together. *The meat of the tree*, I thought, *is the bone of the tree*. Earnest was right: In any kind of wind, the tree would split and crush anything nearby.

We unloaded the gear as Earnest explained our strategy for the felling. The clients, an elderly couple, came out to watch. Everybody was glum, and Earnest and I a bit brittle with each other. Clanking in his fetishistic leather and steel harness and burdened with coils of rope, Earnest paused before he started to climb, to stroke the big wall of bark with his hands.

It was an apologetic farewell, like a compassionate veterinarian calming a horse he's about to put down.

Then he climbed, and again I witnessed his miraculous transformation into a weightless being, an acrobat of the inner space of the tree. Swinging and alighting, climbing, rappelling, he reconnoitered its architecture for a time, then commanded me to start sending up the tools and big ropes. The clients watched until the first of the big branches swept down, crashing and fanning onto their lawn. A few minutes later, when I looked up from my chainsawing, I saw that they had retreated inside.

This was harder work, by far, than the elm we had done before. The branches, so light and airy on the tree, came down heavily, weighted with their leaves and innumerable small branches that I had to slash and battle through to make my cuts. At intervals, Earnest descended and drove off with truckloads of brush as I continued to saw. Even with my headphones on, I felt myself going deaf from the whining and snarling saw. My hands grew numb from its vibration, from wrestling and rocking it into the wood. Its oily blue smoke gathered in my lungs and on my clothes.

The elderly couple made us pitchers of lemonade with ice in it, and I was glad we weren't in Deputy Dickhead's jurisdiction. But the labor was unrelenting. No rest breaks, no time to converse. Earnest had set as our goal for the day the removal of all the branches; he planned to come the following day to topple the main trunk.

Toward evening, I was so exhausted that I almost told Earnest I had to quit, couldn't do it, was afraid I'd cut off my own leg. But as long as he kept going, I felt I had to stick it out. And just as it got too dark to continue, we loaded the last branches onto the truck, strapped them down, found places for the tools, and rattled away.

"PPP," he said as soon as we hit the bigger road. "You're right. It's a rotten way to say it. It's a pretty horrible idea. Like original sin or some other bullshit you're supposedly stuck with from birth."

"Yes."

Clearly, it had been bothering him all day, and now he was wrestling with how to express it. "When I was a kid, my mother called people like that 'accident prone.' That's observably true of your neighbors."

"I wouldn't know. Jim says so, yeah."

He sighed again. "Diz could've given you the genealogy of some of them up there, in detail, and I suspect you'd see patterns that posed risks to genetic inheritance. And yes, I'm sure socioeconomic factors play a major role, too. When you're poor and dropped out of school at fifteen and maybe aren't very bright, who are you going to marry? Marie Curie? Albert Einstein? It comes around full circle in the next generation."

"You're taking a very academic approach to explaining this."

"Because I'm talking to a white, college-educated, politically correct schoolteacher and I'm trying to speak her language." He said that carefully, without scorn.

"Okay."

"So let me rephrase it. Some of the people living uphill from you often demonstrate 'a lack of good judgment.' They're about a mile away, straight through the woods. They know those woods better than you do. And it sometimes ... gives me pause."

I nodded.

He looked over at me as he drove. "Can we leave it now? Is it done?"

I nodded.

He still wasn't sure, so he reached over and we shook hands to seal the deal that it was done.

WE FOUND A steak house near the interstate for what I now understood to be a ritual celebration of a hard day's work getting done. We got some glances from the other customers, but I felt righteously proud as we walked in, in our honest filth and stink.

We read the menus. We both commented on how, when you're hungry, really hungry, your mouth waters just from reading descriptions of the meals.

I ordered a pint of beer along with my food and only after the waitress had left did I remember Will's tales of the bad times on Brassard's farm.

I looked up at Earnest, alarmed, and blurted, "Oh! I'm sorry!"

"For what?"

I gestured randomly, table, menu, disappearing waitress. "Beer. The beer. I forgot—"

"I take it somebody told you some history. Will, huh?"

"I'll have her take it back. I forgot!"

He shook his head as if I were a lovable but dim child. "Ann. Ann. Amazingly, in the last thirty years I have witnessed people drinking beer and even enjoying it. I drink one myself now and then. I am not an alcoholic, not even a perpetually recovering one. That's more Jim's situation. I just ... avoid it a bit."

I nodded. "Okay."

The waitress appeared with a basket of sliced hot bread; Earnest folded a slice around a couple of butter pats and stuffed it whole into his mouth.

"Why didn't you tell me about Charlotte, about all that?"

"What's the point? Thirty years ago."

What *was* the point? I wondered. I was curious, yes, but was that any reason to expect someone to spill about difficult personal events, no doubt painful in their recollection? At that moment, I realized there are different kinds of curiosities. There's the idle variety, and mine was not. There's the prurient sort, which mine was certainly not. Rational, scientific inquiry, no.

That left the *it matters to me* kind.

Then the waitress presented me with my beer. Amber, bubbles rising merrily, it filled a heavy frosted mug, and it looked glorious. I was dying of thirst. I glanced up at Earnest to confirm his amused approval, and then I picked up that mug and gulped and it was bliss. The bitter hops cut through the oily chainsaw taste in my mouth.

"What was she like?" I asked.

He exhaled slowly. "I don't know. You replay memories enough times, after a while it's just memories of memories, don't connect with anything real." He tipped his head to think about it some more. "Mainly, what I remember is the feeling of being with her. Then the feeling of being without her. But it's not something I think about every day. Almost remarried a couple of times, as my recent egg-timer adventure demonstrates. Dodged the bullet each time."

I just nodded and swigged some more beer.

After a little while, Earnest asked, "Was Char part of your five-item agenda?"

I was astonished that he remembered my morning preamble. "Yes."

"What else?"

"A matter of ten grand nobody but Diz thought to tell me about." I took another swallow. "That I didn't ever thank you for."

"Goddamn Diz. Just another way to make you feel shittier than you already felt."

"No! Really, she just sort of stumbled into it, we were milking and she mentioned it. To say how great a person you were."

"Diz said that? Huh!"

"'Saint Earnest.'"

He grinned to himself. "Who'd a thunk?"

"Back to the ten grand."

"She said something almost nice about you, too, you know."

Truly, I rocked back in my seat. "What?"

He frogged his lips, hesitated. "Well, I can't exactly remember at the moment."

"The ten grand, Earnest."

"It was no act of chivalry on my part. I'm part owner of the farm. It got everybody through a tight spot. The farm needed another hand. You needed some money."

He watched as I processed that. Of course he was part owner! Brassard's father willed it to Jim and Charlotte, Earnest was Charlotte's husband, her half descended to him when she died. Another revelation. I thought back to the first day I set foot on the farm, the oil-smudged man who, when I asked if he worked for Mr. Brassard, had grinned and said, "Looks that way." It *had* looked that way, but was not that way, just Earnest's understated, self-deprecating humor, a joke just for himself.

The waitress came with our meals—Earnest's huge slab of meat and two baked potatoes and separate bowls of coleslaw and peas, mine a half of a roasted chicken and a steaming mound of rice topped by slivers of toasted almonds and surrounded by green beans. "Another?" she asked, gesturing at my empty mug, and I nodded.

We tore at our food. We attacked those plates, ravaged them. I guzzled half my second beer in one swallow and by now the buzz of the first one, on an empty stomach, was filtering into my fatigue and it felt great. As he wielded his knife and fork, Earnest's forearms seemed as big as my thighs.

"I figured Will Brassard would be on your agenda," he said blandly.

"Why'd you think that?"

"Why? He's your age, you're single, he's more or less single now, you're both good-looking, he's smart like you, and you're both ..." he paused and looked caught out.

"Both ...?"

"Both don't really want to be all that single at this time."

I took that in. "What makes you think that?"

He shrugged, making light of it, tossed his head to one side, carelessly, *Whatever.*

"Just to be clear, I am *not* man-hunting or pining around for—"

"I didn't say you were."

"I've been enjoying the hell out of my independence! I've got my agenda and I'm feeling stronger every day because of it. It's—"

"I believe you." He put his hands up: *Okay already, I give up.*

"I mean it, Earnest. Yeah, I came here in a sort of desperate state of mind, but it was to sort out some shit on my own. Which I've been doing. What, I'm gonna move out to the fucking wilderness to find a guy?"

He nodded, taking the point. "Still," he said mildly.

We went back to eating, and my huff faded. The beer no doubt helped.

"Actually," I said after a while, "he wasn't. On the agenda. But as long as you brought the subject up."

"What do you want to know? Always been the quiet type. He's kinda mostly sorta divorced, his daughter's six and is named Isabelle. Master's degree. He makes good money, but with keeping up two households and child support, he's as strapped as the rest of us."

"Nice to have the vital stats," I told him. "Should I be writing this down?"

"The thing about Will is, he's not a good self-promoter. Especially with women, in my humble opinion."

"Hence the joke book? Give him some ice-breakers?"

He ignored me. "He's won awards for his videos—hasn't mentioned that, has he? Ran track and field at UVM and took trophies at some inter-state competitions. Plus, I've seen him coming out of the shower, and the guy's what in polite company one would call very well endowed."

"Earnest!" I glanced quickly around us, worried that other diners had overheard. "This is a little more information than—"

"I'm just saying. He's not a great advocate for himself, especially around women." Clearly Earnest was enjoying my discomfort.

"Anything else I should know?" I tried to say it scathingly, but I was getting looped enough that amusement trumped sarcasm.

Earnest pondered for a moment. "Let's see. His political views are somewhat to the right of mine, so there are places we don't go when we talk. But I like Will and he tolerates me pretty well."

"Like what? Political, I mean."

"Oh, he's more of a mainstream capitalist, that's all. Nothing as extreme as I am."

"How extreme is that?"

"Want a discourse on Native American culture?"

"Sure!" By now I was just plain drunk, greatly enjoying my license to ask questions and digress on any tangent.

"The Oneidas have a little reservation up near Green Bay. Tribe owns all lands in common. Has its own health-care system, universal coverage— at least it did when I was a kid. It's a corporation and if it makes money, like from capital gains on investments, the money's distributed equally among the tribe's members. I got a thousand bucks two years ago, my share of timber sales from tribal land. Works pretty well."

"So you're a *communist*?" I tried to look horrified.

"No. But I am pretty red, I guess, yeah."

"That's funny! Red—like Indian? Redskin?" I thought it was a scream. Two beers, not used to it, I was blitzed.

He made a sad face, a commentary on the sheer poverty of the joke.

Onward we ate. Then: "Even Diz mentioned it," Earnest said. "That's what it was."

"Mentioned what?"

"Will. You. She detested Will's ex and after one of Will's visits she was expounding on the woman's failings. Said something like why couldn't he land a girl with more guts, 'like Ann.'"

My jaw literally dropped.

Shrug. "Or to that effect. I don't remember her actual wording."

"What virtues could I *possibly* possess that would make me worthy?"

Shrug. "I don't know. She'd been railing about the ex's lack of 'spunk.' Or was it 'grit'? Wait, I remember now! 'Even *Ann* has more grit!'"

My pleasure deflated. *Even Ann* was simply a way of establishing the lowest imaginable standard of comparison: Even malaria wasn't as bad as smallpox. Still, I felt vaguely flattered and I had to laugh at myself for momentarily thinking that Diz had thought I possessed even the slightest utility. Earnest laughed, too. I felt giddy and silly, alcohol in my bloodstream, a good day's work under my belt, well-deserved fatigue creeping into every limb.

We continued chowing down, and I forgot whatever else I thought I needed to discuss with him. I suppose any thread of conversation I attempted unraveled before it wove. At some point I realized I was going to burst if I ate another bite. Earnest mopped the last juice off his plate, paid, rousted me out of my seat, shepherded me out to the truck.

Sitting on the wide bench seat, I lolled against the passenger door as Earnest buckled himself in and cranked it up and pulled out onto Route 2. Dizzy, amiable silence in the dark for a few minutes.

I felt blissfully sleepy, happy. I'd had a really great day. Made two hundred dollars, fun to be with Earnest, Diz had thought I had spunk, sort of ish. I shut my eyes and just surrendered to the gentle gravities of the truck's turns and accelerations. Sack of potatoes. Diz had been one hard nut, but maybe worth the cracking after all. Earnest was such a sweet guy, the best. Through thick lips I said, "So. Vietnam. How old does that make you now?"

"That makes me fifty-five."

I was skunked, half asleep. "Too bad," I mumbled.

I AWAKENED TO find myself still sprawled in the truck, in the dark. Earnest sat doing some paperwork on a clipboard he'd set on the steering wheel, reading and jotting by the metallic streetlight glow that angled into his window. We were at the Williston park-and-ride, abandoned now except for my car. The dashboard clock said it was going on midnight. He'd been sitting there with me asleep beside him for over two hours.

He looked over when he noticed my stirring. "I didn't want to wake you," he said. "I wasn't going to let you drive like that."

Earnest counted out four fifty-dollar bills and made sure I pocketed them securely. My head had cleared, but I was so stiff and sore that my legs almost buckled when I jumped down from the cab. He was watching me carefully, so I mocked him by standing on one foot, successfully, for fifteen seconds. He smiled. He waited until I started my car and turned on the headlights and backed out with enough precision to reassure him again. He honked and then his taillights sped off and I cruised back to the farm.

Chapter 29

JUST AS YOU can't talk about dairy farm life without discussing manure, you can't talk about it without considering business—money and the lack thereof. Manure is the more pleasant subject.

Toward the end of August, Brassard called Will and Earnest and me to his office. Almost four months after Diz's death, he was no longer so stunned, so numb. But he had acquired a kind of resigned melancholy at odds with the genial, shyly humorous personality I'd known in my first year at the farm.

As I learned that afternoon, it wasn't all about Diz.

I know, the plight of America's small farmers has been a trope of rural America since well before Woody Guthrie mourned it and railed against it in his Dust Bowl–era songs. It's not a new topic, but this was my first personal exposure to its complexities and emotional urgency.

I was aware that Brassard was running on the edge—that's why he sold my acres in the first place. But in the back of my mind, I still held on to the grand mythology of the *Grapes of Wrath* saga: drought or flood, failed crops, greedy bankers. If farms fail, it's *Grapes of Wrath II*, full of high drama.

But on a modern small farm, it's more a matter of shrinking margins. Death by a thousand cuts, not by a biblical storm or plague. The need to borrow too much, changes in markets, higher fuel prices, aging farmers, aging equipment, rising interest on variable-rate loans. The distance between income and expenses shrinks and shrinks and then goes negative, and … then what?

Back when Brassard's grandfather bought the place, eastern small farms could still bring fresh milk to nearby markets at competitive prices. But the scale of farming in the Midwest changed. Flatland corn-belt dairy farms produced so much milk, so cheaply, that Vermont's rocky-soiled, steep-sloped farms couldn't compete. Federal supports provided a price floor, but the floor varied, leaving small farmers in perpetual suspense.

The year I started at Brassard's farm, milk prices had fallen to only about half what they'd been two years before. The newspapers said that between ten and twenty small Vermont dairies were going out of business each *month*. To put it in urban terms, I'd been making thirty-nine thousand a year teaching at Larson—how would I have fared if suddenly they paid me only nineteen thousand? I'd have to make my car payments and buy groceries with my credit card. And start running up interest, with no assurance I could ever get out from under.

You may have read the dire statistics in newspaper editorials. But it's very different when it concerns people you care for, a patch of ground you've worked. I had been there less than two years, and though I still planned to leave, I had grown loyal to the sweet breezes of Brassard's little valley and the people who made their living from the soil there.

This is, it really is, a love story. But the farm's misfortunes were part of learning and building that love, and love is certainly as much about learning and building as it is about passion, romance, or serendipity.

Jim Brassard was no old-timey farmer. He'd kept up with computers, had a slow but functional connection to the internet; he did his accounting using QuickBooks, and he kept track of every cow on Excel spreadsheets.

He read farming journals, toured agricultural websites, and went to farm shows to keep up.

But as he explained that afternoon, the accumulation of debt and fluctuations in milk and grain prices had made the finances precarious in recent years. And then the loss of Diz and the obligation to take on extra paid help—the balance had tipped into the red. Thanks to selling off my land and cash infusions from Earnest, Brassard had met a balloon payment on a loan, but he had not enough cash flow and no more borrowing power. Earnest told me that a single tire for the Harvester might cost eight hundred dollars; the failure of one of the summer's hay harvest cycles would require the purchase of about five thousand in hay from off the farm.

I was astonished—and flattered—that I was included in this deeply revealing meeting. To me, it meant that I had truly joined "we." I wasn't Diz—not by any stretch of the imagination capable of her workload or possessing her range of skills—but I was somehow "the woman" of the farm. I looked at the faces of these three men and loved their trust of me, and their need.

Is needing the same as loving? No. But to the extent you seek to love yourself and the life you've been given, you recognize that need and love, giving and receiving each, are closely linked. I had glimpsed one type of need—felt it still—during my divorce. But the kind of need Brassard's farm had is a different and more complex linkage. It is an honor to be so needed. Maybe Diz had been trying to explain this when she made me swear to "take care of these good men." Being Diz, she'd summed it up not as some philosophical abstraction, but in terms of *what one must do* to love. You take care of each other, you meet each other's need; you do whatever you must to see to their happiness and sufficiency.

Brassard's projections showed that the farm would go broke by midwinter. Then there would not be enough money to pay the vet or buy diesel fuel, and certainly not enough for the property taxes due in spring.

I just listened as the men considered the range of possible scenarios. Bankruptcy? Brassard bristled at the idea, and Will said it was unlikely to succeed unless a hefty portion of capital assets—cows, equipment, land—were sold to partially repay creditors. And then there'd be no source of income. And the bankruptcy process itself would incur substantial legal expenses.

Earnest said he had about twelve thousand in savings, but he didn't want to put it up unless there was some plan for a turnaround in the farm's finances. Which there wasn't.

When Will suggested that his father borrow some money from his widowed sister in Rutland, Brassard scowled. She didn't have enough to make a difference, and, again, what was the point without some longer-term change in the business plan?

Brassard could sell the whole place outright to another farmer who felt he could run it at profit, or more likely had the capital to convert it to a confined animal-feeding operation, use all the pastures for corn and buy a lot more feed, expand the parlor's milk throughput capacity. Brassard didn't like the idea, but if he got a decent price, he'd be tempted. Not that he had any buyers on the radar or could find one in time.

Another possibility was to sell just the cows and equipment, rent out his fields to another farmer, and live out his life as a marginally solvent old widower. I had gone with Brassard and Earnest to an auction of another farm's estate, where every cow and tractor and baler and tank and stepladder and bucket was paraded before a crowd. I'd found it deeply upsetting: the apologetic but eager bidders, the seller's tight, shame-filled face. Jim told me afterward that the proceeds were disappointing. The prices fetched were not great, because the equipment was outdated and because the bidding farmers needed good bargains as desperately as the old guy needed cash.

Or Brassard could sell off some more of his land, open land that would bring more bucks per acre, and a few houses would get built up around the old farmstead. I knew he was revolted by the thought. I shared the feeling. I had a completely self-interested stake in that possibility: I didn't want my land, my wild home, to overlook a housing development or trailer tract. In any case, it could be years before an offering for sale resulted in cash in the pocket, and the farm didn't have years.

The happiest but least possible was that Brassard could radically change the business plan and develop a solvent farm adapted to emerging market opportunities. Lynn and Theo, down the road, had found a niche for their organic produce and goat's-milk soap, and so far it was working. Something like that was by far the most palatable solution overall, but there was no capital to invest in such a change, and it would take years to create new farm products and build a market for them. And while we knew organic anything was a growing market, Will explained that "organic" was a strictly regulated term, requiring certification of soil chemistry and usage history. Given the fertilizers and herbicides applied on it over the years, none of Brassard's land would qualify.

After two hours, this discussion petered out due to the sheer depletion of morale. All we knew was that the farm had entered a glide path toward failure.

BRASSARD DROVE INTO town on errands. Earnest went off to repair something unspecified. Will and I headed to the barn to do the afternoon milking, with Theo's sister due any minute to help.

I took first shift on cow flow while Will worked in the operator's pit. We had settled the first four cows in their positions and Will had started along the line of udders when he asked gloomily, "So, did you pick up on any of the subtext in all that?"

"Subtext?"

"In what Dad said. In how he said it."

I thought back. "Well, *how* he said it ... he was pretty blue, obviously. I'd think it would involve some ... shame or embarrassment ... it's got to be a monumental disappointment to—"

"Disappointment, yeah."

I puzzled at the bitterness in his voice and looked at him for some kind of clue. "I guess I missed the subtext, Will. This is all a new universe for me."

He sighed, frowned, flipped his forelock off his forehead. "He couldn't look at me. Because he feels like I let him down. Back of his mind, I sort of caused this because I didn't, won't, come back and take over the farm. Three generations of farmers, and I'm the one blowing it off."

Now that he explained it, yes, I realized that Brassard had seemed to tighten up when he spoke to, or listened to, Will.

"But what difference would that have made anyway?"

"I'd have been free help for the last twenty years. And my wife and kids would have helped, too. And I could have skipped college and saved all that tuition money. Or—"

"Will!"

"What?"

"I think you're exaggerating this."

He was having a hard time attaching one of the claws, shaking its tangled outflow tubes in frustration. "We've had talks over the years. He blames me for some of it. Justified or not, it makes me feel like shit and pisses me off."

"What'd Diz think?"

"Huh! Diz thought I should get my ass back to work."

"But you *do* work! You're always working!"

"*This* work. Work the kind she did, work the *way* she worked." He got the claw straightened out and suctioned onto the teats. "Also I should have married someone who wasn't a *princess* who was 'too *special* to get her hands dirty.'"

I wondered just how much of a "princess" Will had married, and I was a little taken aback by the depth of his confession and vehemence. After a strained silence, he straightened, slapped himself on both cheeks, and grinned. "Okay. Sorry. You don't need to hear anybody's self-pitying rant. Really, that's not who I am. It's just a tense time."

A thump and clatter came from the outer door, and then Robin bumped through and called hello.

She bustled in, a robust twenty-two-year-old who resembled her brother: tall, big-boned, dark hair, blue eyes. "Sorry I'm late!" she said cheerfully. She smacked her hands together and got her earbuds ready for insertion, ready to boogie with the cow crowd. "So, what's new?"

"Not much," Will said. "Same old shit."

Chapter 30

I WAS DISAPPOINTED that no inspirational lightning had struck during our brainstorming. It saddened me that Will went through life feeling that he was letting three generations of Brassards down.

He seemed so downcast after milking that instead of heading up to my camp, I invited him to dinner at my chicken-coop apartment. I asked him if he ate quiche and he said, "Any chance I get," so I borrowed various ingredients from the house kitchen.

I had occasionally spent nights in the help dorm during the summer, but rarely, only when the weather was truly horrible or I was too exhausted to make the climb to my own place. When we came in, I realized that I was not used to seeing anyone in here, certainly not someone as tall as Will—the ceilings suddenly got lower. It had a tiny entry alcove where you stamp off mud or snow, hang up your coat, and leave your muck boots, then a little living room with a kitchen at one end, and a bedroom just big enough for a bunk bed and two bureaus. The bathroom had a shower but no tub, a stacked washer-dryer setup, and just enough room between fixtures to turn around.

The second thing I realized was that I had not made quiche in a couple of years, and though it's pretty foolproof, I suffered a sudden lack of confidence in my ability to not screw it up. Also, I had no wine to ease the transition from work mode to socializing, so we both felt a bit awkward at first. I put on some water for peppermint tea instead. Will sat at the counter that separated the kitchen from the living room proper, while I went about breaking eggs and chopping vegetables. For a moment the room was silent, just the noises of cooking and ticks and snaps of the oven heating up.

"I'd volunteer to help, but I'd just get in the way," he said. And it was true, the kitchen was not roomy—pull out a drawer or open a cabinet and it cut off movement.

After a while, he said, "Anyway, thanks for feeding me. I'm glad I don't have to eat with Dad and Earnest. After today's discussion. The suppressed atmosphere of accusation aside, it's depressing."

"Do you think Earnest feels the same way your father does?"

"I doubt it. He has a pretty forgiving outlook. People need to be able to make their own choices. He gets that."

"Do *you* get that?"

"My brain understands that my position is rationally defensible. My gut hasn't gotten the message."

I nodded, didn't come up with a follow-up conversational tack. Neither of us wanted to return to the subject of the farm's finances. I was fortunate that I had something to do with my hands when conversation stalled, but Will didn't.

"Do you have a DVD player?" he asked. "Or a laptop?"

"Laptop."

"Want to see one of my productions?"

"I'd love to!" I told him.

So he went out to get a DVD from his car. The teapot shrieked while he was gone, and I put teabags into two mugs and poured them full. When he returned I set up my laptop on the counter where we both could see it.

"How long is it?" I asked as he opened the DVD case.

"We don't have to watch the whole thing, I can just hit the high points—"

"I don't mean that! I'd like to see the whole thing, I just want to know if I should get the quiche in the oven first, and then we'd have enough time without interruption."

"Or we can play it while you're cooking. Or while we're eating."

This created a lot of choices, each loaded with social implication—how interested was I really, how closely should I watch it?—that we sort of stumbled over.

"How long is it?" I asked finally.

"Eighteen minutes."

"Perfect. I'll get this in the oven and then we can drink tea and watch without distraction." Will seemed pleased that I'd decided on the immediate agenda—he needed some script guidance here.

With the quiche in the oven, I sat on the other counter stool as he got the video going. The scene opened to show a bunch of cows with a fence in the foreground, a low steel-roofed cowshed in the background. Over that image, the title faded in—*Brucellosis: Is Your Herd at Risk?*—accompanied by some easy-listening-style bluegrass music. The credits slid by, showing that the film was produced by the Interstate Dairy Practices Council, and that Will was editor-in-chief and had a hand in scripting, videography, and editing. When the credits finished, the scene cut dramatically to a tiny calf lying on the ground, covered with blood and slime, a lumpy rope of umbilicus draped over its twitching body.

"Brucellosis," said the bland voice-over, "otherwise known as spontaneous abortion disease or Bang's disease, is a highly contagious bacterial infection that strikes not just cattle but can be transferred to humans who consume milk products." The dying miscarried calf dissolved to a dairy farmer, talking to the camera as his name appeared in a tag that unfurled at the bottom of the screen.

Will brought down the volume to explain that Vermont is pretty well brucellosis free, but the rising popularity of raw milk could create an increased brucellosis risk to consumers.

Watching the video, I learned that not only do cows abort, they have a hard time eliminating the infected placenta. The disease can be transferred from cow to bull and bull to cow. The close-ups of enlarged bull's testicles and brucellosis-affected placentas were no doubt of great practical value to farmers, but I was relieved when the focus moved from the farm to the laboratory, where bulk milk samples were being tested for brucellosis in sterile white-and-chrome environments.

I went to check the quiche, which didn't need checking. "It's a very professional job, Will. It must be challenging to keep all the pieces of a big project like this organized."

He brought down the volume again. "You know what's amazing? This thing is eighteen minutes long. We had to shoot about eighteen *hours* of footage to get those eighteen minutes."

I kept my eyes on the screen as I refilled the teakettle. "And as many hours in the editing studio, I'd bet."

He nodded. "I know the start is pretty grisly, but I wanted to go for a sort of shock effect, to let people know how serious it is. The middle is more scientific, but then I got very graphic again at the end to remind the viewer."

"Sounds like a good approach. Drive the point home at the end."

I worked at minor food preparation tasks; Will sipped from his tea, watched the screen, then looked over at me. "You're handling this very gracefully, Ann."

"What?"

"Brucellosis videos before dinner." He reached over, ejected the disk, and waved it in the air. "Not great first-date material, is it?" He smiled ruefully, then appeared caught out. His ears reddened. Neither of us had acknowledged this as a "date"—the thought hadn't even occurred to me.

"I just grabbed it out of the car," Will said. "I wasn't thinking."

"Will, it's fine. I'm glad to know more about what you do."

"The only other one I have with me is about mastitis. Infection of the udder, clogging of the teats. More relevant to this place. Really hits some Vermont farms."

"Please leave me a copy," I told him. "I really should learn about this stuff."

He laughed and shook his head. "There you go with the being gracious thing again."

"I'll just take that as a compliment and leave it there."

Then I told him it was time for him to set the counter for dinner, that I was going to make a salad, and that while I did I'd love it if he told me more about his family, meaning his wife and daughter. Again he seemed glad to have an agenda established.

The quiche turned out better than I'd expected. We did talk about various topics, mainly about Will's daughter, whom he adored. He didn't mention his wife and I didn't tell of my catastrophes in Boston. Conversation stalled at around eight o'clock; I intuited that Will wanted to say something that stuck in his throat. Eventually he gave up on it and decided he'd turn in early. We told each other thanks and goodnight.

I don't know what he'd been unable to say—a request for another "date," a question about my marital situation? As a social interlude, date or otherwise, it had been a little awkward. Still, I liked Will's innocence, his lack of finesse in hanging out with me, his lack of premeditation in showing me the video. Earnest was right: He was not a great self-promoter around a woman. But he struck me as honest, and I appreciated that.

Chapter 31

Sept. 7

Brassard figures the only way out is to auction off half the cows and then sell off some of his fields, fifty acres subdivided into four lots. Earnest, even though he's legally co-owner, defers to Brassard on these matters because ultimately it's Jim's family's heritage. And anyway, he can't offer a better course. Will can only shrug.

The parcel he's chosen to sell is right on the road—flat, pretty, well-drained acres at the lower end of his fields, so if he can find some buyers who want to live this far out, it'll bring in a decent price. Having made the decision, this big, quiet, gentle man now goes about his days in a kind of mourning. It doesn't help that this change comes so hard on the heels of losing his wife. He's a man going through the motions, a man surrendering his past. In a rare moment of confession, sitting at the kitchen table with a cup of coffee growing cold at his elbow, he told me it's hard to accept that the skills he'd acquired through a lifetime, all that devotion and hard work, mattered not one jot.

At the same time, he says, he's had it, he's had enough of this. "It probably is time to cut back or call it quits, with these damn knees and knuckles the way they are."

So, another Vermont dairy farm down the drain. Four houses popping up on another rural road. Brassard will see them from his living room window. I might see them from some spots on my land, at least when the leaves fall.

But what's the matter with that? Four families will have nice homes. They'll plant little trees along their driveways and do that cute thing with circles of redwood bark around their shrubs. There'll be more traffic on our road, maybe even school buses, I'll probably hear their lawn mowers from my little patch of wilderness. But that's modern times, right?

I'm ashamed to write this. As a "flatlander" myself, I have no right to criticize, no right to mourn the passing of the old ruggedness and honesty and ragged edges of the working landscape. I've spent so little time in it, have devoted too little of myself to it. I haven't earned the right to mourn.

But I do mourn. I have been nurtured by this, strengthened by it. I've taken solace in the fact that there are still tranquil corners of America where people make do even if roads are muddy or cell phones don't work. I've just started to get my feet under me and I know living this way is the reason. I can't help but see the pending loss as another verification that my need to flee my prior life and "get away from it all" is doomed and pointless. There is no "away."

Chapter 32

A LOT CAN change in a few days. The lesson applies to despairing predictions just as much as to counting your chickens before they hatch.

About a week after that business meeting, I got an outlandish message from Cat on my voice mail. She'd left it the day before, but I didn't hear it until I drove to town on errands and had both the time and the cell reception to get messages. She said she'd met a man, and she really wanted to, *had to*, bring him up to meet me ASAP, *this can absolutely not wait another minute.* The message went on with an inordinate number of superlatives. Of course, she's always been irrepressible, her enthusiasms infectious and impossible to argue with, but after twenty-some years you learn to gauge a friend's degrees of urgency. *This is the real deal, Ann, this is huge, you know I'm not into premature and excessive enthusiasms.* That was not entirely true, but something in her voice—an unfamiliar, lower note of earnestness, a sort of husky breathlessness—gave me pause.

She also said she wanted to come up Tuesday, the very day I got the message. It was not a good day for visitors. I had a rain cloud over my head, the farm was melancholy, and there was so much work to do. Going on mid-September, the last hay had to be got up, we had a bull coming to impregnate the next round of cows and some new heifers and still had some preparations to see to. Also, Brassard had asked Earnest and me to come to another business discussion that night, and it could only mean more bad news. Much as I wanted to meet Cat's new guy, to indulge her as a good friend should, I had to tell her this wasn't the best time to come.

I was sitting in Brassard's truck, top of the ridge road, when I called her back. She was peeved that I was calling a day late, so I told her that it had been a very busy period and this was my first chance to get up the hill, in fact this wasn't the best time for …

She swept aside everything I said, went on again about this guy, she was in heaven, I had to meet him and he was handsome as bejeesus, smart as hell, really intriguing past, had the requisite ironic attitude about the cosmos. Et cetera.

That much I could understand, but then she threw me for a loop. She lowered her voice conspiratorially and said something like, "In fact, it occurred to me, I mean I know this sounds strange, but maybe he's someone, I mean, better for *you* than for me. I can see it, Ann. I can really see it."

I was gobsmacked, bewildered. So the whole "I met the right man" thing was a clumsy ruse to connect this guy with Cat's sad, lonely, out-of-touch friend? Next came anger at the condescension implicit—that I was so badly in need of matchmaking.

She was going on again, so I shouted to interrupt her: "Cat!"

"What?"

"This sounds all wrong. What's really going on?"

"*Trust me on this!*" she hissed. It was a dodge, but she had got her back up, too, angry at me, and again I heard that husky tone in her voice.

"You're pissing me off," I told her. "First, it's not a good time to have people coming. I'm depressed, we've got to get a bunch of cows impregnated, there's a lot of stuff that has to happen when it has to happen. I don't have time for fun and games. Second, I don't need or want anybody's fucking help with romance. Are you out of your *mind*? And right now I have to get back to work. Do not come now, are you hearing me? And don't bring anybody up to see me. I'm not available."

She made a sort of growl. "Tough luck, toots. We're already on our way. At a gas station in White River and he's filling up the tank even as we speak. What's that—hour and a half, two hours out? So get your ass prettied up and give me the benefit of the doubt. For this guy, you are available, bet on it."

She cut off the call before I could respond. I called back but she didn't pick up.

I drove Brassard's truck aggressively as I went about my errands. I parked it with a jolt and threw gravel when I pulled out. Big truck, double cab and double wheels in back, I'd learned to wrangle it like an old hand. Lumberyard, gas, grocery store, pharmacy for Brassard's blood thinners. *Get your ass prettied up—you are available, bet on it.* It was beyond condescending. A creepy, clumsy attempt at a setup. I was angry at myself for telling her too much about my inner state over the past two years, furious with her for whatever this was. I bashed my way back over the ruts that corrugated our back roads.

Brassard was far out across the lower fields, flinging manure; Lynn had gone back to her place. But I found Earnest on a ladder in the main shed, up installing a new ventilator fan where one of the old ones had gone defunct. It was a job that would ordinarily require at least two people—the fans are about five feet in diameter and heavily built. I wasn't there to see him bring it up the ladder, but I didn't doubt he'd carried the thing with one hand, like a lady's purse.

I gave him the parts he'd ordered, then sat on a stanchion to watch him as he continued to work.

I tried to calm myself. With the cows still outside for another few weeks, the floors pressure-washed clean, it was a spacious and pleasant space. The open doors and side windows were open so daylight flooded in and a breeze came through, carrying the woody scent of a billion leaves just starting to turn. Really, a beautiful day and a tranquil place, comfortably upwind of the manure spreading. And there I sat, feeling ill with anger and resentment.

Always happiest in high places, Earnest whistled as he clanked away. I didn't say anything for a few minutes, long enough that he was startled when he turned his head and saw me still there.

"So, how's your day going?" he ventured cautiously.

"There's a stupid, shitting, stupid thing about to happen, and it's making me sick. I'm embarrassed that you or Lynn or Brassard have to witness it."

Startled, he dropped a socket wrench. "I can hardly wait," he said.

I retrieved the wrench and met him halfway up the ladder to hand it to him.

Back on the stanchion, I told him the situation: fucking Cat, conceiving of this fucking crude subterfuge to bring some Romeo all the way from fucking Boston.

Earnest, balanced easily half on the ladder and half on a horizontal beam, drove in a screw with his impact driver, *bra-a-a-a-a-t*, drove another, setting the brackets I'd brought him. He examined the result, experimentally spun the big blades by hand, lifted and dropped the louvers. A few more rattles and clanks, another *bra-a-a-a-a-t*, and he climbed down. He came over to me, wiping his hands on the bib of his overalls. Back on earth, standing in front of me wearing his tool belt laden with drill driver, wrenches, pliers, coils of electrical wire, he was a broad and firmly planted presence.

"You guys ever done this before? I mean, set things up—"

"Yeah. In fucking seventh grade."

He nodded thoughtfully, then leaned back against the ladder. If I had expected some pearl of wisdom, I was mistaken. "You know," he said, "I don't think I've ever heard you say 'fucking' so often in such a short period of time."

I was able to smile slightly.

But then he went on to say that maybe I should give Cat the benefit of the doubt, maybe there was something here. I couldn't tell whether he meant it or was baiting me, being ironic, but if it was a joke his timing was bad. When I interrupted to tell him to fuck off, he just made a check mark in the air, still counting each "fuck" and "fucking."

I remembered the groceries sitting in the truck. We left the shed and carried things inside and put them away. Earnest made a sandwich for himself. I tried to drink a cup of coffee, but it struck me as bitter and I put it aside. My stomach was full of bile.

The September sun slanted through the windows and cast a band of brightness across the dining room table. Earnest was clearly upset by my distress. "We could turn the tables on Cat," he suggested. "Call Lynn, go get Jim, four of us stand in a row, scowling, arms crossed. Make him run the gauntlet of our disapproval. Intimidate this little bastard—who must have a lot of brass himself if he's letting Cat do him the same way she's doing you."

"He may not know the whole plan. Probably doesn't. Long way to drive for a blind date."

He nodded, chewed thoughtfully. I checked my watch.

We improvised schemes to discourage Cat and this guy and after a while got pretty absurd, which helped considerably. Earnest suggested that if Brassard parked the manure spreader in the driveway and had it accidentally start spraying, that would put a crimp in the guy's style. We laughed and my hackles went down a few degrees.

Another weak brainstorm struck me: "Earnest. Could you be my boyfriend for, like, ten minutes?"

He tipped his head, puzzled, biting his upper lip as if waiting for the punchline.

"I mean, when they come, you and I go out there holding hands or otherwise being, you know, 'demonstrative' in a way that says—"

The humor left this face, and he said, "That would require quite a stretch of their imaginations, Pilgrim—a guy almost twenty years older? Just meet this twit, pretend you never heard Cat's pitch. My two cents, there's absolutely no reason for you to bullshit anybody, no reason to play any game at all. Just tell them to go to hell if that's how you feel."

That last cheered me. Of course he was right. We sat for a bit, then went out to do some raking and cleaning up of the porch and lawns, waiting for Jim to get back and the bull and my unwelcome guests to arrive. Making it look good in honor of Diz. I pictured her doing this chore, brusque and ruthless, keeping things in shipshape, and missed her. She would have had some advice to stiffen my spine! Or she would have given Cat and her little gigolo a glimpse of her hard side, and they'd be gone in minutes.

We worked silently, thoughtfully, under Bob the dog's amiable supervision. Earnest seemed to have run out of ways to lighten the mood. The afternoon milking was still a couple of hours away.

I can't really describe what I felt for that last half hour. Initially, all I'd felt was outrage at Cat, resentment, disappointment in her. You don't do this kind of thing. Even if, especially if, you know someone is lonely and living so far off the beaten path. I questioned the state of our relationship: Maybe we were moving beyond each other; maybe this friendship had run its course. But another voice told me this was so off the charts that I should consider the remote possibility that Cat was onto something. Hadn't I learned that love comes at you from strange angles? Wasn't this better than internet dating?

Strangely, to my own irritation, I did in fact feel an uptick of excitement. A premonition of something imminent—a revving of the engine of curiosity, anyway. It grew as the hour passed, and it was not entirely unfamiliar: I realized I had vaguely felt something like this for months, a growing awareness of some change approaching. It starts with the faintest tickle at the back of your mind, the base of your brain, then swells into a microscopic electric thrill or tension in your chest and shoulders. I have to believe that future events send signals backward in time to us, and we can sometimes feel them coming with some sixth or seventh sense for which we have no name.

But of course I didn't know what form it would take. And thinking about romantic love just then, I also felt a twist or turn, a knot of confusion that I probed and couldn't recognize. Something about the whole equation had changed; an integer had shifted in the calculus of love, needing, loneliness, desire. I was truly more on my feet, more balanced despite my sometimes intolerable longing. There was certainly a lonely hollow place in the center of my being, but its shape had changed. If I had arrived at my land and the farm as a box of disconnected Lego pieces, now it seemed that a few of them had connected, locked together here and there amid the jumble.

I decided I'd be reasonably gracious, but businesslike. I was in the middle of my working day. Brassard's friend Jack Pelletier would be delivering a bull tomorrow, a rare event, and we needed to isolate the six cows and heifers that the bull would tend to, and to set out feed and water for the visitor. And I had milking and cleanup to do, and I did have to join—I liked joining—the ritual of cooking dinner with the men. Cat and this guy would have to entertain themselves however they could while I did what needed doing.

My eyes were drawn to a flash of reflected sunlight as a car crested the hill, and instinctively I knew it was them. I groaned and wished this whole thing were over with and I could just have a normal evening: finish the day's work, then climb gratefully up the hill to my own land and my tent. The veeries hadn't yet left, and I wanted nothing more than to listen to their down-spiraling *whirly-whirly-whirly-whirly* calling all to tranquility as I stared into my campfire, absorbing the surcease that only being alone and sufficient in the evening woods can provide. I wondered whether Cat thought they were going to spend the night and where they expected to spend it.

Cat's beat-up BMW trundled down the road with a white van trailing some distance behind it. Cat put on her blinker, turned into the driveway, and to my surprise the white van followed and pulled up beside it. My puzzlement grew as I approached the BMW and couldn't see anyone in the passenger seat. Then Cat exploded out of her door and practically leaped over her own hood, smiling hugely, crazily. I had planned to give her a dead-eye gaze, but things were moving too fast and too strangely.

"This is so fun!" she said. "This is TOO good! God help me, I'm gonna have a heart attack!" She turned back to the van and yelled "Get the hell out here, for Chrissakes! She won't bite!"

The van's parking brake ratcheted, the silhouette of the driver moved inside. The driver's door opened, and then around the front of the van stepped a guy with buzz-cut brown hair and that kind of facial stubble that looks so careless but that I always figure must take a lot of effort to maintain. He walked reluctantly, his face paradoxical with mixed emotions—a man guarded yet undone, unprotected.

My heart did a flip, literally seemed to tumble upside down. Yes, it was destiny and it was love at first sight, overwhelming. Earnest came up beside me and I fell against him slightly.

Then I was in my brother's arms, holding him. Locking Erik against me, swearing I'd never ever *ever* let him go. "You little shit bastard bastard bastard!" I said. Cat burst into tears, and it ignited Erik and me. We cried and rocked as poor Earnest stood there looking baffled.

Chapter 33

We went in and had coffee and all talked stiffly and safely for a bit. Then Cat and Earnest sort of went away on some pretext, and in the absence of observers, Erik and I eyed each other cautiously. He was shorter than I remembered, leaner in the face, slim but clearly fit—in the warmth of the house, he rolled his shirtsleeves off his forearms and they were sinewy and branched with veins. Tattoos—a line of Chinese characters, bruise blue—ran up one arm.

That moment of silence and observation was the default response for both of us, in itself a family resemblance. We didn't try to fill the gap with inanities. His eyes moved over me, up and down, and then he looked around at the kitchen and the view out the windows as if they were part of me. His eyes, his mind, just as I remembered, seemed quicker than mine.

"You look … terrific. I mean, I always knew you were pretty, but I didn't realize …" He gestured at the whole of me. "I mean, *beautiful.*"

I was wearing a shapeless oversize Carhartt canvas jacket, jeans, and mucking-out boots, and I'd tied my hair back severely to keep it out of my face.

"Where were you?"

"I went to some strange places. I'll tell you all about it, but not right now, okay? I gotta just … try to catch my breath."

I was surfing alternating waves of joy and resentment. "Did you know you were hurting me?"

"I don't know about that, but I thought about you an awful lot."

Silence. I wanted to cry again. I had so much to tell, so much to ask, that it all dammed up and jammed up. I managed: "You here for a while?"

"As long as I'm welcome."

"I ask because we've got a bull coming tomorrow and there's still prep to do for that. And then I've got cows to milk. And other stuff that can't wait. You'll have to come help out or sit here with Cat or something. That is, if you're not leaving in the next ten minutes." I was trying to be hurtful.

He dipped his chin. "Sure. But I have a question for you. Personal question."

"What's that?"

"Are you happy here?"

I actually thought about it for a few seconds. "Sometimes."

"So … How many options, life options, do you have right now?"

"What? Oh, Christ! I know what Cat thinks about—"

"No, I mean it. Nothing to do with Cat. I really want to know. Me."

I thought of a lot of things to say, mostly ways to defend myself or say it was only temporary or turn it around in a way that would punish him. But I said, "What you see amounts to the sum total. For a variety of reasons."

"I ask because I'm pretty low on options myself. Lots of … reasons at my end, too."

I was moved. He was approaching intimacy by telling me we had to take each other's existential temperature first, no beating around the bush. I remembered now that his quick intuition and candor had often pissed off his insecure teenage sister and had not improved his popularity at school, except among the smart-ass crowd.

"Yeah, I've got exactly one iron in the fire." Then he added, brightening, "But it's a good one!"

Before I could answer, the phone rang. It was Jack Pelletier, Brassard's friend and the owner of the bull, calling to remind us he was coming by with Maximillian in the morning. We joked about how the ladies would have to hold out for another day. Then Will's car pulled up in the driveway, and there came Brassard driving the Deere around the far side of the barn, returning from the joys of manure spreading. A moment later, Will stamped his feet in the mudroom. Then I saw the Agri-Mark truck turning into the bulk tank access drive on the far side of the old barn.

"I gotta go see to the Agri-Mark guy," I told Erik. "The milk pickup people. This is how it goes around here."

Chapter 34

Sept. 16

Erik has what is for me a disconcerting way of meeting people. He smiles, shakes hands, says the requisite polite and blandly positive things, but then tips his head back and watches, still holding a small smile, eyes ever so slightly lidded. It's not supercilious, not at all, not judgmental, but you can almost hear his synapses sizzling. He's just observing. He's letting the other person show their hand first. It only lasts a couple of seconds, and I doubt anyone notices.

He did that momentary assessment when I introduced him to Earnest, standing in the front yard: Earnest who was radiant with pleasure, truly happy to discover who this unknown visitor turned out to be, shaking Erik's hand and squeezing his shoulder hard.

Erik did it again when Will got back, as Will more reservedly shook hands, remarked on our family resemblance, and told him how much the Brassards had enjoyed having his sister "join the team here." When Will asked, the way one does, what Erik did for a living, Erik chuckled or coughed and said, "It's kind of an overused answer, but I guess I've gotta say 'a little of this and a little of that.'" Will was courteous enough not to push him for more. I have the same question.

Brassard had towed the manure spreader around to the far side of the barn, to its home near the other really stinky things, and when he joined us and learned who Erik was, his eyebrows popped above the rim of his glasses. A weather-front odor of manure had arrived with him, so he mimed shaking hands, made a small grin, and left us, saying he had something of a hankering for a shower and a change of clothes.

I took Erik on a tour of the farm, with Earnest and Cat tagging along tactfully well behind us: The dog's name is Bob. Here's the old barn, here's the milking parlor, here's the skid-steer, that over there's the manure stack, and that's the manure spreader, I had a hard time back in Boston, I really felt I had destroyed my whole life, this is my special buddy the old Ford, that's Brassard's Deere, there's the tedder and that's the roll baler and that's the feed mixer thing, it got so I missed you and worried about you so much that I learned to cut you out of my thoughts, do you even get that? This big shed is where the cows will live come cold weather, here are the workers' quarters where I live in winter. Off that way, up to the left, that's all pasture, Brassard's land ends on the ridge above it, in the woods past the cows. Over this way, downhill over the curve of the slope, is where the hay and cornfields are. On the other side of the road, that long strip of open land, up to the base of the hill, that's just scrub, not used for anything.

But above that, all those woods there, that's my land.

Erik and Cat spent the night with me up here. Brassard invited them to dinner, said they could stay in the house or the help dorm, but Erik said he wanted to see my place and get a taste of my lifestyle. Will had already started preparing a huge pan of shepherd's pie, but I asked Earnest if he wanted to join us up on the hill for some canned stew by firelight, and to my surprise he said yes. So after milking and equipment cleaning, the four of us headed up.

Orange-pink sunset on leaves just turning to warm hues: In that rare rake of light, the woods glowed like a jack-o'-lantern's eyes when a candle's lit inside. Cat learned her lesson during her first visit and wore hiking boots and down parka, Erik seemed used to hardy living and brought up a couple of army surplus mummy bags. At intervals, he stopped to look at the farm and up and down the valley, from different vantages, stroking his stubbled cheeks, nodding appraisingly and appreciatively. Earnest had stolen a few edibles from the house.

Marching up the hill, I told Cat, "I still plan to kill you. Just not tonight."

Dead serious, she shot back, "I had to keep you in the dark. No way, no imaginable possible way, was I going to miss being there at that moment."

Erik told us he'd driven across from Oregon in four days, sleeping at night on the ground or across the seats at highway rest stops. He would have called me but had no way of finding me—why didn't I keep a Facebook page? So he called Cat, who still has a landline and an actual listed number. Cat said, "I was eating spaghetti when I got his call and I nearly choked to death. I had to give myself the Heimlich maneuver." They'd caravanned up in two cars because Cat had to get back to her job and Erik wanted to spend more time with me, if that was all right.

It's odd, when you bring a stranger to a place familiar to you, you see it differently, as if through their unbiased eyes. When I came into my camp it looked orderly and beautiful and, strangely, "sensible," a not-entirely-unreasonable abode. The sun had dropped by the time we got there, leaving just the tops of the trees still radiant, casting now a pinker light through the darkening lower forest—illumination like a magical theater set. We got the lanterns going and I showed Erik where I keep the outhouse. Cat gathered twigs and oversaw the opening of four cans of stew, Earnest and I built and lit and encouraged the fire. Back among us, Erik showed quick reflexes and nervous energy, not just picking up my ladle but flipping it up spinning and deftly catching the handle, rattling a quick drumroll with a couple of my metal cups. He carries a harmonica in his back pocket and though he didn't play it, he took it out and fiddled with it, balancing it on the tip of one finger. The woods had gone dark by the time the stew pot steamed. Earnest shined a flashlight into the grocery bag he'd brought and discovered a loaf of bread, a bunch of carrots, and a bag of corn chips.

We sat around the fire, eating stew off plastic plates, drinking peppermint tea out of metal cups with rims that burned our lips. Cold pressed against our backs while our faces singed. Three faces dear to me, bright-lit by the fire, framed by flickering columns of trees that shaded dimmer and dimmer and finally faded into the curtain of full dark: my heart truly overflowed.

Chapter 35

BUT IT WASN'T long before discord joined us in the campfire circle. Erik's mysteries were not so easily plumbed. He didn't appear reserved—he wisecracked and shared anecdotes, gestured energetically, took off his billed cap and flipped it with vaudevillian flair back onto his head. But he deflected a lot, somehow turning questions about himself into another interesting but unrelated narrative. Between eating and joking, I saw Earnest shoot glances his way. Cat, only a little reprimand in her voice, asked Erik how long he was going to keep us in suspense before telling us what he'd been doing for seven fucking years.

When Erik stalled on that, Earnest reversed the question: "So what's next? What's the plan? Stick around for a while or …?"

"Actually, there's a project I've been thinking about for quite a while. And I really needed to get away from the West Coast and I *really* wanted to see my sister, so here I am." He gestured around the woods and down toward the farm. "It's pretty serendipitous—I mean, that you've gone rural, turned farmer, Annie. Think there's any chance Mr.

Brassard could find room for me here?"

I shrugged. "The farm's not in a great position to take anyone on. But you can ask Jim."

"Any experience at farmwork?" Earnest asked.

Erik laughed hard enough that he slopped scalding tea onto his jeans. "Me? *Extensive* experience in agriculture. Or rather horticulture."

"Like what?" Earnest said. He sat forward, put his elbows on his knees, rolling his metal teacup between his palms.

To me, his posture signaled heightened interest, but apparently Erik saw it as suspicious or aggressive. Erik's body went very still. "Like it can wait for another time." It was an in-your-face, up-yours comeback.

"Got me interested now," Earnest said, absolutely without expression. "And it's your business because …?"

"Erik? Erik! This is *Earnest,* my *friend*! What … I don't get …" I tapered off, unable to fathom what I was seeing, hearing.

My brother winced, drew a hand across his face as if wiping away something blurring his vision, or rubbing sleep out of his eyes. "Jesus. Sorry! Rusty social skills." He shook his head as if to wake himself up. "Also, I'm tired as shit. Three thousand miles, driving's fried my brain."

"No sweat," Earnest told him, still watchful. "I know that one."

I heard Cat exhale. She had held her breath for the past minute. The men looked frankly at each other, taking each other's measure, but the swell of tension that had risen so quickly now started to slip on by. Strangely, I saw a common feature in their faces, not in bones or color but in the lines and lights of character. I felt as if each recognized it in the other.

"I've got a regular *saga*," Erik said wearily. "But I figured I'd start with my sister before I lay it on anybody else."

"I can understand that." Earnest tossed a glance my way. He dipped his head minutely as if to reassure me, *I'm okay with him, Pilgrim*, and eased back. He drank off his near-boiling tea, oblivious to the burn. We listened to the fire crackle for a time. A few early-falling leaves fluttered down, like bats descending from darkness into our sphere of light.

"Anyway," Earnest said, "this's past my bedtime. I'm gonna turn in."

He stood, yawned, brushed off his pants. "Anyway, yeah, you guys have some catching up to do. So I bid you goodnight, adieu, and hasta la vista. Ann, got some entertainment scheduled for the morning, remember." Then his bearlike form faded away from the campfire's light and disappeared downhill.

Cat and I sat there, unsure where to take it.

"You know," Erik said, gesturing after Earnest with his cup, "I like that guy. He's got a keen eye, that's for sure."

"For what?" I asked.

He shrugged. "For losers."

ERIK WANTED TO sleep in the woods, said he could use it, and anyway three would have crowded the tent. He gathered his mummy bags and headed off into the shadows uphill. I heard him moving about at some distance, scuffing, probably seeking enough flat ground without rocks to make a nest for himself.

Cat and I washed the dishes in my aluminum sink, using warm water from the teakettle, then dowsed the fire and took to the tent. Exhaling steam, we settled into our bedding. Cat wore an Incan-knit hat pulled well down over her face, the earflaps' braided strings tied beneath her chin. I blew out the last candles and shut off the Coleman lantern.

"That was … weird," Cat whispered. "What the …?"

"Why's he so closemouthed? What's he told you?"

"Not a lot. Nothing, actually. We've spent almost no time together. When we did talk, we mainly talked about you."

"Oh, yeah? What'd you tell him?"

"Huh! I was as cagey as he is. Figured you should tell him whatever it is you think he needs to know. I wasn't going to tell him that you … ran into some hard weather and all that. Figured you should put your own spin on it."

We were quiet for a while. A slight breeze had uncoiled from the sleeping woods, bringing down a loose scatter of leaves that landed invisibly on the tent fly with soft dry thuds and then slid rasping down the nylon.

"I guess he strikes me as someone who's had some hard weather, too," I said.

"For sure."

"Back when I used to call him, out in California? He was hanging out with a druggie crowd. He sounded like a stoner. Wasn't surprising. Remember, he got busted in high school?"

"I remember a very tense period at your house and a mandatory haircut for Erik."

"It made me sad, because he's too smart to waste himself that way. He never mentioned having a job. I kind of figured he'd gotten into the marijuana business. He sort of hinted at it sometimes. He was up in Northern California. That's where a lot of it's grown, isn't it?"

"That was his 'agricultural' experience?"

"An inside joke, I guess. An insider's joke."

"Thus the defensive bristle."

I didn't know. I was getting drowsy, but Cat seemed to have a hard time getting comfortable, shifting and rearranging and rolling over and resettling her pillow.

Then her voice, tiny in the darkness: "His van? It's really packed. I mean, I haven't gone inside it, just stood in the door, but it's packed to the ceiling. All these boxes, taped, sealed tight." She paused and added reluctantly, "It … has a plant smell. Earthy, sort of sharp plant smell. Sorta like … pot."

My heart plummeted. But I couldn't bear to ask anything more. And I had to be up at four to milk the cows.

Chapter 36

BUT OF COURSE, I didn't sleep after that. In my jagged imaginings, I could only assume that Erik had come across country with a van felony-full of dope that he planned to sell on the East Coast or, for all I knew, here in Vermont. And that the van was now sitting on Brassard's property, and that Erik was *extremely* touchy about it all. I replayed our campfire conversation and saw hints of danger throughout. *I needed to get away from the West Coast.* What—needed a change of pace, a new "headspace"? Or that the law was after him? Or he'd gotten into trouble with some other California drug suppliers? Needed to escape child-support payments? The creaky hyper hamster wheel of my mind spun all night.

At some point, I heard an irritating noise that was, of course, my little alarm clock: four a.m. Whatever else, the cows had to get milked. Cat didn't wake. I dressed and stumped downhill, exhausted, and crossed the road just as Will came out of the house to take his shift with me. The motion lights switched on in the farmyard. Erik's van had no side windows, but I shaded my eyes to peek through the windshield, and back in the dim interior I could just make out what Cat had described: a wall of stacked boxes, all the same size, floor to ceiling. I fled to the milking parlor.

Once you've milked for a couple of years, you become sort of a machine yourself. You could do it in your sleep. Diz probably could have done it after she was dead. But the mix of extreme fatigue and tension and relentless routine is not a good one.

Will noticed. Kindly, he asked if I wanted to skip it this morning, he'd ring Lynn or wake Earnest up. I told him I was fine for it.

"You must be over the moon to see your brother!" he said as he settled a new group of cows into their stations and I began to move down the row of bony angular haunches and swollen bags.

"I sure am!" I said heartily. I didn't want to go further down that track, so I turned it around and asked him about his own long-estranged half sister: How would he feel if he saw her again?

"I can't imagine what it would be like. Also can't imagine it happening."

"Not even now that Diz is gone?"

"I get Christmas cards from her. With the folded news update inside? Her job, kids, husband, vacations, son's team wins soccer tournament, Herb's knee surgery. I drop her a note about once a year. I don't know anything about her problem with Mom, but I don't think it's about anger and resentment anymore. Now it's, what, just a matter of distance. Time and distance. Life moved on. Jane's got her twenty-four seven all lined up, more than enough to keep busy, and it's working for her. Me, half brother, I'm way out, barely on the radar."

"But you grew up together! Don't you ever miss her?"

"Huh. Well. Sometimes. But in the female companionship department, my sister isn't my problem. My wife is my problem."

"The absence thereof, or the presence thereof?"

He laughed. "I love that! Gotta remember that one!"

Earnest had kept me up to date on Will's divorce and custody issues. That he lived at the farm now had less to do with its moment of need than with his having to move out of his place in Rutland. He claimed that the divorce was by mutual agreement, but he often seemed sad in a chin-up, quietly burdened way.

Another few minutes passed as Will let out another four cows and positioned four more. "Absence, presence," he said. "Both. More gone than you'd like, but still there more than you'd like."

"Both, that's exactly right." Wipe and strip, then confession: "I had a tough one myself."

He smiled gratefully from over the backs of the cows.

I DIDN'T HAVE time to wonder where Erik or Cat was, because just as we emerged from the barn, Brassard's old friend Jack Pelletier turned into the drive. His sparkling-clean white truck pulled a covered white trailer with side windows revealing something huge and black and white moving inside. We called Bob inside and shut the door so he wouldn't get underfoot.

Pelletier's bulls were regionally renowned for their quality. Like Brassard, he had taken over the business from his father, who had provided bulls to Jim's father—an intergenerational bond. I had met him at Diz's memorial event: French Canadian ancestry, black haired, a small wiry frame that he carried with an outsize swagger. The two men shook hands, then turned to face the paddock fence as they discussed logistics.

When I first came to my land and heard farmers mention "AI," I assumed it had to do with artificial intelligence, and rather than reveal my ignorance I'd spent hours trying to relate the concept to the context of overheard discussion. Actually, as I learned when I began working on the farm, "AI" means artificial insemination, which most dairy farmers use to impregnate their cows.

Observing the process for the first time further helped dispel the mythical image of the small farm that lingered in my mind. Surely, I had thought, there was a dashing bull out there in the pasture, proud and fearsome but gentlemanly. He'd be a Clark Gable of cattle, adored by his paramours, his gallantry adding a touch of romance to their otherwise boring lives.

But there was no such bull: Brassard had used AI since the 1990s. At intervals throughout the year, he bought cryogenically frozen bull semen in long, thin ampules called "straws." When a cow went into heat, he—in the past, with Diz assisting—reached his whole arm into her intestinal tract, where he could then use his fingers to guide the long wand of a semen "gun" that he inserted into the birth canal. When he could feel that the wand had gotten all the way to the uterus, he pushed the plunger on the gun and emptied the straw. If all went well, the cow gave birth nine months later.

I hadn't yet donned the armpit-length rubber glove and done the internal groping and finessing. The task held no appeal for me. But I had learned to thaw the straws, load the gun, and otherwise assist.

AI allowed Brassard to keep his herd's calving cycles at optimum, select only the best sires, and introduce genetic diversity into the herd, making sure that he didn't mate heifers with their own fathers. Like most Vermont farmers, he kept a vat of liquid nitrogen, about the size of a wastebasket, containing a stash of straws to be used as needed.

But farmers didn't use the practice when he was growing up, and his father had always kept a bull or two to service the herd. In fact, Brassard was still dubious about AI. One reason was that when a cow has a date with a bull, she's 95 percent certain to get with calf; AI was only half as reliable. Brassard and Pelletier had in common the belief—which Will insisted was totally unfounded—that natural insemination produced healthier calves that ultimately delivered more milk.

Also, Pelletier liked to do "pen testing" of his young bulls with Brassard's cows and heifers. One of the key criteria for a bull's value was his sex drive—how motivated was he, what was his "service capacity"? A bull demonstrating good libido could be counted on to produce more sperm and thus more money. Pelletier was proud of his animals, always eager to show off his latest breeding masterpiece; Brassard, this time with three heifers and three mature cows ready to go, was grateful for the favor.

The pending arrival of the bull had required some preparation. Over the years, Brassard had kept the farm's old breeding pen—a strongly built board-fenced paddock set into the near pasture—in pretty good shape.

Still, the morning before Cat's telephone call, Will and I had gone out to check the condition of the fence. We hammered in every nail head, checked every board and replaced older ones with fresh lumber, tested gate hinges and latches. As we worked, Will told me horror stories about bulls trampling and goring farmers, injuring cows so badly they had to be put down, killing farm dogs, crashing through fences. They were preposterously strong and had volatile tempers—another reason farmers preferred AI.

By the time we finished battening down the pen, my imagination had conjured a new and unsettling image of bulls. They weren't Ferdinand, the callow youngster sniffing flowers under the cork tree, nor chivalrous bovine Clark Gables. They were monsters, demons so savage they were effectively carnivores. Max's imminent arrival added to my anxiety about Erik and his van: I envisioned the bull coming to the farm strapped and chained to a sort of a dolly, the way Hannibal Lecter got transported, to be rolled to the breeding pen.

Chuckling, Will also cautioned me about Pelletier himself. He was Brassard's age, but he had a lascivious persona, liked to chat up women and exploit his profession and his animals for suggestive narratives. I could expect some ribald commentary.

LYNN HAD MOVED the harem into the breeding pen while Will and I did the milking, so by the time Pelletier arrived we were ready.

Brassard and Pelletier talked some more, then Pelletier started up his truck again and expertly backed up so that the trailer was closer to the paddock gate. When at last he swung aside the doors to reveal the monster, I was impressed but not terrified. Max had shoulders and chest like a pile of boulders, and a neck thick as a tree trunk, but he did not have horns or a surly attitude. He was not Hannibal Lecter and this was not Pamplona. He clomped daintily down the ramp from his trailer, lifted his nose, then moved toward the cows. He actually was quite handsome. Jack Pelletier walked next to him, holding the rope to his nose ring as Brassard flanked him on the other side. Charged with gate duty, I stayed well ahead, intimidated by

Max's sheer mass more than his disposition. Earnest followed with an extra rope in case of any unexpected turns of events.

Pelletier told me he had a particular fondness and great hopes for young Max, who was fourteen months old and had a scrotal circumference of thirty-eight centimeters. Mistaking me for someone who knew anything about the subject, he rambled happily on, using acronyms and specific measures of health, vigor, muscle-to-fat ratios, and so on.

This was Max's first date, Pelletier explained cheerfully. Sure, he wanted to pen test the boy's service capacity, but just as important, it only seemed fair that a bull—most likely doomed to mechanical mates for the rest of his life—should experience the real thing at least once. Six or eight mounts in a day, Pelletier said, would be good for the boy's morale and qualify him as a gigolo or porn star with excellent career prospects.

The men introduced Max to his harem, and we all lingered to watch. There were no fireworks. The cows didn't seem to care much, and even the heifers showed very little agitation. Max didn't rip around, snorting and kicking up turf, but just nosed his way among the girls, mildly interested in their behinds but not aggressively so. None of them seemed particularly focused on the task at hand—tails switched at flies, ears swiveled this way and that as they listened to sounds from around the farm.

I was standing next to Earnest, arms folded over the paddock fence, watching, when hands came around my waist and held me hard. Erik kissed the back of my head, Cat joined us at the fence. At the far end of the pen, the small mountain of Max's body reared high as he made his first mount of the day. "Attaboy," Pelletier said quietly, fondly. The cow seemed hardly to notice. When Max came back to all fours, he rested his big head on his mate's hindquarters.

"And people ask what you do for fun up here," Cat said.

Erik looked much better—last night, he had indeed been exhausted by his drive. Now his face was smooth and shiny, and though my immediate desire was to demand information about him and the contents of his van, nothing about him struck me as cloaked or caped. His eyes showed only interest in the proceedings, not calculation.

"He took a shower, an *ice shower*, in your stream water. Your brother is a *hunk*, Annie! He's got muscles on his muscles! And then he shaved with your dish soap and a *straight razor*, which gave me the willies to watch."

"I invited you to not observe my ablutions," Erik said dryly, "if you didn't want to."

Earnest chuckled. Cat turned back toward the slow-moving commotion in the pen.

LATER, PELLETIER DROVE off on other errands, leaving Max with us for the night. Cat and Erik, Earnest and Brassard and Will and I went to the house and milled around the kitchen and dining room, improvising a lunch of leftover shepherd's pie, leftover chicken, a two-pound chunk of cheddar, loaves of bread from a local bakery, coffee. The oven, reheating the shepherd's pie and chicken, cozied the rooms with warmth and savory scent.

It was a gathering that would change the lives of everyone there, though only one of us suspected it at the time.

I was wound tight, supremely uncomfortable. I hadn't had time to take Erik aside to grill him or threaten him or whatever I needed to do. I loved my brother, but I'd acquired a powerful protective love for this farm and these people, and I was not going to let him put it at risk any more than it already was.

We sat at the oval dining table, six of us, Brassard at the head, and talked about Max; Brassard recounted a few of Pelletier's infamous exploits. Married young—"Seven kids!" he marveled.

"Jeez. Could put *himself* out to stud," Earnest muttered, then looked abashed.

"Well, he more or less did, back in high school."

Everyone laughed, much pleased. It had been a long time since Jim Brassard had shown any levity.

"So, Erik, tell us about yourself," Brassard said.

The laughter quickly died away. Though he was a weary and blunted man, Brassard's authority came across—nothing accusatory, but a simple inquiry from an honest, elder man is not easy to deny.

Cat jumped in: "Yeah, and I want to know what your tattoo says!"

Erik rolled his sleeve farther and held up his arm so we could see the whole line of characters, stretching from his wrist to the inside of his elbow. "It's Chinese, and it basically says 'Let him who is without sin among you cast the first stone.'"

This morally loaded choice for a tattoo changed the dimensions of everyone's curiosity.

"Churchgoer?" Brassard asked.

"No. Never been in my life."

"Well, it's sure good advice. Why that one?"

"I guess so I could show it to good folks like you."

The clink and scrape of eating continued, but the easy bustle of lunch-making had become something very different. This was, as Erik would have said back when, *heavy stuff.* Earnest and Will leaned back in their chairs, as if clearing the air space, the line of sight, between Erik and Brassard, surrendering control of the transaction to the patriarch. If Erik had hoped to tell me his story first, the option seemed to have been lost.

Brassard took off his glasses, tipped his head forward and thoughtfully scratched his left ear, and I saw that it did indeed bear a scar, a pale braid of raised skin that started at the top of the shell just at his temple and disappeared into the whorls below.

"Out on the West Coast all this time, Ann says," Brassard said. "Kept yourself busy, I guess."

"Wasted some years with a decadent lifestyle. Got a little smarter and got some schooling, though."

"What'd you study?"

"Last five years, I got a bachelor's degree in business administration with a concentration in marketing."

"Good choices, this day and age." Brassard, burdened again, was wiping his glasses on a napkin. "Huh. Maybe you can give us some advice on that score—could sure use it. Farmin's not what it used to be, put it that way. What school?"

Erik had been toying with his fork, balancing it across one finger, tipping it almost to the point of falling, then letting it settle back into precarious balance. Nervous, but maintaining a wan smile.

"Mostly the school of hard knocks. But for the degrees, let's just say I got the best public education money could buy."

Earnest chortled, bobbed his head once, as if finally putting together the pieces of the puzzle. He leaned back into the table. "Where'd you serve?" he asked good-naturedly.

"Up in Elk Ridge, Oregon." Erik seemed to be playing out a long joke, and clearly Earnest had anticipated the punch line.

"In the service!" Brassard said, pleased. "What branch?"

Erik stopped fiddling. "Mr. Brassard, I served *time*—seven years at the Oregon State Penitentiary in Elk Ridge. I got out twelve days ago." He tipped his chair back, hands clasped behind his head to observe our reactions, both resigned and defiant. *Let him who is without sin among you cast the first stone*, his forearm insisted, in Chinese.

Silence. These were not overly judgmental people, but such an announcement demands a moment to consider and adapt to. Do you ask, "What were you in for?" Do you sit and wait for more explanation? Do you really want to know?

Then Cat asked, still on about his tattoo, maybe trying to kick-start the conversation again on a more positive note: "So ... why'd you write it in Chinese?

Erik's face grew serious. "So people would have to ask what it says. And then I could say it out loud."

Chapter 37

ERIK DROPPED OUR jaws about five times that day.

His tattoo, his whole approach, brought back to me just what a complex person he was—wired a bit differently from the rest of us, seeing the world through multiple lenses. He had always known that about himself. Back in high school, he'd gone through a period of being big on "cognitive dissonance," usually considered a negative and stressful psychological state in which a person's mind struggles with conflicting thoughts, opinions, emotions, or intentions. It can be paralyzing and painful.

But Erik had decided it was a positive state, essential to good mental health and moral integrity: "Ever think what would it would've been like if the Catholics and Protestants in Northern Ireland had been able to entertain a little fucking cognitive dissonance about their differences on religious dogma?" he'd ask.

Except that nobody got it, so mostly nobody got *him*. Those who did like him, those he therefore hung out with, were kids who liked his dashing negligence, his disaffection for convention and authority, not his

smarts or subtleties. One likes to be liked; his social choices took the path
of least resistance.

The way he explained it to me was that you could be a rabid Red Sox
fan, as we all were, and still admit that the Yankees were the better team
in any given year. You could be into heavy metal, as he was, and still love
Mozart, as he did.

The problem was that he too often induced the state in others who
couldn't endure it as well as he did.

One particular Sunday afternoon gathering at our house, when
Erik and I were in our teens, provides a perfect example. My father had
invited several friends from Wilkinson Academy, my mother a few of her
adjunct-faculty colleagues. The adults sat in various chairs and couches
in the living room, sipping martinis that everyone praised—my father
had prepared a pitcher and set it on the coffee table along with a plate of
toothpick-impaled olives and pearl onions. Erik and I sat invisibly at the
periphery, mostly bored but curious enough about adult social behavior,
especially when the martinis kicked in, to stick around.

One of my mother's colleagues was a music composition teacher, a tall
man defined by the angles of his elbows and knees, high bald forehead,
and a degree of tweediness that struck me as a little overmuch. At some
point the conversation meandered its way to music, and the group found
a pleasant consensus about Mozart—how wonderful, how cheering, that
lovely weightlessness, that effortlessness fluidity. How prodigious a talent.

I was as surprised as anyone when Erik, piping up from his crouch
on an ottoman, offered the opinion that Mozart was sometimes
"self-plagiarizing" and that his lifetime oeuvre had suffered from it. Erik
believed he recycled too many of his own ideas, which no doubt helped
get some of those commissions done on schedule and maybe explained
the time he famously completed a symphony while bouncing around in
a stagecoach racing toward the work's premier. And didn't he supposedly
write one while bowling?

The music teacher was aghast. Erik had blasphemed. He could only
assume, he said in a kindly but patronizing tone, that Erik, being his

age and of his generation, could not be expected to understand or enjoy Mozart.

"No, no, I totally love Mozart!" Erik insisted.

"You just provided a pretty withering critique! Which is it?"

"The two are not mutually exclusive," Erik said, stiffening.

Growing impatient with such a puerile discussion with an uppity juvenile, the music professor took Erik's tone personally and returned it as such: "And, might one ask, who are *you* to have an opinion about *Mozart*? You're what, fifteen? Do you know anything about classical music?"

Erik was taken aback. He couldn't comprehend how anyone could fail to understand his viewpoint or get so worked up about something so obvious. He hadn't meant to roil the social waters, just wanted to join the conversation at an adult level. Not yet in possession of his later bravado, he was intimidated by this circle of adults, gone silent now to listen to the exchange.

"Not much," Erik admitted.

"Have you studied composition, or harmony? Or any music at all?"

"No."

The music teacher flung his hands out to each side and dropped them onto his thighs, his argument sealed, Erik dismissed.

But Erik had a legalistic mind. He detested prejudice, especially in the form of underestimation, and he never backed down from anything. "That's like … like, I mean, what would you say if I asked you if you're for or against nuclear power?"

"Nukes? I was part of the Clamshell Alliance! You're too young to even remember that, of course. We protested the Seabrook plant, laid *siege* to it, did our best to shut it down. And I'm damn well proud of it. What does that have to do with Mozart?"

"So … are you an atomic physicist? A nuclear engineer? What expertise entitles you to have any opinion at all about nuclear power?"

The music professor opened and shut his mouth, frustrated at having his ad hominem bounced back at him, his logic dismantled, and flummoxed by the continuing effrontery of this upstart kid.

"I'm just saying ..."

"Honey," our mother cautioned.

"I'm just saying," Erik continued, not without a tinge of malice, "I think Mozart's Fortieth and the Requiem—especially the "Lacrimosa"?—have gotta be among mankind's greatest achievements. Totally. *And* I think he self-plagiarized too much of his own stuff."

At that moment, my father stood and picked up the pitcher of martinis. "Who's for a refresher?" he asked brightly.

ALL THAT CAME back to me as we got to know Erik that day. His tattoo, his philosophical complexity: *Ah, yes, right. My brother.* His knowledge of Mozart had not been due to his being a scholarly type, an intellectual—anything but. He detested all things academic. For all I know, that argument with Ichabod Crane was one of the catalysts for his determination to graduate early, to "get the hell out before the bullshit gets any deeper." He was just really smart and broadly curious, could pursue a subject with fanatical intensity if it interested him.

Jim Brassard broke our silence after learning about Elk Ridge State Penitentiary, our reluctance to ask, *What were you in for?*

"What were you in for?" he asked.

He put his glasses back on, the better to see Erik with, the black plastic arm of his glasses hiding once again his scarred ear even as the reflection on the lenses hid his eyes.

"For farming."

"Huh! Why not?" Brassard asked rhetorically, gloomily. "Next thing for us, I wouldn't wonder."

ERIK TOLD US: Since I last saw him, he'd gotten into raising marijuana in Northern California. He and his partners grew about twenty acres of a "dynamite" strain for a few years. Erik, among his other duties, kept watch: You lived right there in the patch to water, fertilize, and prune during the day and to keep watch for other growers who might "interfere with productivity" at night. Too many structures on the land would have attracted the interest of the DEA or state police conducting aerial surveillance, so he and his compatriots slept outside, kept their visible footprint small, and scattered their crop among small trees and bushes.

They had a pretty good business plan. They grew, harvested, hybridized, and maintained their own seed stock; they shrink-wrapped their product, transported it, and sold it in the Bay Area to local distributors they trusted, and had a pretty good sideline, even mail-order, in handmade pipes they whittled while the plants matured. Made good money for three years, except that so much was in cash and they had limited laundering capacity. For the most part, the only ways you could deal with it were burying it, starting lots of savings accounts and never depositing more than $4,999 at once, and spending it on relatively lavish living. You couldn't buy a new car for cash, but greenbacks could still get you a pretty nice used Merc from the right dealer.

Still, he and his partners—"good people, a tight bunch"—lived with unrelenting stress that began to wear on them. One night, they got stoned together and everybody realized that the other was feeling the same thing: *I gotta get out of this.* Plus, the marketplace had become more competitive, resulting in aggressive encroachment from some new growers nearby who were "less oriented toward a mutually supportive local economy." Actually, they were the sort of guys "with a different kind of ponytail," wanting to consolidate a larger market share and connected enough "in other circles" to boost Erik's group's collective blood pressure. Erik slept with a shotgun and finally used it one night, firing over the heads of some intruders to scare them off. In retaliation, the other growers beat up one of Erik's group, and retaliation seemed unwise: These guys seemed more willing and able to escalate than Erik's people were.

So they did their best to vanish. They took their last crop and seed stock and set up again in southern Oregon. After a year or two, they started divesting and diversifying. They figured that their horticultural skills would help them explore other promising products without so much anxiety attached to them.

"So, second year in Oregon, we had about five hundred pounds of prime bud and leaf to deliver and I was the designated driver. We were moving it to some new connections in Portland and Eugene, avoid the long drive to the Bay Area. Bad plan—we didn't know them well enough. Long and short of it, I got caught. I elected to take the rap on my own, keep my friends out of it, and got twelve years. Got out in seven for good behavior."

What to say to *that*?

What Brassard said was "Mother of God. I smoked hooch a few times over there, couldn't see as it had much goin for it. Hard to believe there's such a market for it. You did too, didn't you, Earn? Smoke?"

"A bit. Never got the taste for it," Earnest said. "Lot of guys did, though."

By "over there," Brassard meant Vietnam.

Brassard, turning back toward Erik, staying on topic and now hardening up a bit: "So what brings you to our neck of the woods? Anything besides seein your sister?"

Chapter 38

THAT DAY, FOR the first time ever, we ran late with afternoon chores. Erik kept us utterly caught up in his narrative.

Watching him tell his tale, I saw just how much he had grown. Prison, or maybe just life, had knocked off the sharper edges and rounded some of the harder angles. He expressed his certainties in ways that allowed more room for others' opinions; his monologues were interspersed with pauses that invited others' responses. And where he used to dramatize and emphasize, he now tended to speak with wry understatement. That said, there was a toughness to him—not the showy machismo of his younger years, that piratical dash and panache, but a slower, pragmatic kind that I supposed must be earned in, say, a state penitentiary.

He didn't tell them everything—he saved some details for me alone, shared over dinner here at the camp tonight—but covered a lot of territory.

As Erik told us, he'd been betrayed by his buyers, and the police never learned the origin of his stock—he refused to incriminate his partners, who were also his dearest friends. They'd always agreed that if anybody got caught and didn't talk, they'd reciprocate and preserve his or her share in the business, to collect later. Their experiences in California and his arrest discouraged them from continuing in the marijuana industry, but they continued as a corporation, more formally now. Erik got twelve years. Fortunately, the state had a progressive prison rehabilitation program, including access to college classes, and he had used it to develop skills he figured he'd need when he got out: business administration, marketing. He was determined to run his own shop—he wasn't the employee type, he knew that much about himself.

So he got out, went to see his old partners. They were doing very well. They reimbursed him for his efforts on behalf of the corporation—"they stuck to their principles." They offered, and he opted for, the van and its contents instead of cash.

At lunch, Brassard cut to the chase: "I guess here's where I need to know what's in that van that's sittin in my driveway."

Everybody's eyes went to Erik as he absorbed the question. He stood up. He said he'd be right back. We heard him go out and, faintly, the opening drag of the van's side door and a moment later the drag and slam. Cat kept her eyes on me.

"I'm sure you can understand my outlook, Ann," Brassard said. This was the boss speaking.

Frankly, I was grateful for his taking charge. I hadn't relished the idea that I would be the lone bearer of some bad secret, or the solitary carrier of difficult news from—or to—my brother.

Erik came back inside with a Styrofoam container about the size of a pizza box but six inches thick. He smiled like a chef about to serve his pièce de résistance as he brought it up to Brassard and set it on the table. He used a table knife to slit the tape and then lifted the top half of the box.

Brassard moved his glasses down his nose to look. "Roots?"

"They call them crowns, but basically they're roots, yes," Erik said.

IN THIS CASE, it was the root mass of the hops plant, the flavor basis of beer. As Erik explained it, these were called "crowns" because, while they were the center of the underground part of the plant, they actually had two purposes. The roots headed out and down to suck up water and nutrients, but the crown also included rhizomes—underground stems that grew horizontally, sending up shoots as they went. It was a highly effective way for the plant to spread, because each shoot then turned into its own plant. Most new growers started their hop yards by buying mail-order rhizome sections cut from the crown—just sticks about as long as a hand and thick as a thumb. The advantage of having crowns instead of rhizomes, Erik said, was that they could be planted right away, that fall, and produce a robust hops yield in the first year. He would also take rhizome cuttings from the crowns and plant them in the spring.

Hops actually contained some of the same chemicals as cannabinoids, Erik went on enthusiastically. It had a lot of the same hands-on crop management needs and harvesting procedures as his prior crop of choice. His former partners were making good money selling it to the emerging artisanal beer-brewing industry in California and Oregon. In prison, with plenty of time on his hands, Erik had done market research and figured he could get in on the ground floor of the "as yet immature, but primed" East Coast artisanal brewing trend.

This was a lot of information to absorb. Brassard, the authority only moments before, pondered and, as he did so, faded thoughtfully back into the grieving, run-aground man he had been since Diz died.

Erik had come east with about twenty-five thousand dollars' worth of hops crowns in his van and was looking for a place to set up raising them. He'd planned to head to Vermont even before he knew I was here, because he had identified several start-up Vermont breweries and figured that with Vermont's "brand" there'd be a huge market for superior aromatic hops, especially if they were organically grown. It was, as he said, serendipitous that I had gotten in with a farm. He let that comment hang.

Will put it all together first: "If you're thinking of growing anything organic here, we've already considered it. We don't have any organic land. Dad and Grandad have used commercial fertilizers and herbicides and insecticides on these fields since basically forever."

Brassard nodded, still lost in thoughts or terrors of loss and loneliness. "How about those scrub strips below Annie's land?"

Did *everything* Erik say induce a stunned silence? That day, yes.

Brassard roused. "Never used em," he muttered. "Couldn't put a crop on em because they're full of rocks so we couldn't drag a tiller or combine over em. Didn't need the extra headache of cleanin em out. Brush-hogged em every few years, that's why they're not just woods now."

"I kept up with it the last few years," Earnest said. "Just because ... I don't know. Brassard tradition?"

"My dad grazed over there sometimes," Brassard put in. "Thought it would be smart to keep it open in case we ever needed."

"How many acres?"

Another silence as Will, Brassard, and Earnest did some mental calculations.

"Well," Brassard said, "we got about six hundred feet above Ann's right-of-way, another, oh, eight hundred feet to the south end. Width varies, but I'd say maybe six acres total."

Erik: "That never got sprayed or—"

Earnest, smiling: "That got logged off a hundred fifty years ago and never got used. The first farmers here cut the timber, probably grazed over there back when, but it's never been crop fields. So no—no pesticides and whatnot."

"So it won't be hard to certify as organic," Erik said. "What do you think, Mr. Brassard? Think I could plant hops there?"

BRASSARD EXPLAINED THAT the farm was hard-tasked right now, any extra hassle would break the camel's back and he wasn't even sure we'd be able to hold on to the place anyway, financial problems. It pained him to admit this to Erik.

"I mean, can I lease it? I'd pay you a thousand an acre for a year. And whatever you need for letting me use a tractor once in a while, some manure if you can spare it, make it ten thousand? I can pay you in advance."

"Man who's just out of the penitentiary," Brassard said darkly, "isn't goin to have any money. Unless it's from before he went in, and I don't know as I want anything to do with that brand of money. Come back to bite me."

Erik laughed and for a moment looked like he did when he was a kid and his heart was light. "No, nothing like that! I get out of Elk Ridge and my friends tell me there's this lawyer been trying to find me. They didn't know what it was about, maybe some other trouble, so they didn't tell him where I was. But then I contact him and discover that my old aunt Theresa had died and left me a pretty good pile. Annie, you must have gotten some too, right?"

I smacked my hand against my forehead. Of course. Right. Of course. When the lawyer notified me of the inheritance, he had asked me where Erik was. I told him I didn't know, hadn't heard from him in seven years, but he must have kept sleuthing.

Brassard still looked skeptical. "Thousand an acre is pretty high," he said. "Worth that much to you?"

Brassard's dark mood intimidated me, but Erik faced him straight on, clearly the look of an honest entreaty. "Where I'm at? Where I've been? I've kinda got only one shot here, and that shot's worth a good deal, whether it's on this farm or another one. The crowns have to be planted in fall if they're going to bear anything next year. They won't survive till spring out of the ground. So I've got a rush on."

I will not pretend that my heart didn't soar at the prospect of some money being pumped into the farm's finances. It could make all the difference. Earnest and Will were almost goggle-eyed at the rapid pace and unexpected turns of this discussion, but I could see that in each of them a little sprout of hope had suddenly uncurled.

Brassard looked overwhelmed. He knew the chores were calling. He said he'd have to think about it. Then we were clearing the dishes, cleaning up, each in our own thoughts. Cat headed back to Boston, crying joyfully again. The Irving Oil truck came and refilled our diesel tank. Max snorted in the pen. Erik shadowed Will and me as we shunted cows around and did the milking and equipment cleanup and parlor poop removal, then went inside to talk with Brassard again.

Earnest had been clanking at some machine in the old barn, but he came to find me as I finished purging the milk pipes.

"Your brother sure knows how to make a dramatic entrance. Quite a splash. I think he's left us all a little breathless." He put a hand on my shoulder, looking at me in a way that told me he was concerned for me and, I could tell, for the farm. "Think he can make something like that work?"

"I have no idea," I said.

Chapter 39

Sept. 17

I am writing by candlelight in my tent home. Cat returned to Boston today, forgiven, and Erik is sleeping out in the woods somewhere nearby. Another clear night, not particularly cold, silent but for the occasional falling leaf sliding down my tent fly. I'm exhausted but can't sleep—the day cranked up the voltage of my nervous system and now I can't dial it back down.

Erik and I headed back up here at sunset. The light was not splendid, because a thin overcast had dulled the sky, like your breath on a windowpane. As we got the fire going, lit some lanterns, I really went at Erik.

"Why didn't you contact me? How could you do that to me?"

"I was ashamed," he said simply.

"What," I said, "I'd find it so morally reprehensible that you'd grown pot? I wouldn't care! Half the people I know smoke now and then—myself included, back in Boston!"

"No," he said. He seemed close to tears. "No. For being asshole stupid for so

many years. Getting arrested was just the cherry on top. Pop said I was wasting
my talents. You said it! You all said I could do better than the buddies and
girlfriends I chose to hang with. I grew pot and I also did a little on-and-off
dance with H, okay, I fucking wasted how many years of my life? And, trust
me, putting on the ol' orange jumpsuit really brings that shit home to you. I
wasn't going to do you much good for twelve years anyway."

"You're my brother," I reminded him.

"I was fucked up and it was all coming at me faster than I could handle
it and by the time I got a grip I was like two years in and it was a habit—
being alone."

"You're my brother!"

And he said, "What can I say? It's done. It happened the way it did. I'd
love it if we could leave it there. Leave it back where I'm trying to leave a
bunch of other stuff."

I could see that. Given that I am trying to leave a bunch of other stuff
"back there," too.

He seemed to read my mind: "When are you going to tell me what
happened to you? Because some shit happened, that much I know."

I told him I wasn't up for it right now. I made a big omelet for each of
us, eggs folded over cheddar and diced tomatoes and onions. We ate in silence.

When he talked again, he told me more about why he'd felt compelled to
leave the coast. The only reason he hadn't gotten a longer sentence, the way
he'd avoided implicating his partners, was that he'd done a plea deal in which
he revealed instead the location of the "different kind of ponytail" guys back
in California. For which he felt no remorse at all. But when he got out, his
former partners said they'd heard rumors that the guys still "on the outside" had
long memories and vengeful souls. Also, upon returning to his old friends, Erik
discovered that his wife—had he mentioned he'd gotten married?—who was
one of the partners, lived with another of the partners and had had a kid with
him. Cute little girl, four years old now. And while he understood—after all,
seven years is a long time—it was the first he'd heard of it, which he kind of
resented and anyway it would have made working together pretty tense.

I asked him what it was like in prison. He said Elk Ridge was not what you'd call a spa but not the kind of place where you had to worry about bending over to pick up the soap in the shower. Still, it behooved one to stay in shape, so he'd worked out in the gym every day.

I assume this was more of that wry understatement, but can't be sure. I asked, "But how about your mind? Morale? How'd you ... a person like you, especially, how'd you stay sane?"

"What is a person like me?"

"You know what I'm talking about."

"Yeah, well, it was touch and go sometimes, he admitted, especially around the third year. They'd been long years and I thought I still had nine to go. That's when I got my first tattoo. Tattoos, it's one of the things you do to fight boredom. This one I did at that low point. And it actually helped." He unzipped his jacket and rolled up his shirt and yes, as Cat said, he is muscled, slim but rock hard. Over his heart he had tattooed "I Am Free." He explained that that was his heart talking, reminding him every day that no matter what, it would never be imprisoned, not in Elk Ridge or anywhere. "The one on my arm, that one I did later when I knew I was getting out. By way of explanation, I guess."

After a while, he went off to sleep in the woods again. "As you can imagine, I'm enjoying the hell out of open spaces," he explained. The absence of walls.

I heard his harmonica for a few minutes in the distance, quiet and spare and plaintive.

One more rather wonderful thing happened this afternoon. As we did our chores, Will called me "Annie," the way Erik does. It just came spontaneously. I guess, after hearing Erik call me that all day, maybe it just seemed to fit. Later, Brassard did, too: "Annie." Earnest hasn't adopted it, maybe because he already has his own personal name for me.

But Annie: I like it. "Ann" seems formal and stiff, an overly frilled English queen. "Annie" is less pretentious and more countrified and it's also the name I'm called by family.

Chapter 40

It was mid-September, meaning there were only so many weeks until the ground froze and working in the soil would get impossibly difficult. Erik had to work fast to plant his crowns. With any other crop, there would have been no chance, given the rocks: The tillable fields Brassard and his fellow farmers had enjoyed for the past two hundred years had been hacked from this land by families willing to gouge out each stone and stump with shovels and mattocks, ropes and ox-pulled sledges, over many years.

But hops is not a ground-growing crop. It's a climber, so the farmer builds it a vertical field—a trellis. As Erik explained, you set twenty-foot posts into holes in the ground every forty feet, string cables between them, and then put down vertical ropes for the hops vines—actually, "bines"—to snake their way up. The hops farmer can just leave the biggest rocks where the glaciers did and work among them. Erik needed to get the crowns into the ground as soon as possible, but first he had to soften the soil, erect the posts, and string the trellis cables so that in spring they'd be ready to go.

Erik's deal with Brassard had included use of the tractors and implements at an hourly rate. But Jim's Deere was off limits unless he drove
it himself, and the big gray Harvester was not designed for this kind of
work. That left the Ford and the little Bobcat, available when not needed
elsewhere.

I could only observe the process in glimpses caught between chores,
but there was something ceremonial about the day Erik started carving out
his hop yard. At the very least, it was one man trying to build his future,
to put his ragtag life on a better footing, much as I had done in buying my
land. It could also be the beginning of renewal at Brassard's farm.

He started by brush-hogging that long strip between the road and
my land. I had always assumed that brush-hogging involved pigs—I
don't know, putting a bunch of them on some land and letting them
root around and eat all the vegetable matter. But it doesn't. It involves
a tractor, to which you attach what is really just a bigger version of a
domestic lawnmower—a broad flat platform covering two monstrously
powerful spinning blades and supported by little caster wheels. You drag
it up and down, and the whirling blades hack through grass, reeds, bushes,
saplings—anything. It makes a terrifying noise of rending and thrashing,
and sometimes a hair-raising metallic gunshot when a blade hits a rock.
It's a crude tool, but all growing things fall behind it, turned to chips and
shreds fine enough to work into the soil.

Erik spent a bruising day cutting brush from those six acres, and he
came back to the farm deaf, exhausted, and coughing from breathing so
much diesel exhaust. He'd had to give some of the bigger rocks a wide
berth, so the next day we delivered a more nuanced shave with a huge
walk-behind cutter, a Gravely. Partly to show off my hardihood to Erik,
I volunteered. It went like this: You grip the two-wheeled, four-hundred-
pound Gravely by handles extending to the rear, controlling it with levers
for clutch and blade and braking. When you engage the drive wheels and
try to navigate around rocks on uneven ground, it flings around a person
of my weight like a dog shaking a rabbit. After about an hour, you are
exhausted. Then Earnest takes over and the bitching thing becomes docile

and compliant for a couple of hours while you watch, lying torpid and dead useless against the windshield of your car, trying to gather enough energy to milk the cows.

Erik had towed the prehistoric metal-wheeled tractor out of the field earlier, but when they finished brush-hogging he repositioned it at the edge of my parking area, where my uphill trail began and where we went in and out of the scrub field. I liked the look of it there.

Erik's most grueling challenge was opening up soil with so many rocks in it—the same dilemma every early Vermont farmer had faced. He couldn't use any of Brassard's implements, which were too wide and designed for broader, softer fields that had been cleared of rocks and long since leavened by a century of regular tilling.

Will and Earnest and Erik and I considered the problem as we looked out over the freshly bristle-cut field, swigging coffee from big plastic cups. The boulders humping up here and there from the mash of shredded grass and brush were not the problem. Beneath the surface, the ground was full of rocks ranging from the size of my hand to the size of a gunnysack of feed grain. Now Erik had to break that soil, soften it, aerate it, and fertilize it with fermented manure. Fortunately, he didn't have to open up all the soil, just thin strips with fourteen feet of unbroken ground between them. Still, it was a daunting prospect: eight strips, each two hundred feet long, per acre.

Will proposed using the Ford's backhoe attachment, a jointed arm and digger bucket that, when folded, resembled a scorpion's stinger tail. You'd move the tractor along the trellis line, stop, dig and scrape with the toothed bucket, lift out the larger rocks and set them aside, then smooth the dirt back into place with back-of-bucket swipes. Then drive forward another ten feet, stop, and repeat the process. Somebody would tag along with the Bobcat, making off with the bigger rocks in its loader bucket and piling them where they wouldn't get in the way.

Erik's van held enough hops crowns for three acres; the other three acres he would plant with rhizomes cut from these crowns in the spring. He estimated that even with leaving fourteen feet of unworked soil between planting rows, he'd need to break and soften and smooth about a quarter mile in each of those six acres. He and Will did some math and figured it would take two weeks of ten-hour days, barring equipment failure or weather delays. And only then could Erik start drilling the holes for the six hundred poles he needed to erect. And, after that, start planting before the cold came and the ground froze.

As Will and Erik discussed this, Earnest had been quiet, frowning, chewing first on his upper lip and then on his lower lip. After a while he drifted off to the barn, and while we all kept talking we heard a tractor fire up and then saw the Ford chug away down the slope of pasture and out of view.

Watching him go, Erik slumped as if he just now realized the scope of what he had planned. He jabbed his thumb over his shoulder in Earnest's general direction. "I guess he got discouraged, huh?"

Will and I glanced at each other. Being discouraged by a physical challenge was not something either of us could easily associate with Earnest.

Will had to go up to Burlington and I had other work to do, so we left Erik sitting on one of the ancient tractor's wheels, flipping his empty coffee mug by its handle like a flashy cowboy gunslinger spinning his Colt, and staring forlornly at the acres he'd already worked so hard to tame. He was no doubt second-guessing his determination to plant on Brassard's farm. He'd done it because I was there, Brassard needed the money, and the deal could be concluded fast. But he could have kept looking for some other organic acres for a week or more and might still have had the time to get the crowns in—probably could have gotten them in sooner, in fact, if the soil had been worked before. I had even asked Theo and Lynn about putting the yard on their place, but they said they simply didn't have enough land to spare. Now it was too late; he'd made a deal with Brassard and had paid him in advance.

And anyway, there I was, and Erik and I needed to be near each other.

He cut a solitary figure on the tractor's wheel, flipping his coffee mug. As I walked away, I knew that he'd left a lot of his story untold, and that it would ultimately reveal a person struggling with a loneliness not unlike my own. And the self-questioning: It no doubt ran in the blood.

ABOUT AN HOUR later, I heard an unusual noise as I was doing supply inventory. I came out of the barn and joined Bob to watch Earnest driving the Ford up the road, pulling one of the derelict implements from that overgrown patch of field below the house. Its tall, skinny iron wheels squeaked, and it trailed strands of the grass and blackberry canes it had been half buried in. A metal seat rose on a single shaft between the wheels, just ahead of a triangular frame mounted with what looked like a witch's spindly fingers curled into claws.

Earnest dragged it into the farmyard. It was a chisel plow, he told us, made to go deep into hard soil. Its name made sense: Each of the three curved claws ended in a sharply beveled arrowhead. The beauty of it, Earnest explained, was the ingenuity of the tines' curve, which rose high above the frame before continuing down to the chisel tip—actually more of a spiral than a semicircle. The bevel of the spade-shaped heads would draw the fingers down into the ground, but if one of them hit something it couldn't get through, the spiral would open wider and allow that particular tine to momentarily rise above the obstacle. The fact that it had a seat told him it had once been pulled by horses.

Farm implement manufacturers still made variations of chisel plows, he said, but he figured Erik would want to hang on to his money. This one was in pretty good shape—it hadn't been abandoned because it broke, it had simply become outmoded.

Earnest and Erik worked on it for two hours, patch-welding parts as needed, greasing the axles, oiling the control levers, sharpening the chisel blades with an angle grinder. To get it out of the bushes, Earnest had attached it to the Ford's tow bar using loops of heavy wire, meaning the men also needed to build a proper hitch.

They finished just before milking, so I got to watch the first test of it in the hop yard. Earnest sat on the seat to manipulate the levers that set the tines' depth. Erik drove, starting out in crawler gear, twisting himself around in the Ford's seat to check on the action behind. The blades bit and pulled themselves into the ground; the spirals opened out a bit; Erik notched up the throttle lever. On the surface, the tines cut only slender furrows, but their real work was below the surface, where each arrowhead sliced and jumbled the soil. And hit rocks—the curved tines rose and fell independently of each other, a slow three-fingered pianist.

It was not a straight shot by any means. The old spring-steel tines had lost much of their flexibility and one of them broke off the housing; Earnest welded it on again along with a piece of old leaf spring from another implement. At intervals, a big rock stopped forward motion entirely. When that happened, they backed up, lifted the tines, drove past the obstacle, and then set up a little stick with surveyor's flagging tape on it, marking the spots that would need the backhoe. Then, the second day in, the poor thing gave up the ghost, breaking two tines and cracking the frame. Earnest didn't believe it could survive another round of repairs. So they towed it back to the parking area and set it up opposite the old tractor, the two forming a rustic ceremonial gateway to my access path and to what we hoped would become Erik's hop yard. We admired the relics' optimism: *History meets future here*, they seemed to proclaim.

Erik scouted the back roads looking for another antique that might do the job, but eventually he had to go spend two thousand dollars on a modern chisel plow from a farm implement store in Rutland. It was utterly without the slender grace of the old one, more like a weapon of war. Its frame was painted a gaudy red, and its three, heavily built, straight tines—shanks—were black and cruel looking. Appropriately, he said, they were now called "V-rippers."

Erik claimed he liked the old one better, but this one allowed him to drive faster and needed only one person to operate, allowing Earnest to catch up with tree jobs he'd been putting off.

That autumn is hard for me to recall and even harder to recount. We saw each other, all of us, through a fog of fatigue and urgent preoccupation, and with a disconcerting intermittence. Earnest here then gone, Will here then gone, Lynn and Robin coming and going when goats and gardens allowed, Brassard appearing and disappearing. We were like a juggler's pins, spinning end over end, passing each other in the air in every imaginable recombination.

We all had more work than could be accomplished in twenty-four hours. With Earnest still at his tree jobs at least three days a week, and Will editing a video project that often took him away, I became the Swiss Army knife—small but with every tool you might need. We all helped Erik whenever a window of time opened up, and devised a meticulously planned staffing schedule to make it all mesh.

For the next few weeks, Erik worked in a frenzy. He used the Ford's backhoe attachment to remove the larger stones he had flagged on the first pass. He located sources for the trellis poles, got them delivered; he bought big spools holding, literally, miles of steel cable, and hundreds of fittings such as cable clamps and turnbuckles and anchor pins. He and I drilled hundreds of holes with an auger attached to the Ford's PTO. He hired a contractor with the right equipment and worked with the men to erect the poles and string cable along their tops. Once the poles were up—visualize a sparse, geometric forest of telephone poles—he further softened his planting strips using a big walk-behind tiller, like the Gravely, that he rented. He worked in the rain until the ground got too soupy to continue. He skipped lunch because he forgot to eat. He worked after dark by the light of the Ford's or the tiller's headlamps and a big handheld beam he directed where he needed more light.

One night, just a sheen of sunset light gilding the inverted bowl of the sky, I saw Brassard come out of the house, cross the road, and limp into the hop yard. He flagged down Erik, shouted something up at him. The tractor motor chattered to silence. Erik creaked stiffly down. As they walked back, Brassard put his arm over my brother's shoulder, talking seriously with him.

Later I asked him about their exchange.

"He told me I was done working for the day, flat and simple," Erik explained. "Said it was time for some chow and some R and R. 'No point in workin the ground if you end up in it before your damn hops do.' He took the key out!" This was testament to Brassard's determination on the point: No one ever took the keys out of the tractors.

Another moment that gave me a sweet pang in my chest: Earnest and Erik, working together, jive-talking, insulting each other's proficiency at all things, laughing. At one point, they started shouldering and shoving, roughhousing like brothers. Erik has probably done his share of fighting, but it was like a bear playing with a puppy. Erik laughed about it later, marveling at Earnest's power.

I did a lot of the hole drilling that preceded the installation of the poles. This required a twelve-inch auger attached to the PTO of my— the—Ford. The auger is a broad drill bit, an Archimedes screw about five feet long, that the tractor motor rotates and that the hydraulics push down into the soil. Erik had gone out earlier with a tape line and chalk powder to mark the drilling spots along the trellis lines. I'd position the back end of the Ford a few feet beyond the chalk spot, engage the hydraulics, and slowly jam the auger into the soil. We had to get down about five feet so the bottom of the pole would settle below the frost line.

This soil hadn't been shattered by the chisel plow, had never been forced to do anything and wasn't inclined to acquiesce now. Again and again rocks stopped the auger and broke the shear pin, an insert on the shaft that's intended to self-destruct rather than let the shock destroy the whole rig. When a pin sheared, I'd stop. Then, with Erik's or Earnest's help, I'd twist and wrestle the auger and the vertical shaft into alignment, punch out the mutilated pin, and bang in a new one. Then I'd lift the auger and look into the hole to see what we were up against. If it seemed an immovable object, I'd scoot the Ford a few feet farther along the line and start drilling a new hole. Fortunately, the hops trellis formation didn't have to be absolutely precise.

After a couple of days' drilling, the math began to discourage us. The top three acres required around three hundred poles. Three hundred five-foot-deep bores through rocky soil broke dozens of shear pins and bent and nicked the auger's blades so that Earnest had to hammer them straight and weld in new patches of steel. The Ford proved indomitable, but the humans got sheared, bent, and nicked, too. Drifting off to sleep, I saw the auger pulling up soil between its blades, spewing and dumping the earth as it rose. I heard the laboring engine and the groans of the straining PTO rig, the awful screams and scrapes of steel against stone, deep in the ground. I'm sure Erik unwillingly relived his day's striving as he tried to sleep, too. The job was getting done, but it was taking its toll.

This sounds like misery, and often enough it was. But I also felt, I think we all did, a lovely sense of community. No, of *unity*. The seven of us had become a sort of single organism, a collective entity, cohering by common purpose and the shared state of exhaustion. Fingers of the same hand. It was unconscious and probably unnoticed by the others, a natural product of our coordinated labors and our exertion. No need to apologize for being too tired to converse or for rambling on like an idiot, no need to explain laughing your head off about nothing. One day we all cracked up about "having high hopes for the hops" and then trying to decide whether a single hops plant was a "hop." From there we went on to explore other plurals and singulars. If you were a member of the New York Yankees baseball team, you'd call yourself a Yankee, no problem. But if you were with the Boston Red Sox, would you refer to yourself as a Red Sock? We laughed till we groaned, and offered no apologies.

Hidden within all that desperate fuss and fury, derived from it, rose a glow of reawakened purpose and hope.

And, getting out of bed one morning, tired but more confident again, I thought about that ground: This is what the good round world is made of, this tough, stubborn, fertile stuff. Thanks be. And I thought, *I shall be tough stubborn stuff, too, and one day fertile as well.*

Yes. That was the day, the moment, that I realized I wanted to have a child. I was stunned and thirty-seven and so often lonely and empty at night and thought I knew myself, and at that moment I entered a new era of my life.

Chapter 41

WE WERE FORTUNATE that the cold came late that year. The maples' brilliant foliage faded and browned, and then let go all in a single day's wind-borne blizzard. Again the pines magically appeared, deepest dark green in the gray of the shorn woods. Though October's bright, dry days lingered on into November, and at night the temperature rarely got below freezing, every single task of constructing the hop yard took longer than estimated. Erik worried that the crowns would not get in the ground in time.

But the weather stayed mild. The rest of the crowns went in, and still the soil in the southern three acres remained soft enough to break with the V-ripper, churn with the tiller, and drill for postholes. We got better and faster at it as we went. By the time the first snow came, a second field of telephone poles stood there, stark and strange, south of my access track. The two fields resembled a primitive version of a power transformer station, rows of those posts with a skein of cables taut between.

ERIK'S ARRIVAL AND the potential of hop farming had boosted the morale at Brassard's farm, but while the cash helped, it only slowed, not stopped, the downward spiral. Again, it all came back to Diz, the hole left when she died. We all agreed that getting the hops into the ground was an urgent priority. It might be the "turnaround business plan" that Earnest had spoken of. If the hops did well next summer, Brassard could feel secure in the money he made from Erik's leasing the land. The farm would have a little more financial ballast. He and Erik had also discussed the possibility of Brassard putting up his own trellises on a few acres. If Erik made good wholesale contacts, Brassard could consider shifting from dairy even if his land was not certifiably organic.

But that was all long-term pie in the sky, and at odds with the short term. With Will and Earnest and me putting time into the hop yard, Brassard had to hire Lynn and Robin every day for milking and other dairy chores. It helped that Erik started paying two hundred a month to rent the twin of my apartment in the chicken coop, but that didn't begin to offset the low milk prices, barely recovered from the prior year. Brassard had decades of financial planning experience, and he knew how tight his margins still were. And he was a man hurting in a lot of places. I soon learned that he was unraveling even as he tried to heal, but carrying himself like a good soldier.

Once the hops were safely put to bed and I had dismantled my camp on the hill, there was nothing more to be done on my side of the road. Earnest followed his tree jobs south, planning to return in late November or early December. Will stayed at the farm most nights but was usually gone during the day.

My moving back into my tiny apartment in the guesthouse-help dorm meant that Erik and I became neighbors and could spend time together after the working day. Sometimes we all had dinner in the house, Brassard and Will, Erik and me. Mostly, though, it was just Erik and me cooking for each other in our Spartan workers' quarters.

Those dinners allowed us time to talk unhurriedly, and we slipped by degrees into the familiarity and honesty that we'd had when we were younger. In prison, he had gotten into Celtic music, particularly the lovely mournful Irish tunes of lost love and homeland, and played them from his iPod as the musical score for my tales of miseries and mistakes in Boston. I confessed in serial fashion during dinners and evening card games; Erik bristled in outrage on my behalf, mourned in commiseration, and agreed with me, shaking his head incredulously, about what a complete "dumb-ass wimp-out" I'd been. I had told it all to Cat, of course, but this was the first time I'd revealed the whole pathetic saga—including the desperation of physical need—to a man. He served not just as a foil for catharsis but also, unknowingly, as an ambassador for the male gender, easing me toward rapprochement. He was sympathetic but didn't coddle me or try to persuade me that I hadn't, as he said, "screwed the pooch." Once I had primed the pump, he revealed more about his own burden of hurt and shame, and I know our talks relieved him of some of that weight.

Erik was always moving. He picked things up, looked at them closely but distractedly, put them down again. He fidgeted in elaborate ways, doing improvised prestidigitation with a can opener or spatula, balancing a saucer on one finger, flipping the cap of the soy sauce bottle into the air and vanishing it with a one-handed swipe as fast as a cat's. It seemed to me his nervous intensity was mounting.

One night we were sitting at my kitchen counter, empty dinner dishes still in front of us, and he explained his state to me.

"I hope the elder sister recognizes the self-control the younger brother has shown," he said as preamble. "As a sign of his maturity and determination."

"In what way?"

"Annie, I spent seven *years* in the *pen*. I got out and drove here and started planting *hops*. I'm sitting here having dinner with my *sister.*"

"And …?"

"'*And?*'" He laughed and shook his head at my stupidity. "I want to get laid! Jesus H. Christ!" He stood and looked at the ceiling and spread his arms like an opera tenor belting out his passion. "*I want to get laid!*" he bellowed to the gods. "I want a *woman!*"

When I stopped laughing I told him I couldn't help him there. "Unless … maybe you and Cat? I mean she showed a certain—"

"Cat? *Cat?* Get real! Cat's been my other big sister since I was ten years old. Hey, I can get a little kinky, but not *that* kinky!"

"I can't think of a local source for available women your age. They don't carry them down at the feed store."

"I'm hip. So what are my options? Where are the good bars within a fifty-mile radius?"

"You're asking me? I haven't been in a bar in years."

At that, he frowned. "Speaking of which. A subject in its own right."

"What?"

"What about you? I never saw you as the nun type. You've been up here how long now? Two years? And you don't want some romance?"

"I came off a really bad one, Erik. I've been giving it some time." This conversation was getting uncomfortable for me—I didn't need a reminder of the void in my life. "That said, yes, I want some romance. But it's different with me now. I'm older. I want different things from a relationship."

He kept a suspicious frown on me. "Not sex?"

"I didn't say that. Just not only. For you it's simpler."

"What about Will?"

"Huh?"

"He's got a little something going for you. Haven't you seen the way he looks at you when we're all together? Very attentive? Responsive?"

"I haven't noticed," I lied. "Has he said something to you?"

"No," he admitted. Then he went on, picking up momentum: "But he's good-looking, seems like a decent guy, and he's close to hand—"

"We were talking about your love life, not mine."

"He told me his divorce has come through."

"I heard. Let's get back to bars within a fifty-mile radius."

"How about Burlington? College town, right? They say college girls go wild for ex-cons."

We laughed. Who knew? Maybe they did. I couldn't help him with this, but I was beginning to suspect I'd be seeing less of him.

WE BOTH WERE yawning by the time we finished the dishes that night. I figured Erik would head over to his side, but instead he sat at the counter again with a small, thoughtful frown.

"What we were talking about earlier. Can I tell you something?"

"Of course."

"It's something Pop once said. A man-to-man comment, not the father-son wise advice thing? Just an observation. About women."

"Okay …"

"This was before I left home, I was what, seventeen. We were going on some errand, nice day, spring. Yeah, that's right, I was on my way outta there, and he wanted to buy me a watch, like a goodbye present? We stopped to get ice cream from a woman who had a cart there; then we sat on a bench and ate our cones. Pop watched the ice cream woman as she served other people. She was late twenties, early thirties, an old lady by my standards at the time, but I couldn't take my eyes off her, either. She seemed to *glow*. I mean, she was sort of pretty, but when I did that kind of assessment a guy does, you know, up and down, the inventory, like hair, breasts, hips, legs, checking off the … her …"

"Virtues." I was enjoying his difficulty explaining this.

"Yeah, virtues. She was pretty, but you couldn't say what 'part' of her was pretty. The checklist didn't apply to this woman. And anyway, she was wearing a big apron so you couldn't even get, you know, a good sense of … But she was sexy and alluring as hell. Totally alive in her moment. What's the word? *Vibrant*, that's it. It was in the way she smiled when she talked to her customers—she *meant* it! The way she rang up a purchase and handed back the change. You wouldn't think serving ice cream is sexy, or like ballet, but every move she made was beautiful. Opening the lid of the freezer, for Chrissake!"

"So you two were gawking at her. And Pop said …?"

"We weren't gawking! We were appropriately surreptitious. But we were spellbound. Pop said, 'You know, that kind of beauty, I've seen it before. That effulgence.' I didn't know what effulgence meant, so he explained it was like radiating, burgeoning, blooming. 'And every time I've seen it, it's from a woman who has come into a certain moment of her life. She's sending out rays. Every time, every time a woman like that is ready to take a man and have a baby, her aura, that strength, is sending out a signal. She'll have a baby within a year.'"

"How would Pop know!"

"He said Mom had been that way and he came to her 'like a moth to a porch light.' Then he named a woman he'd known in college, and the daughter of one of his friends, then one of his colleagues at work. He'd noticed their 'effulgence' and before long they're shacked up with some guy and pregnant. He said Mom had noticed it, too."

I tried to picture my father talking this way. He would never have been so forthcoming with me, but that was reasonable—this was one man to another. And he knew Erik was leaving soon; he probably wanted to connect intimately with his soon-to-be-gypsy son. I wasn't scandalized that he'd been talking about a woman twenty years younger. He'd said nothing prurient or lecherous. I couldn't see it as sexist, either, one of those elbow-in-the-ribs comments about the amusing peculiarities of the weaker sex. Pop was not at all that kind of man. It struck me as honest admiration of a natural phenomenon, and an observation made from experience.

"Was he maybe warning you that if you encountered a woman like that, like 'be careful unless you want a kid'?"

Erik thought about it. "No. He was just appreciating the whole thing. He thought it was a beautiful fact about life. We finished our ice cream and went on our way. Never mentioned it again. But I've seen it myself since then. He was right. There comes a moment."

I would have asked him about that—had he seen that moment in his girlfriends, his wife?—but he yawned and looked weary and I figured I should let him go to sleep.

"Nice story," I said. "Dear Pop. Our dear Pop."

He roused as if he'd forgotten why he brought it up. "Right. Annie, I don't know if you feel it, or know it, but you're *there*. You are effulgent. You're putting out that signal. You're ... effulgent."

"Go to bed," I ordered him.

He shrugged, kissed me goodnight, and went out the door. I heard him moving in the next room over as I got ready for bed and turned off the lights.

Chapter 42

FOR THE NEXT few days I checked to see if I felt effulgent—a rather ugly word for a beautiful phenomenon, lending the whole premise a somewhat comic quality that Erik and I joked about. I kind of knew what he meant. But I had known women of every age, very young and very old, who seemed to overflow with vitality, to exude burgeoning energy and magnetism; surely it was not only linked to readiness to take a life mate or have a child.

Still, coming so soon after my discovery that I wanted a child, his comment seemed to warrant serious consideration.

My assessment: Compared to the wreck I was when I first came, I was certainly better. Whereas before I'd been a black hole, emitting no light or energy, I did feel as if I possessed some degree of luminosity again. I felt a strand of resilience inside, strong yet supple, in body and psyche, as if I'd been at least partly woven back together. I was conscious of being fertile—the word wouldn't have occurred to me if I hadn't been working the soil and using the word as a farmer does—a new awareness, almost a sensation, like a sphere of potential I carried, cradled between the bones of my hips.

But sometimes I still curled grublike around loneliness at night, one spoon alone in a drawer without a fellow spoon to nestle into. I realized that the nighttime physical proximity of a loved one provides an existential reassurance in ways that daytime company can't. Your mind may be far away in dreams, but your sleeping body absorbs the warmth of the other, unconsciously counts your bedmate's heartbeats and breaths, and these provide deep and timeless affirmations.

And I was working on a dairy farm. I figured it was hard to feel effulgent or come across as effulgent when you're wearing knee-high rubber boots covered with cow manure, layers of dirty, fraying jackets, a man's knit cap, oil- and shit-stained leather gloves. But when I mentioned this to Erik, he said it didn't matter. To a man feeling those rays, that kind of thing *contributes* to the effect.

Another puzzle, maybe more about men than about effulgent women. In any case, I was usually too busy or too tired to give it much thought.

THE FIRST SNOWFALL set the hop yard into sharp relief. The shadows of the poles doubled the effect of the rows: hundreds of horizontal stripes converging with vertical ones. They confused and dazzled the eye. But they served as marvelous solar clocks. As the sun crossed the sky, the forest of shadows swung across the ground, pointing west in the morning, straight uphill in the middle of the day, and east, toward the farmyard, in the evening. As the solstice grew nearer and the sun sank lower, the bars of blue dark grew longer and longer.

As I predicted, Erik spent less time at the farm. He didn't tell me of his adventures, or where he spent nights when he didn't return. I deduced that he had acquired at least one steady date, because he often drove up to the ridge to make calls on his cell phone. We had no phones in the bunkhouse, but he could have used Brassard's landline; the conversations he was having must have needed privacy. At times I worried about his falling into the bad habits and bad company that had landed him in Elk Ridge, or making other mistakes of judgment a college town and a pretty face can induce. But I didn't probe him and saw no outward indication of it.

Every day, I joined Lynn and Robin for milking and cleanup, then did manure management, scraping the aisles with the skid-steer, pushing poop soup into the grate that pumped it to the lagoon. I shoveled dirty bedding sawdust out of the stalls and replaced it, moved hay and corn silage to the feeding alley. Between daily chores, I plowed snow off the driveway and farmyard and raked it off the eaves of the house and chicken coop apartments, shadowed the vet on her occasional visits, kept track of supplies and drove to town on shopping runs—there was plenty to keep me occupied.

By the second week of December, Earnest still hadn't returned from his southern swing, and I started to worry about him. I left messages on his cell answering service but didn't get a call in return. I imagined run-ins with rednecks who objected to his skin color or police who weren't as accommodating as Officer McGillicuddy. But then one day, his big stakeside rolled into the farmyard, and there he was, climbing out of the truck, that wonderful barrel-bear-shaped form, stretching and rolling his neck to work out the kinks, looking around to check on things.

"Everything okay here?" he asked when I went out to greet him.

"It is now," I told him. "We were getting worried! I left half a dozen messages. Why didn't you call?"

He fished in his jacket pocket and brought out his cell phone. It was broken nearly in half, shedding bits of screen and electronic guts. "Fell out of my pocket and I dropped a chunk of log on it, *ka-smack*. I kept it for a souvenir."

I took his elbow and we headed for the house.

"Jim's good?"

"Jim's okay. Still gets pretty blue, but he's surviving. He's inside."

"What about Will?"

"Seems fine." In fact, since our dinner together I hadn't seen that much of him. He had started another big project and usually came home too late to help with afternoon milking or even to join Brassard and me for dinner. Also, I suspected he'd stayed more embarrassed than necessary about the brucellosis video.

"And your brother? He's good?"

"Erik's not around that much, but he seems to be doing well."

"Women," Earnest stated.

"How'd you guess?"

We went into the mudroom, stomped off, hung up our jackets. Through the doorway, I saw Jim Brassard standing up from the kitchen table, smiling at the return of his friend.

"What're you two chucklin about?" he asked as he shook Earnest's hand.

"Erik," I told him. "And women."

"Well, maybe he'll bring somebody home," Brassard said. "We can always use the extra help."

Chapter 43

A COUPLE OF weeks later, I was puzzled to see Earnest standing at the end of the driveway, inexplicably sending semaphore signals with his arms. As I headed toward him, I spotted a white car at the top of the hill, descending at a rate that suggested uncertainty. It sped up when Earnest stepped into the road and waved his arms more vehemently.

"Old friend," he said. "Haven't see him in quite a while. He's not good with directions."

The car pulled in and parked, and a man about Earnest's age climbed out. From his copper skin and the planes of his face, I could see that he was an Indian, but he was Earnest's physical opposite: tall, slim, narrow shoulders—the shape of a man used to an ergonomic office chair. He wore a blue nylon windbreaker insufficient for the weather.

The two men hugged and then turned to me.

"This my friend Larry Hoskie," Earnest said, beaming.

"Lawrence," corrected Lawrence. Bob the dog moseyed out to nose his crotch, and Lawrence scrubbed him around the ears.

"Hi, I'm Ann," I said.

"Ann! *The* Ann? I've heard a lot about you!" We shook hands.

"Yes, Earnest has told me about you, too," I lied. Earnest had never mentioned him, hadn't even told us he'd be having a visitor.

"Larry is one of these high-tech nutcases," Earnest explained. "Computer-programmer type."

"Lawrence," Lawrence said.

"See what I mean?" Earnest said.

"So," I said, "you're an Oneida, too?"

"Fuck no," Lawrence said. "I'm Diné. Navajo. We were both in the army but didn't cross paths over in 'Nam. We had the misfortune to serve on the same base back here in the States."

"I was in mess and I saw this guy, the only one who had the same … complexion as me. But it turns out he's *Navajo*." Earnest said the tribal name with a disappointed and disapproving inflection. "You know what I mean?"

"Asshole," Lawrence said to me. "You know what I mean?"

They were both grinning broadly, and I recognized this kind of reconnection. With deep friendships, years apart make no difference. You start up right where you left off. There may be plenty of new detail to relate— the life you've lived since you saw each other last—but the fundamentals remain unchanged.

Earnest swatted him on the rear to head him toward the house, and we went in to sit at the kitchen table. Earnest and I drank coffee; Lawrence wanted only tea. "I'm the high-strung type," he explained. "That stuff makes me want to jump out of my skin."

They spent some time catching up. Lawrence said he had come within two hundred miles of Earnest only because his company had secured a contract with a Boston firm and he had flown out to meet their people. He liked the gig because he could still live on the rez and do his work entirely via the internet.

"Navajos, they've got it knocked," Earnest told me resentfully. "Reservation the size of New England. We ended up with a postage stamp in the middle of Wisconsin. And another token patch in New York."

"I'm guilt-tripped, okay, Earn?"

"Earnest," Earnest said. "With an 'A' in it."

"I'll try to remember," Lawrence said.

We drank our hot beverages and I learned some of Lawrence's story: After the army, he went back to Ganado, on the "Big Rez," for lack of other great ideas. He attended Diné College, the Navajo community college up in Tsaile, got his associate's degree, then moved on to Northern Arizona University for his bachelor's. Computers were not a happening thing yet, so he studied electrical engineering. "I figured someday we'd get electricity on the rez," he said drily, "and such skills might be needed."

He met a girl at NAU, got married a couple of years later, and had three kids.

"My oldest daughter, she's thirty. We had another daughter and a son, a few years apart. Out of the house now, but they kept me busy for twenty years."

"Remind me, what's your son's name again?" Earnest asked, baiting him.

Lawrence sighed. "Earnest," he told me reluctantly.

"With an 'A' in it?" Earnest asked.

Lawrence ignored him and showed me a family portrait that, from the age of the kids, had to be a decade or more out of date. They were posed in front of a smudged backdrop in a photographer's studio, dressed up for the shot. His wife was a plain-faced woman, uncomfortable in front of the camera's merciless eye, but the daughters had vivacious smiles and young Earnest struck me as a happy-looking knucklehead.

Earnest asked about reservation life. Lawrence said it was coming along.

"It's not as poor as when I was a kid, not even as bad as when you were out last time, Earn. We got some of the mineral rights worked out in the last few years, collected some major back-due royalties. Lined the pockets of the politicians, even had some left over to build some new housing and water infrastructure. It says something that a guy like me can make a living out there now. There's broadband in Window Rock!" He shrugged and his enthusiasm deflated. "Of course, along with came a heapin helpin of modern America's problems."

I suspected that the men wanted time together alone, and there were chores waiting, so after a few minutes I shook Lawrence's hand and excused myself.

I WAS PLEASED to meet Lawrence and touched by their jive talking. But the encounter made me realize how little I knew Earnest. I didn't know that he'd ever been out west or that he had friends there, including one to whom Earnest was so important that he'd name his son after him.

Later I saw the two men walking, Earnest pointing out features of the farm and landscape, Lawrence nodding, Bob tagging along behind. Neither of the men was smiling anymore; in fact, though I couldn't see that well from my distance, Lawrence seemed downcast, almost in tears. Earnest had draped one of Brassard's checked wool jackets over Lawrence's nylon-clad shoulders. When I came out of the barn again an hour later, Lawrence's car was gone.

LATER, I WENT looking for Earnest and found him in the shed that he used as the farm's repair shop. Coming in through the adjoining room, I could tell from the fluttering light and smell of hot steel that he was welding. I backed in, found an extra face shield, and put it on before I turned to face him. The faceplate was so dark that I could barely make out Earnest's form hovering above the brilliant burn star. He gave me a signal to let me know he'd seen me.

At last he finished, snuffed the torch, and flipped up his visor. I did the same.

"How about taking a break? I'm making some sandwiches."

He gave me a thumbs-up and started putting away his equipment.

We went to my apartment, where Earnest sat on a stool at the counter, shedding cold from his coveralls and giving off the smell of burnt gases and molten metal.

"What are you making in there? Or fixing?" I didn't recognize the long, elaborate but decrepit machine he'd been working on.

"Just adapting an old conveyor that Jim doesn't use anymore."

"Adapting for what?"

He shook his head. "It's a hops-related secret. On a need-to-know basis. Your brother got me going on it."

Impatient, I slapped a plate down in front of him. "Lots of secrets. You haven't caught me up on Larry Hoskie's visit. Every time I learn something new about you, it just opens up a bunch of new mysteries."

He looked offended. "Not so. My life is an open book."

"Maybe so, but I can't read it. Greek? Sanskrit?"

Ordinarily, Earnest would have at least smiled or offered a rejoinder, but now he seemed somber. I put two bologna-and-lettuce sandwiches on his plate, then sat at the counter with my own.

"Larry is a good guy," he explained. "I love the man. He's got a problem, wanted to talk with me about it in person. Came two hundred miles each way from Boston—that's a sign of how serious it is."

I didn't want to offend by asking what that problem might be. "How did you two get so close?" I asked instead.

"If you're thinking about battlefield heroics again, you're wrong. I didn't meet him till we were on base, back here."

"Where you were an MP ..."

"Right. And he ran the PX. PX is basically the store where the enlisted men can buy consumer crap—shaving cream, soda pop, cigarettes, stuff like that. He did the same in Vietnam. Never fought."

"But somewhere in there, you earned his affection or loyalty to the extent that he named his son after you."

My probing irritated him. He glanced impatiently around the kitchen, stalling. "You have any orange juice or something? Welding gives a man a powerful thirst."

I brought out the carton and a glass and put them in front of him. I sat again and waited him out.

He poured, drained the glass in one long swallow, then frowned speculatively at me. "You white girls are pretty smart. Perceptive."

"We like to think so, yes."

"So I told you, I mainly broke up fights and hauled guys to the brig or to their superior officers, or put them back to bed or whatever. Lawrence got into a lot of fights, so I had to … intervene on his behalf on several occasions."

"Lawrence? *Fights?*"

A pause as Earnest folded his second sandwich in half and took it in with two bites. I went to make another.

"Exactly. Not an imposing physical specimen, is he? That was the problem. His build, the fact he'd never seen combat. That meant he was queer, which meant he took a lot of shit off the other guys, which meant he took offense and then needed to be rescued. I looked out for him."

"You'd think the other guys on the base would've gotten the message. After you stepped in a couple of times." I could picture Earnest piling into a group of men and scattering them like bowling pins.

"Oh, they did. It wasn't a problem after a while. They were all good guys, really, just needed a broader perspective."

I smiled inwardly at that. We ate. Earnest checked his watch, I checked mine. Again I waited him out.

"His son," Earnest said. "For Navajos, an uncle is the same as a father. When Earnie was born, Larry asked me to be his uncle and I said yes. In their tradition, that's a great honor and a serious responsibility. Kid and I got to be pretty close after I'd visited a couple of times. Last time was back when he was maybe fourteen. He was having a tough time and badly needed an uncle-type at that juncture. We've always hit it off. Smart, sweet kid. Like his father."

I got up to clear our dishes.

"Some of those modern American problems Larry mentioned— meth and oxy have come in, it's not just booze anymore. There are Navajo and Mexican gangs making it and selling it and killing each other over it. My godson-slash-nephew has a problem with drugs and with the Navajo police. Arizona State Police, too, but the Navajos are touchy about jurisdiction, they've got a lot of sovereign rights, and they won't extradite him to the US. So for now Earnie's still on the rez, but he's not doing well. Larry wouldn't like me to tell anyone more than that. He asked me to help out."

"What—you'd go out there?"

"Got to." Earnest stared at the floor. "There are two other uncles, but one of them was the guy who sold the kid drugs in the first place, started him off. The other is the opposite, so pissed off and ashamed that he refuses to help. Larry wouldn't ask me if it wasn't urgent, if he had other choices."

"What will you do? That his father can't?"

"I don't know yet. Sometimes being the father makes it harder, though. Sometimes a young guy needs an outside voice he trusts, somebody without all the knots and baggage. Apparently I was of some help to the kid last time."

I nodded. Selfishly, I was thinking not about Earnie or Larry but about the farm, in winter, without Earnest. "When was that?"

"Ten years ago." He rubbed his forehead as if working out tension there. I could tell he was already thinking ahead to his trip west. "When I went out for Larry's wife's funeral."

I took that in, and we sat there, saying nothing, for a moment.

"You have my cell number, right?" he asked. He knew I did. I took it as an invitation and felt a little better.

"I think I might have it around here somewhere," I told him.

Chapter 44

EARNEST'S DEPARTURE, AFTER only two weeks at home, began what would be a lonely and difficult winter at the farm. Part of it was the absence of Diz, of course—her continuous activity had made the commotion of at least two people. But Will was also gone a lot on an assignment that took him to Massachusetts for many days in a row; Erik was off seeking love somewhere within a radius of fifty or who knew how many miles and often coming home only once a week, if that. When he did, he seemed in good spirits but revealed nothing of his time away from the farm, not even in contented grins of conquest or pouts of frustration. I didn't grill him, figuring he'd tell me what I needed to know when I needed to know it.

The hardest part was a second long and unexpected stretch without Earnest, in January. He had barely gotten back from Arizona when his sister in Milwaukee called with another urgent errand for him. She had to move out of her duplex because of a rent increase, and the guy she'd married had become nowhere to be found for the past year or so. Two kids, working full time, she needed help. Earnest drove out in his pickup to move her belongings, do some repairs on the new place—"a dump"—and help her get her household set up. We hadn't even had enough time to catch up on what happened in Arizona with young Earnie and Lawrence, and the troubles of modern America hitting the Navajo Nation.

At intervals, I called Earnest on his cell from Brassard's landline after dinner, just to check in with him. He always seemed glad to hear from home, but preoccupied and remote. Within a few days of his arrival, he had helped his sister pack up and they'd taken ten trips back and forth in his truck. His next job was to help set up her new place, which would require some rewiring and wall patching that the new landlord wouldn't have paid for and didn't need to know about. His niece and nephew were great kids, talkative and helpful, but his sister said their pleasant disposition was an illusion; they had put their stubborn, sullen teenage ways on temporary hold only because he was there. Earnest's voice seemed too small coming over the wire when one was accustomed to the bigness of him. And our conversations were always too short, Earnest giving indications of wanting to get off long before I'd let him. In that, he was like my father, Matt, Erik, every man I'd known; I tried not to take it personally.

A big snowstorm blew in just before New Year's, so I got to have fun with the Ford, building mountain ranges at the edge of the farmyard and along the driveway. The tractor and I also enjoyed breaking the three-foot banks left by the town road crews with their enormous trucks and giant plow blades that curled like the perfect surfer's wave. But in the stark white of late December and early January, I was pretty sure that my ostensible effulgence had gone into hibernation along with bears, raccoons, porcupines, and skunks.

ASIDE FROM BRASSARD, Lynn and Robin were my main company. On those cold predawn shifts, it was the headlights of their Jeep I saw in the darkness as I bumbled out for the morning milking. Lynn and her sister-in-law were very different—one slim and blond and graceful in her movements, the other strong boned and with a lovely dark-Irish pale complexion, black hair, and startling blue eyes—yet they were in accord, good friends, working in easy harmony. Three women: We called each other the Fates, sometimes; at other times, when we made more mistakes than usual, the Three Stoogettes. If one or more of us were in a bad mood, we thought of ourselves as the three witches, the Wayward Sisters, in *Macbeth*. I enjoyed these twice-daily interludes of female company and saw them drive off each time with a pang of loneliness.

In the year since I'd met her, Robin had matured, filled out as a person, and I began to think that maybe this was what effulgent looked like. I took to covertly studying her for indications, while we worked, without coming to any firm conclusions.

In midwinter, Vermont is a hard, ragged place. People start to fray. Those cold, short days established a pervasive chill that couldn't be banished by the woodstove or furnace in the house or the kerosene heater in my chicken-coop apartment. The long shed stood full of silent cows, warming their space only by their collective body heat. On moonless nights, the pasture and lower fields became dim gray smooth curves and planes, lonesome, and my land a dark and mysterious mass looming over the near valley to the west. When the moon waxed close to full, the fields gave off an eerie glow, as if lit from beneath the snow. The motion lights that snapped on over the barn and house doors created an island of artificial light, increasing the sense of isolation and blinding me to everything beyond the driveway and farmyard.

I often had dinner alone with Jim Brassard at the house. At first he insisted on trying to help me cook despite the fact that he'd done little of it when Diz was alive—"Wouldn't let me. Kicked me out if I tried." I could see why she had: He was a large man who crowded the space, slow moving, clumsy with his leathery fingers. It was easier for me to take charge and tell him to relax while I pulled something together. Anyway, it was a luxury to have a full-size kitchen and all its gadgets, and I fully indulged in it. I roasted whole chickens with potatoes, carrots, onions, and garlic cloves alongside. My mother, being a Midwestern woman, had been fond of meatloaf and had taught me to cook it at an early age; Brassard claimed he loved it. Beef and pork roasts, winter squash, baked potatoes, chicken pies, baked apples—in the cold times, we enjoyed anything that required using the oven. Sometimes a stew seemed in order, so I'd throw whatever was available into a pot and simmer it for a couple of hours, steaming up the house, Brassard commenting at intervals from the living room, "That smells good enough to eat!"

When Erik and Will were there, talk flowed more easily: more people rowing the conversational boat. But Brassard was not a talkative person, and when he and I ate alone the silences often stretched overlong. Sitting with this midsixties man aching from arthritic joints and still wounded by his wife's death, there in the dark of the deep winter, entailed a lot of patience. I didn't feel right filling the silence with jabber, and there was only so much news to bring from the cows. He knew I could manage only limited discussion of the articles he'd found interesting in the farming journals. To take the edge off the silence, I sometimes brought my laptop over and played music—Celtic tunes I'd borrowed from Erik, or indie singer-songwriters I had downloaded in prehistory—which sounded small and metallic coming through the tiny speakers. I didn't know what sort of music Brassard enjoyed, if any; he never listened to the radio, because here between the arms of the hills the reception was so poor. Sometimes we sat for long intervals during which the only sounds were our small noises of eating, air sucking through the woodstove grate, or wind nagging at the shutters and eaves.

But I don't think he found the silence particularly awkward, and he sometimes surprised me with his candor and insight.

"You doin all right, then, Annie?" he said one night. "After all this. Probably not what you thought you were buyin into."

"I'm doing fine. We've had some teat chap, but Lynn and Robin and I have been—"

"Well, I'm glad to hear you're takin care of the cows. Never had a doubt. I was talkin about you, though. If you're holdin up." He forked some chicken into his mouth, looked up and held my eye.

I wanted to answer glibly, glide past it with one of the many conventions and easy ways out we're accustomed to, but Jim Brassard knew how to cut to the chase and how to spot evasiveness when he saw it. I wasn't sure whether his probing was simply good human-resources management or personal concern, but he did carry authority in him and could show it in a range of circumstances.

"I consider myself fortunate that I came to work on Brassard's farm," I told him. "And I'm glad my brother could land here, too, however it pans out with the hops. The winter's getting a little long, but I'm doing pretty well."

"Came here a little beat-up, though. We knew that, Diz and I. What was it—man trouble?"

"Everything trouble."

He took that in and said, "Times like that for all of us, I guess." He paused, and I could only assume that was how he saw the current era of his life. "But you're doin better now, looks like. Hasn't entirely disagreed with you. And you've been good for this place. For me, Earn, Will. God help me, even Diz would agree if she wasn't dead and so stubborn."

"I am much better now. It helps to know I'm being of some use. I mean, that I'm working, I'm earning my keep, I've got … people to care about."

He nodded and attended to his eating. It was a spacious conversation.

"Question I have is, a woman your age, I'd think you'd want to marry. Good to have a companion. It's a lonely road sometimes, you know that. This farm isn't helpin you there."

"When the time is right, I figure I'll know. Or somebody will discover it and let me know."

He chewed, pondered that for a while. "Well," he said, "Will's got out of his marriage. Guess he's in the same boat now."

I had to smile. Brassard went on eating contentedly, apparently guileless. A farmer, planting a seed and knowing well that patience was required thereafter. It seemed that everyone on the farm thought of Will and me more than I did.

"And a good thing," he went on, hardening. "That gal he married— not right, never was, not for a farmer's kid even if he did go to college. Diz couldn't take the sight of her. Took her to task if she came out here, put her through the wringer. Poor gal. We didn't see much of Will for some years."

"Ouch."

He sighed heavily as his thoughts moved along. "You didn't know her too long," he said. "Diz. More to her than you'd think. Than you saw."

"Well. Sometimes I got a peek inside. And the things she said about me—she was *right*, Jim. She had me pegged right."

He looked at me gratefully. "She wasn't soft anywhere, I'm not sayin that. Just she had parts of her where she wasn't so prickly. Very smart woman. You'd be surprised the things that interested her. Hard to believe, she wanted to raise orchids. Orchids! In Vermont! Just a few, to look at, to play at growin. Years, she was a member of the American Orchid Society, read every issue of that magazine. We'd've had to build some special little greenhouse and we just never got around to it. I guess I let her down that way."

His reminiscence was drifting toward the melancholy, and his face began to sag. "Even got *me* interested. Orchids, for Chrissake! Most amazin damn things! Twenty-eight thousand species of em."

"I doubt she saw it as you letting her down, Jim."

Bob came over to put his head in his master's lap. Brassard stroked him thoughtfully. "Always plenty else to do, I guess."

Chapter 45

IT TOOK ME a while to see that something was changing in Brassard. If I'd had more experience in this domain, I'm sure I would have spotted it sooner. His melancholies lasted longer and got deeper, and he seemed older than his years. When he came to the table, his hand would reach for the chair back, miss, and have to take another try. One morning, he dropped his truck keys in some puffy new snow and couldn't find them, and he had to come out to the barn to ask me for help. I couldn't find them, either, but then I thought to use the magnetic roller we used wherever we worried about nails getting into cows' hooves, or metal into their feed. It's T-shaped, like a push broom with little wheels, except that where the bristles would be there's a powerful magnetic bar. I swiped it through the snow between house and truck until I heard the satisfying click of the keys latching on. Brassard was pleased with my ingenuity.

But I was getting worried for him. Around the first of January, he missed paying a bunch of bills and had to pay some late fees—not for want of liquid cash, just from forgetting to pay, or losing the envelopes.

He left the dome light of his truck on one night, and it would have run the battery flat if I hadn't come along to turn it off. Still, I didn't become consciously aware of this overall drift until he came into the house and didn't take off his boots, didn't even stamp them clean, tracking slush through the kitchen and dining room.

Alzheimer's? I wondered. Depression? Some other sickness?

It was the latter, I discovered. One comparatively warm day—a good old-fashioned January thaw, Brassard said—I opened the cowshed door to the near paddock so they could get some sun and fresh air; they'd drift out on their own. Then I went to the upstairs of the old barn and threw hay bales down through a trapdoor into a utility room that also opened onto the paddock, so I could give the animals something to chew on out there. When I figured I had tossed enough, I took the stairs down and around and was surprised to find Brassard standing precariously on a short stepladder in one of the workshop rooms. He looked over at me as if startled by my appearance.

"And here's the girl, in person," he said.

"Yeah, I'm letting them out for a few hours. Putting the hay out."

He clambered awkwardly down and sat on a bale. "Suppose you're wonderin what I'm doin up there. Gentleman of my years, and all." He chuckled uneasily. I glanced at the ceiling and saw the branching copper gas pipes that radiated from the corner and across the ceiling.

I looked at him questioningly, clueless.

"I've been thinkin," he said, "there's another way for this to go."

"For …?"

He made a big, floppy, encompassing gesture. "For all this. The whole damn business."

"I'm not sure what you're saying. Another way to go … you mean money? I thought Erik had helped out on that score, things were tracking better now."

"Oh, definitely does help. It does help, sweetie. Just not enough. We're still going down the drain, just slower. Damn milk price is stranglin us."

"Would it change if the hops came out well, if next year we put in some acres on this side of the road? They wouldn't be organic, but they'd still bring in some decent money. Erik says his strain is really good and once the brewers get—"

"Oh, it's a grand scheme. Problem is, no vegetable thing is gonna do just what you want. Not ever, especially your first time through. Anything can go wrong. *Everything* can go wrong. Turns out the deer or groundhogs like em, forget about a crop. Couple molds, mildews, aphids, there's a beetle cuts em down like a weed whacker. Looked it up on Google. It'd be easier if they weren't organic, could spray em. What's he gonna do, pick the bugs off one by one?"

"Knowing Erik, he will if he has to."

He laughed grimly. "Talkin to your brother, he says hops're hands-on, cuttin em back and weedin all spring, then pickin em pretty much by hand. Time intensive—he'll have to take on help, and that'll cut his net to hell. Sure, maybe next year we could take out some of my corn and put in more hops, but that still puts the first harvest two years out. Don't know that we'll hold out that long."

Then, to my shock, he reached down and picked up a bottle of vodka from the floor behind him. He didn't drink right away, just sloshed it around, pondering the liquid through the glass. It was two-thirds empty.

He glanced up at me sideways, a cunning look. "Now, don't tell Will or Earn, right?"

"Jim—what are you doing?" I stuttered.

"Oh, don't get on some high horse. What, we're growin six acres of beer across the road and can't take a drop over this side?" Now he took a big slug that he swished through his dentures before he swallowed. He exhaled the burn with satisfaction. "See, the secret with vodka is you can't smell it on the breath," he said, pleased with his ingenuity.

"That's a really bad idea, Jim," I said, gesturing at the bottle. I was stunned, unable to respond coherently. I thought back to the many times I'd noticed his fumbling or mumbling, and realized it must have been going on for weeks.

"Well, I guess I've always been good at bad ideas." He took another mouthful, chewed it and swallowed, then waved one hand in a loose circle around his head, indicating his whole world, whole life. "Got a knack for it."

My thoughts scattered like pigeons when a dog comes along the sidewalk. I didn't know what to do, where to start dealing with this. First thing would be to keep booze out of his hands. I might be able to snatch this bottle, but he could have hidden bottles in any of a hundred places on the farm, stashed in the house or barns or sheds or his truck.

Brassard's face took on that clever, confiding expression again. "You haven't been here long enough, but we used to have a problem with the propane feed. Out back the barn there? Got a sort of a main, comes out of the tank, then branches off to the space heaters in shed and parlor, water heaters, workrooms. Went through a time when we had a problem with leaks. Must be a hundred valves and fittins in here, took Earn a long time to find em and fix em all."

The propane tank was shaped like a giant vitamin capsule: fat, white, blunt-round at both ends, mounted horizontally on two concrete brackets. I guessed it contained at least a thousand gallons, enough to burn down or blow to pieces the whole farm. I glanced up again at the ceiling above the stepladder, the snaking pipes.

"See, you can't use accelerants, like gasoline or diesel, the fire inspectors know that one, figure that out in a heartbeat."

The strange drift of this terrified me. "What is this bullshit, Jim?"

"But an accidental propane fire, insurance would bite on that. Happens all the time. We've never made a claim in forty years, not a nickel. How much they've made off us, we deserve something in return. Forty, *fifty* years—not a nickel!"

"Don't say another word! I'm going to the house. You're coming with me. We're going to call Will."

He just shrugged and remained on his bale, rocking his big torso from side to side. He didn't resist much when I took the bottle out of his hand, but he didn't get up, either, and he was too heavy for me to lift.

His thoughts turned inward. "Hasn't this been just one hell of a year?" he asked himself as I left the room. "One hell of a year?"

I KNEW THAT Will was deep in his project with his production team, but I called him anyway and left a barely coherent message on his answering service. I called Erik's cell with the same result. Then I called Earnest in Milwaukee. He picked up and listened as I spewed the tale.

"Okay. I'll head back. Still, can't get there right away. It'll take me at least a day, probably two, to wrap things up here, I've got wiring hanging from the ceiling, gotta close it up. Then a full day of driving if I go straight through. Say, minimum of three days. You and Will are going to have to manage till then."

"What should I do? What did Diz do?"

"You're not Diz. You can't be Diz. Don't be Diz."

"But what did she do?"

"Ann, I was blitzed myself. She beat the shit out of me, and it scared me to death. This little woman at me like a Tasmanian devil, I never want to see a sight like that again. And what could have happened if I had … reacted wrong. Thinking about it makes me want to puke my guts, literally. She laid down the law for Jim, too. Probably the same general plan. I don't remember it all that clearly." He got silent, then whispered to himself, "*Fuckfuckfuck. Damn it, Jim.*"

By the time we hung up, I had been gone from the barn for ten minutes and my fear mounted. What was Brassard doing in there? I ran back out and was relieved to find him sitting where I'd left him.

I had no script for this. At the legal aid office, we had often dealt with alcohol-fueled domestic abuse or street crime or car accidents, but I always had a desk and a wall of paperwork to protect me from my clients. I never got close enough to their lives to get my hands dirty. I had no experience with the murky ambivalences and painful betrayals and family-shattering choices they faced. I could recommend interventions, rehabilitations, restraining orders, custody transfers, but I had never implemented them or enforced them, never saw how they played out, face-to-face, in real people's lives.

At a loss, I knelt down in front of Brassard and put my hands on his knees and stared into his face as if, by force of will, I could wake him from this awful spell.

He looked at me with blurry affection. Then he said, pleased at the revelation, "I know what it is. My daughter. Jane. Sometimes you look a little like her, Annie. Same age, about. Hair, same. Pretty girl, Jane. That's what it is."

"Let's go to the house."

"Broke my heart she and Diz couldn't get along. Couldn't talk sense to either of em. Damn Diz anyhow."

"Let's go. Get up now."

He shook his head, no, mimed a pugilistic pout of resistance. His affect had changed: A sly humor crept into his expressions and gestures.

"You're not going near the gas, Jim. You're not going out of this room except to the house."

He tried to lean back against the workbench, but it was farther than he'd expected and his shoulders fell hard against it. He reclined there, legs spread wide, boots planted flat, apparently comfortable despite the awkwardness of his position. I hated seeing him like this, pathetic and visibly slackening.

"What did Diz do? When this happened before? Your drinking."

"That business back when?" He yawned. "Yes, Diz. Didn't want to cross that gal. No, you did not!" He chuckled at the very thought.

I realized that whatever Diz had done, I couldn't do it. I could argue, I could threaten, but I'd never be able to strike at someone I loved. Of course I held a pocket of anger deep in me, that awful pit where every resentment and hurt lodges, but couldn't imagine turning it against someone I cared for, even for the best of reasons. Diz could, had.

"Get up," I said. "We're going to the house."

"I'm fine right here. You go on ahead." Still being clever, a disobedient boy. The booze was hitting him hard now.

Without planning it, I stood and with all my strength lifted his big feet up off the floor. His weight shifted and his shoulders slid past the edge of the workbench so that he toppled back under it, clattering into the haphazard buckets, tools, and odd machine parts that had collected there. He lay there for a moment, confused, lower body still up on the bale, shoulders and head tangled in gear. Then he twisted and thrashed, clanking, trying to right himself. He couldn't do it and after a moment lay back, flummoxed.

With a series of jerks, I got the hay bale out from beneath him so that his body slid to the floor. That allowed him to get his arms under him, and he half rolled and curled forward to get his head clear of the workbench top. I took one arm and heaved to help him up. He leaned unsteadily against the workbench as I swiped dirty hay off his clothes.

I gripped his hand and pulled him back to the house. He had passed the point of resistance. His affect of sly humor had vanished and left no emotion or attitude at all in its place. He was simply flat, void. I sat him on the mudroom bench, pulled off his boots, and wrestled him out of his wool jacket.

"Go to the bathroom," I told him. I led him to the door and pushed him inside.

I heard him peeing, then the water running in the sink as he reflexively washed his hands.

When he tottered out, I led him to his recliner and positioned him and let him fall into its embrace, a dead weight. I pulled the lever so that he was almost horizontal, deep between the chair's overstuffed arms. He wasn't asleep, just flaccid, a man made of melting plastic.

I checked the answering machine, but nobody had called while I was out retrieving Brassard. The problem was that I had cows to deal with. They would be milling into the paddock. I had to get some hay to them, and I needed to run water to the drinking troughs out there. And fifteen other chores to do before evening milking. The day's cycle was relentless, and I couldn't stay in the house to make sure Brassard didn't get up and do something dangerous. I waited a few minutes hoping that Will or Erik would call, then gave up and went to rummage in the chest of drawers in the kitchen. I found some duct tape that I used to attach the chair's lift lever to its frame. He wouldn't be able to pull it back to sitting position and, I hoped, wouldn't be able to stand up.

WILL RETURNED AS Lynn and Robin and I were doing the afternoon milking. I heard his car rev in the farmyard and ran out to greet him. He threw open the door and our eyes met and we trotted up the stairs into the house.

"In the living room," I said.

We found Jim safely asleep in his recliner, snoring. His hands lay relaxed on his thighs like contented animals. Will stroked one of them gently, but Brassard didn't stir.

"But what now?" I asked. Will just shrugged, at a loss.

Chapter 46

WILL DIDN'T KNOW anything about dealing with alcoholism, either, but his project management skills stood him in good stead. His first act was to get Brassard's pickup truck out of his reach, keep him from going into town to replace the vodka I'd poured down the sink. I drove the truck to Lynn and Theo's place, and Lynn gave me a lift back in her Jeep. By the time I got back, Will had done a quick search of the house and found another bottle, which also went down the drain.

Then he wrote a letter and emailed it to his lawyer, detailing Brassard's threat and committing the lawyer, as an officer of the court, to tell the insurance company in the event of a suspicious fire at the farm. Finally, he called the state fire marshal's Barn Fire Prevention Task Force and asked for an inspection of the farm's gas systems.

Two days later, the inspector came, checked every inch of pipe and every fitting, valve, and regulator, and declared the gas system compliant. Will showed his father the certification and the letter he'd written to his attorney, driving home the message that Brassard's plan—if indeed it had ever been more than a despairing drunken fantasy—had been preempted. The insurance company would never believe that a propane fire was an accident. There'd be no cash coming in from fraud and the destruction of three generations' legacy.

I'd never seen Will angry, but I caught a glimpse of it when Brassard went looking for his truck keys and couldn't find them. He was in a surly mood, feeling condescended to, hungover, thirsty for what he couldn't have, and as he rumbled through the house opening drawers and cabinets he was frightening: well over six feet, easily 250 pounds, huge hands, face blunt and sour.

After half an hour of searching, he asked Will if he'd seen his truck keys. Will handed him some keys.

Brassard looked at them and said, "What the hell?"

"Those are tractor keys," Will said. I didn't know there could be so much ice in Will, and as he spoke he looked and sounded much like his mother. "You are a *farmer*. You drive a goddamned *tractor*."

WAS THERE A code hidden in that exchange? If so, I think it had several dimensions. On one hand, it was Will's channeling his mother's voice and the deathly chill of her contempt for any weakness or abdication of duty. On the other hand, I have to believe it was also an appeal to Brassard's pride, or a reminder of the pride he should feel. *You are a farmer.* Brassard blinked and started to reply, but his son's words confused him, tripped up his anger and tumbled him into a mix of other emotions. He went away to his office and sat in front of his dark computer screen.

I admired Will for his skillful management of Brassard's fire threat and for standing up to his father about the truck, which must have been agonizing for him.

Earnest returned the next day, exhausted from thirty hours without sleep, and a long drive. I was running the skid-steer down the alley, pushing a tide of slurry, when his bulky silhouette appeared in the brightness of the wide door at the other end. Seeing that familiar shape, my heart bounded. I backed up and met him in the middle of the shed.

Without saying hello, he asked, "Where's Jim?"

I tossed my head in the direction of the far door, where the big green Deere appeared, a small mountain of bedding sawdust in its bucket. It dumped the load, backed up, turned, and rolled out of view again.

He nodded, a little relieved. Otherwise, his face was gray and haggard.

"You look like hell," I told him affectionately.

"Thanks."

I realized he was too exhausted from sleeplessness and anxiety to enjoy my attempt at humor. Having reassured himself that Jim was functional, probably unwilling to walk through a moat of manure to get to him, he started walking back toward the house. But I backed up the Bobcat to keep pace with him.

"Earnest!" I called. He stopped and looked over. "Do you have any idea how good it is to see one's Earnest again? Any *idea*?" And tears flooded my eyes. I don't know why I framed it that way; maybe my odd choice of grammar kept it safely impersonal. But I truly wasn't sure—*did* he have any idea, *did* he know what a marvelous thing an Earnest was? I very much wanted him to know, and saying it relieved an unbearable pressure in me and that was what released the tears.

He smiled and put his hand to my wool-padded arm, softly. "I'm just tired," he reassured me. Then he was walking away again, and after a moment I was going down the alley with the Bobcat for another long scrape.

Chapter 47

AND SO BRASSARD's farm limped into the New Year. Earnest's being there helped. He was ballast for the place, kept us right side up and sailing straight. Especially for Brassard. Sometimes I'd go into the house and I'd hear the two of them in another room, conversing quietly. I don't know what they talked about, but I knew that Earnest wouldn't presume to lecture, shame, or instruct his friend, whom he'd always respected as the elder man.

We were all on guard, watching Brassard, checking for signs, keeping track of his whereabouts. A couple of weeks later, when we finally allowed him access to his truck, one or another of us accompanied him on his trips to town, claiming errands of our own. The farm settled back into a simulacrum of its prior rhythm, but with an added edge of vigilance.

The traditional January thaw never really ended. February was a rotten month—raw, unseasonably warm. Early January's stark, crystalline beauty morphed into dull overcast skies, sleet, freezing rain. The Himalayas of snow I'd built shrank to dirt-crusted little ridges, and the farmyard became a basin of muck and slush. When the weather did flash cold for a day or two, it froze the rain onto cars and trucks and glazed them in rock-hard clear ice that was impossible to scrape off. All the snow melted off the fields and the hop yard, making Erik and Brassard nervous about having adequate water in the spring. Though it was often warm enough to put the cows out, we seldom did, because they came back so slimed with mud that we couldn't manage adequate shed and parlor hygiene; Bob the dog was functionally under house arrest for the same reason. Trips to town became arduous due to the early melting of the dirt roads and the deep mud that resulted.

But the dark sky—that was the worst. Without the drama of a thunderstorm or high winds, no crazy whimsy of snowfall, that static pewter gray weighed on us. The sky literally seemed a burden we carried on our shoulders.

Still, I can now see that something good emerged from that gray smear of a month. You must understand that this is not just my Pollyanna penchant speaking, but one of those insights that can reveal themselves only over time. Nor does it have anything to do with Nietzsche's dour cliché "That which doesn't kill you makes you stronger." No: It's that when people endure troubles together, and stand up to them, they witness the best of each other. There's no other way to discover that resilience but through shared hardship. Earnest, Will, and I had observed one another's varied approaches to dealing with Brassard's and the farm's difficulties, the scope of determination we revealed. We came to greater respect for each other as a result. Greater loyalty.

And Brassard: He cranked himself back upright, inch by inch, marshaled his willpower. Ultimately, it was he, not me with my duct tape or Will with his tractor keys, who bound himself to the mast, kept himself away from the Sirens of anesthetizing spirits. The mast was the work that needed doing and the responsibility of being the elder and, ultimately, the captain of this particular ship. I suspect this was the perspective Earnest had been nurturing in those long-closeted conversations they'd had. Brassard rose to it.

February slipped into March, windier but not much brighter. The wind blustered erratically down in our valley, rattling the branches of the apple trees around the house, but it hit the ridgetops hard and steady; at night I could hear the vast, diffuse roar of my own forest, like distant surf. Looking over the fields without the snowpack, Brassard and Erik grew still more anxious about having enough soil moisture for the crops. Brassard said he had noticed this trend over the past decade: warmer winters, changing rainfall patterns. He read us an article from the *Agriview* newsletter about likely impacts of climate change on Vermont's farming—a dismal prognosis.

ERIK FINALLY BROUGHT a girlfriend home for dinner with us. They had connected at a gym in Barre, where he'd taken a membership and she divided her time as receptionist and fitness trainer. Kiera was plain of face, with unconvincing blond hair, but her gym-toned muscles gave her a nice shape and a lithe step. Though she'd never lived on a farm, she was a native Vermonter and had been around farmers all her life—in more ways than one, definitely not "a princess." In common with Will, she was an avid Celtics and New England Patriots fan and could match him stat for stat. She was about Erik's age, I figured, and they moved easily together.

Still researching the topic, I took Erik aside at one point and asked him if she was effulgent. He rolled his eyes. "No, Annie! Jesus! She's just a good pal."

After that, I added *good pal* to my relationship-cataloging process. I assessed women in the grocery store or hardware store to see whether they were effulgent or were good pal material. Some were obviously contenders for neither, such as Millie, the short-spoken, laughless woman at the general store who had explained to Cat why she kept night crawlers in the fridges. Mostly, though, I had no basis for judgment and so came away no wiser from my inspections. Anyway, I knew there were more categories to be added to the list. Was Cat effulgent? I couldn't see it, but Robin was a definite maybe. Was Lynn a good pal? No, she was much more, too keen and balanced to be dismissed so lightly. What was she, then?

WE HAD SOME good times despite the relentless weight of the sky and the anxiety created by the absence of snow.

On Valentine's Day, Brassard, Will, Earnest, and Erik each gave me some token. I felt very appreciated. Given the diversity of their approaches, I don't think it was a coordinated effort. Brassard's was a Hallmark card with a note written in his careful cursive, wishing me a *Happy Valentine's Day* and telling me "we" were lucky to have me in the family. Will bought me a set of four much-needed earthenware plates, suitable for pasta, playfully colorful, for my chicken coop apartment. Earnest's gift was a cupcake he'd had specially made at the Grand Union's deli counter, red frosting topped not by a sugary heart but by a licorice-looking Pilgrim's hat with an arrow through it, which I considered sublime wit. Erik knocked on my door, opened it before I could answer, tossed me a red rose wrapped in green tissue, and blew me a kiss.

Toward the middle of March, Erik and Kiera decided that we should have a big dinner together. We invited Lynn, Theo, and Robin, and Brassard invited John and Sarah Hubbard, the middle-aged farming couple who owned the land on the other side of mine—eleven of us in all, a big crowd compared to what we were used to. Outside, the weather was raw and miserable, but inside we were a merry bunch, baking chickens and pies and whipping up mashed potatoes and sizzling onions for gravy. Thanksgiving in March. The kitchen and dining room turned tropical. Will and Erik and Kiera argued about sports, Erik's loyalties being with West Coast teams, putting him at odds with the other two. Brassard and Hubbard had a lot of farming to talk about, and Earnest joined them for a discussion of various new implements that were coming onto the market. Brassard, clearly enjoying the crowded rooms and the bustle, looked better than he had in a long time.

I had never seen Robin in anything but dirty jeans, muck boots, and rubber coveralls, had seldom seen her face without a smear of brown on it, but for this occasion she wore an actual dress, simple gray and belted with a thin red strap at her waist, and had her dark hair loose and lush around her shoulders. She was effervescent and vital—stunning, actually. I noticed the men's inadvertent responses and Kiera's less appreciative appraisal, and at one point Brassard came over to me and chuckled: "That girl is a clear and present danger to herself and others."

I decided that Robin was exactly what effulgent looked like, and I was pretty sure I could never meet such a standard.

Chapter 48

THAT GOT US through to April. There was no snow on the ground, but in the end the season turned out happily for all the fields, including the hop yard. The unseasonably warm weather thawed the ground early, and then we had a period of regular rains that put Erik's mind at rest.

Then the spring labors began.

Brassard went to work his fields, days and days of preparing the soil: manure spreading, fertilizing, harrowing, and planting. The cows moved outside, but milking continued and the shed needed spring cleaning. Spring calves began to come, taking every spare minute. And, as Brassard had pointed out in that very first discussion, the hop yard needed an enormous amount of work that strained to the utmost our ability to handle the other chores.

Erik's business plan required six acres to make a net profit, and he'd planted only three last fall. But hops propagate through their rhizomes—those parts of the stem that grow horizontally under the ground, among the roots—which need to be planted as soon as the frost leaves the soil.

The hops grower harvests rhizomes from mature crowns, which flourish despite being pruned.

That meant Erik, and whoever else had a spare moment, had to kneel in the wet, icy-cold soil to carefully expose each crown, clip off sections of rhizome, then mound over the root mass again. We collected hundreds of rhizome sections, filling galvanized buckets and grain bags and plastic bins. Erik worked from sunup till sundown, and by nightfall his knees and back were so stiff he could hardly stand. Working with him, I actually looked forward to milking as a relief from the stoop-labor discomfort and numbing repetitiveness of rhizome collecting. After the first day, we had a good sense of how long the surgery took for each crown, and with around 2,500 to be unearthed, clipped, and mounded back over, Erik realized that it would never get done.

"I didn't take enough courses in human resources management," he lamented bitterly. "My staffing model for this project was for shit."

Ultimately, he hired three enterprising Vermont Tech students, two boys and a girl, out on spring break. Tim, who insisted on being called by his last name, Bailey, had a basketball player's build; Jason was chubby and looked soft, but he was actually quite hardy and put on a good macho act. Jennifer had been brought up among a lot of brothers, so despite her slight build she had a solid punch when it came to rough play, and could hold her own in the badass-insults department. They worked well together.

As much as we worried about the crop and Erik's bottom line, we welcomed their enthusiasm and energy. They got a kick out of thinking they might someday drink beer made from these very plants. Every day at sunrise, a rattletrap pickup, a rusted Toyota like mine, and a jacked-up but hard-worn muscle car parked in my pullover as muffled rock or rap music pounded inside their cabs. Later, even from inside the barn, I could hear the young people's laughter and catcalls from out in the hop yard. But when Brassard saw them, he chewed the inside of his cheeks. I knew he saw Erik's net income shrinking with every hour of help he had to pay for.

At lunchtime I slapped together sandwiches for them, which they inhaled. Lunch at the house, or on the front porch on warmer days, took on a party atmosphere. When Earnest and Will joined us, they answered the kids' scandalous tales of campus life with anecdotes of comparable misadventures on base in the army. Brassard enjoyed it from a distance. He had gotten cortisone shots in his thumb joints and had taken up his pipe again, putting a leathery cherry scent into the cool air.

But the work didn't end when the young people went back to school after break. They had clipped almost three thousand rhizomes, and with the frost safely gone from the soil, all those sticks had to get planted throughout the lower three acres of the yard. Even though Kiera joined in when she could, and the kids worked right through their last weekend off, only one acre's worth had been planted by the time they returned to school.

I can't remember much about that April except for one day of rapture when I came across the first daffodils, bounding out of the ground to say hello. Between farm duties and hop yard, I worked fourteen hours a day. Somewhere in there I noticed the absence of Kiera. When I mentioned it to Erik, he shrugged it off: "If you can't take the heat, stay out of the kitchen. I warned her when we first started going out."

He didn't mean the heat of passion; he meant slavery on a farm. I drew a better bead on what *good pal* meant.

Ultimately, we got the rhizomes in more or less on schedule. Without pausing to inhale, Erik started putting in the training strings, pairs of them hanging down in a V shape from the high trellis wires. When the hops sprouted above the soil, he'd need to guide them to the strings so they would twine and climb. He would allow each crown and rhizome to send up two bines, then clip the rest.

Installing such a huge number of training strings was too much even for Erik's long days and all the time Earnest and Will and I could spare, so again he had to hire extra hands.

They were a uniquely Vermont pair: a middle-aged gay couple with big beards, callused hands, and hard-slim, gnarly bodies. They lived in an off-the-grid log cabin, eating from their own subsistence gardens and earning some cash from a maple sugaring operation. Lunch was fun: Though they looked like hard-bitten hillbillies—"woodchucks," in Vermont parlance—Perry had a degree in philosophy, James in English lit, and they had a marvelously idiosyncratic sense of humor, rich with scholarly allusion. They had been together for twenty years and had married the moment Vermont made it legal.

They also worked like mules. But despite the extra help, Erik was still stringing when the first shoots began popping up.

As THE WEATHER warmed, my apartment began to feel close, no longer pleasantly cozy but stuffy and airless. My land was calling me. The trees were misting with buds, just as they were when I first saw the place, and the air took on that wet tang of earth and ice. As soon as the ground got dry enough, I packed my belongings into their plastic tubs, loaded them onto the little trailer, cranked up the Ford, and dragged them up the hill. Traces of snow still hid in the north-facing shadows of tree trunks and boulders.

When I turned off the tractor and the engine clatter stopped, the forest's subtler noises flowed around me. A few birds, just back from southern haunts, called near and far among the trees; a faint breeze told quiet secrets among the still-bare branches. Distant cows lowing, the scratchy skittering of an invisible red squirrel racing up a tree, the uneven calls of geese following the valley to their summer nesting sites farther north: From the sounds alone, I knew I had come home again.

I worried for Erik and felt guilty for not helping him at every available opportunity. But I was getting exhausted. From work in the wet soil, my hands were so chapped that no amount of Bag Balm could smooth them or heal the cracks. I was not Diz and had sworn not to become her successor, but I felt myself turning into her. So I made it clear to all—Erik, Will, Earnest, Brassard—that I would keep living on my land and I would spend time there sometimes, regardless of the fortunes of the farm or the hop yard. One of my commitments to myself had been to honor my commitments to myself.

So I had a mostly clear conscience as I swept the twigs and leaves off my little platform and set up the tent. Erik had bitten off his agenda here, and he understood my sticking to my own with the same determination he showed. Brassard had his, his family's, fate to contend with, and though our fates were intertwined, I had by now paid an honest price in cash and labor for my acres.

On the first of May, Brassard signed the deed over to me, formally acknowledging that my indentured servitude had ended. It was the beginning of my third year there.

That didn't mean I could stop working at the farm. It needed me, and it mattered greatly to me. If the land was the home of my soloing spirit, the farm was my home among the human family. I had learned that a family—which by then included not just Erik but also Earnest and Brassard and Will and even Lynn and Robin—is an ecosystem. It is as complex and beautiful as my forest. All its parts, all its members, are continually coevolving, each adapting to each, as every living thing must if it wishes to thrive. It is good to be part of it. My land affirmed that I was a bright and strong thread; the farm affirmed that I was woven into a sturdy and comely fabric.

But that deed—I took great satisfaction in having it tucked safely into my sea chest. These woods were now inarguably mine. It was something like a marriage. But the woods could not confuse me with my own ambivalence: I simply and without any doubt or reservation loved this forested hill. Nor could the woods disappoint or betray me, because I had no illusions about what it was I so loved. The forest was an ancient rugged wild organism, tolerating and, at least a little, accepting me.

Chapter 49

I HAVEN'T EXPLAINED a great deal about the darker aspects of dairy farming, in part because even by the end of my second year there I still didn't know the whole story. Finally coming face-to-face with them was a wrenching experience that brought me up hard against my own hypocrisy. I came to appreciate Will more from working alongside him and for his willingness to talk with me as I wobbled through it all.

A dairy farmer carefully oversees the cycles of cows' lives: their periods of giving milk, drying off, delivering calves, getting pregnant again. It's a testament to Brassard's skills that he can manage his herd to sustain steady milk production throughout the year. Of course, he also has to maintain a consistent herd size—he can't have more cows than his fields can feed or his barns shelter—so he also has to deal with the end fate of each cow. They're born; they must die.

I understood the need to put down the occasional cow that got badly injured or irredeemably sick. Since I arrived, Brassard had twice shot cows who had broken their leg or pelvis, carried their bodies in the Deere's bucket loader, and dumped them into the pickup bed. I myself had sorrowfully shepherded a number of limping, head-hanging cows, declared unsalvageable by the vet, to the truck that would take them to be butchered.

After two years on the farm, I thought I had left behind a lot of my stupidity, but when I took part in the regular culling, I discovered I still had plenty in reserve. This culling was based on hard pragmatism—determining which cows had lived out their profitable milking lives and then selling them off the farm. It occurred regularly, but I had never taken part in selecting culls; Brassard himself oversaw it.

Before coming to the farm, I unconsciously assumed that cows just gave milk automatically, the way hens lay eggs. But that's not true: They have to get pregnant and give birth to lactate. Once impregnated, they carry their calf for about nine months—amazingly, still giving milk to the tube for seven of those months. A cow's milk production is highest just after giving birth, then dwindles until, after about ten months, she's allowed to "dry off"—not be milked—for two months. Calculating these cycles for a hundred cows; maintaining another sixty heifers at various stages of maturity until ready to breed; staggering the timing of impregnation, milk giving, drying off, and calving; *and* projecting cash flow from it all—I couldn't imagine how Brassard or any other dairy farmer did it.

Calves arrived throughout the year. We took them away from their mothers three days after their birth, moved them to a different shed, then fed them by hand on a mix of milk and other nutrients until they matured enough to eat grain, hay, or grass. At first, the calves were bawling, lonely, hungry little animals, and their vulnerability awakened the maternal instincts of Robin and Lynn and me. But they calmed quickly and started eating grain and forage within a few weeks, and their frisking told us they enjoyed the company of their fellows in this cattle kindergarten.

But Brassard didn't need the calves; they were largely a by-product of his need to keep the herd in lactation. He sold the males immediately to be raised for beef or veal; he also sold some females, keeping only enough to replace the older cows who would be culled. The ones he kept would mature to about fifteen months—that's what a "heifer" is, a young cow before her first pregnancy—and then he'd impregnate them.

When I first started at Brassard's place, I helped feed the calves but didn't participate in the removal of the ones to be sold off the farm. As low man on the totem pole—Earnest loved calling me that—I was the designated specialist in manure management, so I was usually otherwise engaged. Anyway, I had too little experience to help choose the older cows to be culled; in fact, it had never completely dawned on me that if new cows were entering the herd, an equal number had to leave it to keep the overall herd size constant. I didn't really know what became of these healthy cows, only five or six years old, when they left the farm. If asked, I probably would have said they went to someone else's farm, or to some vast cow retirement pasture to live out their lives in contentment.

But that's not how it goes. When they get culled, they're trucked away to be butchered.

In big commercial operations, farmers pump the cows full of hormones so they produce lots of milk. Such cows get used up fast, typically lasting for only three lactation cycles before becoming a "loser"—that is, she's costing more to feed than she's earning from her milk output. At four or five years old, she's culled and shows up at McDonald's or in your supermarket's meat or dog-food section.

Brassard's cows were not exploited so hard. He ran an old-fashioned farm in that his cows spent five months outside each year, eating fresh grass along with high-quality foodstuffs we put out for them. Even in the cold months, they ate mostly hay and corn silage grown on the farm, and since Brassard bought less feed, his costs were lower and his cows could remain profitable longer. A few had been around for as long as ten years.

Given that he really was a cow whisperer of sorts, Brassard amazed me by his ability to accept the necessity of culling, while sincerely feeling affection for his animals. His gentle but firm treatment always calmed them and made them more amenable to being compelled to do things. He talked to them fondly and his goadings were more like suggestions. Certainly, I had no such talent.

When he asked me to help with selecting culls, I told him I didn't want the responsibility. I wasn't up for handing out death sentences. I couldn't maintain objectivity about those cows I had come to know as individuals and had given names to. But when he insisted, I understood his rationale: By now, I had seen each cow up close every day and had a good idea of her health and behavior and milk output.

I also figured I should face into this hard fact of where the food I ate came from. Feel like a burger? A cow has to die, I told myself sternly. Put cream in your coffee or have a cheese sandwich, a cow has to be milked, and every cow that's milked eventually gets culled and killed.

Reasonable cognitive dissonance, mentally balancing two conflicting imperatives? Or just hypocrisy? I still haven't entirely decided.

WILL AND ERIK inadvertently made culling much more difficult for me.

One evening after Robin and Lynn left, milking and cleanup done, I came out of the barn to find Will standing with one foot up on the wooden fence, staring out across the pasture. The fields were still lit by a gentle sunset glow, and a faint mist had lifted from the soil of the valley and hillsides, softening all forms. The cows stood out in black and white relief on the distant pasture slope, scattered widely, heads down, cropping up grass.

"What're you up to?" I asked.

"Nothing. In itself rather nice."

It was. I stood with him and shared the tranquility of the fading day. Far across the pasture, in a thin belt of marshy land near the stream, the spring peepers were tuning up: a few questioning calls, then more, then more until, within three minutes, they sang out a continuous racketing chorus. From farther down, the peepers in one of the small ponds at the end of Brassard's land joined in.

"Amphibian love songs," Will said. "My favorite sound on Earth." He got quiet, then asked, "What are your plans for the evening?"

They weren't plans so much as necessary rituals: "I'm going to cook dinner in my apartment down here and then I'm going to head up to camp. Why?"

"Because I just remembered something I used to do when I was a kid.

And I thought I'd try it again and wondered if you might want to come along."

"What is it?"

He laughed. "It's sort of stupid and sort of magical. Why don't you have dinner, I'll cook up something for Dad, and let's get together in another hour or so. When it's full dark."

Mystified, I agreed, and he headed off to the house.

An hour didn't leave time for me to hike up to the tent for dinner, so I went into my tiny Spartan apartment. I blinded myself by flicking on the electric lights, then set to boiling up two packets of the ramen I kept in the cabinet for times when I was too tired, or the weather was too rough, to trek back to camp. The noodles were exquisite, as almost any meal will be when you're very hungry—no other seasoning is as good as a hard day's work.

I had just finished when Will knocked and stuck his head into the doorway. "Ready?"

"What exactly should I get ready for?" I asked.

"Just a short jaunt. Regular boots, a sweater or jacket. Pullover hat is optional. That's about it."

We went out into the night. The motion lights didn't switch on, and Will explained that he'd turned them off for now: "Better in real darkness."

He led me to the wooden fence and climbed over, and when I joined him he headed without a word into the night. I assumed that not talking was part of this; up on my land, I had learned the value of silence. We went diagonally uphill and across the pasture, into the vague dark, toward the peepers and toward the scattered white blotches that emerged from the darkness—the cows' black parts had melded with the night. As we got closer, I could see them react to our approach, lifting their heads from the grass, or standing up quickly if they'd been reclining. Will headed toward the densest cluster of the herd.

We plugged onward. After another few minutes, we were far enough into the darkness that the house lights were no longer rectangles but just a cluster of dots. Then we came over a slight rise and started down toward the wetland where the peepers were now rioting, deafening, and the house lights were lost from view. We were between the roll of the hill and the black mass of Brassard's eastern forested ridge, with no visible lights or any evidence of mankind's existence at all. This could have been the twenty-first century or the Stone Age.

My eyes had adjusted to the dark by the time Will signaled that we should stop. He was a colorless man-silhouette, and the blotched cow shapes were inexplicable as they moved uneasily in the darkness.

Will lay down on the ground, signaling me to do the same.

I hesitated. It was chill and felt wild here, and I knew what a Holstein cow was. Their long-lashed, docile eyes are misleading: They can be stubborn, obnoxious animals and, if you're not alert, dangerous. Each was ten times my weight, and when I was standing, the heads of some were higher than mine. There were times when I could have sworn a group of cows literally didn't even know I was there and therefore didn't obey my shoves and scoldings. Even their absentminded unruliness could knock me over, and the bad mood of one could send the whole herd into uneasy motion that threatened to become a stampede. And Queenie—just the sight of her war-paint facial markings in the milking parlor gave me a flutter of trepidation.

I was leery, but I lay down near Will, belly to the ground, feeling very vulnerable and wondering what we were doing.

The peepers racketed. The white blotches moved in the darkness and after a while I noticed the blotches growing and gathering, and soon I could see the whole cows, dozens, coming toward us. Some were clearly agitated, approaching us sideways, bucketing in defensive display as they came.

Will lay contentedly on his stomach in the grass.

Soon we were surrounded by a shifting, shoulder-to-shoulder circle of Holsteins, craning their necks to bring their noses closer to us, jostling, stamping, uneasy but curious. Did they recognize our scents? If they did, why were they so jittery? I lay there, paralyzed, surrounded by a towering wall of huge animals, rows of knobby forelegs, faces as big as my body.

They were huffing heavily, not at all calm, and their eyes were wide and wary, showing white. Some pounded their hooves an arm's length from my face.

"*Rose! Rosie!*" Will whispered. He held out his hand toward one of the cows, and now I recognized her, too: a sweet-tempered smaller cow whose side markings vaguely resembled roses. Rose cautiously extended her nose, snuffed at Will's hand, and seemed to calm.

Then a commotion started. Back in the herd I could hear scuffling and the shifting of hides against each other. And then Queenie burst her way through the inner ring. The others sidled away, deferring to her. Of all the cows, she was the one I least wanted to see out there.

Her appearance agitated the others and I grew terrified of them all. We humans didn't really command them, I realized. At milking time, they obeyed the demands of their swollen udders, not our goading and cajoling. In the dark, I could feel their animal natures and knew that their fear could easily turn to desperate, defensive aggression.

Queenie shouldered closer, leaned her massive face so close that I felt the moist heat of her heaving exhalations. The peepers seemed to be screaming. Will didn't move or speak.

We spent a full minute in stasis. Then, as if some message had passed among them, other cows moved forward, shoving aside the first circle. I felt them—their individuality, their identity within their natural social structure, the herd. Did Queenie signal her approval of us? I don't know. But one after the other, they approached. I'd named several of them myself and called to them by name as they came near: Bertha, large and rather clumsy, thickset in body but with a relatively small bag. And Twiggy, overcoming her skittishness to satisfy her curiosity. Each one calmed further when they recognized us and felt reassured.

They began to drift away. Perhaps we'd only bored them with our stillness. Or the allure of grassy slopes drew their ever-hungry mouths. We lay there as the circle reconfigured and thinned; after fifteen minutes, the last of them had wandered back into the darkness.

Will rolled over onto his back. I did the same. Through the mild haze,

I could just see the blurred stars. We were alone on the gentle slope of Brassard's upper pasture.

"Cool, huh?" Will said. He put his hands behind his head and looked over at me. There was enough light to see that his face was split by a boyish grin.

We walked back in companionable silence, hugged goodnight in the farmyard, and then I crossed the road and headed up the steep track to my tent home there in the forest darkness.

ERIK ALSO SHOWED me another dimension of bovine character and made culling all the more awful. He always carried his harmonica with him and often improvised bluesy meanders on it when he was trying to make a decision. He discovered that the cows were fascinated by it. When he wheedled near the pasture fence, they'd drift toward him from all over the hillside, a slow avalanche of ambling black and white forms. They pressed forward against the fence and watched with fascination, ears upright, lifting their wet snouts and snuffling for olfactory clues to what this strange sound meant. Within a few minutes, scores of cows would be crammed together in a semicircle, rows of bony backs radiating from its center, Erik.

Their fascination, their wonderment, moved me. Like anyone, they were bored by their regimented lives and welcomed having something new to inspect. As they watched and listened, jostling and craning around each other's head for a better view, they struck me as simple souls—gentle, innocent creatures. They snuffed and shifted, marveling and puzzling. Their faces struck me as expressive, and watching them as Erik played, I realized how individual and distinct each face looked now that I knew them better.

Erik got a huge kick out of their attention and took pleasure from giving them some entertainment. I loved seeing it, too: Erik at the epicenter of this checkered crowd of big, inquisitive animals. I empathized with the pleasure they took from this departure from daily routine. I felt for them and knew them. After all, I had milked them and spoken to them and pushed them and washed their teats and rubbed Bag Balm on their chap, fed them and watched them gratefully chow down. Some of them I had nursed by bottle when they were calves. It hadn't occurred to me that I'd also have to help kill them.

ON THE DAY appointed for my first culling, we herded them all into the cowshed. Will and Brassard and I walked among them with clipboards and pencils, pages of notes we'd taken throughout the year, and Brassard's spreadsheets. We jotted ear-tag numbers to identify likely culls. Will had done this many times before going off to college and knew a lot about it from making his films; he was a good judge of a cow's health. Brassard checked various signs of vigor and energy level and bag health. We chalked the bony rear ends of some and put pink tags on their ears. I knew half of them by name. Bertha got chalked—she was robust in body, but that small bag doomed her. So did Savannah, for whom calving was difficult and required long recovery and vet bills; she was simply not pulling her financial weight on the farm.

Will noticed my increasing reluctance. He took my elbow and asked, "You want to keep going? It's hard if you're not used to it."

"Yeah, I should keep at it," I told him. I set my teeth, and when Brassard asked me I grimly told him what I knew of milk production for each, and read him information about health issues and birth dates from his spreadsheets. As we went, I plunged into the self-punitive state I'd arrived in. I knew how Diz would have put it to me as she scorned my sentimentality: *You want to wrestle with your Inner You? You want opportunities to Prove Yourself? Here you go.* I agreed with her voice in my head and decided that I had to see this process to the end.

We separated seven culls and moved them into a small paddock defined by temporary electric fencing we had set up. They were to loiter here, wondering why they were pulled away from the herd, until the knacker's wagon arrived. Released from the shed, the others wandered off into the pasture, disinterested.

Brassard went inside to call the buyers. Will and I leaned on the wooden fence, looking at the culls in the paddock. We had put in a feeding trough and filled it with good silage, a last meal for the condemned, and they went to it and did what they did best: ate.

"So," Will said, "where are you at?"

"In an urban, stupid, naive place. A hypocritical place."

"Don't be so hard on yourself. We're looking at death row. I can see how it wouldn't be easy, especially first time around."

"Thanks."

Trying to cheer me up, Will told me about Robert E. Lee, the fierce devotion his soldiers had for him, his love for them, and his agony over the fact that "to be a good commander, you must order the death of the thing you love."

"I'm not a commander. I'm a farmhand," I told him bitterly.

He nodded equivocally at that. "Lynn and Theo, down at their place?"

"What about them?"

"Lynn raises goats."

"Yes, she makes *soap* from their *milk*," I snapped, impatient with him.

Will seemed oblivious. "Great soap, too. So … she has to breed her does every year, right, to get the milk? And can't keep growing the herd forever, same as here. What happens to the male kids, or the extra does?"

"Sells them, I suppose." I'd never thought about it.

Will kept on, breezily: "Well, she does sell a couple. But she and Theo butcher three kids every year and put the meat up in their freezer. They had an outdoor roast a couple of years ago, people came from farms all around, one of the kids spitted and slow cooking over a wood fire. I helped baste. The meat was delicious."

I knew that Lynn named every one of her goats, even the new kids. I tried to picture her—her fine white-blond hair, delicate intelligent face, gentle presence—conducting that murderous ritual every year. And I couldn't. I decided I had to ask her how she did this.

Will watched me process this. "I'm not doing a great job of making this easier, am I?"

"It isn't your job," I told him.

He got quiet. We waited for the buyer. I reminded myself that

Brassard's cows had lived very comfortable lives, about the best possible for a dairy cow: They'd never gone hungry or been subjected to pain or lived in filthy or cramped conditions. They had enjoyed many sunny days on grassy slopes, had received veterinary care at the slightest sign of ill health. They ate a better diet than they would have in the wild and they didn't endure harsh cold. I reminded myself that in the wild, hunger or predation or disease would have killed these cows at a much younger age.

It didn't help much.

"Maybe I'm not cut out for this line of work," I told Will.

He grunted. "Tell me about it."

Eventually, a huge pickup truck turned off the road, pulling a cattle trailer with slatted vent windows. I realized I had seen that truck often over the past two years, sometimes coming to Brassard's, sometimes rolling past to another farm on the meat dealer's route. The cows got anxious when the rig backed toward the paddock, and they wheeled and flinched at the harsh metallic scrape made by the aluminum ramp when the men pulled it out.

That was the hardest part: seeing their confusion and fear as the crew goaded them into the trailer. I didn't let myself think of Bertha or Savannah by name as I said goodbye to them.

Then it was done and the tailgate closed and the cows were no longer visible except as abstract black and white forms moving uneasily behind the ventilation slats. Will took a receipt from one of the men. The trailer pulled away and up the hill. We walked back to the house.

Brassard was in his office, pecking at a calculator, reading glasses on his nose, somber but businesslike. Culling was part of his job and he'd done it hundreds of times, and he was glad to have this round done.

He glanced up at my face, which must have been drawn and grim. "I know what you mean," he said as if I'd spoken. "Damn thing is, the culls are often the ones been around the longest, so you know em better. Not my favorite part of the job. Don't know I could ever raise beef."

He turned to Will: "How's about we get a fresh pot of coffee goin? I'm thinkin Annie could use some refreshment."

Chapter 50

May 18

Deep in the woods today, I experienced a moment of heart-kicking fright, an electrical sense of alarm that I haven't felt since that first day I walked my land, when some big animal startled and crashed through the brush near me. I think it was worse this time because it brought me abruptly out of a serene and contemplative state of mind.

I've been trying to rehabilitate myself after the murky discomfort the culling instilled in me. I know there's nothing I can do about the world's appetite for cow's meat or milk, but of course that doesn't mean I can't make choices for myself. Walking up here after giving death sentences to seven cows, I knew I could elect to become vegan: eat no milk, cheese, or meat, wear no leather.

What does it say that my first act upon returning to my hill that night was to make a dinner consisting of a couple of grilled cheese sandwiches, sizzled in butter in my iron skillet?

One way I've been trying to steady out and recharge has been to spend more time up here alone. As always, it's working. Also, I've embarked on a project. Maybe it's a half-assed way to retreat from my animal-kingdom consternations by concerning myself instead with the world of plants, but a few days ago, after a conversation with Earnest, I realized that I know nothing about my woods.

I know my trees emotionally, I suppose. I live among them; they really are the walls and the roof of my "house." I even sort of say hello to a few that have distinguished themselves by their unusual shape or particular beauty. But when Earnest rattles off tree names, I have no idea what he's talking about. For him, "beech" and "chestnut" and "box elder" are real and distinct entities, each with its own lifestyle, each with particular leaves, blossoms, and fruits, each providing homes or food for certain animals. Each offers specific challenges to climbing, trimming, or felling, and he can see them in his mind's eye when he tells me about his workday. I finally got sick of pretending that I knew a cottonwood from a telephone pole, so I decided I should get a better idea of what he's talking about.

And, of course, he had long since anticipated my need to know my surroundings, by giving me that beautiful little guide to Vermont's trees and forest plants. At one point, he asked me, "So, have you read my autobiography yet?" In retrospect, I see that the book was an invitation to his world—a personal gesture than I didn't fully appreciate at the time.

It's filled with photos of leaves, trunks, blossoms, berries, and nuts, along with drawings of their profiles and diagrams of their way of branching, which varies greatly. When I've had spare time, I've taken to walking around with book in hand, inspecting trees and low growth. I can't believe I wasn't paying closer attention all along.

Thus far: Beech trees are the ones with that smooth gray bark. I think of their trunks as the legs of elephants, but lighter gray and without the wrinkles. They have a miraculous way of branching: horizontal limbs, uniformly spaced, their spiky-edge leaves held in spacious flat layers, creating a superbly organized "leaf mosaic." If you lie down with your head at the trunk and stare upward into the green, you can see how neatly the leaves arrange themselves to gather the light that slants through the layers above.

Turns out it's the beech that makes the little shells I find all over, about the size of marbles, split and covered with spikes. The squirrels and birds eat the nuts, of course, but so do bears! In fact, the book shows—and I've been finding—smooth gray bark puckered by four-pointed claw marks made by bears climbing to get at the nuts.

The ash has rougher, spongier bark seamed with vertical grooves, a handsome sartorial choice that reminds me of tweed. They grow tall in this sunlight-competitive environment, but their foliage strikes me as insufficient for such big trees. They have compound leaves, meaning that several little boat-shaped leaves spring from a single stem, and when fall comes the whole cluster detaches at the base. Earnest says it's these ash leaf clusters I've seen sometimes gliding through the woods like paper airplanes. Will says ash makes great firewood and that rocking-chair rockers are usually made of it because it's so strong yet so flexible.

Black cherry trees do make hard little berries, but not the "cherries" we put on top of ice-cream sundaes. Their trunks have almost-black bark in loose scales or flakes and are wigglier than the upright columns of ashes. Will, my advisor on the qualities of firewood, says cherry is responsible for that sweet smell that sometimes fills the farmyard when Brassard's woodstove is going, something like the scent of his pipe tobacco.

Oaks: There are very few here, so I'm especially glad to come across one. "Strong as an oak"—they deserve their association with all things sturdy and durable. And yet, they have a bohemian side, these staid trees. They branch in an improvisatory way—free-form, rebellious dance gestures. When the cold season arrives, the leaves turn a heavily lacquered purple-brown and make a brittle rustle, almost a clatter, in the wind. They're the most generous of trees, and the animals flock to the mat of acorns they shed.

The white birches I recognize because Pop taught Erik and me how to use strips of their turpentine-scented papery bark to start campfires. They tend to grow in groves that stand out bright against the darker woods all around, seeming sunlit even on dreary days. In twilight, they can look like lightning bolts rising up from the ground rather than descending from above.

And, of course, I know maples, the most numerous trees on my land, with their hand-shaped, comely leaves and the showers of helicoptering spinners they send down. What I didn't know is that these seeds are called "whirligigs," the perfect name. Will says I have a good stand and should consider making syrup.

It's a calming sort of "hobby," learning one's trees. I'm doing well with my deciduous trees, but next I need to get to know the evergreens. So far—not a point of pride—all I know is that they're evergreen and we use them for Christmas trees.

I WAS HAPPILY absorbed in this exploration, far to the northwest corner of my land, when an explosion of crashing and crackling made me jump. It was close by, and that shocking primal fear hit me all at once and full blown, my pulse slamming in my neck, hands tingling. Something big thumped and careened violently among the low-hanging branches. Then I glimpsed a man between the tree trunks, hurtling away, disappearing in some low growth.

"Who are you!?" I yelled. I imagined one of the Goslants, come to poach again or sneaking up on me for who knew what purpose. "Stop! I mean it! Stop right now!"

The adrenaline of fear mingled with anger from the memory of those deer guts, and without thinking I ran after him, shouting, "I've got a gun! Stop right now!"

He burst from the thicket and began running pell-mell downhill. Then he tripped, landed hard, and tumbled messily for ten feet. He came upright again, holding on to a tree trunk, looking back at me in terror: a short, thickset man in jeans and a ragged T-shirt. He froze as I ran toward him.

"Who are you?" I demanded. "What do you think you're doing?"

"Ricky!" he said. "I won't be bad!"

The pitch of his voice and open innocence of his face surprised me, and my first thought was that he was just a child of perhaps twelve. Then, as I got closer, I recognized his body shape and the wide, blunt features of his face: He was a young man with Down syndrome, probably closer to twenty.

"Don't shoot me, okay?" His chest was heaving. "I won't be bad!"

The sight of him broke my heart. His arms and face were badly scratched where branches had torn him, and his warding, supplicating hands were bleeding and dirt-smeared, probably from the fall he just took.

"Ricky," I panted. "Your name is Ricky?"

"Yeah. I'm a really good guy!" He pronounced it without a *d*, "*goo'guy.*"

"Ricky, don't be afraid of me."

"Okay. Won't be afraid," he said, terrified.

"Where do you live?"

The corners of his mouth twitched down. "Got lost."

"If you tell me where you live, I'll take you home. Can you point in the direction you came from?"

He looked around, then back at me, shaking his head, disappointed in himself. "Got lost."

I wanted to touch him, reassure him, but was afraid he'd spook and run again. "Why don't you come with me? You're all scratched up. I'll take care of your scratches and then we'll figure out where you live. Okay?"

I turned, beckoned him to follow, but he didn't move.

"I don't really have a gun," I said. I tucked the tree guide into my belt and held my hands out to each side. "I was just scared when I first saw you, that's why I said it." My pulse was only now slowing.

"Okay," he said.

We began picking our way up the slope. After another minute, he said, "Live with Grampa and Gramma now."

"That's good! We'll get you back to them so they don't worry about you. What are their names?"

"Grampa Homer is my grampa. He's a really good guy."

Homer, the patriarch of the Goslants—Ricky was his grandson, or some descendant at any rate, and now in my care.

"I know where Grampa Homer is," I told him. "Let's get you back there, okay?"

"Okay."

I have always loved the look of people with Down syndrome. It is as if they're a tribe or family of their own, living throughout the world, sibling-similar despite variations in the color of skin or hair or eyes. There's something sturdy and trustworthy about them, these short, stalwart people, and those I've known have all been cheerful and touchingly appreciative of any chance to socialize. Their faces remain astonishingly unmarked by age, so I often assume they are younger—a family of perpetually youthful and innocent people. At the legal aid center, I got to know two teenagers with the syndrome: one unable to speak and needing accompaniment wherever she went, but physically affectionate; the other talkative, gregarious, and able to get around town on his own. Clearly, Ricky was more like the latter.

He didn't have anything to say as we walked, so I filled in the silence. "I was out here learning the names of the trees."

"Names of trees," he said, bobbing his head.

"Do you know tree names?"

"Too many." Shaking his head.

As we headed to my campsite, I introduced him to each type of tree and showed him the pictures in the manual; he was hugely pleased to see a photo of the bark or a leaf, and then, right next to the photo, the real thing. His face settled into a companionable smile, and he said the names after me: "Black pine. Yellow birch."

At the edge of a more open spot, we came to a stand of young poplars—they're the ones with the roundish leaves, pale green on top and silvery underneath. They are peculiar in that the leaves flutter in even the mildest breeze, and where most trees receive the wind in synchronous waves, each leaf of the poplar oscillates in its own rhythm. "These are poplars," I told him.

He looked at them for a moment and then beamed. "Butterfly trees!"

And he was right: It was as if each tree were entirely covered with green butterflies, flapping their wings at different tempos. Since then, I have never thought of the poplar in any other way.

Back at camp, I warmed some water on my Coleman stove and washed his scratched arms. He winced at the sting, but he was relieved to discover that the wounds were not as big as they had looked when they were crusted with blood. I took extra care in sponging the scratches and bruises on his face, and when I was done I rubbed anti-itch cream on the fly bites on his neck and temples. He gratefully accepted a drink of cold water and a couple of fig bars, and by the time we started down to the farm we were good friends.

"How'd you get so lost?" I asked him. "You were a long way from Grampa's house!" He'd been at least a mile away from the Goslants' place, through rough country.

"Just got lost," he mumbled, his face closing up.

"Were you ... looking for something?"

He didn't answer, but his expression showed that my questions upset him.

"Were you going somewhere?"

"Johnnie got mad," he said.

"What do you mean he got mad?"

"Said I wasn't a good guy, I was stupid, I should go away. He hit me. Then I got lost." He brushed his cheek with one hand, and I realized that the bruises there were not from stumbles in the woods.

I didn't respond, but this was another notch in the tally stick. I was increasingly beginning to dislike Johnnie.

WILL'S CAR WAS just turning out of the driveway as we came to the end of my access track and onto the road, and when he saw us he stopped. He looked quizzically at me and dubiously at Ricky.

"This is Ricky," I told him. "He got lost and needs to get back to his grampa's house. Want to give us a lift?"

Will checked his watch. "Goslants, I take it."

"Goslants!" Ricky confirmed, brightening.

Though clearly not pleased with the duty, Will agreed to drive us, and we went around the car. I had planned to get in the front seat next to Will, but when I opened the rear door for Ricky, he looked frightened again. I got the sense that Will made him uncomfortable. "You sit in the back seat too," he said. He stayed hunched in the door frame, looking up at me, until I joined him. Will's eyes met mine in the rearview mirror.

"My name is Ann," I told Ricky as we drove up the hill. "I forgot to tell you."

"Hi, Ann," he said politely. He offered his hand, and we shook.

"And this is my friend Will."

"Hi, Will." Less certainly.

Will smiled vaguely and dipped his head hello.

"You kind of look like Johnnie," Ricky said.

"Nope. Not Johnnie," Will said.

The drive to the Goslants' place took only a few minutes, but I could feel Ricky's anxiety rise as we got closer. His blunt head turned uneasily as he took in the landscape. His lips worked; he reached for my hand tentatively, but when I took it his stubby fingers clenched mine hard. This young man was suspended in an agonizing state of relief that he'd soon be on familiar turf, and fear of what would happen there.

As we drove, I began to wonder about that myself—how I'd deal with Johnnie, how far a confrontation might go. My shoulders tightened and I became uncertain of my self-control.

We got to the Goslants' just as a beige pickup swung into the drive. It had a State of Vermont Highway Department logo on the door, and when we came alongside, I could see that the driver was a man in his sixties, gray haired, wearing a checked shirt and horn-rimmed glasses. He looked over at us with concern and suspicion. My first impression: a face conveying great resignation, as if this man had witnessed and endured many hard things and did not expect any end to seeing and enduring them. When he spotted Ricky sitting beside me, his eyes closed and his head dipped forward in weary relief.

I knew this had to be Homer, the Goslants' patriarch and the solid foundation of their world. He got out of his truck, and when I got out— Will stayed at the wheel—Ricky ran to him and hugged him hard.

"I got lost," he apologized to Homer's shirt.

Homer held Ricky's head against his chest and looked over at me. "I was just out lookin for him. Where'd you find him? Where did you go, Ricky?"

"He was way down the hill there, in the woods."

"Johnnie hit me. So I went away."

Homer's face received this injury but didn't explain Johnnie or apologize for him; he held himself with dignity, defying shame, refusing to air dirty laundry in front of strangers.

"Johnnie's not here now," he told Ricky. To me: "Thank you for bringin him back. We were worried. He's my grand-nephew." To Ricky again: "Go see Gramma now, okay? Johnnie isn't here. She'll make you something to eat. Grampa has to go back to work."

Ricky reluctantly let go of his grand-uncle, went staunchly up the steps, waved to me, and vanished into the house. Homer turned to me, a man weary to the marrow. "He won't bother you again. He's just here for a while, got problems at home. I'll see he doesn't bother you again."

"It wasn't a bother," I said. "He's a sweet person."

"I'll have a talk with Johnnie," Homer concluded. The gray of his hair seemed to make an aura of that desolate color around him. His weariness seemed boundless, his burden of worry beyond weighing, his resignation absolute. He climbed back into the truck and waited for us to back out first.

WILL WAS RUNNING late, so he sped back to the farm.

"He was so scared when I found him," I told Will. "Kind of scared to get back home, too, though." I was relieved to have arranged a happy ending for the adventure, but Johnnie hovered in my thoughts. I'd seen him only that once, and yet I'd conceived a fear and something like hatred of him.

"I'd be careful about drawing too many lines between yourself and the Goslants," Will said stiffly.

"Well, I didn't know who he was. I couldn't leave him running around the woods! He seems like a perfectly nice person. Homer, too."

Will didn't answer. In another few minutes, he pulled a U-turn and stopped his car in my parking spot opposite the farm's driveway. "Sorry to be in such a rush," he said.

"No, I appreciate your taking the time."

"Annie. Just … think twice about getting connected up there, okay? Lots of things to feel pity or sympathy for, the instinct to take them under your wing, I know you're that kind of person. But don't ever let them think they're … in with you somehow. I'm just saying."

He sped up the hill, dust swirling behind his car.

I began the hike back up to my camp, thinking about Ricky and Homer and Johnnie. And Will: How many times had he heard that same warning from Diz? She must have instilled a deep aversion in him from infancy, one that wasn't entirely rational and so couldn't be articulated. I wondered whether it was based on some real experience or was just Diz's shame—or, rather, her pride in the distance she had so rigorously maintained from these kin.

Chapter 51

SPRING RIPENED INTO longer, benevolent days, lush with the scent of growing things. Brassard's fields hazed green; flowers burst into bloom in Diz's untended gardens. The hop yard needed endless work. Once the plants had climbed a few feet, Erik—we—had to go along the rows, snip about half the strands, and pull them off the training strings. This would spur the roots to put more energy into the remaining bines and would assure the mature plants of enough sun when they filled out and began producing cones.

But again, the sheer number of plants made it impossible to complete the job within the time frame the pruning cycle demanded. So Erik hired the Vermont Tech kids on a day-to-day basis, and Perry and James came when they had time free from their own gardens. Robin, working long hours with the intent to save enough money to buy a car, arrived on her mountain bike when time allowed. The two-mile pedal, uphill the whole way, didn't seem to tire her at all. And with her strong thighs in cut-off jeans, the flush of exertion in her cheeks, billed cap worn backward, her effulgence had become a palpable force. The Vermont Tech boys could hardly bear to look at her.

We often saw deer at the edge of the pasture or along the back roads, and Perry warned us that if they liked hops, Erik would be in deep trouble. He said James and he had erected seven-foot mesh fences around all their gardens and had even buried the bottom of the mesh two feet below the surface to keep out burrowing groundhogs.

Erik's online research on the topic produced ambiguous answers. No, hops are too bitter, deer will stay away. Yes, they'll eat hops when the bines are young. It depends: Deer in some areas will, some areas won't.

Putting seven-foot fences around six acres would take all summer and cost a fortune, so at Perry's suggestion Erik started a new ritual. Everyone— men and women—had to pee around the periphery of the hop yard. Erik even pissed in a plastic milk jug at night so he could distribute it in the morning, and he led Bob along the roadside verge three times a day to water the weeds together.

When I came down from camp in the morning or returned at night, I stopped to do my share. The Vermont Tech students thought it was a scream, chiding each other for not contributing enough, and making up endless weak jokes. "You're in trouble now!" They cornered Erik and had a mock-serious talk with him, explaining their concern that the uphill urine border might percolate down and spoil the flavor of the hops.

Erik laughed it off. "How do you think Budweiser and PBR get their unique flavor? Brewing's best-kept secret—keep it to yourselves." We must have put hundreds of gallons around that yard over the course of the summer.

Erik also slept out in the yard with Bob and an air horn. "This is a lot like the old days," he remarked sourly. "Waiting for the buds to ripen, keeping interlopers at bay."

Whether it was the pee or the bitterness of the hops, the deer didn't show. The hop yard flourished.

IN EARLY JULY, I had a disconcerting moment with Earnest. One after-noon he came back from a tree job at three o'clock—early for him and surprising because this was the height of his working season. It was a hot day, and as he often did, he used the garden hose to rinse wood chips and dust out of his hair and off his upper body. I happened to be in the kitchen making myself a late lunch, and when I saw his bare torso I was shocked to see red welts all along his left rib cage and up over his chest. He winced as he palmed water onto himself.

I went out to him just as he finished. "Earnest! What happened?"

"Nothing." He hobbled over to the faucet to turn off the water. I stood there until he remembered that I didn't relent when I had questions.

"I took a fall. Not all the way down. My harness caught me, but the rope gave me a burn. That's all."

"You're limping!"

"Yeah, I was hanging there and let myself down too fast." He was angry at his own stupidity. "Twisted my ankle when I hit. No big thing. Not the first time."

I wrestled the story out of him. He'd been working on a long-dead elm, and he'd wrongly gauged the strength of a couple of branches. One broke as he stood on it. He'd rigged a safety rope to a branch above him, but when the first one went and his weight came onto the rope, he felt the upper branch crack and give.

"I'm thirty feet up. All of a sudden it's just air beneath me, I'm holding a slack rope in my hands. I fell about twenty feet and was lucky the rope snagged on something that held. It stopped me hard, like *chonk!* I was sort of stunned, so then I misjudged my release and landed off balance. Ankle went over. I could hardly walk at first. Figured I should call it a day."

I was appalled—at myself as much as the accident. I had worked with Earnest, had seen him balancing far up in the lattice of big trees, seen him swing from place to place with a chainsaw in one hand, and I'd thought only of the danger I faced when I let down a big branch!

There's a simple reason for my blithe, oblivious perspective: It had never occurred to me that what he was doing was dangerous. He was so happy up there, so confident, so in command, that it seemed effortless. I had begun thinking that Earnest was invincible and invulnerable, a blunt-featured, copper-skinned Superman. He was like the sun or some other elemental constant. Just as the rope had brought him up hard, I came up suddenly against the knowledge that he was mortal after all.

My face must have revealed my concern, because Earnest went on: "I thought I was going to die. Seriously, I was so scared, my whole lunch passed before my very eyes."

He'd set me up with that, caught me entirely off guard. "You're such a shit!" I told him.

He limped over to the steps of the house and sat down carefully, body glistening, the waistband of his jeans dark with wet. I followed him.

He scrubbed his fingers in his hair, scattering droplets. "It's my own fault. I wasn't paying attention. I think I'm losing my stuff."

"One mistake doesn't—"

"It's not the first time this summer. Nothing else that serious, but lots of little miscalculations, little oversights." He shook his head, bit both lips, disgusted with himself. "You can't afford that, up in a tree."

I wondered whether I should rub some lanolin on his rope burns, maybe tape some gauze over them, but I decided not to. By now bruises were coming in, blue under the abraded skin, and they'd be painfully tender. I also knew he'd rather forget about it, not have me underline his vulnerability with too much solicitousness.

But, thinking back, I *had* noticed a change in Earnest during the past few weeks. Or was it longer? He had been quieter, more restrained. Blue, I thought, and distant. It troubled me.

I sat there with him. "Did you have a good rope man?"

"He's fine. Good worker. Not his fault. I paid him for the full day anyway."

"Why do you think you're off your stride?"

He glowered at his hands, shrugged. "Preoccupied. Distracted. That's all."

I wondered what was bothering him. Something with his Navajo friends, or the uncertain fate of the farm? His sister? A girlfriend he hadn't mentioned? Or some other aspect of his life?

My stomach growled and I remembered that I was starving and that lunch-making materials were waiting on the counter inside. Finally, I stood up.

"You really lost your lunch?" I asked.

"That was a feeble attempt at wit. Didn't have any lunch."

"I was just making myself a sandwich. How about I make you one?"

He needed a moment to think about the proposition. "No. I'm fine. I should try to get something done as long as I'm here."

"With your ankle like that?"

He rubbed his eyes wearily, still reluctant but yielding. "Okay. I guess a sandwich would be good." He shook his T-shirt to shed some dust, and put it back on with an inadvertent groan.

WE TOOK OUR plates and coffee mugs to the dining room and sat on opposite sides of the table as we ate. Earnest had nothing to say and barely glanced at me.

"What is it?" I asked.

"What's what?"

"What's bothering you. You're not just preoccupied. You don't smile much. You seem ... guarded."

He chewed, swallowed, looked around the room as if the answer were somewhere on the wallpaper or sideboard or china cabinet. "Just another aging fart's midlife crisis."

"That pisses me off, Earnest."

"What does?"

"Every word you just said. First of all, you're insulting a friend of mine! And 'midlife crisis' is flat-out ducking me."

He shrugged. I stared hard at him.

Earnest never did well under an unyielding glare from me. He heaved a sigh of surrender. "It's simple. I've screwed up some things in my life, and now I've got to think about what I'm doing and why. And what's next, what I want. I need to make some changes, but I can't figure out what they should be. So my mind goes around and around and doesn't come up with solutions and then I fall out of trees."

He inspected his coffee, took a swig of it, and finally did look at me. "I'm pretty sure you know something about that state of mind." He didn't smile, but his eyes warmed with the resigned amusement of a fellow sufferer.

"Yes. I am familiar with it." He knew what an understatement that was.

We finished our food, drained our cups. Earnest stood and collected our dishes, but I stopped him as he limped toward the kitchen.

"Is there anything I can do to make it better? I mean your state of mind. Given my expertise in the subject, and all."

He gave one small cough of a laugh. "No. Nothing for anybody but me to do. Thanks, though, Pilgrim." His eyes met mine, and a little arc leaped between us—his appreciation for my concern.

He rinsed the dishes; I dried. Then I went back to the cows, and over my protests, he gimped out to his project in the machine shop.

Chapter 52

By NOW I was fairly competent at living on my hill. But the woods continued to change me, and in ways I could never have imagined.

It's hard to tell all that I've seen and done, because I doubt you will believe it. But this is a fact: When you live in the woods, especially when you're there at night, all night, you experience unusual things. At moments, you glimpse other dimensions of the world that are always present but that we're habituated to ignore. Encountering them can upend your view of life and of your place in it.

I have been candid about the Great Fear and my own foolishness and weakness, and I've done my best to honestly describe the other inexplicable powers and wonders that revealed themselves to me. What happened that summer seems unbelievable, but I can only relate it as I experienced it.

To put these events in perspective: I've never been superstitious. I grew up in a proudly secular family. Though I've always felt that there is something like "God," my sense of that being is not like anything I've encountered in anyone's scriptures, tracts, or sermons. I've never taken LSD. I can't claim to have had a "paranormal" experience. And as far as my primal fear of unnamed forces dwelling in the deep woods, the Great Fear, I know only that in the right circumstances we all can feel it and that when it arrives, one knows one is experiencing something primordial and real.

Here's the thing: The world will teach you. It will. When you've been busted open as I had been and you're on unfamiliar ground, the true world steps in and reveals itself. And it's not what you expect. Most often, your days' events are explicable by all the facts and assumptions you absorbed in science class. But sometimes, very rarely, you are allowed a peek through a crack in the door—no, through a crack or flaw in that misleadingly solid-seeming edifice of assumptions.

I can't explain what the "mechanism" of a miracle is. There is no mechanism; there's a vast living thing that dwells everywhere. I can't further define it. Ultimately, it is beyond definition.

ONE EVENING IN the middle of July, I returned to the tent grubby and exhausted. Erik was still slaving at his hops, using the last of the daylight, planning to sleep at the bunkhouse.

Since the day Earnest fell, I had been increasingly conscious of his mood. He seemed remote, didn't talk or laugh as much. If he smiled at all, it was with a rueful tilt. He became opaque, and I began to feel less at ease around him. And in my solitary times, mostly when I was alone on my hill, I began to experience my own unease, a muddled amalgam of tension and something like dismay.

But this had been a good day, and that disquiet had subsided as I walked up the hill and into the forest's calming embrace. The calves were healthy; we'd introduced the new cows into the rest of the herd with no problems. No equipment had broken; Brassard seemed good. I had snagged Earnest when he got home, and made him visit me in the milking parlor as Robin and I worked. He seemed more relaxed than he had in some weeks as he told us about his day. He stayed only a few minutes before going off to work on his mysterious mechanical project, but this momentary return to our regular sync eased me and contributed to the calm of the evening.

As the sun went down, the forest cool slowly reasserted itself, pleasant on my skin. I made a crude shish kebab of vegetables and sausage slices speared on a stick, basted with an improvised marinade of Perry and James' maple syrup, soy sauce, and mustard, and seared over a hot fire. I ate it with satisfaction, and the world felt in harmony: tired muscles, good day's work done, full belly, dinner music of the veery and wood thrush singing as they headed for their nests. Blackflies gone to wherever they go, and only a few unmotivated mosquitoes.

For once, when the fire burned down to embers and the last sunlight was almost gone, I didn't go into the tent. Just sat on my log, lazy, pleased with life, too tired for the necessary rituals of battening everything down and lighting the candle lanterns. Night came out of the leaves, blue-black spreading into the air, and for some reason it seemed particularly full of expectancy. I didn't exactly like that feeling, but it intrigued me and I didn't retreat from it. In another little while, the trees hid in full dark, no moon yet, no clouds to bounce down the last high rays of the sun. The woods grew quiet. The stealthy noises began.

By now Erik had no doubt called it quits and was probably in his room, showering or eating soup, unheated, right out of the can.

Finally, reluctantly, I made sure all food was put away and the fire safely doused. I thought to read for a bit, but when I put on my pajamas and slid into my sleeping bag, I went out like a snuffed candle.

I awoke to find the tent wall glowing, a palomino mottle of light and shadow. Through the screen I saw the moon rising, just a middling young crescent but enough to send pearly shafts through the trees. I got out of my bed and unzipped the door and went out to look at it. It seemed not an astronomical thing but one closer to the ground, the blade of a slow-moving sickle, slicing harmlessly through the highest branches. I smiled up at it and then, without a thought in my head, I moved toward the darkness uphill. I slipped into it. That sense of imminence had burgeoned. The night was waiting. My mind was utterly devoid of thought or intent.

July 14

I don't understand anything about this, but I'm overwhelmed by gratitude for it. I have just been in proximity to a great mystery, on the dizzy verge of the unknowable. I'm trying to write by moonlight and it's probably three a.m. and my fingers are clumsy as they try to scribble human words. As if I've come back from another shape. What just happened? What did I do? What part of me knew, what was I calling, what was calling me? I'll never be able to tell anyone, because it is too incredible, people will think I was on drugs or dreaming or am lying.

I woke up from a sound sleep and went out into the darkness. In my pajamas and socks! The moon gave enough light to see my near surroundings. I was drawn to go into the woods, into new parts, into the deepest. With just socks on, my feet could feel each twig and shift to avoid snapping it, I didn't step but rolled my feet over the dead leaves, making only the softest wrinkling noise.

I had no destination in mind, but I never hesitated or had to decide which way to go; there was only mindless certainty. I felt an inexplicable sense of high anticipation. It is like fear in that it comes on us in unknown places and makes us hyperalert and we don't know why it's there or what it means. We know it's risky, but it IS NOT fear. It's the call of mystery. That's the only name I can think of for it. The call of transformation.

I walked toward nowhere and—this is the hardest to figure out—for no reason I began making a noise. With my lips pursed as if to kiss, I said, "shhhhhhh," a shushing noise but long, falling from higher to lower and modulated at the end by tightening my lips, more like "shhhhhhhew." It was a long exhalation and very quiet. I made it at regular intervals, not with every breath but maybe five times a minute. It was purely irrational. I had no reason for doing it. Why would anyone do it? I was just doing it. I was supposed to. I drew in deep breaths and blew out "shhhhhhhew," the noise of wind moving through pine boughs.

I went uphill for a while and then my body knew to head downhill and to the northwest. Probably I went well past my own borders onto I don't know whose land. Very thick forest, trees bigger than mine, more pines and spruces. My eyes adapted to the dark more than I'd ever known they could; everything stood out clearly in that dim gray and pearl light.

After fifteen minutes or so I saw a special tree. It was about as thick as Earnest at the base, came straight up to waist height and then one wide branch, thick as I am, came out at a right angle, perfectly straight and horizontal for about four feet. Then it bent sharply and went vertical again, parallel to the main trunk, its high branches lost among the tree's other limbs. I remembered that Pop called these "Indian trees," claiming that in the old days the Indians bent saplings' branches to point toward a route or place, then kept them trained that way, road signs in the woods. I climbed onto the horizontal part, feet up on the vertical turn of branch, shoulders against the main trunk. I kept making my long, whispered "shhhhhhhew." It was crazy. Every fifteen seconds or so, I made that tiny quiet sound. No reason.

I lounged there. That feeling so much like fear was strong and it was wonderful—highly awake except no thoughts and no focus of attention. The woods so glorious, the moon very muted in the evergreens there. Windless. I lay, purposeless, just feeling the pregnancy of the night, expectant but of nothing I could name. Still making that noise.

After about twenty minutes, I heard a series of soft cracklings from the dark, growing closer, and a faint rubbing sound, something passing through brittle pine boughs. I didn't startle, felt no fear, as if I knew it was coming. I just lay still, making my absurd noise. Then the opaque black at the periphery of my vision seemed to bulge and separate, and two big pieces of shadow came my way. They were bears, and instantly I knew they were the same ones who had visited my camp two years before, but much larger now. They were "my" bears. They rolled toward me and as they got closer I could just hear the faint deeper thud of their footfalls. Their muzzles were paler than their bodies and I could see them looking my way, round ears alert, then raising their heads to scent the air.

One approached me directly, while the other took a wider route. They made soft grunts to each other, quick short sounds like a noisy eater enjoying his food, but from deep within their massive bodies. I held perfectly still, lying in my wooden hammock, still making that absurd shushing whisper.

I can't find words to describe my state. Not trepidation, more like intense exhilaration. It was definitely not fear, but the feeling, so much like fear, that is really just absolute alertness and aliveness. I knew them; I knew this was supposed to happen.

Within half a minute of their first appearance, they had moved right next to me. They looked up at me with benign curiosity. One came close and I felt its hot breath on my hand, which rested on my stomach. The other shouldered aside the first to do the same, then grunted amiably.

I kept making my sound, only now it was a sort of song I was singing about loving those bears so, so much and celebrating us meeting each other here and not being afraid of each other.

They were not alarmed to find me there, not even surprised. One partly stood and gripped the vertical part of my branch, its claws making a crackle on the bark, to sniff my feet in their wet socks. The other did the same on the main trunk of the tree to snuffle my face. Its face was only inches from mine, and its eyes were purely curious and devoid of ill intention. They seemed like human eyes, inhabited by an intelligent being, by a soul. Its huffing humid breath smelled rich but not foul. After a few seconds it got back onto all fours, took a few steps away, and sat down. It looked like a fat man resting, taking a breather for just a bit. The other bear came over to it and cuffed it lightly, affectionately, with one huge mitten of a paw.

They sniffed the air, then the ground, looked at me, looked around the woods, grunted a couple of times. The sitting one got back on all fours, came back to sniff my face again. Then it was time to go. They had other business to attend to. As they moved away, they craned their faces around to look at me one more time, and then quietly crackled back into the shadows, merged with them, and were gone. We had been together probably four minutes.

And I was finished, too. I stopped making that call. I was joyous, over-flowing, and sated. I knew it was time to head back to camp. I had completed the intended errand.

I didn't know the way, hadn't paid any attention when I came, but I headed unerringly back here. I glided, my feet had learned the ground, I was sliding along in the silky diffuse moonlight.

Now I'm still so full of joy but my human self is flowing back into me again. Fatigue coming on, blissful, sleepy. What happened? How did I know to wake, to walk, to make that noise, to go to that particular tree? Never done anything even remotely like it. Never felt so at ease anywhere, never so, what, so guided? So released of intention, so without purpose yet so sure of what to do. Didn't seek this, didn't know there was this. I didn't feel impelled by some instructive spirit being, just that emptiness with a story wound into it, me following the story where it went. Playing my part, surrendering. I never had a rational thought, like "bears are dangerous," or its opposite, "there are no known instances of a Vermont black bear injuring anyone." It wasn't a sudden eureka wow epiphany of wisdom awakening in my soul. It was just an easy coming to know, a sweet destined gentle curious meeting of strangers, just the gentlest gift of knowing that could ever, ever be.

I DID TELL Erik and Earnest about the encounter, by urgent necessity, but this is the first time I have ever revealed it to anyone else. I know you might not believe me. But it explains how I changed and why I did what I did not long after.

My bear encounter: Now I think that's how the pull of our larger destinies works, too. For no real reason, we go making a strange small noise, a secret song consisting of, oh, our way of talking, our ironies or mumbles, that Irish accent we affect sometimes, or the clothes we choose to wear, our habitual faces and moods, the music that's on our iPod, as we mosey along in our lives. We get that stupid tattoo on an irrational whim, we buy lunch from that particular falafel stand because we like to look at the Turkish guy's thick mustache. We just do. We're turning this way and that, finding our way in unknowing response to some irresistible gravitation. And others are drawn by it, equally unaware. If we even notice, we think we're making choices, but really we're just fulfilling the same impulse as my bear-calling "*shhhhhhhew.*" It's just much larger and longer-term. We don't know we're making that random sound in all the ways we express ourselves, don't know why we are who we are, don't know we're on such an inexplicable yet destined journey. We may not trust ourselves or the world that deflects us or lures us or obstructs us. But we blithely continue, heading toward whatever meeting awaits. And that's how magic finds us.

Chapter 53

By late July, Erik's hops had climbed eight feet up the coconut-fiber ropes he'd trained them to. Brassard said he'd never seen any plant grow that fast. Erik told him they had hardly started: In the next few weeks they would gain another six feet and then thicken as they exploded with cones. In all, he expected that each acre of trellis would be holding about ten tons of hops plants, all that mass sprouted from tiny shoots in just three months. If nothing went wrong, he would harvest perhaps three thousand pounds—after drying—of hops cones from the top three acres. The lower three acres, grown from rhizomes, would produce only half that in the first year.

Before the plants rose up their training strings, the trellis was an odd place, not pretty, with almost-straight rows of vertical poles connected at the top by wires, just like telephone poles. But once the bines climbed higher than my head, a hop yard became quite wonderful—a series of paths between near-vertical walls of foliage. Deep in the middle of the yard, it felt pleasantly secret, an enclosure like a topiary maze in an old

English garden. When the sun beat hard on it, I could almost hear the bines reaching, stretching, spiraling upward with remorseless muscularity.

Though in many ways my life was now more coherent, I was living in several distinctly different worlds. To my days working on the farm, and to my time in the woods, I had added working among the hops alongside Erik and, often, Will. Earnest's tree business kept him away three or four days a week, and when he returned he had essential farm chores to do. Earnest and I saw very little of each other, and at times I wondered whether he was deliberately avoiding me. I yearned to tell him about my bears—I knew he would hear it without skepticism and would understand the magnitude of it—but I never found the right time or place.

Will was working on a video project that explored new farming trends in Vermont, so he justified his hours of menial tasks among the hops, always with a camera, as possibly worth a few minutes of the planned forty-minute video. He had a hard time keeping Erik from clowning for the camera.

MY MIRACULOUS NIGHT with the bears stayed with me. My mind turned it this way and that, but I still couldn't slot it into any conception of the world's workings I had ever known. I walked around with that wonder and reverence resonating inside. I held it against my heart like a precious thing, a gem of inestimable value.

This reverence—its violation—explains why I responded as I did when a Goslant killed on my land again.

One evening, I was wandering through my woods, loving them but also doing an offhanded inventory of straight hemlocks and white pines—by then I knew my trees pretty well—that Erik might use for another trellis should market demand call for more hops. I was looking up at trees, not at my feet. Up near my northeastern border, I stepped in something that slid under my feet and made me leap away. When I looked down, I saw another heap of guts on the forest floor. Another deer had been killed and field-dressed here, the abdominal contents left to rot.

Then a horrible thought came to me: Maybe the pile wasn't from a deer. Maybe it was the intestines and organs of one of my bears. The thought came like a scream, and I nearly vomited. My night with the bears was transcendent, a guiding if baffling star in my personal cosmos. Killing one of them was beyond blasphemy.

This time, there could be no ambiguous rationale. It was simply poaching, out of season, illegal, on my well-posted land.

My boot was slimed with the wet of that pile. I stood paralyzed for a moment before I could leave the scene. It was fresh; flies were just starting to find the mess, buzzing and whining past me as they headed toward their feast.

I knew that one of the Goslants had done this, no doubt Johnnie.

You must understand that I bore the Goslants no ill will. I saw them as victims of institutions and history, and if they were hungry a quest for protein was entirely justified. But Brassard said Homer, the patriarch, had worked for decades on the state road crew, making decent money. Johnnie's pickup truck was almost new and customized with fat chrome exhaust pipes, pin-striping, and spring-mounted double antennas. Several of the family were seriously obese; they weren't hurting for calories.

I marched down the hill, furious and heart-wounded. The first person I encountered was Will, camera nearby as always, weeding the hills and trimming the bottom leaves from the bines. I was breathing hard and my face burned and it must have shown, because he said, "Jesus! What happened?"

I told him about the guts but didn't mention my fear for the bears. He sat on the ground and signaled me to do likewise. My state alarmed him, and I knew that the idea of a confrontation with Johnnie frightened him.

"This is exactly the kind of thing we don't need," he said. "The others are just PPP, not so bad, but Johnnie's a loose cannon. He's got some bad-apple buddies, too. Best thing would be to call the Fish and Wildlife Department and have a state warden talk to him. But I doubt you could prove he did it."

"What should I do? I can't just let the little shit-ass *fucker* do this—"

"Let me go up to the Goslants'. I was born here, they'll accept it from me better than you, some flatlander getting in their faces." He cleared his throat and glanced away. "And I'm not a woman. And I don't sleep out in the woods by myself up there."

He turned to look at me, making sure I got his meaning: He would not be as easy a target for retaliation after a confrontation.

My fists clenched white on my thighs. Will saw them and put his hands over them, gripping lightly. "Annie. You gotta calm down a little, okay? Please? I'll go up there. I'll talk to Johnnie. We'll sort it out."

I declined his offer of intervention but thanked him and told him he was right, I should think about it and get a handle on myself. I left him to the hops and went back to the farm.

I FOUND ERIK sitting on the front step of the worker's dorm, a rare moment of repose. He had been making phone calls to equipment suppliers and was taking a break. His restless hands whittled a stick with impatient strokes of his sheath knife. He nodded as I told him.

"Want me to go kill him for you?" he asked indifferently.

"Erik, come on!" Meaning take this seriously. Actually, he frightened me. He wore a denim jacket cut off at the armpits, biker-style, fabric frilled around the cut edges, his arms cording as he shaved off curls of wood. His forearm tattoo, if you didn't know what it said, looked sinister.

"Relax, I was kidding. Well, exaggerating," he said with no irony, glancing up at me, dead-eyed.

I saw an edge in him, maybe forged in defending his drug turf and surviving seven years in a penitentiary, and I realized I didn't really know what my brother was capable of.

"Don't," I said. "Don't do anything. I mean it. It's my land. It's my problem. Do you hear me?"

"Okay!" He looked up at me with irritation, then softened. "Okay." He whittled some more. "But if they ever mess with you personally?" His jaw muscles striated and his knife flashed as he hacked a big chip off his stick. "Whole nother story."

Just then Earnest came out of the barn, and when he saw us together he walked over.

"What obtains?" he asked.

I told him about the guts and said that Will had offered to go up and talk to Johnnie. I wondered whether Earnest would volunteer, too. Of the three of them, he'd be the last person Johnnie would want to see on his doorstep.

"I'm afraid it might be one of my bears," I blurted. The thought made my eyes tear despite my fury.

"Your bears?"

"I have a couple of bears that come around," I hedged. "I ... like having them there." I couldn't formulate words that would carry the enormity of my feeling. "They're my ... they matter a lot to me. *They really matter to me!*"

They absorbed my stumbling explanation and vehemence without comment.

Earnest blew out a long breath, then bit his lips as he thought about it. He looked at me as if weighing a decision, glanced over at Erik, brought his eyes back to me.

"Yeah, you should definitely go up there," he said at last. "I mean *you*. On your own."

I was shocked. He wasn't trying to be funny. But I was terrified of Johnnie, of guns, of what might have happened to the minds of people like him, living in such financial and cultural poverty, envying the world they saw on their satellite TV and resenting that world for shoving them aside in every way unless they showed a willingness to violence.

"Yeah, right," I said.

Earnest came up to me, looked me up and down, squeezed my biceps experimentally, finished by stroking my hair out of my face and staring into my eyes in a purely analytical way. "What d'you think, Erik?"

My brother caught Earnest's eyes uncertainly. But he stood up and came over to feel my arms and then my shoulders, like a boxing coach checking his fighter's readiness. He finished by bringing his hand down my back and, clowning, to my rear end. I swatted his hand. Earnest smiled grimly.

"Strong as a house," Erik proclaimed.

Earnest nodded and rolled his head to work a kink out of his neck. "Go for it, Pilgrim," he said carelessly. He walked into the house. Also feigning indifference, Erik stood, stretched like a cat, and headed back to the hop yard.

I HIKED UP to my place, my redoubt, my tent and campfire and rickety outhouse, my forty acres of woods, with nerves sizzling, electric with outrage. I thought: *For two years I have been lifting, pushing, hoeing, hiking up steep hills, forcing chainsaws through hardwood, shoveling snow and gravel, manhandling cranky old tractors, tossing hay bales, goading or restraining recalcitrant fourteen-hundred-pound animals, holding back five-hundred-pound tree limbs, hauling water, shoveling cow shit.* I'd battled the Great Fear and Diz and twenty-below weather and Jim Brassard drunk and the Great Loneliness.

I knew I had lived an unpredictable zigzag life and had come here as damaged merchandise, but my unpredictability had dimensions yet to reveal themselves.

I kept plastic contractor's demolition bags in my supply chest, big heavy black ones that could hold a couple of weeks' worth of recyclables or be used as raincoats in a pinch. I took two of them and put one inside the other and then brought my shovel up the hill to the sprawling pyramid of guts. It was definitely a larger pile than the one I'd seen last fall. More bear-size, I thought. My grief and rage swelled, bulged to bursting.

The guts were heavy and slippery and difficult to shovel, but I got them into the bag. I carried the bag down the hill and saw nobody in the farmyard and got into my Toyota and drove up to the Goslants' place. I had put the bag in the trunk, but the scent of blood and the fecal stink of entrails filled the car. I had gotten some blood on my hands and they were sticky on the steering wheel.

I had entered an alternate state. Adrenaline had washed away an overlay of civilized behavior and by doing so conjured, revealed, another part of what it is to be me or to be human.

In the Goslants' driveway, I pulled up next to Johnnie's tricked-out

pickup and yanked the parking brake lever before the car had even stopped.
I popped the trunk, hoisted the bag, carried it up the three steps, and laid
it on the stoop. I hammered on the rickety aluminum door.

The twentysomething I'd seen when passing the place answered. A
muffled yammer came from inside and I could just see images flickering
on a big wall-mounted television screen.

"Johnnie."

"Yeah. What?"

"I live on the land just below yours."

"Yeah? And what?"

"You just poached an animal off my land. Which I spent a lot of time
posting. The land is posted up the ass."

"Me? It's not season. No way." When I lifted a blood-glazed hand and
held his gaze, he switched to feigned remorse: "Sorry! Really. It was an
accident." Now he thought he was being funny.

I had not scripted this encounter, so I could only resort to an insane
form of honesty. "Johnnie, do you know what PTSD is?"

"What the—"

"PTSD. You know what it is."

"Yeah. It's when vets come back and they're all fucked up."

"What do PTSD vets do?"

An impatient voice called from inside the house, and Johnnie turned
and yelled, "Shut up!" Then back to me: "Fuck you talking about? What
is this?"

"What do they do? PTSD guys."

"They act nuts. Some of them. They flip out. I don't know. Beat up
their wives? There was that one that killed some people. What's this have
to do with the deer? I'll pay you for the fucking venison. Or you take it.
Now, get off our step."

The deer. I felt a wash of relief, but the outrage didn't ebb. I'd gotten
too cranked up, my motor too revved; I had too much momentum to stop.

"Why would a woman go live out in a tent in the woods a mile from
nowhere?" I asked.

"How should I know? This is shit. I got other things to do and you gotta get the fuck off the step."

"Because I've got PTSD. And I act nuts."

"I can believe that," he said, laughing.

"And when I see this …" I picked up the bag of guts, which he hadn't noticed. I had planned to dump it on the stoop, but I *flung* that bag empty so that its contents ended up on the doorsill and in the entryway. I balled up the bag and threw it against his chest. "… it brings it back to me and I go nuts big-time."

He pulled back. There was a speckling of blood on his Metallica T-shirt, and some had splashed onto his shoes. "You are fuckin—"

"Nuts! What've I been telling you? So if I see this again on my land—a footprint, a twig broken—this is you." I kicked some of the guts farther into the house.

He still played it cool, but I was in an alien-strange groove. I believed what I was saying, and he did, too.

"Okay, I got it. You're fucked in the head. Got that. No problem. I got enough screwballs around already, I don't need another one."

Another call from inside the house: "Johnnie, who the hell are you talking to?"

"Shut up! It's nobody." He turned back to me again and said, "Brassard never gave a shit if we hunted there."

"I'm not Brassard. It's mine now."

"Okay. Your land is posted. You're fucked in the head. It's your land. It's posted. It's all yours. Take the goddamn deer, it's behind the garage. Have a ball, fruitcake."

He had to kick a coil of intestine out of the way so he could slam the door.

I GOT BACK into my car with so much adrenaline in my body, I felt as if I could squeeze the steering wheel into a strand of spaghetti.

If you are reading this and you are a war veteran and have seen combat, please understand that I know the difference. I never claimed, I would never claim, that I had served in the armed forces and seen and done what you have. But at that moment, I realized that yes, I really had come up to the land with some injuries inside. Maybe a lot of the wounds were self-inflicted, but they were real all the same. And the hour I'd spent in fear that it was one of my bears, my sacred friends, had dug a knife into me and lanced the awful pits and pockets of every grief and loss, all the anger and pain, the distillation of every betrayal and resentment that hid in me. Remembering Ricky's trembling fear of Johnnie had added to it. And on my way to the Goslants' place, all those secret poisons gushed forth and converged until my blood seethed with the toxic chemistry of rage.

I drove a few miles on the back roads before heading home, the window open so the wind tugged my hair. The sweet forest flowed past while I cried. I cried for Johnnie because he was a sad little bastard stuck in a shit-out-of-luck life. Cried for Ricky, wherever he was now. Cried for relief, knowing my bears were still out there somewhere. I cried for me, too, and for all the injuries and injustices the world inflicts on us all. And for every damn thing.

I know, I do know, how little I have been hurt, compared to what life can really do to you. But there had been in me a hurtling dark freight train loaded with that lifetime's worth of pain and anger—monstrous, mindless, spraying sparks from the rails. And though I'd had so much good fortune in the past two years, so much that was dear and sweet, that black train still had been coming and had to bull and charge at anything in front of it, and this day it had arrived.

Johnnie, for all that he'd trespassed and killed and been smug and insulting, had hurt his helpless cousin or nephew or whatever Ricky was, had absorbed more of its force than he'd actually earned.

I did feel pity for him. But in coming to my land, I had for the first time in my life staked out some turf, forty full acres of it. I was its steward, and I would honor the obligations of my stewardship.

WHEN I GOT back, Earnest and Will and Erik were in the kitchen, pretending to be relaxed. I went to the sink and washed and rewashed my hands.

"How'd it go?" Earnest and Will asked offhandedly, in accidental unison.

"Good. Went well. I don't think it'll be a problem anymore," I said.

And it has proved true: No Goslant has ever trespassed again. More importantly, I have never again felt the rumble of that dark train, never put someone in front of it. It went off a bridge or cliff or off its rails into a night all its own, far from me.

Chapter 54

By NOW, YOU have no doubt discovered that I had fallen in love, and not just with my land and Brassard's farm. Even though I haven't directly stated it, I have not been trying to keep it a secret—just telling it as it revealed itself. I felt it burgeoning but simply didn't recognize it myself through all the days I have been recounting. I was submerged in it, consumed with it, and surrounded by it. And truly, I had never experienced it, not this, before—how could I have recognized it?

I did feel it coming, an inner turbulence I tried to ignore, but as Erik later pointed out, I was "slow on the draw" in these matters.

In the end, I required permission to recognize it, and Erik gave me that permission by acting like a little brother—one who had always put me up against things I didn't want to, or simply couldn't, face.

By MID-AUGUST, THE hops bines had filled out, clustered with the cones that we would soon be harvesting, and they were heavy enough to make the strongest trellis wires sag. The hop yard was marvelous: long, deep corridors lined with walls of foliage, canted forward somewhat, hallways roofed by a strip of sky. The fact that we'd had to accommodate boulders and buried rocks made this grove more interesting and mysterious. The rows were not straight, but zigged and zagged slightly; with the geometry somewhat relaxed, the lanes gave a secret view here, a longer view there, a sense of benevolent enclosure. A scent, at once familiar and indefinable, hovered between the walls: almost but not quite a mix of pine, basil, and marijuana.

Even Brassard, who by then was spending most of his time in his corn and hay, and who you'd think would have had enough of green things, enjoyed the yard.

One afternoon I was searching for Erik, who was somewhere in those six acres, to bring him some lunch, which I knew he would otherwise go without. I came across Brassard, strolling along in the shaded lane, smoking his pipe as he tipped his head up to inspect the knots of cones at the top of this unfamiliar plant. He smiled at me, and I at him.

"Looks like it's comin along well, doesn't it? Not that I'd know. But seems a robust crop. Got lucky this time around, so far." He spoke with the stem of the pipe in his teeth.

I agreed that it looked good, then asked him if he'd seen Erik in his wanderings.

He put his thumb over his shoulder. "Back a good ways, three rows over. He'll be glad to see that!" He gestured at the plastic bag of edibles I carried.

"Yeah. He forgets to eat."

"Pleasant back in here. Peaceful." Brassard removed his pipe from his lips and said, "If you're not the one doin the work."

I FOUND ERIK teetering at the very top of a stepladder, clipping off some cone-covered sections of bine. He untangled a few and tossed them into the lane, then climbed down to inspect them.

"You're going to break your neck doing that," I told him.

"Wouldn't that be nice," he said bitterly.

I gave him some sandwiches and a bottle of Gatorade that he chugged like a collegiate beer-drinking champ. Then he sat down to look carefully at the cones he'd clipped. They were about the size of strawberries, and though they were still a bright green, their scales were paling a bit and becoming almost papery. He broke a few off the bine, rubbed them between finger and thumb, and held them to his nose.

"Another week, I'd guess."

"That's exciting!" I sat next to him.

He didn't share my enthusiasm. "A very scary week."

"How so?"

"Number one, they have to mature just right to develop the flavor components, and I don't really know jack shit about when exactly they're ready. Number two, rain could delay harvest or make them too wet so that they rot rather than dry when we get them inside. Number three, I don't know how long it'll take to clip off six acres in whatever weather the good Lord chooses to inflict on us. And on and on." He fingered another cone, frowned, and passed it to me. "And then there's this."

The one he handed me had slight blackening on its lower scales, and at the base some were peeling back from the core.

"What is it?"

"Hell if I know. But if it takes over, I'm dead." He unsheathed his knife and carefully sliced through the darkening cone, then held it close to his face to inspect it. "Leaf and bine development have been good all summer, so it's not a soil issue. I don't see any aphids. I don't know. It might be bacterial. I just don't *know enough about this!*"

I wanted to console him but had no advice to offer. I suggested that he eat his forgotten sandwiches, and he complied.

Here it was again: Farm, and you live in suspense. You can't predict the vicissitudes of weather, pests, crop yield, or morale. You can't anticipate market conditions half a year ahead, when your crop will be ready. You don't get unemployment compensation if your operation crashes. And what happens if you get sick and miss a few days of work at a crucial moment in the cycle of growing and harvesting that nature, not you, decrees?

My brother finished eating and then flopped onto his back, spread his legs and arms, and stared at the sky, breathing in and out deliberately as he tried to relax. I settled back, too, so that we lay like two kids making snow angels, except that it was August and we lay on cut-over weeds and grass. I was thrilled when he reached and linked his little finger with mine, the way he would when we were kids and two years' age difference was a long time and I could be a comforting big sister. A murther of three crows flew over, and I imagined that from their vantage we looked like Hansel and Gretel, innocents lost in the wide, labyrinthine world and trying to comfort each other.

"I guess what I'm saying," he said after a while, shyly, "is I'm feeling really fucked up right now." An honest request for reassurance.

I said, "You're going to be fine. Okay? You're not alone in this." I tried to say it with confidence, but in fact I'd been feeling the rising pressure, too. The uncertainty was wearing on me.

I had by default taken over banking for the operation—Erik said he was too impatient for accounting, he was a "bigger-picture entrepreneur"—so I knew that he had badly underestimated the amount of labor he'd have to pay for. And that Aunt Theresa's inheritance—his "initial capitalization"—was almost gone. But I had never gotten a clear idea of how much money he might earn from the yard.

As we lay there, he told me that if nothing went wrong, the acres grown from the crowns would produce a thousand pounds or more per acre, when dried. He expected less from the rhizome-planted acres this year, but from the whole yard he had been hoping for about five thousand pounds. If nothing went wrong. If he got a decent price for them, he might make seventy grand this first year. That would mean he'd cover his out-of-pocket expenses and have a little more to live on and to improve the yard for the next harvest. That would be a bigger crop, and the brewers would know what good stuff he was peddling, and he would make some serious money.

If nothing went wrong.

My brain was calculating the other side of the equation: the impact on Brassard's farm. If this year was a disaster for the hops, if Erik fled from the project in exhaustion and despair and loneliness for female company, Brassard would lose the lease income and the other money Erik was paying. That slender path to the farm's renewal would be gone.

How much tension can be transmitted through lovingly linked little fingers? I began to feel a little ill.

Chores were calling almost audibly in my head. I got up and brushed myself off; Erik stood and shook himself all over, like a dog. He would be exhausted tonight, and I knew he had been living off microwaved popcorn and canned soup, so I invited him up to my camp for dinner. I had made a grocery run and set aside some solid fare for the purpose.

I DID WANT to make sure he was well fed, but I had ulterior motives for my invitation. Whatever happened with the hops, I had felt for some time that his real difficulties came from another source: his intimate relationships. Love is an irresistible tide, I had decided, lifting all things regardless of other vagaries of circumstance, so I planned to ask him about it, prod him to think about it a bit. He needed more than a big sister's love and devotion. I worried about his well-being, especially after having endured almost six months of unrelenting labor to the exclusion of every other life activity, including romance. He wasn't happy with the situation, and between overwork and that absence he had become increasingly irritable and, I knew, existentially overwhelmed.

I had thought I would deliver a wise, sisterly sermon about finding "a good woman," and probably every other cliché about the stabilizing and affirming benefits of longer-term partnership. Look at Perry and James, twenty years together, I would have said; look at Lynn and Theo and their stable, productive little farm. Our father would have said something along the lines of "You know, there comes a time when a man benefits from making some commitments that help balance his life."

Erik came up just after sunset, his sleeping bag and mat over one shoulder. He readily agreed when I forbade any talk whatsoever about hops or money.

I had planned to care for him, but during his years minding his marijuana patch he had developed exceptional skills as an outdoor chef, and he insisted on doing the cooking. He didn't appear to take any pleasure in it, but it gave his impatient hands something useful to do, and I could see that it helped him decompress after the day's tensions. I had bought some sweet corn, which he soaked in heavily salted water for a half hour. When he deemed it and the fire ready, he expertly raked and spread the coals, then arranged the cobs so they would singe and steam in their husks. Then he set up some cheese sandwiches with ham slices and thick slabs of sweet onion and tomato in them; my only suggestion was to add a few basil leaves I'd culled from Diz's derelict garden. He quickly seared the ham, then grilled the sandwiches in my big iron skillet until the cheese oozed, and that meal was blue-ribbon, off-the-charts delicious. We were ravenous but tried to eat like civilized humans.

Looking at him, I was dismayed to see how slim he had become—he'd never had any weight to spare, and had lost easily ten pounds since he first arrived.

The night grew dark around us as we faced each other across the fire. It was windless and very quiet except for the muffled hooting of a barred owl—*goo-goo-ga-joob!*—somewhere deep in my woods. With the late-summer foliage dense around my clearing, we were totally enclosed but for the circle of dark star-pricked sky above. It was a safe and private place to talk about serious things, I thought.

My plan was to cleverly maneuver our conversation toward gener alities about relationships and then gradually bring the issue to bear on him. He didn't need any more pressure, but it wouldn't hurt him to start thinking about it. In a low-key, almost absentminded way, I would eventually suggest that if you don't like these periods of singleness, maybe you ought to take a look at your approach to relationships and think about someday checking one out for more than a few months.

Instead, the soul of tact, I said: "So. How's your love life?" I said it briskly, meant it rhetorically.

"However it is or isn't, it'll have to wait until the fucking hops are harvested, won't it?" He spat into the fire. "What I was thinking, I don't know. I'd rather pump gas. Bag groceries. Go back to Elk fucking Ridge! My blood pressure is through the roof. Anything goes wrong, I'm done. Cooked. Game over."

It was true: He had staked everything on this first harvest and had inadvertently staked the farm's future on it as well. I was trying to formulate a reassuring reply when he preempted me.

"Funny that you should bring it up, though," he said. "My love life."

"I was just—"

"What are *you* doing, Annie?"

"What do you mean?"

He sighed and shut his eyes, a pantomime of great, weary patience. "You're the smartest person I know, and yet there are places where you're ... dense. Slow on the draw. Sorta stupid, actually. Sorry, but it's true."

"Gee, thanks, bro. Now that you've totally alienated and offended me, what were you planning to say?"

"You know what I think? I think you can't see it because it's sort of against the rules. Like you're afraid of it, or you're not allowed? And this I don't get, because in every other way, you seem willing and able to break rules and live pretty far outside the ordinary." He gestured at my tidy yet wild little clearing. "I'm proud of you for that, by the way."

"I don't have any idea what you're talking about."

"See? That's what I mean!" He was a very tired man, sincerely frustrated with me. "We were talking about love. I'm trying to tell you something here. Jesus Christ!"

"Yeah? Well, you're not making it any clearer, whatever it is."

"Okay. So tell me, how're you sleeping at night?"

Again his change of tack confused and affronted me. "What's this? Now you're my shrink?"

"Whatever, Annie." He snorted with disdain and scuffed dirt at the campfire. "Whatever."

It bothered me that he was right. I often awoke in the night and lay there in a jittery malaise. It was a physical as well as emotional discomfort, my body drawing taut with tension that I had to consciously dispel again and again. The feeling of fecundity I'd cherished at first, that sphere of warmth cradled between my hipbones, had become more of an ache.

"Of course I can't sleep! I'm as nervous as you are about the hops! It's a stressful period for all of us. We—"

"Do you need 'permission'?" He put quote marks in the air with his fingers. "Is that what it is? Okay, you have my permission. It is totally permitted. Permission City here."

His attitude irritated me, and I almost snapped at him, "I don't need permission for anything from my little brother." But his words had set my mind spinning, thoughts and feelings like rollers in a slot machine, a blur of roses and cherries, spades and clubs, peaches and diamonds. I intuited that the wheels would stop and end up at some configuration that made sense. Even in my confusion, I knew that much.

"I still don't get it," I told him.

He gave me a hard look, utterly out of patience. "I'm going to sleep now."

And he took his gear and crackled away into the darkness.

So that's how I got permission to fall in love. It took another few weeks for the rollers to chunk into place—one, then another, then the last. When they did and the combination registered, my unease rose in a shrill crescendo until something had to give.

Chapter 55

AGAIN, ERIK'S BIGGEST problem was simply a matter of math. How long would it take to pick thousands of fourteen-foot tangles of bine and cones? He had a plan for it, but he couldn't predict how long it would take. As harvest approached, he hired the Vermont Tech students on a standby basis, arranged for Perry and James to come down when they could take time from their own crops. I warned Lynn and Robin that they would have to do the milking themselves some afternoons so I could work with the hops. We all watched the weather anxiously.

Erik and Earnest invited me to the maiden voyage of the bizarre-looking contraption they'd been working on in the repair shop—their secret project. It was a cone separator they had designed based on Erik's glimpse of his former partners' equipment and on YouTube videos of commercial hop growers processing their cut bines. Many of the parts came from an old baler that had been gathering dust in the hayloft for the past decade. Its conveyor was designed to take bales from the tractor's hay compactor and carry them back onto the wagon trailing behind. Earnest had been adapting it for hops.

It was a complex machine. As Earnest explained it, one person was to introduce the end of the bine into a feed hopper, which dragged the bine between a series of whirling flails that more or less separated leaves and cones from the bines. The green stuff that was battered and yanked off the bine strand was then supposed to pass through a rotating chicken-wire barrel and fall onto the conveyor. The conveyor was set at an angle with the belt rolling upward. The cones, being heavier, would bounce down the sloped belt and into a bin, while the leaves and other lighter stuff followed the belt up and fell off the end. Once the bine was stripped, the person at the hopper flail end pulled it back out and threw it onto a waste pile.

That was the theory, anyway.

To test it, Erik came in on the Bobcat with a half-dozen bines, each about ten feet long, in the bucket—they were light but too bulky to carry by hand. Earnest turned on the electric motor that moved the clattering gears and chains, and I stayed well out of the way.

Erik climbed up onto the wooden platform and fed in the first bine—I worried about his hands being drawn in with it—which immediately snarled and wrapped itself around the rollers and axles of the spinning flails.

Earnest hit the switch to shut down the rig. Three or four cones bounced down the conveyor belt.

Earnest dusted his palms together, miming satisfaction. "That went well!" he said.

Erik's sense of humor had been sweated out of him long before. He began yanking the string and bine out in broken lengths a couple of feet long and pitching them away as hard as he could. There was little satisfaction in it, though, since they were too light to fly far.

"Erik. We'll get it right," Earnest told him. "There'll always be a few kinks to work out."

"Yeah, they had a few kinks to work out of the *Titanic*, too."

"That was human error, actually," Earnest retorted primly. "Which we are not going to make here."

He unplugged the motor, got his toolbox, and climbed up onto the thing. First he clipped the rest of the tangled bine off the rollers and then began poking around the top of the flail compartment. Erik stomped off to cool his jets with some fresh air before coming back to help.

"Your brother will survive," Earnest assured me. "I have a good feeling about this."

"Yuh-huh," I said skeptically.

"No, seriously. I can tell." He picked up a wrench and began ratcheting bolts out of the roller assembly. Without humor, as if levity were a demand imposed on him, he said, "Prophetic intuition. Quite common among aboriginal peoples."

I threw a hop cone at him and left. I didn't know how to comfort Erik, or make the machine work, and my Caucasian, colonialist intuition didn't tell me much of anything except that it was a very anxious time and that somebody's hands could get drawn into the flailing rollers and that my brother was falling apart and that I wasn't doing a whole lot better. And that Earnest was doing a great job of being the steady one but a lot of it was pretense and something had come between us and I hated it.

Later, Erik found me as I was loading hay onto a feed wagon. He said his mood was much improved. Trying to reassure me, he told me something he remembered from business classes: "If you want to be a market leader, you need to be willing push your risk tolerance. Sixty percent of all millionaires have gone bankrupt at least once."

THAT EVENING, I was just about to hike up the hill when Will drove in, parked, and flagged me down.

"What's the rumpus?" I asked as he got out.

"I was going to ask you to ask me over to your place for dinner." He gestured back at my chicken-coop apartment.

"That's very generous of you," I said. We both laughed.

"I have a video I thought you'd like to see. One I made. It's not about cow diseases."

"If you cook," I said. He readily agreed.

I told him my larder was empty—I almost never spent time in my "downhill place" if the weather was anything short of nasty, and didn't keep any edibles there but my emergency ramen—so he went to the house to scavenge foodstuffs. I showered, then realized that my closet was as empty as my refrigerator, leaving me with no choice but to put on my dirty working jeans and shirt again. I set my computer on the counter and booted it up, wondering what he had in mind.

Will came in with a paper grocery bag and laid out a box of dried spaghetti, a jar of tomato sauce, and various greens. Last, he tentatively put a plastic-wrapped brick of hamburger on the countertop. He gestured at the meat. "You up for that? I'm not much of a cook, but spaghetti and meatballs I can do. I guess I could get some eggs and make a kind of carbonara. Might be weird without bacon, though." He was remembering my difficulty with culling.

"I'm still working on the larger issues," I said, "but until I figure it out, that sounds great."

He went to work in the kitchen as I sat at the counter and watched. He was about six feet two inches tall, the top of his head barely a hand's width from the ceiling. He got water going, salted it, then liberally sprinkled the burger with various herbs from jars on my shelves, onion and garlic powder, finely chopped scallions. To mix it all, he put his hands into the bowl and squelched the meat between his fingers until they became so clogged with clinging fat that he had to stop and scrape it off with a fork.

"See what I mean?" He scowled at the mash he'd made. "My ex did all the cooking. Any skills I have are left over from my bachelor days. Spaghetti, scrambled eggs, and peanut butter sandwiches. And beer. I can pop a top with the best of them."

"Speaking of the ex, how's that going?" I asked.

"Settled. Papers signed, sealed, delivered. The problem remains my daughter. It's not that I'm deemed unacceptable as a parent, just that my schedule is so uneven. Also, she's in second grade in Rutland and I need to be up here for now. Hard for her to come out here except on weekends, and even that's hit and miss with my schedule. So. For now it's me visiting her when time permits."

He got quiet and distant for a moment as he poured tomato sauce into a pan; then he brightened. "The ex has a boyfriend, though!"

"Is that a good thing, or—"

"Are you kidding? I'm thrilled! Distracts her from thinking up new ways to make my life miserable. Puts her in a better mood. She's been a lot more agreeable since they got together."

"That's great!" I thought back to my own divorce and remembered my initial feelings—no, my feelings for at least the first year—toward Matt: I'd have liked to dissect him and his girlfriends with a dull spoon. But thinking about it just then, all that heat and heartache and wrangle, seemed unfathomable to me—childish, boring, an unpleasant but mercifully short chapter of my life. Was it just the passage of time, I wondered, or had some other change moved me beyond and above crap like that?

"So," he said, "my latest masterpiece. Not on contract, just my own thing. Been working on it since spring, thought you might like to see it."

He dumped the spaghetti sticks into the boiling water, put the sauce on simmer, scrubbed his hands to get rid of the grease, and joined me at the counter. He produced a shiny unlabeled DVD, slid it in, and started the show.

It opened with a shot of my forested hill, of all things, as seen from the hop yard. Then the camera panned slowly down; the top of the trellis appeared, then the tips of midsummer bines, stirring in a gentle breeze. Suddenly the frame moved quickly downward to a midshot of my brother flipping the bird to the camera. There was no sound.

It moved on to a wonderful montage of vignettes from the hop yard. Here was Jason, the chubbier of the Vermont Tech kids, bent to work planting rhizomes, with a more-than-generous view of his exposed rear, pink above his jeans. He turned and made as if to punch the camera. Then, seen through a gap in younger bines in one of the lanes, Bailey-not-Tim and Jennifer, who everybody knew were having an affair that they were inexplicably trying to keep secret. Bailey grabbed her and tried to kiss her; Jennifer shoved him away, laughing and looking over her shoulder to see whether somebody might be watching. I could read her lips: "Cut it out!"

Then came a series of rapid-fire shots that had me laughing helplessly: all the men, at one time or another, urine-marking the border of the yard. Will had done a discreet job, never getting a frontal shot, but the streams were often visible and the postures unmistakable. Each lasted about two seconds and faded into a similar shot of another of the crew, and another, and another, speeding up until it seemed as if the enterprise must have occupied every minute of the summer, that a tsunami must surely have descended on the yard. Even Bob had a couple of cameos, doing his part.

I screeched with laughter, something I'd done only when Cat got on a comic roll. "Fabulous!" I told Will. "Perfect. Brilliant."

"It changes a bit," he said.

By degrees, the tone of the video segued from silly to simply amusing to pleasantly rural to more serious, capturing portraits of the people at the farm, busy with their work. Here was Brassard, sweaty, holding his Agri-Mark hat off his head to scratch his scalp as he puzzled over something problematic. He turned to catch Will filming, mouthed, "Don't you have something better to do?" But after a scene of Earnest flinging huge sections of tree trunk off his truck—eventually to become part of the winter's firewood supply—there was Brassard again, climbing down from the Deere with the wincing carefulness of a man whose knees were killing him. Then Earnest, shirt off, skin sweat-sheened and oil-smeared, muscles balling as he cranked a wrench on the cone separator. I thought it was an aesthetically effective shot, a Rodin of man and machine, force brought against resistance, defined by the play of light on surfaces.

Next, a woman doing cow flow, lightly swatting the back end of a lagger, calling over the backs of the cows to someone in the parlor. With a shock, I realized it was *me*. I was making a joke and smiling, and at that moment, for the first time in years, I thought I looked *good*. I don't mean sexy, but just, I don't know, a decent, competent person in reasonable command of herself. Because I hadn't expected to see her, I had momentarily glimpsed Ann Turner without vanity or defensiveness, and in that instant I had rather *liked* that person. The scene passed in a few seconds but left me pleased and a little stunned.

The vignettes lengthened; the tempo slowed. More often now, they showed tired people: Erik with his hair sticking up crazily, shirt off, sweat drenched, dragging a shovel behind him as if he were too weak to lift it. Me in the big door of the shed, swiping hair off my face and trying unsuccessfully to tuck it behind my ear with my leather-gloved fingers. Brassard with his pipe, looking out over corn in the late afternoon and swatting at a persistent horsefly. Robin, muck boots on, leaning against the Jeep, one hip stuck out, tired but unconsciously glamorous as she shaded her eyes against the afternoon light, apparently waiting for Lynn to come out of the barn. A lingering shot of Perry and James, walking away from the camera, along the uphill end of the hop yard, two bearded men holding hands, talking, absentmindedly bumping shoulders.

Then Earnest and Erik and me, sitting on the edge of the porch, all three of us in exactly the same posture, leaning forward with elbows on knees, hands dangling, talking seriously, thinking something through. Bob lounging at our feet, tongue hanging, oblivious. Again I had a moment of that clear vision that comes with unfamiliarity, this time not in seeing myself but seeing Earnest and my brother: *What handsome men!* I thought.

It ended with a close shot of a single brilliant deep-orange poppy standing tall above Diz's derelict flower garden, swaying gently in one of the breezes of that particular summer of all those people's lives.

Then it was done. I was moved and astonished. I had noticed Will filming now and again, mainly in the hop yard, but never realized he had assembled so many moments. I also realized I hadn't given him credit for such a good eye, or sense of humor, or sensitivity. He had been *looking*, observing, seeing, all that time.

"I love it. That's … *us*. You *got* us."

"Thanks. It's not really done. Just a bunch of clips I pasted together. But it's fun, isn't it?"

"There's someone missing, though."

"Who's that?"

"Will Brassard."

"Well, someone's got to be behind the camera." He went to check the spaghetti, then turned up the heat on the sauce and meatballs. He set me up at the counter with lettuce, carrots, and tomatoes to make a salad.

"I think you should branch out," I said. "With your eye, your sense of timing? I mean, you've landed in an agricultural-productions professional niche. But that's pretty ironic, don't you think? Given your feelings about farm life?"

"Oh, farm life is okay to visit; I just wouldn't want to live there."

We both chuckled. The growing anxiety and fatigue was wearing on me, too, and I was having my own doubts. I remembered getting my monthly check from Larson Middle School, its reassuring predictability, and the pleasure that came from a workday that actually ended.

WE ATE WITHOUT saying much. The silence felt a little uncomfortable, so I played some of Erik's Celtic tunes on my laptop. But they were melancholy, not the best choice. It had gotten dark outside, and despite each other's company, I think we both felt the lonesomeness of a rural night wrap around the farm and around my little apartment. I had heard Erik come into his side, but no further noises, and I knew he hadn't made himself any dinner—he'd taken one look at his bed and collapsed into it.

"Yeah, I thought I should redeem myself after the brucellosis fiasco," Will said.

"Hey, don't put it down! I am now much more vigilant for signs of brucellosis."

He was supposed to smile at that but didn't. Another silence.

"Dad has dropped your name on me about ten times in the last week," he confessed. "Increasingly in the last couple of months."

"Likewise."

You must understand that I have never been any good at moments like this. The nakedness that both parties feel is difficult for me, and I have too little experience, no habitual reflexes, to fall back on. I knew Will was the same kind of person. To our credit, though, if we were not adept we were pretty straight up.

"What do you say when he does?" he asked carefully.

"Nothing. He just … it's very indirect."

We looked at each other frankly for a long moment.

"You're not really there with it, are you?" he asked.

I considered that as he watched me attentively: a good-looking, intelligent, well-intentioned man facing determinedly into a moment of difficult honesty.

"I'm not sure where I am with anything much," I said at last. "Do you maybe mean 'Am I ready?'"

"I suppose that's one way to put it."

"Because I think there are really two questions there. One is if I am. The other is if you are. And I'm not sure you are, because you're fresh off a hard breakup and you don't know whether you're just lonely and unanchored and are … reaching out. I mean, it *is* scary. Being single. When you're not used to it." I knew the feeling all too well but couldn't express it, so I tried to make the shape of it with my hands: "There's this gap in every day, where there's … supposed to be someone."

He nodded. Clearly, he knew that feeling, too.

I wondered whether he noticed that I'd avoided directly answering his question. I thought about effulgence and my brother's crabby but insightful observations. The slot machine tumblers Erik had set in motion were still rolling. But though they had not quite come around to their fated final combination, they were definitely slowing.

"I guess you're a couple of years further along than I am," he said.

I counted up the time in my head. "Yeah. Two years further past it, I guess." "So … what's it like out there?" A sad smile. "Get any better?"

I turned toward him on my stool and put my hands up, resting one on each cheek so he'd know I meant it, and kissed him on his forehead: "Much better," I assured him.

After he left, I thought about our conversation. I decided that Will had after all noted my attempt to deflect his question, had recognized as camouflage my clichés about not being "ready," and had concluded that the answer was probably no.

Chapter 56

I WISH I could say that the hops harvesting went well and we got rich and lived happily ever after. But it didn't, and we didn't. The weather held through most of it, but we didn't have enough experience and we didn't have the right equipment and the seasonal clock ran the seconds down until it was too late.

The upper yard matured first—which was good because it allowed some time for processing the cones before the lower yard had to get cut. When Erik gave the signal, it was all hands on deck. Even Brassard came for the fun.

We fanned out in the upper yard and walked up and down the rows with machetes, cutting the bines off at about three feet above the ground. Now they hung straight down, like curtains, creating more room for Brassard to drive along the lanes in his Deere, towing a low-sided wooden trailer. Up front was Earnest, lifted high in the Deere's bucket, wielding a hedge-trimmer to cut the bines and training strings just below the trellis wire. Perry walked alongside to catch each bine as it fell, and as the trailer rolled by he flipped it up to James, who laid it on the bed. When the trailer became too full to manage anymore, I drove up on the Ford. I left an empty trailer for Brassard and then drove the full one back to the barn.

The men had turned the upstairs of the old barn, the spacious hayloft, into a hops-processing plant. They had set up the cone separator just inside the door at the gable end, at the top of the ramp from the road. Farther back were rows upon rows of chicken-wire bins that the cones would sit in as they dried. Erik fed the bines into the flail rollers as the Vermont Tech kids dealt with debris and cones.

It took the cutting team only two hours to harvest that first acre. But at the barn, the bines backed up in front of the feed end of the separator, mounded into toppling heaps, until we had to stop cutting new ones.

Earnest and Erik had done a brilliant job designing their contraption. It worked perfectly. Nothing broke. The cones bounced down the conveyor at a tempo that allowed Jennifer to pick out bad ones and any leaf pieces that happened to go with them. Jason and Bailey worked in excellent synchrony, handing fresh bines up to Erik, raking leaves out of the chicken-wire barrel, removing the stripped bines, and carting away the heaps of leaf debris that fell continuously off the top of the conveyor.

An air of optimism filled the place—for about an hour.

It isn't my desire to inflict vicarious misery on you, so I will simply say that it took *thirty-two hours* to strip cones off one acre's worth of bines. Thirty-two nearly-continuous hours of racketing drive chains and gears and belts and the relentless thrashing of the stripper flails. The upper three acres took five eighteen-hour days with Erik and Earnest and me, and anyone else who could find the time, working in shifts all day and through half the night. We also needed an extra day just to rearrange the mountains of debris, tune up the separator, and generally regroup.

So by the time the upper acres got processed, the lower acres were going by—the cones losing their lupulin yellow, going brown, losing their bitter odor. Eight days into the project, two successive days of downpour compelled us to abandon further harvesting. In the end, we managed to get in only four acres.

Later that fall, we fed everything on the last two acres into the chipper along with the other hop yard leftovers. It made some great compost.

On the bright side, the drying arrangement worked pretty well. And Erik had been courting buyers all summer, so when the cones were about dry enough, a couple of brewers came by to crumble and slice and sniff them. They made a pretty good offer. We bagged the cones by hand and then did our best to shrink-wrap them using a vacuum setup the men had cobbled together. We delivered them in Earnest's big stake-side truck: Earnest, me, and Erik sitting like limp hay-stuffed scarecrows, speechless blank numb with exhaustion, side by side on the wide bench seat, rumbling up to Waterbury to drop them off.

I insisted on buying the men a steak dinner, honoring the ritual Earnest had established. This time it was Erik who drank some beers and who was asleep, leaning heavily on my shoulder, by the time we made it back to the farm. He toppled out of the truck, lurched through his door, and slept for two days straight.

For a variety of reasons, I had fallen into the role of managing the bank account. By the time the dust settled, I calculated that Erik had lost almost fourteen thousand dollars on that first crop. And the only way he'd managed to keep the loss that small was by getting so much pro bono work from, mainly, Earnest and me. And Earnest's skipping some tree jobs—and losing a few grand in income—to make time to help. And the time Will put in.

But a loss of fourteen thousand wasn't too bad, actually. It meant that he had recouped enough of the money he'd invested that he could live on the cheap until the next harvest. He'd even have some funds to invest in better equipment, and now the big expense of the trellis was out of the way. Later, the brewers told us they were ecstatic about the hops, highly aromatic and bitter with notes of grapefruit that they conveyed to the beer. They designed a new recipe around Erik's hops and placed an advance order for every last cone he could produce next summer.

So it was a loss, but not a total loss. The next year had promise. When

I mentioned that to Brassard, he looked at me over his reading glasses and said, "It's *always* next year that'll do better and put you over the top."

DESPITE HIS EXHAUSTION, Erik didn't renege on any of the work required in the hops war's aftermath. He clipped the rest of the bines from the lower acres, gathered together the other debris, and ran it all through the chipper to get composted. He and Earnest moved the separator to a corner of the repair shed, and then Erik dismantled his drying racks. This liberated the upstairs of the old barn so it could receive the baled hay, which had been waiting under tarps, and Erik did his share of the relocation. He and I went over the books with Brassard to make sure he'd paid every penny owed for tractor and tool use and the manure he had churned into the hop yard soil.

"Got the makins of a good farmer," Brassard commented. Then, dryly: "'Course, you have to stick with it over some years to know if it's goin to work for you or not."

As I expected, when he'd completed the last hops chores, Erik pretty well vanished again. Love called from beyond the valley.

Chapter 57

I HAD ASSUMED that my state of disquiet would fade once the hops adventure had resolved itself. But it didn't. I resigned myself to being an unsettled person. I always had been, I told myself; why should anything be different now? But this was a dismal prognosis and didn't seem quite right in any case. I wished I could talk to Earnest about it—in fact, I was accruing a backlog of things to ask him and tell him—but we had become guarded around each other, and it seemed there was never a time without interruptions and other priorities.

A couple of weeks after we finished the hops, just as the forest leaves began to turn, a minor thunderstorm jostled through. At Brassard's farm, the nearby hills tended to break and jumble the winds, so we seldom had monumental storms. Instead, we had many smaller, chaotic atmospheric tussles; this one was just a bully sticking out his elbows to push his way through a crowd. The lightning rarely struck where we could see its forks, the bombs of thunder stayed distant. It wasn't even enough of a bother to stop work outside, though it did cause Bob the dog to cower and the rest of us to wear hooded raincoats.

It rumbled away well before nightfall, and I walked up to my camp quite confident that my tent had survived in good shape. It had, but a gigantic birch had been knocked over and lay across the far end of my clearing, broken from impact.

I think it is the golden birch that gets so grand and broad in its ancient age. Even using my manual, it's hard for me to tell, because the bark of these old trees has changed with age to the indeterminate color of some baser metal. They can be six feet through the trunk, standing with most limbs broken off, almost dead themselves but nurturing all kinds of living things. Little pines and maples start growing in forks where accumulated leaves have turned to soil, rooted twenty feet from the ground. Shelf fungi jut from the trunks. Small mammals and birds make homes in deep holes they dig here and there, and I had often seen woodpeckers hacking at their bark and ripping away chunks of rotten wood the size of my hand. Incredibly, these ruins often retain one or two slim branches still bearing leaves, fresh as saplings despite the passage of decades or perhaps centuries.

Though I had loved having this birch and its denizens as my neighbors, and appreciated the tree as the probable ancestor of the younger birches all around, I didn't want its bulk lying across my meager clearing. It crushed the blackberry cane that I knew the bears and raccoons and birds needed, and it blocked my path uphill to the spring. My little chainsaw wouldn't reach a third of the way through its trunk.

Of course I went to Earnest for a solution: Earnest, master of trees; Earnest, tree whisperer. And of course he said he would come to check it out and help me deal with it, when he found the time. He'd been working his tree jobs up in Chittenden County until sunset every day. That's why I was surprised when the next evening, well before sunset, I heard his call from down the path: "Pilgrim! It's the Indians."

Darkness was still an hour away, but I had lit my fire for the pleasure it gave. He came up the track in his work clothes, still sawdust-covered.

"Got tree problems? I'm your man. Extensive experience. References upon request." His humor, as it had been for many weeks, was forced.

I told him to shut up. We sat on the logs near the fire as I made some chamomile tea in a pot big enough to give us each several mugfuls.

He looked tired. I was just glad to see his face there in my home. Whatever I'd thought to say, or he had, neither of us got to it right away. We sat on the logs and percolated as the water did.

"Good day today?" I asked.

"Okay, yeah."

"Doesn't sound very okay."

He sighed heavily. "Killing trees in South Burlington shopping mall parking lots." But his face smoothed a bit as he scanned my woods. "Nice to be up here, though. A relief."

The pot reached boiling and I threw in a handful of teabags. We were quiet as we watched the chamomile essence diffusing into the water.

"I have something to say to you," I said finally.

He seemed alarmed at the prospect. "You know, it's late and maybe—"

"It's about when I told you and Erik about the bears."

"Yes."

"You told me to go up to the Goslants' on my own. Will offered to do it, Erik said he'd go up and kill Johnnie—"

"Really? He said that? Good man!"

"Well, he admitted he was exaggerating."

Earnest enjoyed that. I poked the fire with a stick so that a crazy flurry of sparks spun up.

"Meanwhile, the toughest guy east of the Mississippi said I should go up there on my own. By myself. To get into a fight with a screw-loose kid who kills things."

He shrugged. I waited him out. He knew I would wait him out. The tea diffused.

"Those bears. I don't know the story, but the way you were …" He looked at me straight-on. "You couldn't see yourself, but when somebody's vibrating like a tuning fork and their eyes look like, what, a samurai's eyes … When it's that important, one thing I know, you have to deal with it yourself. You can't duck it or delegate it."

I nodded.

"Tell me about the bears." He was very serious, and the power of

Earnest's command to honesty was not something I could resist. "What happened that was so important."

So I told him. I told him everything, about the inexplicable call of the darkness, the silly pointless noise I made, the bears and me together in the darkness, and how I felt afterward. The magic of that night came back to me in all its irrationality and mystery, and sharing it with someone was blissful.

When I finished, Earnest didn't say anything, just let the story hang in the air of my dimming glade, respecting it. The tea was ready by then. I had replaced my tin cups with some big plastic mugs, and poured it steaming into two of them. We each squeezed some honey from a plastic honey-bear and then cupped our hands around the mugs and contemplated them as if they could tell us something. It was quiet except for the fire's small, busy noises and the occasional fat drops of water falling from leaves that had cupped them since yesterday's storm.

"You were strong enough," he said finally. "You are strong enough. I thought you should know that."

THAT WAS GOOD tea. We each savored two whole mugs full and both had to head off in the dimming light to pee, I at my outhouse, Earnest somewhere in the woods at a respectable distance.

When we got back I said without thinking, "You have been *melancholy*, and I want to know why."

"It's not something I can go into with you right now." He picked up his empty mug and stared into it.

"Are you angry with me?"

That startled him: "No! Why would I be? Why do you say that?"

"You've ... you're, like, *cautious* when we talk. You're too *polite*! I *hate* it when you're polite with me, Earnest!"

"I'm just going through my own shit. I need a real change, a major change. Maybe move off the farm. Get my own place up where my work is, not come down so much."

I rocked back a bit, taking it like a punch.

"It's okay for a guy to move on in life! Sometimes you get to a place where"—he gripped the air, fists full of tension—"something's got to give." He looked at me, asking for understanding. "Something's just got to change."

In my head I came up with a dozen arguments against his moving: What will Jim do? You're his dearest friend, he's not over Diz yet, he needs your company! And who will fix the equipment? He can't afford to pay anyone! What, you'd live in Chittenden County, with the malls and parking lots? You hate it up there!

But all I said was, "Whatever it is, moving won't help. It'll come with you. Trust me."

He bobbed his head as he thought that over. "Probably true."

We sat there staring at the fire. If somebody had come upon us, they would have seen a large man in work-sweated, wood-dust-covered clothes, and a smaller female figure in manure-smeared coveralls, sitting on opposite sides of a campfire with their elbows on their knees. If the two had been closer to each other, you'd think they were leaning over a chessboard, utterly still as they pondered their next moves.

But there was no calculation going on. We just hung in a stasis of irresolution.

After a while, pressure grew in me, just as it had in Earnest: "See, where I'm at," I blurted, "I've been trying … this whole thing"—I gestured around me, at the woods—"is me trying to be who I am and accepting who I am. Really accepting who I am. But I don't feel like I'm getting there these days. It's like I'm keeping secrets from myself."

He nodded deeply.

Another long silence. Then he said, "Show me your tree before it gets too dark."

WE BUSHWHACKED TO the big birch. Its main trunk remained intact, but the age-rotted stumps of its branches had broken off when it fell. Earnest stroked its bark, inspected the various animals' holes, walked along it to the broken forks so he could look at the branches. At the breaks, its wood had the strength and texture of stale bread.

"I hate to see these go," he said. "Habitat trees. Where are all these critters going to find another home before winter?"

We talked about how to cut it and move it and where to put its pieces. I wondered aloud whether maybe some of its residents could return to their homes if we set the pieces nearby, but Earnest said that if they lived too close to the ground, they'd become little snacks, canapés, for bigger creatures. We figured we'd bring the Ford up with the bucket on the front, and Earnest's biggest chainsaw.

With that settled, he said he should call it a day and get some shut-eye. I offered to walk him partway down, and he assented. We walked in silence. Our conversation had been all fits and starts and confessional blurts, but I felt lighter. Just talking about something personal, for the first time in quite a while—maybe it had broken the ice; maybe we could talk together again soon and figure out what was ailing us. Surely he wouldn't leave the farm, I told myself. Of course he wouldn't. Would he?

About midway down, I thanked him and said goodnight and went back up to my clearing. I could just make out the great birch, lying like a beached whale among the brambles. The place had taken on a lonely feeling again, after just those few minutes away.

Chapter 58

Sept. 14

I am sitting on my log near the fire, which tumbled by increments and is now nothing but a nest of embers. Still, it puts out a good heat, and anyway it's a warm night for mid-September. Earnest visited and left and tomorrow we'll cut up the huge birch that fell across the upper end of the clearing yesterday. He says he might leave the farm.

I have a poem going round and round in my poor stupid head, one of Lewis Carroll's pleasing, absurd follies I memorized when I was, what, ten? in Mrs. Griffith's class.

> *"The time has come," the Walrus said,*
> *"To talk of many things:*
> *Of shoes—and ships—and sealing-wax—*
> *Of cabbages—and kings—*
> *And why the sea is boiling hot—*
> *And whether pigs have wings."*

Why is it torturing me tonight? Because your life, Ann, has become a catalogue of absurdities and follies? Because your pratfalls aren't funny anymore? Yes, but no. Because the time has come, Ann, to talk of love and loneliness, of woods and farms and yearning, and why your blood is boiling hot and what you're going to do about it.

You're talking about this on a paper page because you're scared to talk about it in your heart.

And as for loneliness: You've become an expert. Now you know there are several kinds. There is the beautiful big kind, where you feel yourself to be a unique thing, a bright singular moment in a vast world—that's frightening but exhilarating. I could not know of it without having lived in these woods, and knowing it makes me wiser and stronger and I wish I'd felt it much earlier in my life. Thank you, my dear hill, my dear woods.

Then there's the curled grub of sad scared loneliness, missing everyone, feeling left out and left behind, unsafe, cold, quivering, shivering lonely. Not being whole and sound in the beautiful woods, just lost in them. So much of that since losing Mom and Pop and breaking up with Matt.

No. I had so much of that. I haven't felt it for a long time, with Erik's coming, all the people of Brassard's farm. But now a third kind has taken its place, Ann, which is what's killing you right now.

What's it like? It's not cold, it's hot. Sort of like the brilliant hot circle you make by angling a magnifying glass toward the sun. Focus it on a dry leaf, and the leaf blackens and begins to smoke and then ignites. And the reverse of that bright spot hovers in your eyes for hours.

It's focused loneliness. Loneliness for just one thing, one person. That focus burns and you are burning, Ann Turner. Accept yourself. Tell yourself your secret.

Chapter 59

THAT NIGHT I lay in my tent listening to summer in the woods. I have told you how this symphony plays: As the light fades, quiet near sounds and very distant sounds come to the fore in a complex weave. The veery elects to be the last bird of the day, singing that most liquid and supple song. It seems the forest's watchman: All's well, it says, hereafter is night, and fare thee well. All to your nests, all to your rest. It sings the day creatures' lullaby and for me is synonymous with the arrival of night.

The blue evening dark slips and seeps in, and things go still. The rustlers come awake and move among the trees and low growth: my neighbors the bears and porcupines and deer and perhaps crepuscular creatures no one has ever seen or heard of, who are unique to late twilight and so subtle they have passed unnoticed by mankind forever.

But I felt no tranquility. I lay in my tent, on my cot, twisting in the sheet I had spread over me—it was too warm for the sleeping bag—unable to sleep, unable to think, unwilling to. The tangle and knot came from my belly, my spine, my thighs. I felt surges and fires, tides and flares, at once unbearable and irresistible.

The night was so fine that the air was silk. The moon had come over—half-moon, the gentle sort, neither the assertive full moon nor the insufficient, wary crescent—and I rose on one elbow and looked through the tent screen to the clearing, lit opalescent, cool and too empty.

I was in an agony you can understand only if you have felt it. I was as twisted as my sheet, I had a knot in my middle, the lines of my life were tangled and snarled and resistant. The feeling was as ancient and certain as the fear of night, tidal in its power. I looked to my memory, to my lessons here in the woods and on the farm in the past few years, and to my life before, and at first I thought they offered no answer to this state.

I could see that the past two years showed a through line, but that I had been, for all my divergence and contrariness, a creature of convention.

I felt an explosion of rebellion against being this dull-witted creature and against this state of tension and paralysis and cowardice. There *was* an answer to this state: *You are strong enough. Accept yourself.*

I flung aside my wadded pillow and extricated myself from my sheet. I stood inside my tent, shivering from the vital awakening in me. I was wearing only my pajama bottoms and a T-shirt and I didn't care and I unzipped the tent and stepped outside into patient moonglow. It was not so bright that it hid the stars above in the darkness. With the light of both, I could see my way as I started down the track to the farm.

If you have lived in the woods, you know that holding a flashlight or lantern does not help you see. In fact, it's self-imposed blindness that makes all near things too bright and all distant things too shadowed— turn your eyes to one side for a moment and you are sightless. If you have walked in the night, you know that you can indeed see, that even simple starlight can be enough, especially when your feet are bare and can feel the subtle textures on the path and remember the contours of the land. On this night, the path was clear to all my senses.

I left my campsite clearing at the downhill end and entered the deeper tree shadows. Here, the moonlight fell through leaf shadows, turning the woods into an impressionistic landscape in which distances were defined by degrees of dappled bright and dark. My body knew these trees, this track, these turns, and gravity told me the way down.

I was just past the first bend when I saw a dark shape moving below me, a shadow detaching itself from the tree shadows. For a moment, I was startled breathless. And it came closer, silent but solid dark, and it frightened me until his voice came from the shadow: "Ann! Where are you going?"

I was no doubt also a shape, suddenly there, pale in my nightclothes, and my pale shape said, "I was coming to meet you on the path." Which I hadn't known until that moment.

And there he was before me, the shadow shape moving purposefully up my track. And if I'd been able to hear anything but my own startled heart beating, I know I would have heard his.

When he reached me, we turned and walked up, back toward my tent, his weightless but solid shadow next to mine.

He said, "I—"

And I said, "I couldn't either."

I could bide no longer alone. I couldn't deny it anymore. I couldn't endure it anymore. I don't care if it's impossible.

Side by side, not touching, we came into the moonlight of my clearing and said nothing, because all had now been confessed, admitted, and needed no elaboration.

There was the tent and inside was the bed and there we knew we would end up, but here was the pale moonlight and the smooth air and the first delicious moments of acknowledgment. There had been long courtship here, and there would be chivalry now. We stood facing each other, holding each other's hands on each side, thinking we should speak, but failing, simply moving, very slightly, in tandem. At intervals, our chests collided and I felt his strength and his honesty. This was not postponement, this was fulfillment fully taken and fully savored. We moved together there in my clearing. I felt a bubble straining in my chest, a laugh of joy that celebrated relinquishing a burden, accepting the improbability and rightness and inevitability of this. He fitted his hands to my waist and lifted me as if I had no weight at all, as if he were wishing me flight, wishing me to touch the moon. He held me over his head as I balanced straight-backed, arms out to each side, legs together straight behind me. We spun that way. The first time Earnest ever kissed me was as he held me above him and placed his face against my belly and kissed me there.

And after a time, we went into my tent, my transient little house, and made our bed upon the floor, improvised but not hurriedly so.

And thereafter, that night, it is only mine and Earnest's to know and to remember.

Chapter 60

I DON'T KNOW whether you think it most improbable that we came together despite nineteen years' difference in age, or find it incredible that we took such a long time to acknowledge something so clearly apparent. Earnest and I marveled at both, but in fact we talked very little about it; it was as moot as moot can get.

For me the greatest irony was that I thought I'd learned that love will most likely come to you in unexpected forms, from unexpected angles. But I hadn't entirely believed it. Still stuck in my wretched brain was some childish mythology about love. It belonged in the same category of notion that made me expect my land to be spacious eighteenth-century English woods, full of wealthy scions but devoid of biting insects and bad weather. The same expectation that small farm life was about happy horsies and piggies but not about overworked people and money problems and cows that actually pooped.

So it took me a while to recognize that for me love was an Oneida tree surgeon built like a bear, no taller than I am, and nineteen years older. Recognize and give myself permission. Took me that long despite the obvious fact that we had fallen into step beside each other within the first week, more than two years before. That from the start we had spoken the same language with such fluency, understood each other's inflections of irony and humor and affection and intention.

Two days later we got to work on that fallen birch. We didn't talk about nineteen years, because it was already so long ago that we had largely forgotten it.

Mainly we talked about the moose we saw in the clearing when we came out of the tent that morning. He was an adult bull, so gigantic he seemed an animal that belonged in Africa, among elephants and giraffes, not here. His antlers spanned at least six feet, and I could have walked beneath his dewlapped, bearded chin without stooping. He regarded us with regal curiosity and a touch of skepticism. We stared in awe. After about a minute, he lifted his nose and must have snagged some signal out of the air, because he turned on his long legs and strode unhurriedly back into the woods. I would have thought that a creature that big, with those antlers, would thrash and clatter through the saplings that bordered my clearing, but he didn't. He slid into and through them smoothly and quietly, neat as a playing card slipping back into the deck. Earnest said seeing him was a good omen.

We talked about the moose only intermittently, between periods of Earnest's chainsawing and my driving the Ford and scooping huge rounds of spongy trunk and taking them away. We had fun disposing of those wheels. We rode together to my western slope and let them roll downhill for the fun of watching them go. Some careened and bounded practically out of view; some smashed into trees and fell over as mounds of fibrous chunks. The critters would feast on the bugs and grubs in there.

I used our rest breaks to ask him some questions. We snacked and drank spring water. For miles around us, the leaves were coloring, and the air seemed infused with the scent of their hues.

I was trying to figure out something about Earnest that I couldn't quite get my mind around. Essentially, it boiled down to this: How could he be so perfect?

"Perfection is in the eye of the beholder," he cautioned me. "You need to watch your expectation management, Pilgrim."

I kept at him: How could he arrive in my life at his age, at my age? How could he be so good and so wise without someone else claiming him long before?

We both were in the best possible mood, further buoyed by the dry clarity of the September sun and the wind rustling the leaves in rushes and sighs.

"I am pretty cool, aren't I? Here's my secret: It's totally self-interest. Speaking to a middle school teacher here, it's about my self-esteem and other sensitive stuff."

"Self-interest."

He continued with some reluctance: "Kind of person I am, I remember everything? Especially things to my discredit? I remember unkind things I said to my *mother*! I said things that hurt girlfriends. A couple of times in the Army I beat up on guys more than was needed for situation control. I remember swatting a *dog* when I was fourteen for chewing up one of my comic books!"

We had that penchant in common.

"I bet most of the people you think you hurt don't even remember," I told him.

"Probably not. But I do. Those things stay with me. They come back and hurt *me*. At some point I decided I didn't need to inflict any more pain on myself. So I got … nicer. That's all there is to it. Self-interest."

We got quiet again, both of us tilting our faces into the sunlight.

"How about you?" he asked.

"What—how do I manage to be a tolerable person? I've never had it that together, the way you describe. Never anything so conscious. I've always just been winging it. You know what I mean? Always winging it into whatever."

I stopped and reconsidered for a moment. "Actually, by the time I got here, I was barely even winging it. At best, flying on a wing and a prayer."

He kept eyes shut and his face to the sun, in no hurry to hear more or to respond. It occurred to me that perhaps moving more slowly with people, allowing more silence, was an important part of being nicer.

"I always liked that expression," he said amiably. "In your case, what exactly was the wing and what was the prayer?"

"That kind of question is why Erik calls you 'heavy.'"

He tossed his head, shrugged.

"The wing," I said, "was getting the damn work done. And the prayer was you."

WE DRANK SOME more water, stretched, then got back to cutting and hauling away the old birch. It was tricky working among the brambles and we both got scratched up despite wearing coveralls. I felt bad about crushing so many of the blackberry canes, but I knew that by next year they'd be back with no trace of our tractoring.

A little later, having cut the last segment into movable chunks, Earnest shut off the chainsaw and wiped the sweat and sawdust from his face. "Actually," he said, "that wasn't the whole truth."

"What wasn't?"

"The origins of my being such a great guy."

"Oh?"

He got a little shy. "Around you, I was always on my best behavior. Seriously. I wanted to impress you." He looked thoughtful for a moment. "'Impress' is probably not the right word. But you know what I mean."

"What, back when you showed me how to seal the seams of my tent?"

"As a matter of fact, yes. Yeah."

That pleased me enormously. I brushed chips out of his hair and off his shoulders.

"Why'd you want to impress me so much?" I asked, fishing.

He gave me a raised eyebrow and said, negligently, "I've always had a weakness for beautiful women. Putty in their hands. Sad, really."

I'd take that, I decided; I didn't mind that.

After a while I had my own clarification to make. "I wasn't just winging it, that's not all there is to it. If I seemed like a tolerable person, it was because whenever I was around you, I felt *good*. I just always felt ... better. Happier. *Always*, Earnest. It's very easy to be tolerable when you're feeling good. To be an okay person."

"That'll do it, too," he said, serious, meaning it. And then something like a vow: "I will make every effort to keep it that way."

Chapter 61

THERE'S NO HAPPY ending to my story, because there is not yet an ending. That is, it ain't over till it's over, and it's never over, as my father liked to say.

I didn't really understand what he meant until now. It will unfold forever, through lifetimes, and they will always be calico, checkered lifetimes. I have now been here for seven years and I have changed in a thousand ways. Certainly, I am wiser and sounder and happier and stronger, but the ups and downs have never stopped rising and falling. We at Brassard's farm continue to surf those waves with varying levels of confidence.

Erik: What's to become of him? My worry grew by the tiniest of increments. It started innocently enough. I got my mail at a box at the local post office, because I'd rented it before I started working for Brassard. Erik preferred not to get his own box; any mail he did get—bills from hardware suppliers, for example—arrived to him care of me. Neither of us got much mail. Why pay rent on two boxes?

Same with banking. When he first came, he asked me if he could deposit the cashier's check from Aunt Theresa's estate into my bank account. It made sense—he had just arrived, wanted money fast to pay Brassard in advance and assure him he wasn't a flake like his sister. But he never got around to opening his own account. After a while, it didn't seem particularly necessary, because I ended up being the owner of Brass Valley Hops, Incorporated, and am the one who pays the bills.

It's true. Erik didn't register himself on the articles of incorporation. He decided that I should be president and CEO, and Earnest and Will and Brassard should be board members. He said he wanted to honor me, and anyway he figured I was more responsible than he was. He had the brewers make their checks out to me or the corporation, not to him personally.

He is a persuasive talker, an escape artist of sorts. We were all so hard-pressed for time, had such work-fogged brains, it all seemed somehow reasonable. And Earnest and I: We had entered a whirlpool of convergence that, whether we knew it or not, made all else seem a little vague. I agreed to everything Erik suggested.

His van: He never got Vermont tags, because apparently, it was still registered in the name of a friend out in California, who every two years sent him the new paperwork and plate stickers. It had taken me two years to switch over my Massachusetts plates, so at first I understood his lack of hurry. But eventually, I did mention it to him—sooner or later, some state trooper would notice that he'd seen that same van for too long, that it should get Vermont plates. He'd pull Erik over, kindly remind him to register in Vermont, and ticket him. Erik shrugged it off. But whenever I rode shotgun with him, I noticed his impeccable driving, something I wouldn't have expected from my renegade brother. If the sign said thirty-five, he drove thirty-four miles per hour.

On the farm, he used Brassard's landline, as we all did; in town, he used only disposable cell phones. He said he just didn't want to bother with account statements and all the rest of it, or pay for an expensive phone he'd just lose or break in the hop yard. It was easier just to buy a new one every few weeks and always know where you stood with your remaining minutes. It was a choice that seemed consistent with his lifelong persona of the footloose desperado, contemptuous of anything as bourgeois as monthly bills, so I never gave it a thought until later.

There were a dozen other little clues that, one by one, slid past me at first but after four years could no longer be ignored.

I invited him up to my campsite; we cooked dinner together, and then I confronted him: "You are trying to be invisible. You're working hard to leave no tracks." Before he could deny it, I ticked off all the indications on my fingers.

"Why? Is it those guys with grudges from California? Do you think they'll really work that hard to find you?"

He got a little cocky. "I doubt those shitbags have the attention span to stick with it. Anyway, given their … habits, they've no doubt picked up other more pressing grudges to settle in the last few years. Keep em busy!" He chuckled at that.

"Then what?"

He stood up off his log and came over to me, knelt, and put his hands on my knees. "You really want to know? You sure?"

"Yes."

"I was released from Elk Ridge on parole. I skipped parole to come here, Annie. I am a fugitive. Interstate flight—there's no doubt a federal warrant on me."

I didn't believe him at first. Then I told him he was an idiot and he should never have done this and should think about maybe growing up some year. I stamped and picked up sticks and threw them at him. We got into a childish sibling shouting match for which there could be only one outcome. It was too late, he'd made the choice, the chips had fallen, I could be as mad at him as I liked and it wouldn't change the facts. It pissed me off and broke my heart and scared me. Here everything was rolling along so well, the hops in high demand among some very successful brewers who were paying top dollar. The farm had been in a reasonably stable economic state and a very agreeable emotional state.

Erik, who had turned it around, might also be its undoing: Is that ironic, or is it inevitable?

So there's that sword hanging over Erik, and the suspense sometimes becomes difficult for all of us. Except for Brassard—he knows nothing about it. He's seventy-two now and has earned some respite from such things.

But what happens if the sheriff pulls Erik over to let him know his turn signal isn't working, and does the obligatory record check? It can keep me awake at night—at four a.m., it's almost unbearable.

The best solution I could come up with was that Erik could petition the governor of Oregon for clemency, on whatever improbable grounds we could dream up. If his taking up farming was any indication, he could maybe plead temporary insanity.

Earnest didn't seem particularly surprised when I told him. He thought about it for a while, stroking a nonexistent beard. "That girl Erik's been seeing—how long do you think that'll last?" He wound an invisible egg timer.

"Well, it's been about six months. Seems to be about his average run, so I'd guess not much longer. Why?"

"Larry Hoskie's daughters are gorgeous," he said offhandedly. "The younger one isn't married yet—Larry says it can be hard to meet the right guy out there. Navajos can't marry inside their clan, even if they're not related. Plus, she's too smart and she intimidates the local guys. She'd be in her early thirties now."

"So … Erik should try to date someone he's never met and who's never heard of him and who lives two thousand miles from here? Good plan. But what does it have to do with his parole violation?"

Earnest shrugged. "Just thinking out loud. The Hoskies are great people. I've met the extended family. Marry into the family, you marry into the tribe. The Navajos don't like to extradite, remember?"

Later, he added: "And your brother could use someone to steady him out a bit. I'm given to understand that the Native American makes an excellent spouse."

I had indeed given him that understanding.

At the time, we laughed at this absurd plan B. But Earnest has been corresponding more frequently with Larry and they've been talking about Earnest visiting him on the Big Rez. Earnest even proposed a brotherly adventure to Erik—why not go out and meet some more taciturn Native Americans? On the way, you can tell me all of your sister's secrets. Erik, sick to death of hops, said he wouldn't mind. They'd take the bus so they could see the scenic USA on the way. Also, avoid identity checks at airports.

If they do go, I hope some good magic happens—who knows when or how it will come into our lives?—but it still doesn't strike me as all that likely. And I would miss my brother terribly.

I KNOW IT is not fashionable to be romantic, idealistic, or sentimental, but, truly, before Earnest I didn't know what love was. I had garnered no idea whatever from the Matts and Daniels and whoevers from before.

But even this has not been an easy process. Our first child miscarried. I was devastated, and for a while I feared that the dream of raising a family of my own had crashed and was dead along with the child, and that maybe another time of crashing dreams had come upon me. My mother and father lost their first, too, and I had to wonder whether I carried some inherited deficiency in my DNA, my woman's apparatus, or my karma.

But we didn't wait six more years, the way my parents did. We conceived again within a year and now have twin daughters, exquisitely fascinating and beautifully formed and smart and utterly courageous about entering our uncertain world. When Earnest first held them, they looked like little squirrels against his broad chest. It was the first time I've ever seen him scared. No, terrified—I have the photos to prove it. But by the time they started walking he felt safer around them, and now when he lies down they pile onto him and give him great joy. They're only three years old, but it's good to have some other women in this household.

And yes, Robin was indeed effulgent in that drear February and not long afterward got together with a man she'd met back in college on an exchange visit to Ireland. They live on Lynn and Theo's land in a converted shed hardly bigger than my old chicken-coop apartment, and they seem ecstatic when they visit us with their daughter. In fact, Robin remains as effulgent as all get-out, and I suspect this child is only the first of what will become a big family.

I have continued to spend time on my hill, which has changed very little. I don't "improve" it or civilize it, because it is just as it should be. I still sleep alone in my tent sometimes so I can immerse myself in the mysteries of the forest and of solitude. From those mysteries, even from the Great Fear, I always gain strength. The woods enfold me as I hike up; my family embraces me when I come back down, renewed.

Will has been getting more commissions from out of state, so we see much less of him. The summer after that first hops harvest, he got together with a woman from Rutland, lived with her for a couple of years. He broke it off, but he has a new girlfriend now, and we all agree she has potential.

Brassard planted six acres of hops, then six more, and though we had a disastrous third year due to powdery mildew, now they pull in good money through the connections Erik established. Together, we invested in a small commercial cone separator with, as Erik calls it, "better through-put capacity" that can process the yards' harvests fairly quickly. We've set up the whole upstairs of the old barn to dry the cones, now on racks of big screens vented by fans. The "as yet immature but primed" East Coast artisanal brewing industry matured explosively; Erik and Brassard have more demand for hops than they can supply. If you are a beer aficionado, I can almost guarantee you have drunk beer made from our hops.

My pregnancies made it hard to keep up with the milking. Brassard hired on another couple of hands, and they're all right if properly supervised—which I found I could manage even with a couple of babies on my hips.

Milk prices recovered and, as Brassard says, almost allow a man to make a living.

WHEN YOU ARE a farmer, you tend to pay close attention primarily to what's right there, the next task, the next seasonal change, the next problem. You have to deal with the wolf at the door, not the pack coming down the hill, even though you know you'll have to face them soon.

But, of course, the rest of the world rolls along, oblivious to you. Since I came to Brassard's farm, things have changed. Our country is going through what feels like an upheaval, one that's not entirely comprehensible to us here in the valley. It's not just here; it seems as if it's in every nation, even the dear planet itself and all its living creatures. We hear the news; sometimes we are frightened for the future.

But I console myself. I remind myself that tyrants have risen, reigned, wrought havoc, fallen. Some we remember; most we have long forgotten or have learned about only from their tombs. Nations, cruel or kind, wise or foolish, have reared up and believed themselves grand and eternal; we know of the most recent of these, of course, but the vast majority we discover in archaeological digs, their time-worn traces buried by the years and cryptic to us.

Throughout history, wars have raged, engulfing lands and people, but inevitably, green has returned to the ravaged and bloodied ground. That's because there is a through line, an unsevered strand. We—I am now we—we who work the land are still here. We never went away. Our way of life endures and we are anything but fragile. Here in Brassard's valley, on all the farms, the spirit of Diz resides, strong, indomitable. Cross her at your peril.

And capable men like Brassard, good men like Earnest, wise women like Lynn—they're here, their spirits and backbones are here and they are not just worthy but durable as well. We fall in love as people have always done, and have children as people have always done, and we toil alongside each other as people have always done. We even enjoy each other's company, mostly. Other things come and go, but these good things endure, and when you work among them, you know with certainty they always will.

We're farmers. We know about uncertainties and bad weather and pests. They do give us great concern, but we have seen them come and seen them go. We're used to sticking it out and seeing the other side.

THEN THERE IS love. This is a love story, after all. I came to love so much, in so many ways, in large part because I, believing myself to be falling helplessly, to have no choices, was compelled to accept what came to me from even the most unexpected quarter. I would never have guessed that I'd learn to love a scraggly forest, a hard-pressed farm, or the man who loves me as I do him.

I know many people find themselves to be similarly falling. Of course I cannot speak for your fate, only wish upon you understanding of the most important thing I learned from my stumbling, flailing, falling arrival at Brassard's farm: All those years I was falling and so frightened, I was always falling home.

THE END

Acknowledgments

ON BRASSARD'S FARM wouldn't exist without Rick Bleiweiss of Blackstone Publishing, who tracked me down and urged me to write the kind of book I'd always wanted to. His encouragement and enthusiasm made all the difference. I'm very grateful to him and to the others at Blackstone who read the book and truly saw what it was and what it could be.

Thanks are due to Michael Carr, whose marvelous editing gave the book some class and whose conversation, not just about this book but about style and mechanics in general, made it an enjoyable process.

I owe sincere thanks to all Vermont farmers, the women and men who put food on our tables every day and who are too seldom acknowledged for doing so. President Eisenhower got it right when he said, "Farming looks mighty easy when your plow is a pencil and you're a thousand miles away from the cornfield."

In particular, I owe special thanks to dairy farmers Jerry Kill and Mark Rodgers, who helped me understand the daily realities of farming. Any misrepresentation of dairy farm practices in this book results from fictional license or the thickness of my skull, not from any want of expertise or effort on their part. I am also indebted to Diane Bothfeld and Dan Scruton of the Vermont Agency of Agriculture, who first introduced me to the challenges of dairy farming in the Green Mountains. Thanks also to Dick Waybright of Mason Dixon Farm for giving me so much of his time and knowledge.

I thank my brother Nicholas Hecht, artist and wizard, who opened my mind and heart to the mysteries of the deep woods and the magic that can find you in unfamiliar forest at night. Nick guided and accompanied me on many vision quests, including that night when we lay on the ground, far up in a Vermont hill pasture, to be surrounded by fifty uneasy cows. It was thanks to Nick's calm and charm that we befriended them.

I could not have portrayed the character Earnest without the examples of four men. Elmer (Menominee) was the tree surgeon for whom I served as rope man and who really did jam ice cubes into his canteen with one finger. My brother-in-law Ken Schuyler (Oneida) remained my dear friend despite my messing up his trucks and tractors when I lived in the Schuylers' chicken coop. Bob Kirk and his brother Ernest Kirk (Diné) are wise, strong, talented men who introduced me to Navajo culture, let me live in the goat barn while I wrote *Land of Echoes*, and showed me firsthand the grace and trust that comes from not talking so damn much.

Ultimately, this book must be dedicated to my wife Stella, without whom I couldn't do much of anything and who, along with Jean, Willow, and Amie, helped me understand a bit about women, love, and life.